We Are
Gathered Here

~

MICAH PERKS

A WYATT BOOK for ST. MARTIN'S PRESS ≈ NEW YORK

WE ARE GATHERED HERE. Copyright © 1996 by Micah Perks. All rights reserved. Printed in the United States of America. No part of this book may be used or reproduced in any manner whatsoever without written permission except in the case of brief quotations embodied in critical articles or reviews. For information, address A Wyatt Book *for* St. Martin's Press, 175 Fifth Avenue, New York, N.Y. 10010

Song lyrics from "The Happy Journey" on page 58 published courtesy of the Fruitlands Museums.

"Demeter" by Genevieve Taggard, *Slow Music,* Harper & Brothers, N.Y. 1946. Copyright © 1946. Renewed. Permission by Marcia D. Liles.

Design by Junie Lee

Library of Congress Cataloging-in-Publication Data

Perks, Micah.
We are gathered here : a novel / by Micah Perks.—1st ed.
p. cm.
"A Wyatt book for St. Martin's Press."
ISBN 0-312-15294-9
1. City and town life—New York (State)—History—19th century—Fiction. I. Title.
PS3566.E691487W43 1996
813'.54—dc20 95-33693
CIP

First A Wyatt Book *for* St. Martin's Press Paperback Edition: April 1997

10 9 8 7 6 5 4 3 2 1

For Bob and Polly, and for my great-great-aunt Regina, never known, not forgotten.

In your dream you met Demeter
Splendid and severe, who said: Endure . . .
Find your true kin
   —then you felt her kiss.
—Genevieve Taggard

We Are Gathered Here

1882

*The Town of Hammondville, New York, in the Great
North Woods. Built by General Hammond on the site
of the Hammond ore bed.*

One

～

NOBODY IS LEFT to remember the day Miss Regina Hammond Sartwell dressed in pure white and threw herself out a third story window, but Olive saw it all. This was in March, two thirds through a long grey winter, and Olive was starved for color. In church, she watched the greens and blues of the stained glass until her neck went stiff from twisting away from the pulpit towards the window. She would forget to listen to the minister, forget that the stained glass depicted Jesus on the cross, and fall, eyes first, into the colors green and blue.

In the absence of color, Olive usually looked forward to heavy food and early sleep, but now she looked forward to the train. She stood on the loading platform, surrounded by a dozen women, all in their black Sunday dresses. They were gathered on the platform in four knots—the Swedes, the Irish, the French-Canadians, and Olive with the Yankees. The sky above them was pregnant with snow, resting its swollen belly on the tops of the houses.

Olive watched her mother, Florilla, press her thumb down the back of her hand. That hand was always swollen and a little bent, as if it had been gripping something for too many years. Florilla sighed, shaded her eyes, and peered down the track. If the train didn't come quick her mother would change her mind about wasting half a laundry day to get a look at a lady.

The train was carrying General Hammond and his niece, Miss Sartwell. The general was giving her a tour of the mines. Folks said this Miss Sartwell from New York City had been whisked away on the eve of her wedding, on account it was discovered she had fits. Olive had never seen a fancy lady with the fits.

She imagined this Miss Sartwell on the fourteen-mile train trip up from Crown Point. She would wrinkle her fine nose at the smell from the charcoal pits. She'd pull her thin lids over her eyes to block out the ugly bare hills, just tree stumps up to the highest peak. And then, when the train ran over those shaky pine trestles, fifty feet from solid ground, maybe that delicate miss would cry out, Mercy!, and swoon away. The train would screech to a halt, back down the mountain, and no one would get so much as a glimpse of her ribbons and satin and bows.

Olive pushed a mess of orange curls back into her bonnet. Her pale skin was blotched pink from the cold. She pulled her shawl up over her neck, then bent down to yank her stockings up over her knees.

"Where do you think you are?" Florilla pulled on Olive's elbow to straighten her up.

Olive laughed and batted her mother's hand away. Florilla smiled. Then they heard the train whistle. The deep rumble of the train shook in Olive's chest. The engine barreled towards them, then threw itself into a stop, chuffing and steaming. They watched General Hammond leap off the train.

He was a dashing, small man with a white goatee and waxed mustache. As soon as Olive saw him, she stepped back a little, behind her mother's shoulder.

Florilla sighed. "He won't bite, Olive. Just smile and show your respect."

Olive grimaced.

General Hammond helped his niece off the train.

Miss Sartwell was exactly what Olive had imagined, all dressed in white cashmere. She carried a white silk parasol and wore a white felt hat with blue feathery plumes curling around the top.

Miss Sartwell stopped and glanced around. Her face was a small heart: tiny chin, rosebud mouth, big brown eyes, honey-colored hair surrounded by feathers. She had a long nose with flared nostrils.

"That's just the nose I'd put on a rich girl," Olive whispered to her mother.

"That dress is a trick," Florilla whispered back. "Look at the bustle, and that fabric there, gathered over the hips. And a false front too. Just a flat girl inside a curved dress."

General Hammond called to the lady, "Why your aunt didn't warn you against wearing white to the mines is past imagining." General Hammond had been with the cavalry, and when he spoke he thrust his hand out, parrying. His voice called across battlefields in common conversation.

The lady slit her eyes. General Hammond took Miss Sartwell's elbow. She wore white calfskin gloves over small hands, hands in calfskin fists. The fists didn't seem right to Olive. A lady like this ought to be trailing her hands from her wrists.

"Now, Miss Sartwell, most of our miners are foreigners, but good Christians all, and we have two churches to accommodate them. If we can't recruit Yankees, we try to get Swedes of clean, country stock, but there are never enough of those to go round. There is a baseball team, a free school, and monthly dances in good weather. Of course, no intoxicating liquors permitted." He flipped his hand out. "My aim is to bring civilization to the desert, no more, no less. You see before you the seed of this civilization."

General Hammond's smooth blue gaze found Florilla. "And here we have Widow Landry. One of our oldest families—real Yankees from Vermont, just like President Arthur." He waved her towards them. Olive followed, hiding behind a big smile.

"Now, Widow, test me. See if my ancient memory fails me. Your husband fought in one of my regiments in the war, lost an arm. One of my first engineers, too. Died in that typhus outbreak a few years ago."

"Yes, sir. Except my husband lost his arm when he was a brakeman on your rail—"

General Hammond held up his hand. "No hints, now. As I recall, you've had bad luck with children—five or six of them passed on. Tragic. But here's a strapping daughter."

Miss Sartwell turned to Olive and stared at her with those large, circled eyes. One of her gloved hands moved towards Olive's hair, then dropped. A tiny smile tipped up one side of her mouth. "Lovely," she said. Her voice was scratchy as a man's.

"My daughter's married just this past summer, a Swede name of Ren Honsinger. Both nineteen years old."

General Hammond turned away. "Thought you'd forgotten us, Simon."

The chief engineer, Mr. Simon Putney, stood beside the general, pushing his glasses up, pulling at his hands. "I lost track of the time, sir. Going over some papers, important—"

"No harm done. We used the time well." General Hammond pressed Miss Sartwell's elbow.

Olive watched them walk away. "Your lip," Florilla said. Olive had a snaggletooth, and when she laughed or smiled too much her lip would hook on that tooth—flip inside out. She smoothed it down.

The visitors strolled past the doctor's house, and the groups of women followed at a polite distance, from the visitors and from each other, over to South Pit. Everyone seemed to be discussing fits. Olive's mother and her best friend, Mattie Stone, were arguing, in their nasal New England voices, over foxglove as a cure. An Irish woman said fits came from anger steaming up the brain. You had to drill a hole in the head to let the steam out. Another Irish woman said fits were a visitation from evil spirits. A priest could cure them every time. Mattie swore the cause was too much butter eating.

Olive touched her cheek where the soft glove had brushed her as it dropped down.

There was a rickety log bridge over one side of South Pit. The lips of the pit were slick with ice. Damp air blew up from the deep hole. The ground near the opening was strewn with barrels, rusty pick heads, broken boards.

There was no railing, and Miss Sartwell walked towards the edge of the bridge. General Hammond grabbed her elbow. Olive could see flecks of dirt beginning to cover the bottom of the white dress. "Shall we tour the store, Miss Sartwell?"

Miss Sartwell was still leaning into the dark mine, General Hammond anchoring her by the elbow. The silence piled up until the General turned to the chief engineer. "The store?" he asked.

The engineer touched the bridge of his silver glasses. "Yes. The store." The engineer always seemed flustered. His watery eyes studied the ground and his walk was awkward, as if he were made of wicker.

They moved towards the biggest building in town, the three-story company store where the miners spent their weekly chits. The troupes of women followed. They stood outside while the gentlemen stopped at the entrance to talk to the store manager. Miss Sartwell disappeared inside. Olive wondered if she would touch the bolts of calico and rough wool or lift the lids off the spice jars and sniff, the way Olive liked to. She saw a swish of white move up the stairs to the offices and storerooms.

"Ain't much more to see, Olive. And it is so cold," Florilla said. Then Olive heard a window unlatch on the third floor.

There was the white lady, framed in the open window. Olive memorized the picture to take home with her for later.

Miss Sartwell put a hand on each side of the window. She raised her boot onto the sill. Her eyes grazed over their upturned faces, then caught on Olive. She smiled that small, off-kilter smile again. Then she pushed herself out the window.

Olive breathed in hard, and she felt all the women around her breathing in too, a painful breath in of cold, still air, faces towards the thing falling towards them. Miss Sartwell's dress puffed up, then swung over her head. Everyone saw her pure white petticoat, her cashmere stockings, her high black boots. Her hat flew off like a turquoise bird.

A groan rose from the women, and their arms rose, as if they might catch her, but Miss Sartwell landed on the hard ground, amongst them. Her neck jerked. Her arm touched the ground and seemed to fold up, as weak as a handkerchief. Then her face smacked into the rocky path. There she lay, a white bundle, perfectly still. The women stood, arrested, shoulder to shoulder. They watched her hat land and skid into the store.

The creaking sound of the mining work went on. They heard General Hammond call again, "Miss Sartwell?" Then he leapt out the door, setting the world in motion. He strode up to Miss Sartwell's body, and asked Olive's mother to put her ear to the lady's chest to tell if she be living.

The chief engineer stumbled out, carrying the plumed hat.

Olive's mother rested her head on the muddied white chest and closed her eyes. Then she looked past General Hammond to the others, "She's alive. Praise God."

General Hammond called out, his head jerking every which way, to bring clerks from the store to carry her on boards to the train. He said to fetch the doctor, but the store manager told him the doctor was in Buck's Hollow for the day.

Underneath his orders, Inga Peterson whispered, "Like an angel."

"A miracle," someone else murmured.

"Jumped from the third story and survived!" Mattie Stone clicked her tongue. "Puts me in mind of the virgin birth."

General Hammond flourished his fighting hand at the women. "Give her some room, now. Miss Sartwell has fallen trying to get the best view."

But they stayed put. As the clerks reached for her, they all clicked their tongues. Florilla moved forward. "General Hammond, sir. I know something of broken bones."

The hand flipped. "We'll wait for the doctor in Crown Point."

$\sim$

6

Olive's mother returned to her place and the group gathered around her, huffing in irritation. Then the lady groaned. The clerks jumped back. She raised her head out of the ground. That grand nose was flattened, already swelling purple. Blood rode on her lips. "I'm not dead, am I?" The voice was clogged. She looked down at her twisted wrist, then around her. They all held their breath, leaning forward.

"Damn." She laid herself down on the boards.

The general stared. The chief engineer gasped. Etta Clark whispered loudly, "I know that feeling, I wake up with it near every morning." There was hoarse snickering and avoiding of eyes. For some reason, Olive felt that she might scream at any moment and that everyone would join her.

"For pity's sake, someone bring her a drink of whiskey," the engineer said. "She's delirious."

But Mattie Stone said, "Mr. Putney, have you forgotten General Hammond outlawed intoxicating liquor in Hammondville?" The women could not smother their hilarity. Olive pinched her nose to keep from laughing, but it just popped her eardrums. The engineer gave them a reproachful look, but they didn't care. All of a sudden the day had opened into a holiday. The skinny clerks carrying the lady on two boards seemed like clowns, slipping and skidding over the ice. General Hammond and the chief engineer hovered near, ridiculous. As the women watched them carry her to the train, the sky loosened. Fat, soft flakes began to fall. The women were not surprised.

"And the sky came tumbling down," Florilla said, and for some reason everyone thought that the wittiest remark. Just as they were wiping their eyes, Inga Peterson said, "I'm thinking we could all use some of this whiskey, in getting over the shock." They all gasped, "Mrs. Peterson!" and fell apart again. They drifted in an uncertain group, teetering on the edge of laughter, unwilling to give up the miraculous event and go back to their washing. Snow covered their dark dresses in white.

Olive saw a small, bright blue feather shaking in the snow. She bent down and picked it up, brushed the pure color across her face: a souvenir.

The fire in the stove was down to ash and red embers by the time Olive and her mother drifted back from the train station. A skin of ice stretched over the washing tub. Olive wanted to talk over the afternoon, but it was near five o'clock, the sun falling away, and supper not even started.

Olive forgot Miss Sartwell. She concentrated on heaving the tub of washing out the door, tipping it up, pouring the ice and water over the hard ground. She hung the washing on the line that ran between her house and the Clarks'. It had become a bad day for hanging clothes. Snow coated her light-colored eyelashes until she could hardly see. She put her shawl over her head, heaved the sodden clothes onto the line. The rope sagged under the weight. The washing water froze on her hands, making her clumsy.

Olive brought a bucket of charcoal in for the fire. In the dusk of the kitchen she could hardly see her mother's face.

"We're out of water." Her mother didn't turn from the stove.

Olive pulled her shawl over her head again and walked through the slanting snow and grey dusk. She filled up her bucket and headed back, chin down, walking evenly so as not to slosh the water. She could see her mother light the lamp and then the homey yellow shine from behind the small front window.

Olive brought dusty hay for the Holstein, tied up in the tiny shed built against the side of the house. She let herself down on the stool by the animal's side. Olive clenched her hands a few times, working out the frozen stiffness so she could milk. It was so dark in the shed, she had to feel for the udders. She started the twisting pull on the teats. She heard the milk hit the bottom of the tin bucket. Olive rested her cheek against the warm side of the cow and kept pulling. She closed her eyes and saw Miss Sartwell's gloved hand reaching out to touch her hair.

By the time she was done milking, snow was falling on a moonless night. As she heaved the bucket from the shed to the house she could see the flickering lights from the miners' headlamps trailing up and out of the mines, like fireflies.

The warmth of the house flushed her cheeks and turned her head dizzy. Olive's mother had set the table. The beans were on the stove. Olive poured some milk in a pitcher and lowered the bucket into the dirt hole in the floor. She pulled off her boots and her shawl.

Her husband, Ren, ducked through the doorframe. "Snowing, I guess," Ren said. His headlamp was still burning—he pulled it off his head and blew it out. He hung his jacket on a peg. Olive smiled at him. He nudged her. "Out of my way now so's I can wash." Olive nudged him back as she stepped aside.

Florilla gave the beans a stir. "Married nine months and still ain't used to each other. It's a wonder. Every day the same thing. Ren Honsinger spends his first hour home like he's gathering courage to ask Olive to dance. Olive smiles so wide, her face is like to break."

Olive and Ren laughed, but they couldn't look at each other. He stuck his hands in the washbasin, the dull gold bowl of his hair flopping over his eyes.

"She was always sweet on you," Florilla said.

"Was I?" Olive said. "I thought I just took pity on him on account he couldn't speak English."

"Oh, you was sweet on him," Florilla said. "You just didn't know it."

Ren shook his head. As he rubbed his hands, the water in the bowl turned brown. He left a brown smear on the hand towel.

He sat down at the table, rested his chin on the loose weave of his hands. Olive's mother served the food from the stove. Olive sat down. Florilla mumbled a prayer. Ren stared around, tipped up his plate of beans and bread, looked under it. "Someone's thieved the roast beef." He looked Olive in the eyes for the first time, and smiled. Ren's smile always reminded Olive of the V of a flock of geese. His lips were chapped almost white, disappearing into the flame of his cheeks, but when he smiled, there were the geese—simple, airborne.

Olive smiled back. "Be quiet and eat."

"Tell Ren what we saw today," Florilla said.

"The general's niece jumped from the third floor of the store. She had on a hat with blue feathers."

"Oh, Olive, the hat ain't the story. Ren, that young lady was bent on killing herself, but Someone must have wanted her to live."

Ren kept eating. "She should've jumped down a mine if she was serious."

"Thank the Lord she wasn't as clever as you."

"Her dress was pure white." Olive sagged in her seat, heavy lidded, dreamy. In the half dark, with the hot food and the heat from the stove, with her mother and Ren—she felt peaceful, wanting nothing.

After supper, Florilla read aloud, first a hurried, smudged letter from Olive's only living sister, Ida, who boarded with relatives in Vermont, caring for their babies. Ida always sounded irritated and rushed. In this letter she declared she couldn't stand children. She had big plans. They all smiled, shook their heads.

Then Florilla read the Bible, her rheumatic hand wrapped in a poultice. Olive looked out the dark window at the snow pouring from the sky. They had a clock in the house, its pendulum rocking: seven-thirty. Ren's head dropped onto his chest and he began a low, clogged snore. Olive was finishing patching up a hole in his other pair of overalls. She heard scrabbling and turned to watch a mouse run over the counter.

If Olive could stamp on a mouse, she would, but it was no use spending much energy on it as there was an endless supply of them. And it was not just mice. Bats liked to sleep in the rafters: little black packages hanging by day, squeaking, their droppings falling to the floor. Olive or her mother would cuff them out with a broom, but soon others would move in. One summer, they did not use their stove for a few days, and the bats built a nest inside the pipe. When they finally lit a fire they heard frantic shrieks and the sound of wings against tin. Then the charred black bundles fell into the fire.

A weasel lived in the dirt under the house. And once they found a small green snake curled around a leg of the stove.

Not only that, but Ren had brought Swedish spirits with him when he moved in. There was Tomte, the black dog spirit that slept by the fire and protected them from evil. And the tiny Houseman, who liked a clean and orderly home. When things grew too messy, he came up at night and twirled and twirled in the middle of the kitchen, sending nightmares and tangling hair. He slept under the floor with the weasel.

Then there were the bitter New England ghosts—the spirits of Olive's father and her sister, Submit, both gone with the typhus, and her mother's four babies, born too weak to live—their cries disguised as the settling of the house or the rustle of rodents or a sudden draft that scared the candle flame. It was a full house, especially at night, when the one puddle of light was swallowed up by the darkness that seeped in from the greater darkness. Then the walls between the spirit world, the night outside, and their fragile inside home, thin to begin with, shimmered and disappeared.

Even now, snow was washing under the door, fanning out into the kitchen. Olive could just see her mother in the rocker, reading one of those begets passages, lines of old-time Bible families and their children. Her mother read like a chant, comforting, rocking, until Olive could no longer watch the needle. "We'll go to bed, Ma."

"Go ahead. I'll just read and let this poultice soak in awhile."

Olive wrapped the warming stone in a scrap of flannel and climbed the ladder to the loft. Ren pulled himself up. "Good night, Mother Landry. Nice Bible reading." He climbed the ladder into the cold.

Ren groaned himself down onto the pallet. He strained for his boots, but couldn't reach them. Olive yanked them off for him. When she unbuttoned her dress to put on her high-neck nightgown, the blue feather dropped to the floor. She tucked it under the mattress. As Ren undressed to his underclothes, the candlelight licked his broad, flat chest, his narrow hips. They snugged into bed.

"Don't put your cold feet on me," she said, as he slid his long, icy feet between her calves. She could feel the empty place on his left foot where frostbite had taken his little toe. She pressed her own feet on the warming stone. She turned her back towards him, and he began rubbing her shoulders. She sighed.

"Hurts?" he whispered.

"Uh-huh." His hands were rough, like bark.

He turned his back on her. She rubbed at the snarled muscles of his shoulders.

"You think I didn't know it was snowing, down in the mine, but I did." Ren's whisper was thick—it ran over her like molasses. "I'm working, and then I feel something wet on my cheek. Am I crying? I think. Then I see it's one snowflake, drifted down through the dark, a hundred feet or more, to kiss my cheek. Only one, no more. Did you send it, Olive?"

"Yes," she said. Soon she heard his snoring. She felt her lids closing and her hand slipping off his back.

Then she was sitting up in bed, afraid, not knowing why.

"What. What," Ren said. She knew he was sitting up, too, though she couldn't see anything. Then she heard it again, the pounding on the door. A fist over and over.

She heard her mother's voice. "Ren!" He stood up and hit his head on the slanted ceiling.

"Wait. I'll get the candle." She knocked it over and heard it roll along the floor, felt for it and lit it. Ren pulled the bottom of his coveralls on and lurched down the ladder. He fell the last few rungs. She grabbed her shawl and followed, the tilted candle dripping hot wax on her fingers.

"Patience!" Ren yelled. Olive's mother rushed out from her

bedroom holding another candle high, carrying a bag of medicinals.

"Who is it?" Florilla said. "Is it one of the Calahan babies again?"

Ren pulled up the string latch. A fat man leaned against the doorframe, huffing, covered in snow, holding the reins of his oxen and cart. Olive squinted. It looked like that Cutter man from Crown Point. He stamped his feet. None of them said anything, waiting. "I have a message for you, Mrs. Honsinger," he said.

"Is it Ida?" Florilla clenched her hands tighter on her bag. It could always be one of her babies. Always. The five that had slipped through her fingers stirred, moaned, began to waken.

"No, ma'am. It's Miss Sartwell."

Olive wondered whether they knew she had stolen the blue feather. Cutter came in, and they shut the door.

"I come all the way from down to Crown Point," he said.

"Want coffee?" Ren asked. Cutter nodded. Olive poked up the fire. Florilla put the kettle on.

Cutter was still wheezing. He stood with his hands on his hips. "It's just this. My wife and me, we work for the Hammonds. She's the cook. Miss Sartwell fell up here to the mines today and hurt herself, though not as bad as she could have. Fell in a mine, slipped on the ice, who knows with them good-for-nothin' shoes she was wearing, so the wife says. Anyways, she needs someone to nurse her, more than just the housekeeper. So's Old Mrs. Hammond was fixing to hire some girl from town, but Miss Sartwell screams, 'Oh no you don't.' She wants that girl with orange hair, she says, and none else. Old missus thought young miss was just fevered from the fall, but my wife figures out it's Widow Landry's daughter, Olive Honsinger." Olive's mother handed him coffee. Cutter warmed his hands on it, held it under his chin for the steam.

"So they sent me up here for you. That Miss Sartwell is a handful. Need to keep her quiet. She upsets old Mrs. Hammond with her screaming. And of course, the old missus herself can get hysteric. Wants what she wants when she wants it. Even if it's driving

13

up to the mines through a snowstorm in the middle of the night."

"You're saying she's asking for Olive to stay down there in the big house, and take care of Miss Sartwell? Like a job?" Olive's mother said.

"That's about it."

"In General Hammond's house?" Olive touched her lip.

"Yep. Could be a while, too, because she has the fits, so she needs help, not just from the fall. That's what they say. Needs her own private maid. Mrs. Hammond says she was told you just married, but she'll pay two dollars a week, plus let you off Sundays. Oh, and there's this." He pulled a small rectangular white card out of his coat pocket and handed it to Olive. Olive ran her fingers over the bumps of the engraved script: *Miss Regina Hammond Sartwell.* At the top edge, in smeared ink, it said, "Please come."

"What's your answer?" Mr. Cutter said.

Olive looked at Ren and her mother. "Can she get her pays in real money, not chits?" Ren asked.

"Course. We don't do with chits in Crown Point."

"Two dollars a week," Olive's mother said. "I can manage for a while."

Olive touched *Miss Regina Hammond Sartwell,* again. She closed her eyes, opened them. Nodded.

"You come down on the train tomorrow. First thing." Mr. Cutter set his mug down.

"Will you stay the night?" Ren said.

"No. Wife will think I froze if I don't come home. Plus I have to work tomorrow. But don't you worry, they paid me a dollar to come up here." He grinned and winked at them. "Crazy rich folks." As he walked out to the oxen he began wheezing again.

They pulled in the door string and sat down at the table. "Two dollars a week," Florilla said.

"We could order a velvet couch," Olive said. "A green one."

Ren pressed his knee against hers. "We'll save it, maybe. Yes? For out west. We could leave sooner if we have this money, maybe in the year."

Neither Olive or her mother looked at Ren. "Let's bring Ida home," Florilla said.

"Of course." Olive gave the table a quick pat. "We have to bring Ida home."

Ren nodded. "But there'll still be left over. We can save that for out—"

Olive covered Ren's voice with a groaning yawn. "Two hours till sunrise." They climbed back up the ladder to bed.

Ren pulled her into him, cupped her with his body. "Who's goin' to warm my feet?" he whispered. "I guess Ida and your ma will have to take turns."

"At least we'll have Sundays."

"We'll be on the way west next year, maybe all the way to Minnesota." Ren's breath warmed her ear.

"Ma will never agree to go, and she's been sick as a dog all year, with rheumatism and the change. Anyways, a farmer's wife works as hard as a miner's wife. And with nothing but prairie grass for company."

"But the colors, Olive, the colors," Ren said, dangling a bright lure.

"Tell me," she said, giving in. She listened to Ren's voice describe oceans of green grass and forever blue skies, soil so rich it would push up the brightest tomatoes, as many flowers and fruit trees as they could handle, a land closest in character to the Garden of Eden. She let the words wash her to sleep, but what she saw were the big, circled eyes of the white lady.

Two

Regina opened her eyes and hated her father. It was her first thought of the morning, and that small shock of rage strengthened her. She felt as if her skin had shrunk in the night and was now in danger of bursting.

She lay still, but she could still feel her eyelashes pressing down on her swollen skin. She could feel her skin pull off her ribs with every breath. For more strength, she lined up the people she hated in a row: her father first, next her fumbling sister Eliza, then the doctors—the one in the city, and now this Corning, this female specialist with the beard that grew under his chin. She threw in all the doctors in the world she was ever likely to meet—every one.

Next came her newest acquaintances. That whining Aunt Hammond and that arrogant ass, her uncle Hammond—her mother's older brother. And Mrs. Fisk, the stingy housekeeper, who looked as if she hadn't visited the privy in years.

If she went on, lining people up in order of hate, there was no longer the energy of pure rage. She was left with more exhausting emotions: her sister Maryanne for traveling in Europe, too far to help; her mother for weakness and early death; her friend Lovina for preoccupation with marriage. Regina felt tears begin to take hold.

Quickly she went back to thinking about that pompous doctor in New York. He had told her in a mournful voice that her memory would slowly fail. "An epileptic's memory deteriorates," he had said, swinging his gold watch as if to mesmerize her, to begin the process.

But Regina remembered everything. She remembered where she was—in the back room of the musty house her father had banished her to, in a house kept by her father's in-laws, who hoped she was the type to die gracefully like her mother, needlepointing until the last. And the dark house was jammed between a wide frozen lake and a circle of burned-out tree stumps. She was nowhere.

Regina remembered the jump—all her body rising to her head, a pins-and-needles feeling, and a huge sound like the rush of a gas lamp being lit.

And she vaguely recalled women—those shabby miners' wives—hordes of them. She remembered that girl in calico the color of boiled cabbage. The girl with reddened skin, almost no eyebrows or eyelashes, squinty pale eyes, lip twisted up over big, crooked teeth. But her plain face was surrounded by heaps of orange gold hair. When Regina reached out to touch that beautiful hair, the girl's face held the startled look of love. No one had looked at Regina like that since she'd been hidden away.

After they brought her back down to Crown Point, she remembered Corning, this new doctor, had tried to touch her all over. The pain had been so strong, it felt as if it were pouring out her nostrils in steam. She had needed to concentrate on pain, alone in a dark room. Instead there was Mrs. Hammond sighing and snuffling at the door, the housekeeper holding a lamp too close, and Dr. Corning brandishing his magnifying glass.

Regina screamed and swore at him. The doctor tried to clamp a damp handkerchief to her mouth and nose, to quiet her or to stop the blood. But she yanked the cloth out of his hand with her teeth and spit it on the floor. Her aunt had swooned then and had to be helped out by the housekeeper. That cook with the big potato hands held her down while the doctor prodded her, over the top of her clothes. Then he cut her dress off in strips with long shears. The cook had whispered in her ear on the breath of onions, all about the good food she would make for Regina. The doctor's hands pressed all over her body, but the voice in her ear chanted: jumbles, mock turtle soup, mutton broth, Indian pudding.

Then she heard the doctor at the door, telling old Fisk to engage a girl for her. She began yelling again. She had to yell, to be heard over the pain. "The orange-haired one, only the orange-haired girl. Please. The miner's wife. The widow's girl." The doctor came back in and told the cook to hold her down again. She tried to get up. The doctor wrapped a stick in a strip of her white cashmere dress and began to press it in her mouth. I'm not having a fit, she tried to say, but she had to clench her teeth to keep out the stick, so she couldn't speak, and then, as if the stick had wakened it, she had felt that feeling: something cool slipping up her arms and legs towards her heart. Her vision began to blur, except for her foot. She could see it as if it were under a magnifying glass—her bare foot twisted at a strange angle, the toes straining back, stiff and shivering. Then the cold reached her heart, and she was falling somewhere, and she remembered this, too.

She was falling in darkness, but there was a woman beside her. Sometimes she couldn't make her out, but she knew she was there, holding out her arms. The same woman she had seen in her other fits. This woman put her arms around her, comforting her, cool and bitter as parsley. With her long, vaporous arms wrapped around her, the woman told her: There is a place for you to find.

Now Regina lay in bed, remembering the vision inside her fit. She had a headache that stretched down to her toes. Then she remembered the widow's daughter would come. Unless it had been a dream. Sometime in the night the cook had stood in the doorway and told her they were going to fetch Widow Landry's girl up to Hammondville. Regina had told the cook to find one of her calling cards, and Regina had written a message on it—something enticing, she couldn't quite remember. Regina lay in bed now, in the dull morning light of the curtained room, holding herself against the pain, waiting for the orange-haired girl.

Olive left Hammondville at dawn, on the first train down to Crown Point. It was a cold, high blue morning. A glittering top had hardened on the new snow, and she crunched through it on her way to the train station. As she walked towards the loading platform, windows slid up and doors shoved open, letting out warm air and the smell of cooking grease.

"Where you going so early?" Mattie called.

"Down to Crown Point. Got a job to General Hammond's house."

"Leaving your sweet mama and husband for the general. Hope he don't eat you for breakfast some morning!"

Other women called to her: "Tell Miss Sartwell we all pray she's cured."

"Don't forget a thing you see, Olive Honsinger. Tell us what they eat down there to the general's."

Olive nodded and laughed. She trudged up to the loading platform. She stamped up and down to keep her feet from freezing. Then she heard the whistle and felt the platform begin to shake. She stood on the tips of her toes, then back down again.

Small billows of fog came out of the mouths of the miners set to unload whatever the train had to offer. The clouds from the men's mouths met the steam curling from the engine and covered the platform. The miners slid open the doors of two wooden boxcars. They heaved out huge slabs of ice packed in sawdust. They slung canvas between pairs of men and carried the ice gently between them, towards the icehouse by the store.

Dr. Lenard, the company doctor, stepped carefully off the train, back from fixing someone up in Buck's Hollow. Olive thought of her mother, scrubbing hard on his store-bought trousers, just now. On a flatcar a large object was tied in canvas, and Dr. Lenard hovered near it, patting and soothing. The doctor always wore a

blue silk scarf, even in summer. Most said the scarf was given to
him in Utica by an opera singer. Dr. Lenard had narrow, bent
shoulders, as if his work in Hammondville were a penance, perhaps for the opera singer.

Six miners loosened the ropes and pulled off the canvas. There it
stood in the smoke: the first piano in Hammondville. Olive moved
a few steps closer.

"Play us something, Doc," one of the miners said.

"It's really too cold, boys." He shrugged and rubbed his hands
together to show how cold.

"Sure, Doctor, play us something nice."

The miners didn't move to pick up the piano, so the doctor
sighed and opened the top. The men surrounded him. He pulled
out a little velvet-covered stool, set it down on the flatcar, and arranged himself, cracking his fingers, blowing his steamy breath on
them for warmth. Then he took out a tuning fork from his inside
breast pocket. He placed a finger on a white key and struck the
fork against his teeth.

Six miners surrounded him. Finally Dr. Lenard began playing
something that sounded old and sore. Other men kept moving the
ice, calling to each other below the music. It reminded Olive of old
John the Baptist, a voice crying in the wilderness. An Irish miner
leaned on the piano and put his face in his hand.

Dr. Lenard broke off in the middle of the music. "Dreadfully
out of tune." He tucked the velvet seat under his arm.

The miners rocked the piano onto their backs and slowly inched
towards his house. He noticed Olive. "Off to the Hammonds'?
Now, that's an honor. I put in a good word for you, you know."
Olive nodded, bared her teeth. "I hope your mother isn't going to
try and wriggle out of her duties, just because you're off on your
little adventure. I don't know what I'd do without your mother's
assistance. She's quite the old nursie, you know." He glanced
up. "Oh God. I believe they've actually dropped my piano." Dr.
Lenard's face twisted, but when he called out, his voice sounded
high and false. "Has there been a little mishap, boys?" He

walked slowly towards the group clustered around his instrument.

There was no one else in the small passenger car. The piano still tapped out its music on her forehead—making her think of all those Bible trips, back and forth across deserts and seas. She thought of Ren and his older brother, Magnus, on a ship from Sweden to New York Harbor. All they'd had to eat were dried lingonberries and hard bread for the whole trip. And you would think they would never want to eat either again, but Ren said he dreamed of the bitter red berries, and Magnus brought hard bread with him every day into the mine.

She wondered what her chores would be. Lighter, she imagined, than she was used to. Watering plants. Shining silverware. Reading to the sick lady. Untangling her hair maybe. It gave her the shivers to think she would be so close to the lady as to have her fingers in her hair. She imagined she smelled clean and sour, like spruce. She made sure she thought of the lady only, and not that she would be in the same house as the general, not that she might meet him in the hall, not that she would ever have to light his cigar, her hand shaking so bad that the flame would scorch his pretty white mustache.

The train screeched through Irondale, the midway point. Up on the rise she could just see the cemetery where the babies and Submit and her father were buried. She flattened her hand against the window of the car. A nice place to lie, she thought.

A while later, the whistle blew three times. The engine began to grind down. She heard the brakeman running over the top of her car to set the breaks.

They made a long, slow stop, sliding past the Crown Point town square and towards the ironworks, a half mile away. The brakeman threw open the door to her car as he ran by on the platform. The whole world filled with noise and smoke and yelling men. Olive walked back towards town, mittened hands covering her ears until she came to the first houses of the village. She stepped onto the sooty wooden sidewalk of a street filled with strangers. Some of them stared at her. She stared back, smiling big, then running her hand over her lip. The cold feel of her callused fingers comforted her. Telegraph wires swung down the street. The smell of the town surrounded her—horse manure and woodsmoke, and the heavy stench of the furnaces underneath it all. Olive's breath had frozen on her scarf. Her cheeks hurt.

The general's big, brick house stood just off the village square. Three chimneys—a stingy bit of smoke coming out of one, nothing out of the other two. The house must be colder than a barn, Olive thought. It perched on a rise, as if to get the better of an enemy, with a long row of stone steps off the side, leading down to Putts Creek. It was surrounded by three old maples, as if trees were decoration.

Olive stood on the first porch step until her toes started to numb from the cold. She thought of Daniel in the lions' den, but still she wouldn't touch the lion's-head brass knocker. Finally she hit her knuckles on the door.

The housekeeper, Mrs. Fisk, answered. She was a woman with a proud posture, turned out at the small of her back like a dancer, dressed in black up to her neck. White lace puffed out of her high collar, brushing her long, horselike chin. There was one wide, grey streak in her dark hair, like a mane. Olive had seen her at a prayer meeting once. "Yes?" Mrs. Fisk said.

"I'm Olive Honsinger." She gave her a big smile.

"Go round to the side entrance by the kitchen." The door closed.

Olive stood on the doorstep, working off the smile. Then she walked around and knocked on the back door. Mrs. Fisk answered again. "Servants use the side entrance."

Olive followed her into a large kitchen filled with steam and the smell of burning feathers. The cook was there—her hands slimy with the blood and fat of the partially hacked up chicken that lay on the counter. She had a plump stomach, a skinny neck and small round head, and a sharp nose. She looked a little like a turtle. People said her daughter SuSu was a half-wit. SuSu rocked on her haunches by the stove, plucking the singed feathers off another chicken. A stain the color of sumac washed down one cheek, swelling her lips, lapping at her neck. The cook smiled. "Good morning, I'm Mrs. Cutter." She wiped her hands on her apron. Big wooden drawers were pulled open, filled with white flour and oats. There was a whole drawer of white sugar.

"Put your basket in this corner for now," Mrs. Fisk said. "Have you brought an apron?" Olive pulled her apron out. "You ain't using that yellowed, wrinkled thing in this house." The house-keeper took out a starched apron from the closet.

Olive tied it on. It felt like armor.

"Watch your manners with Mrs. Hammond. Remember she is a lady. She won't put up with miners' talk."

Olive stopped tying her apron. "I'm not like that. My ma taught me everything. I can read and write."

"And don't put on airs." They climbed a steep stairway at the back of the kitchen that ended in a wide second-floor hallway. Mrs. Fisk knocked on a door.

"Enter."

"This is Olive Honsinger, come from the mines to care for Miss Regina," Mrs. Fisk announced, then turned and left Olive there.

"I am Mrs. Hammond." A woman about Olive's mother's age sat in a big, blue armchair in the middle of a pastel blue bedroom, wearing a loose blue morning gown. Her hair looked like grey scissor ribbons. She had a quilt over her lap, and she was painting a plate with a tiny paintbrush. Olive stood in the doorway, feeling large and broad and country. Mrs. Hammond was large too, but covered in silk, the large didn't show so much. Mrs. Hammond continued painting her plate with short dabs of robin's-egg blue. "I used to enjoy painting. Now I seem to detest it. But my doctor believes it may distract me from my illness." Olive wondered if she was so rich, why she didn't hire someone else to paint the plates. The room smelled like brush-cleaning fluid. Mrs. Hammond sighed and dropped the brush on the floor. The paint made a little light blue splatter on the dark blue velvet floor.

"Are you from the Kingdom of Sweden, Olive Handslinger?"

"Honsinger. No, ma'm. My family's from Vermont on one

side, Moriah to the other. My father was Wealthy Landry, the engineer. My husband's a Swede, though. Ren Honsinger?"

"I'm afraid that lineage will have to do, as my niece has a sudden desire for you. We'll just have to hope you haven't picked up diseases from your foreign husband. You never know, do you? They could look as healthy as oxen, but inside, their bodies stuffed with typhus and cholera—poison gusting out on every breath. Doesn't affect them at all." Mrs. Hammond's voice had a tired, airy sound, like bellows. "But, you see, the Hammonds and the Putnams— that's my side—have always had delicate constitutions. Why, I doubt if I, or my niece Miss Sartwell, could fight off a teaspoon of typhus."

"Yes, ma'am."

Mrs. Hammond sighed. "I have a terrible feeling here." She patted her chest. "It's not a pain, it's more of a pressure or a flutter." She fluttered her hand on her chest to show. "And I wake up with it nearly every morning now."

"My mother has that. She takes rosemary, dandelion, and shave grass in a tincture for the flutter, and if you got the flush too, try water lily and witch hazel."

"Your mother will soon see that weeds will not suffice. Without the help of a good physician, it will only worsen. Mine has lasted these five years now, and I can just bear it with all the treatments Dr. Corning can think of. Dr. Corning has studied in Europe. I have engaged him from his practice in Albany. He visits us once a month." Mrs. Hammond looked down at the paintbrush. She nudged it with her slippered foot. The paint smeared a few more inches. "He is with us now."

"Should I clean that, ma'am?"

Mrs. Hammond shook her head. "I must give you some instruction for my niece's care. She is ill, not just from her fall, but from a constitutional disturbance, namely, epilepsy. It affects her mind. She tends towards hysteria, even exaggeration, I'm afraid. It will be your task to keep her steady and calm.

"Take no notice of her imaginings. If she asks you to do anything . . . strange, go to Mrs. Fisk immediately. You see, there has been much strangeness in the poor girl's life. Her grandmother, on the other side, was, to put it kindly, an extreme eccentric. And the unfortunate girl spent her childhood with this grandmother. The blood will out, I always say. Miss Sartwell herself caused such a disaster at her engagement party, scrabbling on the floor like a wild beast, attacking her fiancé, from all reports a shy, lovely young gentleman from an excellent family. Apparently he has gone to Europe to recover. I believe some of the ladies in attendance have never recovered from the shock. I thank Providence I was too ill to attend.

"I must warn you, she may be physically dangerous. But you look sturdy enough. Dr. Corning believes her path to recovery lies in the curbing of her fantasies. He has given so many instructions. Have I forgotten any? Somehow, I must muster the strength to care for this girl. We are both so ill, but she has such an un-Christian temper, it may carry her through.

"Oh yes, before I forget, over on the table there are two items to carry with you at all times. The smelling salts may revive her if she is entering a fit. If they do not, place that cloth-covered stick in her mouth to prevent her from swallowing her own tongue. And above all, girl, keep her quiet. Her noise does incalculable damage to me. Incalculable. My doctor is with Miss Sartwell now, so you may ask Fisk for a chore while you are waiting. Fisk will instruct you from now on. I don't have the strength."

"Yes, ma'am."

Someone tapped lightly on the door. "Enter."

Mrs. Cutter's daughter tiptoed in. A singed white chicken feather stuck to SuSu's wrist. Mrs. Hammond pushed the half-painted plate away from her with her foot. She leaned her neck on the back of the chair; her silver and ruby earrings slid along her neck. The holes in Mrs. Hammond's ears were inch-long slits. Mrs. Hammond sighed and closed her eyes. The Cutter girl went over to a dressing table and picked out a silver tweezers. She stood in front of Mrs. Hammond, braced her hand on the back of the chair, and began plucking the grey stubble that grew out of the lady's chin. Mrs. Hammond grunted as each hair was yanked from the skin.

"You must be busy about your duties now." Mrs. Hammond didn't open her eyes.

"Yes, ma'am." Olive gathered the stick and the smelling salts and left the room. After she closed the door, she turned the little bottle of smelling salts around. The bottle was a pretty deep blue. She uncorked it and took a sniff. Her eyes teared. Her nostrils burned. She grabbed on to the stair railing. "That'd wake the dead," she said out loud.

Olive found Mrs. Fisk writing some sort of list in the kitchen. "Fill the lamps," Fisk said. "You will find the kerosene in the hall closet. I believe there are thirty-six, so be sure you've found them all. Don't go into the general's study or Miss Sartwell's room, the second and fourth doors on the hall. When you've finished with the lamps, come back to the kitchen to fetch Miss Sartwell's breakfast."

Olive had never seen so many things, not even in a store. Throw rugs over Oriental rugs over tacked-down velvet. Even though the morning was brilliant, the heavy damask curtains hung in folds across the windows. There were no fires in the fireplaces, but pure heat seemed to be gusting up from grates in the floor. In the front of the house were two parlors, one of wicker, one of heavy wood and velvet. Her footsteps made no sound on the cushioned floors.

Olive kept forgetting to breathe. In the wicker parlor there was a whole wall of framed seeds and shells. The other walls were covered in landscape paintings with wide gold frames. There were arching areca palm plants, fuchsias, geraniums, dried grasses in standing vases. There was a big glass jar filled with flower petals and cloves. Olive took a small handful and dropped it in her apron pocket. Then she put it back. She rubbed a drop of kerosene on the pocket to cover the smell.

And the other parlor—the colors. She ran her gloved hand over the yellow couch, both ways, smooth and against the nap, over her palm like a sweet animal. A plum-colored chair with leaves and vines carved into the back. Two huge glass cases. In one every sort of china figurine stared back at her, row after row, precarious. She tried to control her breathing, so that everything wouldn't totter and fall. In the other cabinet were the china plates—scores of them, painted with flowers and birds and Bible quotations. There was a case of leather-bound books whose gold-edged pages had never been cut—Cooper, Virgil, Dickens, Dickens, Dickens.

In front of the fire was a stained-glass screen. Brilliant purples and blues in the shape of a woman holding a vase or bucket on her shoulder. Above the fire screen on the mantel stood an upside-down photograph framed in silver. Olive righted it: a lady dressed in white, reclining on a fainting couch surrounded by long-stemmed lilies. She had the tiniest smile on her rosebud lips. She cradled a lily in her long white fingers. The lady must be Miss Sartwell. Olive backed up and sat on the edge of the yellow couch. Her body, which had always felt completely solid, was fading, curling around the edges, thinner and thinner. All that was left were eyes and a shallow, panting breath. All these things are clogging my heart, she thought. She concentrated on her job, looking for kerosene lamps.

Olive was carrying a tray down the hall towards Miss Sartwell's room. Tea sloshed onto the biscuits. She balanced the tray in one hand and knocked on the closed door.

"What?"

Olive's heart started up. Behind the door lived the white lady. "Breakfast, ma'am."

"Come in."

Olive pushed the door with her shoulder. The door swung open. She heard heavy, nasal breathing. The curtains were drawn and there was no fire. Olive squinted. In the far corner of the large room, on a huge four-poster bed, slumped a monster. The face was bloated, purple and veiny. The eyes had sunk, swollen almost shut inside the monster face.

"You're staring, and you're spilling the tea." The words were all gathered at the front of the mouth. Olive righted the tray and tried to find a place for her eyes. She moved closer and slid the tray onto the table by the bed. The monster lady smelled of medicinal alcohol.

"Closer. I can't see your face." The monster lady reached out with her unbroken hand and clenched some of Olive's apron. Olive had to hold herself still to keep from bolting back.

"I don't know your name."

"Olive Honsinger, ma'am."

She let go of the apron. "I just wanted to make sure you were real." She turned to her tray.

"I'm sorry, ma'am, it just—tipped." Olive tried to use her apron to sop up the tea. She could feel a nervous laugh at her throat.

"Don't worry over that. I don't care for food." Olive looked up from wiping the tea. The face was a little like the half-wit's. Olive put her hand in the pocket of her apron and touched the cloth-covered stick.

"I know what you could do for me first thing, Olive Honsinger. You could spy. The ass, my uncle, is consulting about me with that other ass. The doctor. Corning. I want to know what their plans are for me. Go out in the hall, to the right, the double doors—it's my uncle's study. Pretend you're cleaning and listen to what they have to say. Be crafty."

"Pretend I'm cleaning, ma'am?" Olive said.

"Use that feather duster in the corner."

Olive picked up a green dyed bunch of feathers. "Clean with this?"

"Hurry. I want you to hear all of it." Those bruised little pig eyes blinked at her. Olive blinked back.

"*Hurry.*"

"Yes, ma'am." Olive stood outside the closed door she had left and stared at the feather duster. She heard a grating whisper from inside: "Hurry up!"

I'll tell Mrs. Fisk, Olive thought. She walked with the feather duster down the hallway towards the kitchen. As she passed the large, sliding double doors of the study, she heard the grand voice of General Hammond asking if the doctor would like a drink.

"No, General, it's too early in the day for a man who knows as much as I do about the digestive system." Olive stopped. The doctor's voice continued: "I have a letter from a specialist down below, in New York City. He says here that he believes it possible she suffers from hystero-epilepsy, not true epilepsy. I believe this leap from the store does point to a hysteric origin. Although it is just as likely what we call epileptic fury—a kind of madness that comes on just before or after a fit. You see, she has only had two, what we call *grand mal* attacks, and both since the onset of her womanhood. Epilepsy has been linked with a diseased uterus. It is very lucky that in such a remote village as this you are visited by a doctor familiar with female diseases. I studied in London, as you know."

"Mrs. Hammond has told me many times."

"I would like to try a six-month cure—adherence to a healthful diet, which I will describe for your cook. I will also give her Dr. Pierce's Pleasant Pellets to regulate the bowels. Have her maid bathe her with red pepper once or twice a week. That is all the excitement her nervous system will need. Do not allow anything else that will overexcite her. And lastly—"

"Tell your prescription to Fisk. I don't wish to know."

"Ah. You are concerned with the broader diagnosis. If this is epilepsy, she will deteriorate into insanity or clouded intellect. A surgical treatment may be her only hope. I came across an innovative technique in London, practiced by a Dr. Brown. He's written a book on it. I would explain it, but it might seem shocking to a nonmedical man."

"Shocking. How old were you during the war? Eleven?

29

Twelve? War makes medicine look like a parlor game." Olive waved the feather duster around on the wall.

"You're right, General. We are living in a singular age. Here in this room we have both a venerable veteran of the Union army and a man of the twentieth century. I freely admit it. I am possessed with innovation. This particular technique is especially efficacious in curing epileptic females, although it has other curative possibilities, including menopausal hysteria, I might add. The surgeon simply removes the useless flaps of skin surrounding the vulva, the labia—"

"Enough. I'm not interested."

"I understand. In any case, her injuries from the fall are slight. Bruised. Nose broken, which will impair the delicacy of her beauty but not her health. Wrist—a clean break. It should heal in six weeks time. She is fortunate she arrived in your little outpost. I have had articles published on the female change of life, you know. So, sir, what do you say we give her six months to improve? If the cure works, she may be a comfort to your wife, and I will certainly write a paper. If she seems incurable, we will try that unmentionable surgical operation. If that doesn't work, she will be better off in the state lunatic asylum at Utica. The assistant superintendent is my cousin, you know."

"I leave it to you, Corning. I know nothing of medicine. I've never been sick a day in my life. Not even in the war. I grant you that most women are sickly, but this seems a coarse disease for Mary's daughter. My sister Mary had consumption. Never complained. Died quietly. When she passed on they laid her body out as if she were asleep. My wife likened her to Snow White. There is a photograph of this in the parlor.

"I carried a likeness of Mary in my breast pocket during the war. I believe that photograph spurred me on, reminding me that we were fighting for angels like Mary. Mary's bone structure was not so different from this epileptic's, but the expression on this one's face! No wonder her father washed his hands of her. And after her fall the words she uttered seemed evidence of insanity, right there. But we'll give you six months to work your miracle." The general coughed. His voice lowered. "Perhaps you will turn her into Mary's daughter after all."

The doctor laughed. "It's possible that if we lift off the terrible mantle of epileptic fury, we will uncover a girl as sweet as your departed sister. Now, as to this newly hired maid. I've had information from your Dr. Lenard, and I believe you couldn't have hired a better girl yourself. She is from clean New England stock. Her mother helps Lenard care for his simpler cases. And it will be pleasant to have her around the house, as Dr. Lenard says she is not a bad-looking girl—fat-assed and forever giggling."

"I cannot abide giggling."

"Still, she is large and steady, and perhaps best of all, as cheerful and lacking in imagination as her father, who was a great favorite with you, Lenard believes—an engineer. One-armed."

"Yes. Landry—stupid, but honest."

"A dull girl like this is perfect for your excitable young guest. It will be like the company of a cow or a good sheepdog."

Olive heard the chairs sigh as the men rose out of them. She backed rapidly down the hall, the green feather duster in front of her like a shield. She heard something behind her. She twisted around. "I—" Olive reached up to touch her lips, then brought her hand down. "Hello, Mrs. Cutter."

"That feather duster ain't meant for real cleaning." Mrs. Cutter was smiling.

Olive tried to smile back.

"Well, Mrs. Read and Write, don't let Fisk see you walking backwards down the hall waving feathers. They hired you 'cause you was sensible."

"How does everyone know I'm so sensible?" Her voice squeaked.

"I don't hardly know, especially with that mess of fire you call hair. I think you're foolin' everyone, ain't you?"

Olive heard the sliding doors open. "I-have-to-see-to-Miss-Sartwell." She pushed past Mrs. Cutter.

"Ah, Mrs. Cutter, I have some instructions for you as to food preparation for—"

Olive walked into Miss Sartwell's room without knocking.

"You're back."

"I'm sorry I didn't knock, miss, I—"

"Tell me what he said. The ass. Both asses."

"Excuse me, ma'am?"

"My swearing shocks you. You see, my bedroom was on the first floor at my grandmother's when I was a child. Every morning I would hear the hop pickers walk by on their way to my grandfather's fields. That's how I learned oaths. Every morning I was wakened by soft, growly swearing. When I was a girl I would run off down the fields to the lake and practice the swearing for myself. I always held my hand over my mouth when I practiced, to be ladylike. But now that I'm an epileptic, there is no need to hold my hand over my mouth, is there?"

Olive sagged into the rocking chair by Miss Sartwell's bed.

Miss Sartwell's wounded face watched her. "So? What did they say?"

"I'm not sure how to start. I'm a little winded."

Miss Sartwell laughed a narrow, mouthed, painful laugh. "Then I'll ask you specific questions. This will be fun." She pulled herself farther up on the pillows. "Do the questions need to be yes or no?"

"No. Ma'am."

"Why don't you leave off the 'ma'am' and the 'Miss Sartwell'? We must be the same age. I'm twenty-one."

"I'm nineteen, ma'am."

"Just call me Regina. I like my given name. And my father and I no longer wish to be associated."

"If you don't mind then, I'll call you Miss Regina, until I get comfortable."

"Fine. Back to the questions."

"I just needed to take a breath. I can tell you, ma'am. The doctor said—" She gave her head a shake. "He said your fits could be hysteric or real. Either ways he says you have to follow what he calls a strict regimen—nothing more exciting than a pepper bath—which I'm supposed to give you."

"That's all he said?"

"He said some other things."

"Exactly what other things?"

"He says if it's real fits, alls you need is rest."

"Then why don't they let me rest somewhere else? With Mary-anne or Lovina." There was a sharp double knock on the door. Olive stood up to answer it, but Miss Sartwell put up her hand to stop her. "Who is it?"

"Fisk."

"What do you want?"

"I have here a list of instructions the doctor has given your new maid to help you recover, miss."

"Slide them under the door, then."

"Is Olive Honsinger in there with you, miss?"

"No."

"Do you know where she might be?"

"I sent her to empty the slops."

The note slipped under the door.

"Must you stand outside my door eavesdropping, Fisk?"

Footsteps marched away.

Olive picked up the note. "Miss Regina, why did you lie—"

"I don't care for that woman. The only person in this house I can stand is the cook. I've always liked cooks. It's not that I like food, I don't care for it. But cooks are so comforting, because of their own simple faith in food. Perhaps in the spring this cook would bake me a strawberry pie, and coax me to eat it. If I picked the strawberries for her. Those wild ones that grow in pastures. If I'm still here." Her mouth had widened into a grimace. A thread of blood slipped from a cut that had opened on the edge of her lip. "Come back later. I find I want to sleep."

Olive left, balancing the untouched tray in one hand and clenching the list of cures in the other. She stood in the hallway, unable to think where to go. She could hear gasping sobs on the other side of the door. She knocked. "Miss Regina?"

"Come back later."

Olive walked into the kitchen. Mrs. Cutter was sitting in front of a small fire in an enormous fireplace.

"I like a little fire to warm my toes, even with the furnace. Have a cup of tea, Mrs. Honsinger?"

Olive poured herself one and sat down in the chair across from Mrs. Cutter. She wrapped her hands around the cup. She put her feet closer to the heat. She couldn't hear Miss Sartwell's sobs from here, anyway. "I can't figure the heating in this house, Mrs. Cutter."

"This house, Mrs. Honsinger, is a fine puzzle. Now, we got the fanciest heating you can buy, but we ain't bricked up the fireplaces. We ain't got those gaslights, but we got a indoor convenience all set up these two years—bathtub, indoor outhouse—all porcelain and the tub with lion-claw feet, but they ain't brought a man in to hook her up."

"But why? Don't they got the money to finish?" Olive brought her voice down. "Is it like some say? The mines are drying up?"

"No, no, it's domestic. See, Mrs. Hammond started through the change of life about five year ago. And she's been having a bad time of it, too. She give up all her pretty clubs and charities and take to her bed. She pays for a doctor to come all the way from Albany, stays at the house, every month a new cure. Don't think I'm not having to fix a new kind of food every month, too." Mrs. Cutter sat back and sighed. "Ain't this satisfying, tootsies warming, a cup of tea and some good gossip."

"Yes, Mrs. Cutter, it is."

"Anyways, the general gets the idea that this sickness is all in Mrs. Hammond's head, and if she was to keep a stiff upper lip, it would disappear. So he gets up a plan. For every month that the missus stays out of bed and away from her doctor, he'll add a modern convenience to the house. This was the missus' main dream. So the first month she stays out of bed, sewing in the parlor mostly.

You can see she feels poorly. She got sweat on her lip, and she runs to the outhouse every few hours." Mrs. Cutter's voice went low. "To tell the truth, once the poor lady didn't make it and messed herself. She cried then, and almost went up to bed, but Fisk reminded her of the general, so Fisk cleaned her up, and she sat back down and sewed and sniffled all day. Pitiful. Finally the month ended. The general got right to work on the heat, ordered from somewhere, Albany, I guess. True to his word, I'll say that.

"Her next trial was for an indoor convenience. She was determined. But that month she got a new ailment, these hot spells you've heard about. They scared her. She would sit like a statue when they come, and there would be the sweat popping out all over." Mrs. Cutter stood up. She went over to the counter and began cracking eggs into a big brown bowl. "All goes well. The general even starts the work, though the month ain't up yet. But one day, the general's away somewheres, and it turns out the missus has wired for the doctor, planned it out for him to come while the general's away. He tries something new on her." Mrs. Cutter paused in her beating of the eggs with the wooden spoon. She went into her whisper again, her thin turtle's neck craned towards Olive. "I know what that doctor done too, 'cause Fisk was called in and later she was so broke up, she spilled the whole story. The doctor took ice water, had me melt snow on the stove special. Then Fisk brung it up and he shoot it up inside the missus. And I don't mean into her mouth neither. Into the other part—her arse." Mrs. Cutter nodded, then went back to beating the eggs.

"Fisk said missus was so sickened, she just laid her head down on the pillow, tears leaking, ice water leaking. And there she was in bed when the general come home. He found out she had the doctor in, and he washed his hands of it. Told the workers to go on home. And they ain't had another improvement in two year. The general is never at home no more, and the missus ain't left the house, since."

Neither of them spoke for a while. The only sound in the kitchen was the wooden spoon frothing the eggs in the bowl. Then

Mrs. Cutter said, "Quite a mistress you got yourself. This young miss, huh?"

Olive nodded. She leaned back in her chair and closed her eyes.

"That's it," Mrs. Cutter said. "Just you close your eyes and rest a minute. I'll let you know if I hear Fisk."

Olive concentrated on the feel of the fire on her eyelids. But words began to slip through: Fat-assed. Cow. Sheepdog. She could feel tears wobbling against her lids. Olive pressed her lids tighter. She hated blubbering. Like her Ma said, Olive had a face like a daisy. Even as a baby, never a tear.

Miss Sartwell didn't call for Olive all afternoon. The house was quiet. Olive was told to help Mr. Cutter haul coal down to the basement. He worked with that same wheezing she'd heard the night she met him. The basement was cool. Down there in the root cellar were two wooden crates, one of apples and one of oranges. Rows of preserves. Wine bottles.

Later, Mr. Cutter split wood in the back, near the horse barn, and Olive brought armfuls into the house. She liked the raw, sappy smell and the rough feel of the wood on her wrists and palms. The sky was already low—orange and grey. It hadn't snowed much lately down here to Crown Point, and the lawn was covered in stiff, frozen, brown grass. But now snow was falling. Big, light flakes like torn paper floated every which way. The dark, icy puddles on the lawn had a light sprinkling of white over them. Olive liked the lonely sound of the grass crackling under her boots.

Mrs. Fisk came to the back door. "Common sense should tell you that the lamps need to be lit when the sun goes down. The one day the general decides to entertain at home, and here I am busy with Mrs. Hammond. Light his study, if he hasn't already been forced to do it himself."

Olive could hear the voices of men coming from the study. She tapped on the door. "Should I light the lamps, General?"

"Did it myself." She was turning away when she heard, "Stop. Come in."

It was hard to slide the door with one shaking hand. She looked in. The room was bright. There was wood and green leather and books. Men with cigars and dark clothing. Who knew how many, but she saw the general. His small blue eyes stared at her. No one spoke. She kept her eyes on the Oriental rug and counted the green swirls by her boot.

"You may go." She backed out. She struggled with the door. It stuck. When she finally pulled it closed she heard a burst of laughter that reminded her of gunpowder.

Back in the kitchen there was a tray for Miss Sartwell. "After, you can have some supper with us, Mrs. Honsinger," Mrs. Cutter said.

Olive carried the tray down the hall. She knocked on the door.

"Who is it?"

"It's me, miss, Olive."

"Come in." The room was dark. Olive set the tray down and lit the lamp by the bed. Then she made a little fire, for friendliness. She liked the way the room looked, orange shadows, the fluffed-up white comforter, and the bunch of small, lace-edged pillows. Miss Sartwell was propped up in bed, holding a book.

"How could you read in the dark, miss?"

"I just held my face close. In truth, though, it even hurts my fingers to turn the pages." Again, the strange, narrow laugh.

"I'll ready your bath while you eat, miss."

"Have you eaten?"

"Me, miss?"

"Share this with me. I can't eat this great bowl of soup and this elephant-sized bread."

"You'll never get your health back unless you eat up, miss."

"Will you please stop calling me 'miss'? It feels as if you were pushing me away with that word. Stop rushing around and sit down."

Olive walked towards the bed and sat on the rocker. Miss Regina split the bread in two. "Miss, it ain't regular to eat with the maid, is it?"

Miss Regina looked at her with that tiny smile on her face. Olive checked her lip.

"In Geneva I took my meals in the kitchen with Libby. She was the cook. I don't like eating alone. Here, there's no one I care to be in the same room with, except you. Not that I know you. I just liked your hair. And now I like your face."

Olive smiled at her. They finished their food. Then Olive brought the tray back to the kitchen, dragged in the tin tub, and filled it with a few inches of heated water. Water splashed a little over the boards. Steam curled up.

"Let me help you to the tub, miss," Olive said. She took Miss Regina by the good elbow. She edged her feet off the bed. Her teeth were clenched, her good arm stiff. When she slid down Olive saw that her legs, too, were scraped and bruised.

"I was sure no one could live from that height. Still, I tried to jump in the mine, but he wouldn't let go of my elbow."

Olive let go of Miss Sartwell's elbow now. "You're not going to try again, are you, miss?"

"If I didn't die, I must be meant to endure. It's a sign that I'll find what I'm looking for on this earth." She creaked to her feet and groaned. "I'll never try it again. It makes me too sore."

"I forgot the red pepper." Olive found the sack of red pepper in the kitchen. When she walked back, Miss Sartwell was standing by the tub, holding her nightgown above her knees. She dropped the hem.

"Ain't you goin' to get in the tub, miss?" All that water, at this time of night, for nothing.

Tears started leaking out of Miss Sartwell's eyes.

"Are you crying, miss?"

"I don't know why. I've had a good day. I've started plans and met you. I'm on my way."

"You're crying 'cause you're hurt and tired and lonesome." Olive walked over to Miss Regina and edged her nightgown off over the broken arm.

~

38

Miss Regina's body was sinew and bone, flat, like Ren's before he grew up. It seemed to hurt Miss Regina just to lift her leg into the tub, and she continued her quiet rain of tears. Olive was about to drop a pinch of pepper into the bath when she imagined what it would feel like in those long, red-beaded scrapes.

She set the sack aside until Miss Regina healed over. Olive took a rag and dripped warm water on Miss Regina's neck, down her back, then over the shoulders onto her chest. She washed her head gently, with soap. Her hair was thin, like summer grass. Miss Regina stopped crying and closed her eyes. She held the broken arm off to the side like a broken wing.

After Olive dried Miss Regina, she wrapped her in a flannel nightgown and sat her in the rocker and combed out her long, flyaway hair. Miss Regina hardly opened her eyes, but tears leaked now and then. When Olive was finished, and the lady's hair lay in neat, wet ridges like a plowed field, Miss Regina said, "I'll brush your hair now, Olive."

"Mine's a tough job, miss. Snarly."

"I'll be careful."

It was so steamy and clean from the hot water, and the lamp flickered shadows around the warm room. Olive walked around to the front of the rocker and sat down on the floor, near enough to the fireplace so that the cold on her butt felt pleasant. Olive edged near Miss Regina's bony, bruised knees, careful not to touch them. She heard Miss Regina's breath turn into little, irritated huffs as the hurt fingers picked uselessly at Olive's thick braid.

"I'll do it," Olive said. She let down her pinned-up hair and then unplaited her braid. "I like it soft, anyways," Olive said.

Olive felt the comb flicking at her hair, as light as a moth. "Even my good hand isn't working so well." Miss Regina kept flicking.

Olive closed her eyes. "My sister Ida has thick hair too, but not so snarly. Hers is straight brown. She and Ma used to comb my hair out on Sundays. Ida wasn't patient, though. She ripped the knots out more'n untangled them."

"My grandmother brushed my hair. It would tear out if anyone pulled too hard. It's so thin my scalp sunburns in the summers if I forget to wear a hat."

"What about your ma? Didn't she ever comb your hair, before she died?"

"My mother was too ill to have me with her. I'm the youngest, and the others were all grown before my mother came down with consumption. I remember when I would visit the house in New York City my mother would call for me to come to her. She was almost always in bed. I didn't like to go. What she coughed up smelled horrible, and her eyes so big—as if they were made of gelatin. The last time I visited, she was almost yellow, like old lace. And she was as vaporous as lace too. Except for the nails on her hands—they were livid, red and purple. The only colored thing on her." The comb stopped fluttering. "My mother and I are alike in that way, no matter what anyone says. It's just that what she had in her fingernails has taken me over entirely."

Olive twisted around. There was something in Miss Regina's face. "I should empty the water. And you need your rest, miss."

Miss Regina put down the comb and allowed herself to be tucked into bed. Olive surrounded her sore body with pillows. Before Olive turned down the lamp, she asked, "Do you want to say your prayers, miss?"

Miss Regina laughed her thin laugh. "No, I've died and come back—I think I'm past that. God will have to take me as He finds me now." She turned her face to the wall.

Olive twisted down the lamp. She stood for a minute in the room to get used to the dimmer, redder light from the fire. She couldn't lift the water tub, so she dragged it. "Sleep peacefully, Miss Regina."

"Isn't that what one says about the dead? I hope our sleep is filled with dark, long-armed women."

Olive crossed her fingers to ward off the evil eye, the way a French-Canadian girl in school had shown her. She emptied the tub out the back kitchen door.

Mrs. Fisk was sitting in the kitchen, candlelight lapping at her wide jaw. "Will you stay with the epileptic this late every night?" she asked.

"I don't know, ma'am. If she wants me."

"Then I will put out the lamps each night and bolt the door. You will fill them each morning and light them at evening. Mrs. Cutter left you supper."

"I'll take it with me to my room."

"If you eat in your bedroom, you'll draw mice."

"So I ain't allowed to eat in my room?"

"And they said you were mild tempered. But maybe that wicked epileptic is already influencing you." The candlelight slid over Mrs. Fisk's chin and onto her dark hair as she turned away from Olive.

Olive took her plate filled with leftover chicken pie and potatoes, and sat beside Mrs. Fisk. She shoveled the good food in with her hand and her knife, trying to make pleasing conversation. She told Mrs. Fisk too much, even about staining the apron. Mrs. Fisk made no response to anything. Finally, when Olive was finished and had washed her plate, she stood awkwardly with her lighted candle. "Mrs. Fisk, I'm sorry about my rudeness. I was just tired, is all."

"Another thing," Mrs. Fisk said. "I don't know how she does it, but every time I enter the parlor the epileptic has somehow snuck in and turned the photograph of her mother upside down. Devilment. See that it doesn't happen again."

In the little room Olive locked the door and undressed to her union suit. She climbed under the covers and blew the candle out. "Please, sweet Jesus, keep Mama and Ren and Ida and Magnus safe, and please God, don't let me dream of dark women with long arms." She made the sign against the evil eye again.

The sheets were as stiff and starchy as her apron. Outside the sky was clear again, a million stars. A clear day tomorrow. She thought of Ren, curled around himself in their bed, long since asleep, and her mother, snoring slightly, her long grey braid against her shoulder . . .

Six months and then the operation. That's what he'd said about Miss Regina. And if this cutting operation didn't work—the lunatic asylum. Olive was awake again. She imagined sitting on the edge of the lady's bed, whispering a warning to her, and then Miss Regina going wild—shrieking, smashing windows, scratching. Olive begging, wringing her hands, Oh, please be quiet, miss, please. But Miss Regina would not be quiet.

The general's voice would thrum through the house, moving towards Olive: It was your job to keep her quiet.

His ice blue eyes would make her weep.

Three

~

FISK RAPPED ON her door before dawn. The three bangs on the wood shook the bottle of smelling salts over. Olive felt as if she had slept for five minutes. She got up in the dark, dressed, and went about the same tasks as yesterday: pumping water up from the basement, filling the lamps, helping Mr. Cutter load wood and start the fire in the furnace in the basement, surrounded by nothing but Mr. Cutter's wheezing and the dark, predawn shapes of the Hammonds' furniture.

It was getting light when Mr. Cutter went off to feed the horses, and she and Mrs. Cutter and Mrs. Fisk sat down to breakfast in the kitchen. It was bread-baking day, and Mrs. Cutter's hands were floury. Her daughter poured them tea, then sat on the floor by the stove, whispering into the cup she held in both hands.

Mrs. Cutter saw Olive watching SuSu. "Born slow is all," Mrs. Cutter said. Then she said, "Mr. Cutter said last night on his way home, about five miles out of town, he passed the far field by the old Dade farm, the one that burnt down. He says the Gypsies has set up camp. Said it was a chilly sight—those open fires on a night so cold."

"I've never seen a Gypsy," Olive said.

"Dirty beggars," Mrs. Fisk said.

"They might stay for a while." Mrs. Cutter scraped dough out from under her nails with a knife. "A few years ago they camped all spring. Arla Stevens swears they can cure anything."

"They'll stay as long as it takes to steal and cheat thoroughly, until the sheriff drives 'em away. Gypsies are cousins to Indians, and that's something to think about." Mrs. Fisk held her cup so firmly, Olive was afraid it would shatter.

"I heard General Hammond knew General Custer in the war," Mrs. Cutter said.

"Did you ever hear the story of the Indians who slit open the farmer's stomach, tied his entrails to a tree, and left him there, still living? It was around here it happened, too." Mrs. Fisk sipped her tea.

The hall clock struck seven times. Olive fixed the tray for Miss Regina. Mug of milk, boiled-up prunes, and corn mush. Mrs. Fisk had readied a tray for Mrs. Hammond that had on it a glass of wine, several bottles of medicine, and the prunes. The leftover smell from the general's breakfast, ham and eggs and fried potatoes, filled the kitchen.

Mrs. Cutter said, "I just feel awful. I promised that girl I'd feed her real good, but that doctor give me orders before he left, to make her the most plain, awful food you can imagine. She'll die of boredom 'fore she's cured, sure. That doctor may as well come in here and cook his own self, he's been planning the meals for so many months in this house."

Olive walked the breakfast down the hall. She balanced the tray on one hand to knock on the door. The bowls clinked into each other, and milk sloshed out of the cup.

She was sitting up in bed. Her face had yellowed a little more, and her eyes seemed less squinty. They were bloodshot. "I have two adventures planned for us today. The pain is making my head clear. It's not even pain anymore, just plain old ache." She spooned up a little corn mush and gulped milk. "The first adventure is dressing, and the second is an excursion to the outhouse."

"The chamber pot is right there in the corner, miss."

"I know, but I don't want to use that, miss. I want to go to the outhouse. I want to get out of this building even if it's just to relieve myself."

"Mrs. Fisk'll probably think I'm too lazy to empty the pot, miss."

"As long as I'm not making a fuss, they'll credit you. I want to get dressed. Eat the rest of my food."

"Miss Regina, shouldn't you tell Mrs. Hammond, or someone, that you want to step out?"

"No, I don't think I need to let the whole house know every time I want to pee. Now, eat this up for me."

"You need it for your strength, miss."

"Eat it, Miss Olive, or I'll throw it out."

"If you throw it out, I ain't helping you to the outhouse."

Miss Regina laughed, surprised. "I always have to hold my nose when I eat slop, but now it's broken and clogged and I can't taste a thing. Lucky."

After Miss Regina ate, Olive brought out her clothes and laid them on the bed. There was a brown dress made of taffeta and velvet. It was so big and stiff, it could have stood up by itself. Olive helped Miss Regina edge off her night gown. Miss Regina instructed Olive to help her pull on two cotton petticoats. Then she eased herself into a sitting position on the edge of her bed, still naked above the waist, and Olive carefully rolled black wool stockings over her bony knees and up her thighs.

"Just bring me that," Miss Regina said, already out of breath, pointing to a corset trailing pink ribbon.

"My ma says corsets make you sick."

"I'd look common without it. Everyone wears corsets."

"Never saw a woman wear a corset. But then, I guess I'm common."

"Oh, put it away. I'm sure all my maternal forebears are fainting in their graves. What's next? Crossing my legs at the knee?" Miss Regina tried to cross her legs, groaned. "Not yet, I guess. You can put that corset cover back, too." Miss Regina had to stand again while Olive slipped her into a knee-length flannel petticoat, then two more petticoats over that. She was beginning to thicken. Olive pinned layers of flounces to her rear. Her behind rounded. Next her false breasts—tiers of ruffles pinned on the flannel. Lace-up pointed boots. The sleeve of the stiff dress seemed impossible to edge over Miss Regina's broken arm, but she insisted. Olive coiled her hair onto the top of her head. She was glad Miss Regina couldn't see the wispy mess. Finally, a brown hat. Olive convinced her to drape one side of the brown velvet coat over her sling instead of trying to squeeze into it. Miss Regina was again the curving, elegant lady that Olive had first seen. But the strange, bruised face rode on top, ruining the picture.

"Here we go, out of my cave and into the world." Miss Regina hitched one of her legs up higher than the other, gasping after each step. Olive opened the back door at the end of the hall.

"Lord, it is cold. The air is waking me up," Miss Regina said.

"It does just the same for me sometimes," Olive said.

They hobbled towards the outhouse. Olive gripped Miss Regina's arm tightly over the slick, frozen lawn. "Why don't they open the curtains, miss? It looks like someone died."

Miss Regina turned to look at the house. "There's one of the dead now," she said.

Olive felt her neck crawl. She whipped around, but it was just Mrs. Fisk, watching from the kitchen window. Miss Regina slowly bent down. She scraped up a shard of ice and frozen grass. She tossed it underhand at Mrs. Fisk's window. The face disappeared.

The outhouse door slammed closed behind them. It smelled of lime and urine. It was a two-seater, with a neat stack of newspaper piled on one side.

"Here goes," Miss Regina said. Olive helped her lift her skirts, and she sat down. "I can't do this with you standing over me. Sit down and pretend."

Olive giggled and pulled up her skirts. She checked for spiders, then settled herself. It was freezing.

"Who are your friends, Olive Honsinger?"

≈

46

"My friends? I don't know. My school friends mostly moved on. There's Minnie, but she has three babies, plus her husband's younger brothers to care for. I talk to her after church sometimes." Olive could hear Miss Regina's pee splatting on the frozen mess below.

"Are you married, Olive?"

"Yes. To Ren Honsinger, just this past summer."

"Do you enjoy it?"

"What?"

"Do you enjoy marriage?"

"I like it fine."

"Do you have any children?"

"Not yet."

"Why is that?"

"I don't know why, but I ain't even been married a year yet."

"Do you love your husband? I can't imagine you married to a rough miner."

"I'm not," Olive laughed. "I just married my friend since I was a girl—Renny Honsinger."

"But do you really love him, like in the yellowbacks?"

"The what?"

"Those dime romances one's not supposed to read. They were passed around at boarding school from girl to girl. We all read them."

"They never got passed around up to Hammondville. Hardly anyone can read, anyways."

"I was engaged once, but I never loved him the way the girls did in the romances. In fact, I believe I hated him."

"Why did you promise to marry him, then?"

"Do you really want to know?"

Olive nodded.

"Then I'll tell you the whole awful story, like in the yellowbacks. Except my bottom is freezing off. Let's go back. You're finished, aren't you?"

"Yes, miss."

~

They hobbled back inside. Olive peeled Miss Regina's clothes off, layer by layer. She put her back in her nightgown and pulled the covers up to her neck. She picked up all the clothes, one by one, smoothed and hung them in the closet. It would take a whole laundry day just to clean one outfit like this.

"Come sit on the bed, Olive."

There was a fire in the fireplace and Olive added a log. Then she settled on the edge of the bed.

Miss Regina wriggled so the blanket fell down to her middle. Olive edged a pillow under her broken arm. "My troubles began the year my grandmother died. My father sold Grandmother's house in Geneva. I never saw it again. Then, a few months later, I graduated from boarding school. My mother was dead by then, and my father lived with my older sister Eliza and her husband. I had to go back to New York to come out—into society, you know. Eliza was in charge. My eldest sister Maryanne likes to travel. Maryanne was always the strongest. She never married, and she and her dear friend from boarding school, Mrs. Hartson, live together in one of those Boston marriages."

"What's a Boston marriage?" Olive asked.

"It's when two ladies simply enjoy each other's company for their whole lives. Maybe we shall have a Boston marriage, Olive."

"I never even been to Boston."

"The two of them just travel all over the continent, maybe even Africa, I don't know. Maryanne always wanted to see Kenya. Anyway, I liked boarding school, but I hated New York. I had never lived there before I was eighteen. I couldn't make friends with other young ladies my age. Everyone was so nervous about the way they were supposed to act: the proper manner in which to eat an artichoke, greet a gentleman, faint. And I wasn't good at it. Eliza would say, 'I know it's tedious, but there is no other way to find a husband.'

"And I'd say, I don't want to find a husband, but she would just repeat, 'It's a bore, but things will settle down once you're married.' I hardly saw my father. I know I irritated him. Maryanne had irritated him, too. I wondered if my friend Lovina would run away with me like Maryanne and her friend did. I wrote letters to Lovina in Philadelphia, proposing the idea. She would always write back, imagining the house where we would live in the country and with lovely promises and poems and what sorts of apples we would grow. But Lovina thought it was a game. I was in deadly earnest. Lovina and I had exchanged balsam pillows when we graduated from Miss Parker's. We embroidered 'Forever' on them, but Lovina's forever meant reunited in heaven, while I saw forever as a day-to-day affair."

"How did you know Miss Lovina didn't feel the same as you, Miss Regina?"

Miss Regina tossed her head. "Because she always included news about this awful gentleman she was engaged to, that's why. In any case, Father was bent on marrying me off, too. Father had let Maryanne fall into spinsterhood—twenty-seven and unmarried. So he had to do right by me. There was this gentleman I was introduced to. He wasn't much older than I. A Mr. Liston. We were given an introduction through my sister Eliza's husband. I became fascinated by his nose. It turned up and the nostrils flared. When I looked at him I could see right into his head, almost. I couldn't decide if I hated it or loved it. So I let him come calling and so on."

Olive laughed, but Miss Regina held the sides of her mouth. "Oh, I can't laugh—it hurts too much." She squished her mouth out of the smile. "No more laughing. Eliza was always there, making sure the conversations held up. Then he wrote me a letter asking me to marry him. He signed it, 'Sincerely, Mr. Harold Liston.' I hadn't known his first name until then. My sister Eliza said it was a good match. I didn't know how to discuss it—about the nose, and if that was normal love. So I wrote back and said I would marry him if we could travel on the continent with Maryanne for our honeymoon. He agreed.

"Then he came calling as my fiancé. It was the first time we were ever alone. He said that he thought of me often. He took out a small, oval mirror. He said he would like me to gaze into it, and then he would take it home so he could have my face with him always, until our wedding. Then he would give my reflection back to me, and own the true face forever. Perhaps it sounds charming, but I didn't care for the sentiment. It appalled me. When I didn't answer, he walked behind my chair. He held the horrible little mirror out so that his arms were by my head. I kept staring at his thumb on the mirror edge. How absolutely revolting it was. Actually, every digit was revolting. He had thick fingers which he caressed my face with, not my actual face, of course, but my reflection in the mirror. He kept touching it. And his breath heating the back of my head all the while. Then he slid the mirror down so that it reflected my neck, and then further, so that it reflected my chest. And farther on down until he had sucked all of me into that mirror, caressing the reflection all the while with his fat thumb. He put the mirror in his breast pocket and smiled at me as if we had decided something together. I looked up at that nose of his and realized all at once that I despised it. I wanted to snatch that mirror back and smash it, and I would have too, but then Eliza and the maid came in with tea."

"Not so loud, miss."

Regina brought her voice down. "They set a date for our engagement party. Eliza planned it all as I had no opinion on any of it. Not even what sort of dress I should wear. I recall the dress had real flowers sewn into it."

"Law, I wonder who did that."

"I have no idea."

"What kind of flowers?"

"White or blue, I can't remember. Now, the secret is that once, in my last year at boarding school, I woke with muscle ache. I didn't tell anyone but Lovina. And she said that in the middle of the night she had wakened and found me shaking. Somehow we made it charming, as if I had been on a journey at night, like in the fairy tale of the dancing princesses.

"In any case, I didn't want to marry this horrible Mr. Liston with the mirror. But if I waited, I would just have to marry another stranger who could be worse. Everyone was set on my connection with Mr. Liston. I thought maybe Maryanne would help me, but we weren't sure where she was traveling, although we knew she was to winter in Nice. I wrote a letter to Nice asking her to save me. Anyway, I believed that once the marriage was over, I could go on honeymoon with Maryanne and then settle down to visiting Lovina for half the year. That's how married women do it, I've been told. So the night of the engagement party arrived.

"I had to stand at the door and let Eliza introduce me. I hardly knew anyone at my own engagement party. Or hardly remembered anyone's name. I had invited Lovina, and that was all I thought of. Finally, she arrived. I nearly yelled, 'Lovina!' and she smiled that old wicked smile of hers. She grabbed my hands. But then we looked at each other, and with all those people crowding around, we couldn't think of one word to say. And there was some horribly important person behind her waiting for an introduction. Eliza was pinching my arm. And then Lovina said, 'I'll write to you,' and she moved on.

"I began to feel funny. That's the only way I can think to describe it. We had to walk two by two to dinner. I was on Mr. Liston's arm. I remember trying not to look at his nose, but then I noticed his thumb on my arm. It was like a slug. Then the thumb began to blur.

"Something was happening. I could no longer feel his thumb on my elbow. Something was moving up my arms and legs towards me. I can't explain what. Then I felt as if I were falling into a cyclone, and I lost sight of anyone else. And then I saw a woman made out of the cyclone. She didn't say anything, but she moved closer and closer, darker and darker, and I felt her kiss, a dark, unexplainable kiss.

"Then I was looking up into these strange men's faces, including Mr. Liston's. I sat up. I smelled pee. I wanted to get away from those faces that smelled like pee, so I crawled under the table all set for dinner. The smell followed me. I tried to stand and run, but my body ached. I couldn't find that cyclone woman. I heard ladies crying. I saw Eliza's face and I crawled to it. She lifted me up and began to lead me out of the room. As I was walking out, I saw Mr. Liston up against a wall, all pasty and sweaty. I wrenched free of Eliza's arm and went up to him. I wanted that mirror. 'Give it to me,' I said. I unbuttoned his coat jacket to get at it, and I heard more ladies groaning and gasping. Mr. Liston edged down the wall, away from me, and then Eliza said what I wanted was in another room. So I left and fell asleep in my bedroom. No dreams.

"When I woke up the house was silent. I think I drifted off again, and when I woke next a doctor was examining me. I asked him what had happened. He wouldn't tell me. I snapped at him. His questions were so stupid, and I had a headache; all my muscles ached as if I'd been thrown from a horse, which I was once, so I know. Finally, he left. I became sick of lying in bed, so I dressed myself and walked out into the parlor. Father and Eliza were talking there. When they saw me they seemed shaken.

"I asked them what had happened to me. Father left the room. Eliza told me to take stock of myself. I realized I had put on that white dress, all peed in and ruined flowers and dirty. Then Eliza told me I'd had a fit.

"I asked her what she meant by that.

"An epileptic fit, she called it. She told me I'd slept for sixteen hours. She shook a letter she was holding. 'Mr. Liston has written to cancel the engagement.'

"I asked if he'd returned the mirror.

"'Regina! You must try to think logically. You are no longer engaged. Father is convinced you will never be engaged after last night.'

"Do you think he will let me follow Maryanne to Europe, then?

"My sister said that I could experience another fit at any time, anywhere. She said the doctor recommended I go to the country for some fresh air and rest.

"I told her I'd go to my room and think it over.

"But that wasn't allowed either. 'There's nothing to think about,' she said. Father had made all the arrangements. He was going to send me to stay with Uncle Hammond, mother's brother, in the Adirondacks. He thought it best because it was in the country, and so quiet. Eliza reminded me that I had always liked old people.

"For how long? I asked. She didn't know.

"I hardly knew Uncle Hammond. I remembered that his wife had been so taken with the manner in which they had laid mother out that she had a photograph made. The one in the parlor I can't bear to look at, and find myself looking at all the time. That was the extent of my memory of the Hammonds. But I imagined a return to the freedom of Geneva.

"That was the happiest time of my life. The lake is so deep, they don't know what lives down under there. And of course, my grandmother was a suffragette, you know, and an abolitionist. She even wore those bloomers in the fifties, when she was already forty years old! My grandmother allowed me to run and climb trees, play in the hay, anything I wanted. My grandfather grew hops for beer, and I loved to listen to the hop pickers. I already told you that, though, didn't I?

"Did I tell you that once, my grandmother had a women's rights meeting at our house, and the legendary Mrs. Stanton attended? They were sitting on the back porch drinking milk punch, and it was time for me to take my nap. My nurse let me pay my respects before I went down. But I hated naps. So I stalled. I wriggled up on the couch by Mrs. Stanton, told her I had secrets to tell. I sang songs, made up riddles on the spot, performed a dance—anything to keep away from sleep. Grandma said afterwards Mrs. Stanton laughed and laughed and said, 'That brazen girl will go far.'

"I thought I had failed Grandma and Mrs. Stanton, but this epilepsy seemed to be offering another chance. So I didn't make a fuss when they wanted to hide me away in the country. Father never even said good-bye to me. Eliza said I mortified him. Eliza hates father too, but she's scared of him. She believes he's next to God in influence over the world. I pity her. At least I escaped living under the same roof as God the Father all my days.

"Don't look so shocked, Olive.

"I was out of New York in three days on the train north. I didn't even have time to write my friends and tell them what had happened. And I had another fit before I left New York. After that I was never alone. Not even in my sleep. Father hired a huge Polish woman to sleep at the bottom of my bed. She even rode the train with me, then turned around and rode back after she delivered me into the hands of the Hammonds.

"It's as if some seed has been waiting inside me all my life. And just when I believed I was doomed to live the most conventional of lives, the seed blossomed. I know, a fit doesn't seem like a flowering to most people. But the part I know of fits is the way they changed my fate.

"But then I first arrived here and saw how it was—this gloomy house and the sour old people and ruined countryside. The first week I was here I wrote my friend Lovina, asking her to take me in. But I gave the letter to Mrs. Fisk to mail, who gave it to Aunt Hammond, who tore it up and told me not to write letters until I was in a positive frame of mind.

"I couldn't think of a way out. So the second week I decided to try my luck with death. Although I wonder if epileptics go to hell as a matter of course. I hadn't thought of that. And then there is always the chance that it would be empty—you know, no God at all and the worms running through me. That wouldn't be so bad, Olive. It would be nothing.

"Now that I'm alive, though, I know it's a sign. From my mother or Grandma or whoever that woman is. A sign that there is a place for me to find."

"What woman?"

"The one in the fits. And you and she are my only friends now." Regina sighed and lay back in the pillows. "It felt good to tell that ridiculous story from beginning to end. I haven't had any-one to talk to in so long. But I feel I could tell you anything." She gave Olive one of those crooked smiles. "I hope you could tell me anything, too."

Olive's hand went over her mouth, then dropped into her lap. "I got something bad to tell you."

"What could that be?"

"The general and the doctor made an evil plan for you."

"What?"

"It's . . . the doctor give you six months to get cured, then he's going to do an awful operation on you, and if that don't work, he's going to send you to one of them lunatic asylums." Olive's hands pressed against her mouth.

"What sort of operation?"

Olive shook her head.

"Tell me."

"Cut off something—down there."

"Oh, just that."

"I thought you should know. I would a wanted to know if it was me, so I could plan—"

Regina took a tiny breath. "It means I have a deadline, that's all. I certainly won't let them touch me. I'll kill myself again, before that."

"Don't say that." Regina rested her head back against the pil-lows. Olive could see her eyes dulling. "Mrs. Cutter says the rea-son you ain't got any modern convenience here is 'cause the general made a strange pact with his wife." Regina did not re-spond.

"And Mrs. Fisk told us today that Indians, from right round here, once tied some man's insides to a tree while they was still in his body." No response. "Mrs. Cutter says the Gypsies have made camp about five miles out of town. Have you ever seen a Gypsy?"

"You mean real Gypsies?" Regina arrived back behind her eyes with a thud.

"Yes, I hear they come every year, but I never seen 'em. They don't come up to Hammondville, though we had a mesmerist once. And a medicine show with a dancing bear. And once a photographer—Seneca Ray Stoddard."

"I thought they were extinct or all in Europe. I'll run away with the Gypsies." Regina smacked her palm on the soft bed.

"And marry a Gypsy king."

"Tonight."

"What?" Olive stopped smiling.

"We'll sneak out and meet Gypsies tonight."

"You can't hardly walk, much less sneak."

"Tomorrow, then. We'll steal my uncle's velocipede."

"Steal what?"

"Mrs. Cutter told me all about it. That's when I knew I liked her. It's in a shed by the house. It's a peddling machine for two riders. One of the general's business associates gave it to him. The man made quite a show of it, but Mrs. Cutter said it was simply terrible because the general threw it in the shed and never looked at it again. It's there right now, just waiting for someone to steal it and ride off."

"But. Tomorrow is Sunday."

"So?"

"I'm riding the train up to Hammondville to be with my family."

"How strange."

"It seems more strange not to be with them."

"But you'll come back." Regina grabbed her hand. "Promise me, Olive." Regina's palm seemed to be getting hotter. "Why can't you promise me?" Regina pulled her hand away.

"I promise." Olive held her hand out, but Regina reached up and pushed a curl off Olive's face. Even the brush of her fingers against Olive's forehead left a trail of heat.

"Monday night we'll visit the Gypsies."

The church bells were ringing when Olive arrived in Hammond-ville. She tripped on some old boards hidden under the snow when she tried to cut across two paths to save time. She pulled open the double doors to the church and waded into the familiar smell of mildew.

Folks were still settling themselves. She passed Ren's brother Magnus, standing in the back with the other Swedish miners. He nodded to her. She felt his eyes on the back of her neck as she slid in next to Ren. Ren grabbed her hand and held on, smiling at the pulpit. Her mother reached over, patted her knee, whispered, "Praise God."

The preacher walked up to the pulpit. Ren chafed her hands in his, still smiling straight ahead. Olive looked around her at the rows of miners and the smattering of women and children—the church warming a little with their breath and sweat. The wooden seats were hard. A baby was crying over the preacher's sermon. There was shuffling and sneezing. Somebody was kicking the back of her seat. She turned around. It was a little boy. She shook her head hard and turned back.

The preacher cleared his throat: "I take this Sunday's sermon from Proverbs: 'The drunkard shall come to poverty.' Right after church is over and you've thanked our Lord for a Sunday meal—some of you are hiking on down the mountain for drink. The only purpose, to fill yourself with the devil's drink. To spend your last monies on a potion that will lead only to lust and depravity. The good ladies of this nation have set their sights on a temperance drive, to purify this great nation of the drink that impoverishes you, body and soul.

"Do not believe I underestimate the temptation to drink. What with the disappointment in wages. But we must keep our faith with our Father in heaven and our earthly protector, General Hammond."

Ren squeezed her hand; two pink lines ran down his cheeks. The congregation sang that pretty hymn:

*"In the sweet bye and bye
We shall meet on that beautiful shore"*

A woman was crying in the back.

As Olive walked out of church the preacher was bending over the crying woman. The other women seemed to be hustling their men home. The single men stood around in angry clusters.

Olive breathed in the smoky, cool air. She heard the sharp note of a bird, then more. "Ma, look, it's the redwing blackbirds." The dark birds flew high, probably heading down into a valley by one of the lakes.

"That's the first spring bird I've seen back," her mother said.

"Spring's coming," Olive said. She saw Ren's back in a group of Swedes. She touched his arm. "Renny, look, the redwinged black-birds is back." Ren followed her eyes up to the calling birds, now far off. Magnus was jostling Ren's other shoulder.

"Magnus, we're expecting you for dinner," Olive's mother said. He shrugged.

"I'll be home directly," Ren said.

As soon as they were out of hearing, Olive said, "Magnus Honsinger ruined the first spring birds."

"How could he do that?" Florilla said. "But he does seem to slide easily into trouble. 'As the thorn goeth up into the hand,' like the Bible says."

"What trouble?"

"They've cut the wages, again. Ten percent. Men are clearing out. Lucy Peasley's husband for one. And who knows how many Swedes. I'm sure we'll hear about it at dinner."

"Is Ida coming home soon? We got the money now."

"Sent a telegraph. She can't leave just yet, but she'll be here by the end of the month."

"How's your rheumatism?"

"I feel the damp. But I don't care. Just seeing the birds back, that's enough."

"It's bad, then? What about your stomach?"

≈

"I bought a grouse from an Irish boy. So there's stew and corn bread with molasses, and the milk's in the bucket with the rock on it."

At dinner, Magnus didn't say anything. Olive's mother tried: "Magnus," she said, "you know you're welcome to move your things over here. Folks'll say I'm unfriendly to let you stay in Johnson's boardinghouse."

"Mrs. Johnson's is making blood pudding." With his mouth full.

"I could get the recipe."

No answer from Magnus. Olive studied him across the table: He looked like granite. His skin was lighter than a lady's who'd worn a sunbonnet her whole life. That's what all the girls said. He had never married. Some said he visited with a widow outside of Crown Point. And she'd heard talk of tar and feathering the widow too. She looked at him, messing with his food. Everyone said he was the handsomest man in Hammondville, but she just didn't see it.

Magnus caught her staring. "How is this job with the epileptic?"

She dropped her eyes. "Fine."

"They like you down there?"

"I guess so."

"Are they paying you yet?"

"Not till the end of the month."

"So. They're having to be pleased with you for one whole month, then they pay you." He didn't say anything else for a while. Then he said, "Ren, you should be talking to your family now, yah?"

"It can wait till after dinner."

"Nay, I'm leaving after dinner."

"Then stay after dinner," Ren said.

But Magnus wasn't waiting. He turned to Olive's mother. "I know you love this cold rock, but the Crown Point Iron Company swindles us. I'm hearing rumors all the time they running out of ore, anyways. All the good men leaving for this Wisconsins."

"You're going to travel all that way just to mine in another company, not knowing for sure if they're any better?" Olive's mother said.

Magnus kept his voice low. "Now, I know Ren is dream of farming, like in the old country. Good. I'm willing. We'll go all the way out past Indian country for alls I care. But we're going out of here. Look at this land! There ain't no trees, no animals left. The ground so hard, you ain't even growing vegetable. My little brother and me, we end up in the worst land in all this country, maybe."

Olive and Ren kept their eyes down. "You go on, Magnus, if you have to." Olive's mother started clearing the table. "But I'm needed. Only one doctor for eight hundred. Without me, a lot of women would die in childbed, men of infection."

"This place is emptying out. And could be any day and my little brother gets a disease for himself or a mining accident. Cough his chest up. It ain't safe in the mines. I wish to hell you go down there just once and see yourself. You'll never let another man down there again."

"Now, you listen to me, Magnus Honsinger, you think you're such a brave man because you like to cut away." Olive's mother made her fingers into scissors. "Snip snip snip. You cut away a whole country, a mother, and sail to a new land. Well, good for you, but I'm no little boy that likes to see things ripped apart. This dirt holds my babies."

Magnus looked at Ren. Ren looked at his plate. "You have given us a big trouble, little brother. You tie us to this family, and this mother won't be happy until you are nice and dead and planted in this rock. That's the way you like 'em, ain't it, in the dirt so's you know where they is."

"God forgive you, Magnus Honsinger." Olive's mother made a strange waving movement with her hands, as if gathering in all the ghosts, and she left the room for her bedroom.

Olive got up to follow her.

"Olive, wait." Ren caught her wrist.

"What?" She still couldn't look at him.

"Your ma's wrist been real bad; some days she can't even milk the cow. It takes everything just to get supper, then she can't eat it. Ida won't be here for another month, either."

"But what about the two dollars a week?"

"We'll have to do without it," Ren said.

"You can't do without it, Renny," Magnus said. "Just one month and you are having eight dollars. I am having a little money saved, too. Just one month; can't the old woman do for herself for one month?"

"We'll wait until Ida gets here," Olive said. "Then I'll go back to work. I'll write them a letter, explaining."

"Not so easy. You think they are keeping your job while you wait for your sister? Who cares for this epileptic while you are away, huh?"

"I don't know." She turned towards her mother's room. She heard Magnus push his chair back, and Ren call his brother's name and then something soft in Swedish. Magnus slammed the door of the house.

Olive walked to the doorway of her mother's room, pushed aside the curtain at the entrance. Her mother was sitting on her bed, bent over the quilt she'd been working for years, a quilt from all their baby clothes. It was so worn, it was always ripping in Florilla's fingers. It wasn't pretty either, just washed-out grays and browns. Florilla worked over the ugly fabric as if it were beautiful, her stitches even and close together.

"Ma, I'm going to stay until Ida gets here. Don't worry."

An hour later, after Olive had cleaned up, her mother walked over to drink tea and sew at Mattie Stone's, as she did every Sunday afternoon. Ren was greasing his boots by the fire. "Want to go on upstairs for a nap?"

Olive untied her apron and started to climb up. She felt his hand circle her ankle on the ladder, to make her remember.

She remembered that a few weeks after the first Swedes arrived, at dawn in early December, she and her sisters had heard the fragile whine of a fiddle. They climbed down the ladder in their nightgowns and looked out into the grey winter. There were all the Swedes, weaving in a line through the town. At their front marched a little blond girl in a white dress. She walked carefully. On her head a crown of pine boughs surrounded a ring of lighted candles. The Swedes were singing "Santa Lucia."

Ida screamed that wax was dripping down the little girl's back, and she chased Submit, trying to tickle her neck.

But Olive had longed to pat the red cheeks of the little girl, stick her nose in the pine crown and smell the woods. She wanted to wear the crown of light.

A year later, Ren arrived with his older brother, Magnus, and a new group of Swedes, all farmhands off the same boat. Magnus was seventeen, already down in the mines, but he sent Ren to school to learn English for both of them. They shared a single bed in Johnson's boardinghouse.

All the Swedish girls adored Magnus, with his white hair, his milky skin, his flaming red cheeks and red lips. Eyes so light blue, they were almost clear. He was built shorter than Ren, squeezed tight into five feet seven inches. Even some of the American girls sighed after him, though he didn't smile or speak a word of English.

Ren's smile was easy—his lips and tongue stained pink from the beets Mrs. Johnson loved to cook. He was all arms and legs, skinny, hair in his eyes, thirteen—a boy made of broomsticks. They liked each other from the beginning; she wasn't sure why. Sometimes she would help him with English in the school yard. His soft, rounded accent brought out that wanting in Olive, like the smell of pine boughs and the look of candlelight.

He was always there, three desks behind on the boys' side. She felt so comfortable with him, she never thought of him.

A year before the typhus, when Ren was already down in the mines, they snuck away after church one Sunday. Olive teased Ren until he agreed to climb into the abandoned shaft near Swampy Hollow. On order of General Hammond, no one was allowed in the shafts except the miners. They climbed into the cool dark, until they reached the gravelly bottom. They couldn't see anything.

Olive began to whisper the story of the boy who fell in a mine and had his arms crushed. They amputated them both, but he died anyway. Sometimes he was seen at the lip of a mine, on full moons, moaning for his mother to come fetch him. And once Missy Bradfield woke up in the night and saw two small white arms, beckoning to her at the window.

Then Ren's voice was so close in the dark, she could feel his breath on her eyes. "That boy is lucky. He never had to grow up to be a miner. I hate this damned dark. I only see the sun one day a week. I get scared it burnt out, and I don't even know it. Me and Magnus are wanting to buy an ox team and moving out west, to farm. That's what we know. Farming. Will you come with me, Olive?"

His voice spooked her. In the dark, without his face, it sounded like the voice of a grown man. "No, I won't. I'm not ever leaving my mother." She felt for the ladder. She was almost all the way up when she felt his fingers close around her ankle. She stopped still with the shock of it. Slowly his hand began to move up, caressing her calf. Her whole life narrowed until all that was left was the turn of her calf and the feel of his hand over it. She dropped down a rung, then another, sliding into the circle of his body, until she stood in the iron dark of the mine, his breath on her neck and ear, her hand over his, gripping the ladder. His other hand began to slide under her dress.

"What is this girls wear under their clothes?"

"Drawers."

"How do they come off?"

"Like this."

Now, Olive lay in the half dark of the loft on Sunday afternoon, feeling blurred and vague, listening to Ren's clogged breathing. She reached under the mattress and pulled out the blue feather. She ran it over her upper lip. This bed was the safest place on earth. Olive stuck the feather back under the bed. She curled around Ren, let her lids slip over her eyes. Olive whispered, her lips just grazing Ren's shoulder blade, "I could sleep forever."

Four

~

HAMMONDVILLE SHOOK LOOSE of winter in the first week of April, and an early spring settled in. The temperature wobbled at freezing, rain and sleet, wet snow and rain. The snow sunk into the ground and turned to mud. Without the trees to hold it steady, the earth fell off the sides of the mountain. The Whites' house slid down an embankment. Everyone gathered on the edge and stared down the twenty-foot drop at the broken home. Although he was just a renter, Abe White balanced on top of the boards and mud and offered it up for firewood. His wife searched the wreckage for a clock she had loved.

Last spring, Olive and her mother had planted two spindly poplars by the front windows, then shored them up with rocks. The poplars had made it through the whole winter, two poles of thin hope, but now they couldn't hold to the shifting earth. Olive woke to find one toppled over, its roots fluttering in the breeze. The other sapling hung on, tilted and stubborn. Olive fought the urge to yank that one up too, get it over with.

Birds flew over, but seldom stopped. Florilla hung some suet on a string to lure them down. A red squirrel shimmied down the string and ate the white ball of grease. Olive put out some more, shot the red squirrel with a borrowed gun, and made a thin stew, bones and all.

The weather ached Florilla's joints, and their house took on the permanent smell of the bitter poultice she used to soothe the pain. "I don't give a care about my hand, so long as we've seen the last of winter." Olive's mother was absorbed in lists of plants she would soon begin to hunt for—golden thread, mullein, feverfew. Parsley, patience, and sage lined their windows and had to be pulled near the stove and covered with a blanket each night. Florilla checked them often, stroking their leaves with a stiff finger, crooning.

But Olive wasn't cheered. These days she woke up groggy, her eyes gummed shut, and prayed to be allowed to go back to sleep again. Florilla blamed Olive's lack of vigor on illness. She convinced Olive to drink powdered charcoal in molasses, then made her wash in leather shavings and comfrey root. She administered a tobacco and tar plaster to her forehead.

Once Olive caught herself spelling out Regina's name on the roof of her mouth with her tongue.

Magnus was in a fury. His white hair whipped around as he stalked their house, muttering ominous predictions all evening: "Don't be surprise if the mud breaks in the shafts, kill us all maybe" and "Seventy men has leave since the wage cut. All the smart ones is gone, left with the dumb ones now." Olive's mother patched or read and let the bitter smell of her remedies rebuke him. Magnus paced all evening till he worked himself up into shouting: "Goddamn old woman, if I have to tie you up and drag you, we're gettin' out of here!"

Then Florilla would turn on him, wielding God and Motherhood and anything else she could lay her hands on: "Magnus Honsinger, you'll burn in hell for your evilness. You got no idea what it means to care for something. You got to make your life where you find it, you selfish, ignorant boy. Boys are the scourge of the earth." The fight would end when Olive's mother humphed and huffed to her room, and Magnus slammed out the front door or made himself a bed by the stove, battering the blanket.

This new ferocity infected the rest of Florilla's life, so that when laughing, she took in great gulps of air, and when crying, tears burned red lines down her cheeks. Her change of life now seemed to be a distilling. All that was left of Florilla was passion and bones.

Ren woke ten times a night, startled, jerking his head around in the dark, sure the house was sliding away, the roof caving in. Sometimes Olive stroked him, whispering, "Hush." But sometimes she felt too exhausted to bother, and just lay there, watching him twitch and moan. In the evenings, in those few hours between dinner and bed, Ren sat by the stove on a stump. While Magnus and Florilla fought, he acted the fool. He spit on the stove and listened for the sizzle. Grinning nervously, he teased Olive that the Houseman would soon be spinning in the kitchen nights.

"What's wrong? Your dinner's on the table and the house is clean."

"But your smile is gone."

"I never promised a smile, Ren Honsinger."

Ren didn't answer. Two pink spots sputtered on his cheeks.

All evening his right leg would shiver uncontrollably, the way it used to when he had to keep silent in school for long hours. Olive watched the leg. When she couldn't stand it anymore she would say, "Stop that shaking." The leg would quiet for a minute, then furtively start up its twitching again.

Finally, one evening, there was a sharp knock on the door that interrupted Magnus's muttering. It was the telegraph man with a message from Mrs. Hammond spelled out in his own awkward hand. Magnus, Florilla, and Ren watched Olive open it.

Olive Handslinger—
Fifty cents more a week to pay girl to tend mother.
You are expected on Thursday's train.
　　　　　—Mrs. General John Hammond

That night, Olive lay in bed and thought of Ren. She knew what he prayed for without asking him: an end to the fighting, an end to his daily darkness. Time to putter. Every night, Ren faithfully whispered to God, but God kept silent. Instead, He had answered the single prayer Olive had written on the roof of her mouth.

With April almost worn out, Olive took the train down the mountain again. Crown Point had already turned a tender, spring green. In front of the Hammonds', daffodils and tulips were ready to bloom. Near the kitchen door the rhubarb had grown large. She went around the side, opened the kitchen door, hit her boots against the sill to shake off the mud, and walked in. There was Mrs. Cutter, frying eggs at the griddle.

She nodded at Olive. "We missed all your pretty smiles, that we did. And Miss Sartwell has been acting evil. If you ain't come back, everyone was thinking—asylum! Yep, it's true, though I guess the general chose to give her six months, and he's a man of his word, I'll say that for him. Though six weeks is near up, so that would be four and a half months now, wouldn't it?"

"Where's Mrs. Fisk?" Olive asked.

"She's down to Whitehall to visit a dying aunt. Returning tomorrow or late tonight, depending on death. SuSu's with the missus. You go on to Miss Sartwell before she tears this house apart." Olive watched the white of the frying eggs bubble and curl brown at the edges. Mrs. Cutter flipped them off the griddle. "For the general," she said when she saw Olive's eyes on the plate. "Want one for your supper?"

Olive nodded. She hid her basket in a corner of the kitchen and walked down the carpeted hall. She pulled at the fabric under her arms, airing things out. She knocked.

"Olive?"

Olive blinked after the dim hall. The curtains were tied back. Hot sun filled the white room.

"I'm dressed. The first time since you left six weeks ago!" Regina wore a grey and blue dress, plaid in the bustle, striped in the skirt. Her skin was yellowed and veiny over the right side of her face. Her nose had healed with a bump at the bridge, and the tip crooked to the left, looking wicked. Regina began pacing. "I was hateful to everyone while you were gone. In fact, I was so angry at you for your absence, I bit the doctor. Why must everyone place their families first? I reject the idea that blood is thicker than water, I reject it! Water is more pure. But this credo is for little girls, isn't it? It was just a little nip, out of the doctor's wrist."

Olive took Regina's smooth hands.

"Your palms feel like the lick of a cat." Regina looked up. "I find I am shy." She sighed. "But it is passed now. Your face is so good to look at. I'm comforted." Regina settled on the bed, Olive in the rocker. "The minute they told me you were coming, I became docile as a lamb. I even asked for cloth and thread to embroider. When you laugh your double chin makes two smiles. How is it that you didn't run away and come back to me?"

"My mother's rheumatism's been bad. She can't move one of her hands, and it ain't easy for her to do the chores. And her stomach, too. She also cares for a lot of folks, and we wash the doctor's clothes, so her sick hand is hard. And she and Magnus been fighting near every night." Olive's words sounded plodding and ugly, even to herself.

"Do you like your mother?"

"My mother . . . I like her, yes." Olive laughed, looked away.

"The Gypsies are still here. Mrs. Cutter says they made a love potion for a lumberman. He stole someone's wife and escaped out west to the territories with her."

"Maybe the Gypsies'll make a potion for you to stop the fits."

"Or maybe I can run away with them and become a Gypsy witch and tell fortunes and cast evil spells on all the men I meet."

"You would have liked my father."

"I doubt it."

"Everyone liked my father."

"Why? Did he resemble you? Was his voice like honey?"

"He was always working. I remember he had a lopsided walk—he was thrown off kilter by his missing arm. He was redheaded and he laughed at everything. Everyone says I take after him."

"Then I would have married him. And you could have been our sweet daughter."

"Ma used to cut his food for him, and I remember sewing shirts with one sleeve."

"Olive, we have to make our plan."

"What plan?"

"For visiting the Gypsies. My sister Maryanne may come to whisk me off to Europe, and I will already have run away with the Gypsies. She'll have to place notices in all the country papers and hope I'll read one passing through some town or another." Regina stood up and began pacing again.

"Sit down and breathe easy."

"I can't! I've hardly left the room in five and a half weeks. And I'm going to wear trousers, and pretend to be a boy when we sneak out to the Gypsies. When should we sneak away?"

Olive began shaking out pillows. "Stop your teasing, now."

"I'm perfectly serious, Olive."

Olive pushed the edges of the sheet under the mattress. "Gypsies are dirty and dishonest, so says Mrs. Fisk."

"She probably says the same about epileptics and miners."

Olive shook her head, shook the quilt out over the sheet.

Regina dropped herself onto the just made bed in front of Olive. "I have to go." Regina's voice cracked in its effort up towards gaiety. "I'm an epileptic with four months and one week to live."

"Don't." Olive smoothed her hand over the soft pillow. She closed her eyes. "Can't we just sit in this sunny room? Just for a minute or two? Then we'll make a plan to visit them Gypsies."

Olive thought dressing as a boy was silly, but Regina nagged her until she asked to borrow some men's clothes off of Mrs. Cutter, saying she needed a pattern for Ren. Later, she told Mrs. Cutter that Miss Regina had been having nightmares, and that she would have to sleep in her room that night. Olive's face burned and she laughed when she lied, but Mrs. Cutter didn't seem to notice. She wanted to discuss trouser patterns. Mrs. Fisk arrived home that evening at ten. Olive and Regina sat on the bed, listening to Mrs. Fisk throw the bolt on the outside door, and then they heard her heavy, tired steps on the stairs. Regina made them wait. Olive fell asleep across the bed. At one, Regina shook her. "Time to go," she whispered.

Regina undressed, draping layer after layer on the bed until she was just in her thigh-high, black wool stockings. Regina climbed into the trousers and shirt and overcoat. Everything had to be rolled up, cinched closed. She strode around the room, moving from the shoulders, chin pulled in. "They won't give a boy any trouble. Look at how I can move in these trousers." She kicked up a leg, groaned.

"They wouldn't try nothing funny with a scrawny, crippled boy named Regina," Olive said.

"A scrawny, crippled boy named Reginald. I need a hat."

"Mr. Cutter's cap hangs by the kitchen door. We can leave that way." As they snuck down the hall, their footsteps were muffled in velvet. Regina pulled on the hat in the kitchen. They heard a mouse scraping in one of the cupboards. There was a noise upstairs. They both stopped breathing.

They listened to the silent house. "I don't think I can manage this, Regina."

"Why?"

"I been on my feet all day. Too tired, I guess." Olive yawned. Regina watched her.

"Plus, it's taking too many chances, is what."

"Why?"

"Because. What if you have a fit on the road or in the Gypsy camp?" Olive heard the panic gusting in her own voice.

"Maybe I will. I can't say."

They looked at each other, waiting.

"I ain't afraid of fits." Olive took the knob of the kitchen door in her hand, twisted it, pulled, until Regina threw the bolt back. The door opened to a yard filled up with moon and wet chill and midnight.

Regina bent a little at the knees, ready to spring. She loved the skinny moon and the slide of her boots on the wet grass, the swish of the wool trousers and the way Olive's hair shone orangy through the dark. The tight bun felt good, as if her hair were stretching her eyes wide, pulling her smile taut.

Usually Olive's stillness reminded Regina of good things—her grandmother's off-key lullabies, the green roll of a pasture down to a lake, the feel of a smooth stone. But now, Regina grabbed Olive's big hand to get her moving towards the shed.

Regina had to feel for the door handle, a length of rope. The door creaked open on rusty hinges. The noise made her flinch. She put her hands out in front of her and edged into the moldy darkness of the shed. Her foot kicked the machine. She felt along it until she came to the handles. She wheeled it out.

Regina could see it now—two wooden handles and two pairs of wooden peddles, a set attached to each wheel. The rest of the velocipede was iron, except for the hard, solid rubber tires.

Olive wiped the cobwebs off the front. There was a mouse's cache of seeds on the backseat. She brushed it off. "You sure you know how to ride this thing?" she whispered.

"Simple." Regina took hold of the front handles and rolled it over the lawn and onto the muddy road. The jolt hurt her wrist, but she couldn't control the machine with one hand, so she hung on. Regina looked down towards the dark, shuttered town. Then she turned the velocipede so it faced the empty road towards the Gypsy camp. "You take the back and I'll steer. All you have to do is peddle. Don't shift around or we'll go off balance."

"Why don't I run by the side and hold her steady while you peddle?" Olive said.

"You'll never keep up. This is a modern machine."

Olive looked like a sack of grain. The only thing that moved was her head, glancing up to the second-floor windows of the house.

"Better hike up your dress—tie it up so it doesn't get caught. Or you could ride sidesaddle."

Olive slowly knotted her dress. Then she inched a stockinged leg over the bar. She sat down on the seat, her toes just scraping the ground. She gripped the wooden handles.

"Don't get splinters," Regina snickered. She pulled her own leg over the bicycle. The iron bar bit into her crotch. She wouldn't be able to touch the ground once she was seated. She turned her head towards Olive. "Just peddle."

Olive grimaced.

Regina squinted her eyes, clenched her teeth. She put her foot on the wooden peddle, pushed down: The velocipede began to shake over the bumpy road. She had to fight to keep it steady. She felt a jagged pain run up her wrist. She pushed on the peddles. They began to rattle faster. "It's working," she said, and then the pain in her wrist sharpened. She let go of the handle. The machine hit a rut, tilted. They skidded into the dirt. The iron bar banged onto their hips.

"It shakes your bones," Olive gasped, "but it works." She pulled the bar off Regina. They climbed on again and careened forward. This time, Regina held her wrist as if it were splinted. It still hurt, but dully instead of the needle pain. Even the bone-rasping, difficulty of the ride was full of a rattling joy. "Away, away," Regina sang to herself through clenched teeth. Behind her was Olive, steady, heavy breathing, ahead of her was the Gypsy camp, and inside her was the wraithlike lady, burning her insides like whiskey, whispering: There is a place for you to find.

They had to stop to pet dogs so they wouldn't bark. Regina said, "Cur," but she put her fist out for them to sniff. They rode two miles out of town until they came to a fork in the road, then stopped to get their breath. The ramshackle farmhouse at the fork had a shutter torn off, half the fence fallen over, windows covered with blankets.

"Who lives there?" Regina asked.

"A widow and her girl. They say she keeps company with our Magnus, and if it's true, I wish he'd mend the fence." Olive nodded her head towards the right. "That way to Irondale and Hammondville." She nodded to the left. "This way to the Gypsies. Two or three more miles probably."

The road curved downhill, and they rattled faster. Past cows that swung their heads; past a horse that galloped along the fence, a great thumping shadow, racing them to the end of its pasture. Finally, up ahead to the right, Regina saw the remains of a burned house. Olive dragged her feet till they slowed and stopped. As soon as Regina let go of the handle, her whole arm began to throb, as if her heart had slid into her wrist.

At the far edge of the south pasture, against a dark line of trees, Regina could see the flicker and leap of a campfire, the long, swinging glow of lanterns on poles, the dark hulks of wagons. They pushed the velocipede up the drive to a stone foundation. Charred wood and glass lay in a sagging pile. They propped the velocipede on the foundation. Regina felt like an arrow— unwavering, ignorant of her final destination.

Regina watched Olive run her fingers over her lip. "I have a bad feeling," Olive said, but she let herself be led out into the field.

They started across the wide pasture towards the light. The ground was lumpy with stiff, dead brown hay and grass. The dew wet Regina to the knees.

As they moved closer, they heard the mumbling hum of voices. A baby cried, then abruptly stopped. Regina could make out three wagons and some pale tents. Behind the wagons a line of staked horses snorted and stamped.

It must have been close to three in the morning, but the Gypsies were awake. Some hunched around a fire, another group clustered around the opening of one of the tents. Then two dogs yelped and galumphed forward over the hillocky ground. The conversations in the camp stopped. Heads turned. Regina heard Olive's flat voice in her own head: No one in the world knows we are here. Regina hissed at the dogs, "Shoo, you damn things."

For the first time, Olive smiled. She spoke in a crooning voice, saying, "Yes, yes," and cupped her hand on their skinny muzzles. They sniffed and wagged their tails. "Hello, there," Olive called when they were within twenty feet.

No one answered. The men around the fire went back to their business, talking and dipping bread into a pan. A little girl in a sack dress leaned over a man's shoulder, sticking her finger into the pan. The brightly colored knot of women by the tent kept watching them. They were gathered around an older woman wearing heavy jewelry and a head scarf. She stared at them while she poured something out of a little can onto the head of a girl seated in front of her. There was something odd about the older woman's face, as if it had been scoured. When Regina stood in front of them she realized the woman had no eyebrows.

"We're here to see the fortune-teller." Regina directed herself to the hairless woman. One of the men behind them said something in another language, and the men laughed. The older woman continued to watch them as she slid her hands down the girl's hair.

"We wanted to see the fortune-teller," Olive said loudly, spacing her words.

The women washed closer together in consultation. There was a short burst of laughter. The old woman pulled the girl in front of her off her seat and patted her towards Olive and Regina. The girl, who couldn't have been more than fourteen, was wrapped in a plaid blanket. On one side of her head were three glistening braids. The other side hung in loose, dark waves. She had a wide, high-cheekboned face and a long neck covered in strings of gold coins. She grinned with a mouth full of little pointy teeth.

"You're the fortune-teller?" Regina said.

The girl widened her eyes. "All Gypsy women have the gift." Someone snickered, then turned it into a cough. The girl swung up a lantern and walked purposefully into a tent on long, bare feet, trailing the end of her blanket over the wet grass. Olive and Regina followed. Inside, a boy lay on a pallet on the floor. He blinked at them with wide, sleepy eyes. *"Gajos,"* he said, and snuggled back to sleep.

The girl put the lantern down on a wobbly table, then shoved something under one of the legs to steady it. She pulled up a bench for them, kicked over a wooden box, seated herself, let the blanket fall to her waist. The lantern light made shadowy patterns on the walls. Her thin, yellow shift glowed. The gold coins on her neck glowed.

When she leaned over the table, the light turned her nostrils red. "So, you comes late at night, do you? Important troubles." She had an English accent.

"Isn't there someone—more experienced—who could help us?" Regina asked.

The girl exhaled. "Do you know who I am? Just the great princess Delighty, that's all. Last winter I was reading the fortunes of the queen in London, England. This fall I was fortune-telling in Montreal, Canada. I can speak French, English, and Romani—all at once if I have to."

Regina didn't say anything. She thought, I've never in my life seen such a long neck, like a flower stem.

"Why do you think my mother's oiling my hair? Tomorrow is my wedding day. No one is more lucky than a bride."

"How much does it cost?" Olive asked.

"I know what you want. A sign."

"A sign?" Regina said.

"The sign that I can see the future—my mark. The girl held the hand she had kept under the table over the lantern. Her three fingers made long, shadowy slashes on the roof of the tent. She slid her three-fingered hand back under the table. "You are lovers," she said. "Your peoples are against the match. I can read the future in the palm or the forehead. Which do you choose?"

"We don't want—" Olive started.

"We're here," Regina said to Olive. "We might as well learn the future from the great Princess Delighty." She smiled at the girl. "You're right, we are in love. Read my forehead and tell me if we will be together forever."

The girl held out her good hand. "That'll be a dollar."

"A dollar!" Olive said. "I'll answer the question for fifty cents."

Regina handed her a silver dollar. "Will you add it to your necklace?"

"Lean forward," the princess ordered.

Olive sighed. Regina bent her head down. The pads of the girl's fingers began to inch over Regina's brow. "You ain't used to working. You're rich and clever. Your girl knows how to make herself useful, though. Her family's against the match 'cause you got something wrong with you. You're spindly, ailing, no one knows why." She sat back and sighed. "Your forehead is hard to read. I could tell more from the palm, about the marriage, but I need another dollar."

"Regina, this is a waste of good money—" Olive stood.

"Regina?" The girl reached over and yanked off Regina's cap. Her bun sagged down her neck. The girl stared. Then she snorted. "I guess I know why your families are against the match." She giggled. The girl's laughter reminded Regina of soap bubbles. Princess Delighty put her hands over her mouth. There were ten fingers now.

"What happened to your mark?" Olive said.

The girl collapsed onto the table, laughing. Tears streamed. "Oh me, oh my, too bad you ain't Romany."

"We came here because I have fits," Regina said.

Delighty put her head on her hand, still giggling. "Fits?"

"And in the fits I see things. A woman. She speaks to me."

Delighty wiped her eyes with the back of her hand. "You want to know what this means."

"She wants to know if you can cure her," Olive said in her clear, nasal voice.

"Cured?" The girl said.

"Of the fits," Olive said louder.

The princess rubbed at her nose. "Fits ain't so bad. They'll bring you luck."

"How do you know?" Regina asked.

"Everyone knows that. My aunt Gilda had 'em. She had her three boys, a handsome husband, a nice wagon, too. She had a long, sweet life."

"Who are you marrying?" Regina asked.

The girl stopped smiling. "Why do you want to know?"

"You just seem too young to marry."

Princess Delighty waved her hand grandly. "Oh, he'll take care of me. He's my cousin, Ilia. He's been looking out for me since I was a baby."

"What will your wedding be like?" Regina asked.

Delighty faked a yawn. "Not much. Just a whole honey-roasted pig, gallons of French wine, all eyes on us. Just dancing and singing the night long. Me and Ilia, we'll be dancing on candy." She leaned towards Regina, whispered, "After I dance on it, I'm going to gather up the ribbon candy and the licorice, and eat all of it, every bit." As she leaned back her braid swept oil over Regina's knuckles.

Regina put her hand up to her nose. The oil smelled faintly of lemon. "I have the perfect present for your wedding."

"What could that be?"

"It's called a velocipede. It's a machine on wheels that rides two people."

The princess clapped her hands. "I love strange machines, like cuckoo clocks."

"Regina, that ain't even ours. It's General Hammond's." Olive was still standing.

"Well, if you can borrow this machine from your general, bring it to my wedding tomorrow night. Everyone will laugh."

"We have to be going," Olive said.

"What's your name?" Regina asked.

"I told you—Delighty, Delighty Boswell."

"Where are you from?"

"No more questions." Delighty stretched her arms up. "Come back tomorrow night. Don't forget your machine."

Regina started to stand, but Delighty held her down. She gently put Regina's hat back on her head, then tucked her hair inside. "You make a handsome boy," she whispered. The princess Delighty flashed a wicked smile that peeled Regina open from collarbone to hipbone.

They had traded places. Olive was steering. She kept her eyes on the road as her breathing pulled in, then pushed out-out-out. In, out-out-out. The out breaths moved in rhythm with the down push of the peddle and the push of her fears:

It must be going on four.

Five miles to home.

You don't know how early Fisk rises.

If she catches us, we're in for it.

That Gypsy girl is full of lies.

This machine ain't ours to give.

It would hurt your feet to dance on candy.

She pushed steadily and didn't stop for the dogs who ran beside them, barking. Regina kicked at them.

"Just makes them wilder," Olive said.

Regina didn't say anything back. Olive decided Regina's head was filled with nothing but the Princess Delighty and dreams of drunken wedding revels. Olive could see the Hammonds' up ahead. They coasted over the drive that led to the shed, Regina dragging the tips of her boots to slow them down, making a racket over the gravel. Regina did not say one word or move, so Olive took over. "You go in and I'll follow. Be careful and quiet."

Olive pushed the velocipede over the frost-stiffened lawn and into the shed. Regina let the kitchen door slam behind her. Olive closed the shed door and walked into the kitchen just as she heard Mrs. Fisk's steps on the stairs. She grabbed for the kettle.

Mrs. Fisk was still in her high-necked nightgown. Her nightcap was tied in a great bow under her chin. "What are you doing up so early?"

"Miss Regina had a bad night. I'm just making her tea."

"At five A.M.? You look as if you had a bad night as well," she said. "Clean yourself up."

After Mrs. Fisk left, Olive began to pump water into the kettle, her upper arm and neck aching. She had that wavy feeling after staying up all night, as if her head were full of cool air. As if her heart weren't sure how to beat. She put out a teacup. Put it away again. Emptied out the kettle. She made up her mind to go to Regina's room.

Regina was lying in bed when Olive arrived, her face to the wall, her clothes strewn over the floor. Olive looked in the cloudy mirror over the bureau and thought of Mrs. Fisk seeing her with her hair flailing half out of its braid and the smudge of dirt on her chin. She spent some amount of time just watching her face in a trance of exhaustion. She fixed her hair and washed her hands and face in the white china basin. The water turned brown.

She left the room and filled the lamps with kerosene. Then she returned. Her emotions were pressing just under her face, making her feel puffy, as if she could laugh or cry either way, just as easy. She folded Regina's men's clothes. The trouser legs were stiff with mud, and the coat smelled of woodsmoke. Olive sniffed the sleeve of her own dress. It smelled the same way. For some reason that brought tears to her eyes.

"She thinks fits bring you luck," Regina said, as if she had never been asleep at all.

"I was just wishing you'd speak and it come true. Did you hear me thinking?" Olive said.

"No, I heard you sniffing. Delighty looks like a real princess, doesn't she?"

"I pity that poor girl," Olive said.

"Pity her? Did you see the way she walks, as if she owns the world, as if she were naked under that dress?"

"Her name reminds me of Samson's Delilah. And you know how far she could be trusted."

Regina laughed. "That Gypsy girl is the first creature on earth to believe my fits are lucky. I may have found my place."

"You're saying that barefoot Gypsy camp is the place for you?"

"Why not? What's keeping me from it?"

"First it's that friend from school, then me, and now you've fallen for a little girl who isn't even a Christian and who's out to cheat you besides."

Regina sat up. "Could you begrudge me, Olive? You have a husband and a mother and a sister." Regina bit the words out. "I hate this house. All I have is my vision and you. And you're paid to be my friend. I am allowed to have more than one person, Olive Honsinger."

"I ain't paid to be your friend. I'm paid to keep you calm." Olive stared down at one of the cut-glass knobs on the dresser. "Ain't that a joke with you ranting and raving and running off to the Gypsies and riding veloci-whatevers. But today I'm going right on up to Mrs. Hammond and tell her I oughta get paid extra for this friendship 'cause it's causing me nothin' 'cept pain and heartache and there ain't been one solitary moment of calm since I met you." Olive passed her hand over her mouth.

Regina leaned back onto the pillows. "My, my, Miss Olive, you are transforming." She smiled at her.

Olive's smile shook a little on the way back. "What if we get caught sneaking out? What if they notice the machine is gone? I'll be fired for sure, and I'll never see you again."

"We'll be careful. Aren't you curious about this wedding? Don't you want to ride double down the dark road under the moon again?"

"No," Olive said, "I don't. I got aches in my legs only smart-weed and blue vervaine boiled in lye and brushed on with a feather could cure."

"Where did you learn that recipe?"

"Everyone knows that." Olive smoothed down her apron.

"Now I got to do some chores round the house. Help Mr. Cutter with the wood and then Annie's sister brings the wash. And I'll have to wash the Cutters' clothes on the sly. They smell like they been through hellfire."

Regina closed her eyes. "I wish you could sleep. But as long as you've got endless chores to do, you could take care of this as well." Regina held up her forearm. It was swollen, blotchy red and white.

"White bean paste in a muslin bag," Olive sighed.

In late afternoon Olive brought Regina her supper on a tray. Regina had dark circles under her eyes. Half her face was red and imprinted with the lace from the pillowcase edge. Her damp hair stuck to her head. The last light shone in on the carpet, and Regina sat on the side of the bed, staring at the dust dance. Then she shuffled to the rocking chair. Olive unwrapped the poultice. The swelling had gone down. "Have you slept at all, Miss Olive?" Regina asked.

"Not yet."

"I feel as if I've been hit with a hammer. Why don't you lie down while I eat? It would make me feel better."

Olive unlaced her boots and climbed into the soft featherbed. It cocooned around her, warm and damp from Regina's sleep. She closed her sore eyes.

She heard glass shattering. She sat up. The bowl of soup was cracked in half, the barley and brown liquid pooling under the table. Regina lay on the floor, her head in the soup. Her wrists were twisting at a strange angle, and her eyes were open, the pupils rolled back. She growled and choked. Saliva trickled out of the side of her mouth.

Olive felt for the smelling salts. In her hurry to pry the bottle open she waved it near her own nose and began coughing. She waved it under Regina's nose, but nothing happened.

The door banged open. Mrs. Fisk was standing there. "Are you managing?" she asked.

Olive didn't answer. She was trying to press the stick in between Regina's clenched teeth. Olive saw Regina's nightgown darkening at her thighs. She smelled urine.

"I must see to Mrs. Hammond," Mrs. Fisk said, her voice very high. "These fits cause her to faint. You seem to be managing." She closed the door of the bedroom.

Olive dropped the stick and the smelling salts and tried to hold Regina's hand, but it pulled away. The fingers wouldn't bend.

She slid herself under Regina so that her head was shaking in her lap. She felt the warmth of the barley soup seeping into her dress. Olive said, "If you can hear me, come back." She said this over and over, and slowly the shaking seemed to soften and subside. Regina's head relaxed into Olive's lap.

Then Regina stumbled to her feet and began walking to the door.

"What are you doing?" Olive stood in front of her.

Regina's eyes slid off Olive as if she were a stranger. The front of her nightgown was yellowed and wet. She was dripping barley soup from her shoulder.

"Come back," Olive said.

Regina stood in the center of the room as if she'd lost her way. Her eyes sagged half down. She stumbled towards the bed.

"Wait." Olive pulled off Regina's nightgown. She left Regina standing by the bed. She wet some cloth in the water basin. Olive turned around, squeezing the dripping rag. Regina was curled naked on the bed, already asleep. Olive sponged her off between her legs and thighs and on the back of her head and shoulders. She covered her. She cleaned up the floor.

Olive sat in the rocker next to the bed, listening to a gagging snore she had never heard in Regina before. She leaned her head back on the rocking chair and closed her eyes. She concentrated on the rhythmic creak of the rocker. Her hands were in her lap. She could feel them shaking: a souvenir.

Five

AN HOUR LATER, Olive told Mrs. Fisk that Miss Regina was sleeping soundly, but that she felt ill herself. Mrs. Fisk said she could go up to her bed. In her shallow sleep, her waking thoughts mixed with her dreams for hours until Mrs. Cutter called for her to bring Regina supper. Olive stomped down the narrow closed-in stairs to the kitchen. "They pay me good because they'd seen them fits and I hadn't, not until today," she said to Mrs. Cutter's back. Mrs. Cutter nodded.

Olive brought the tray to Regina's room. Regina was sitting on the edge of the bed, her nightgown hiked to her waist, pulling on the muddy trousers, her teeth gritted against their stiffness.

"Have you lost your senses?" Olive said.

"Shush." Regina concentrated on the pants. "Close the door. Everyone will hear."

Olive set down the tray. "No."

"What do you mean, 'no'?" Regina held the pants up around her waist.

"I mean you ain't going out sneaking tonight. You're bound to have a fit, knock yourself on the head, and become a half-wit."

"I promised to bring the velocipede."

"I don't care. You ain't going."

"You're not my mistress. In case you forgot, I'm yours."

"What happened to all that talk about friends?" Olive turned her face away.

Regina let the trousers fall to her ankles. "But I was longing to see the wedding. And she'll think I lied about the present." Her voice came close to a whine. "Will you go for me?" Regina looked sad and weak, her narrow shoulders hunched inside her nightgown. She stared at the floor.

"All I'm doing is just delivering that velocipede and leaving."

"And ask why the princess's mother has no hair." Regina glanced up. "Thank you. I'm sorry about what I said. About the mistress."

Regina shared the tapioca with Olive. Olive was happy to take the edge off her hunger. Later, she would sit in the kitchen and listen to Mrs. Cutter and eat the leftovers from the general's supper. The leftovers she ate at night were rich: cream sauces, butter biscuits, meat with rings of fat. She sucked it all down, didn't care if the pain came later. She had never had the chance to eat food like that, and she thought of it now as she helped Regina finish the thin pudding.

Regina was concentrating on the tray, pressing the toast crumbs with the pads of her fingers, emptying them back onto the plate. "Was it awful?"

"The pudding?"

"My fit. Were you disgusted?" Regina didn't look up.

Olive began picking up the crumbs too. "You was so far away. Where do you go?"

Regina's fingers paused on their trip from the table to the plate. "It's all inside. It's as if I've become some sharp thing and I'm shooting down through layers of darkness. The layers are the consistency of clouds, but thicker. I'm dropping at a tremendous rate and I keep hoping that one of these fat clouds will stop me, but I rip right through them. And then, just when it seems that I will never stop falling, when I am nearly overcome with fear, something catches me. The dark turns into the long arms of a woman.

She is cradling me, and I know if she lets go, I will fall forever, but I trust her. And then there are these words. It's her voice, but it's my voice, too." Regina looked at Olive. "I can't explain it any better than that."

"What did the voice say this time?"

"I don't know, resort or retort. Something like that. It's not the voice as much as the feeling. The cradled feeling. As if she is giving me something I need."

"Do you think she's an angel or a devil?" Olive whispered.

"Neither—something else."

"A ghost?"

"Not a ghost. It ruins it a little to talk about it."

Regina fell asleep right after supper. Olive ate with Mrs. Cutter and SuSu by the kitchen stove, then came back and sat in the rocker. She worked on unraveling an old sweater that Mrs. Hammond had thrown away, so she could reknit it for Ren. The clock in the hall ticked. She could hear the rustle of General Hammond reading the paper in the parlor, and once the voice of Mrs. Hammond, calling down for Fisk. She dozed a little, let the half-unraveled sweater droop to the floor. Through her sleep she heard General Hammond stamp up the front stairs. She heard Mrs. Fisk bolt the doors, then stop at Regina's door. Through the door Fisk whispered, "Olive Honsinger, are you sleeping in Miss Sartwell's room again?"

"Yes."

"Can you sleep through that heavy snoring?" Her voice was tired, almost gentle in its emptiness.

"Yes."

"Are you still feeling poorly?"

"No, I'm all right."

"Tomorrow we shall move the general's old cavalry cot into the room for you."

"Good night, Mrs. Fisk."

"Good night, then."

Olive rocked, hypnotized by the soothing sound of the clock.

Finally she pulled herself up and put on Mr. Cutter's son's wool coat. She tied a wool scarf round her head and snuffed the light. She walked to the kitchen quietly. She stood with her hand on the bolt of the kitchen door, listening to the sounds of the house creaking and the quick slipping of her heart.

She unbolted the door, turned the knob, and stepped out into the night. The sky was low and heavy with clouds. She had to stand still until she could see. She heard the bark of an owl, so far away she couldn't be sure it wasn't a dog. The wind shook the leaves of the trees, turning them upside down, the way it does before it rains. Suddenly Olive felt overcome by exhaustion. She sunk down on the top step, just outside the kitchen door. She didn't know how long she slumped there. Maybe she even dozed.

Finally she hunched up her shoulders, dragged the velocipede out of the shed, and began pushing it towards the Gypsy camp. She refused to think about ghosts or long-armed women, Swedish demons, killer animals, or drunken Gypsy men. She refused to think of the fact that she was stealing General Hammond's personal property to give away to Gypsies. At the first frame house a dog raced out, barking. She steadied the machine with one hand and petted the dog with the other. She put her face down into its damp, smelly fur. She slapped her leg for the dog to follow her, but it just wagged its tail and sidled back to the barn.

Olive came down the long, gentle hill to the burned-out farm, walking on her heels to rein in the velocipede. A large awning had been raised at the camp. She heard music and shouting. It took all her resolve to push herself and the machine forward across that field. This time, the dogs didn't notice her standing in the darkness. There were white candles perched everywhere—in plates, on the ground, dripping wax down table legs. And red wine spilling out of mugs and stemmed glasses and frying pans. A banjo player, a fiddler, and a man hitting two metal cups together worked away at quick music that never seemed to vary. Their heads were tilted and their eyes glazed, as if they were in a trance. People took turns dancing in the center of a circle, making each other laugh. Nobody was wearing coats. A pig turned on a spit, its juices sizzling into the fire. A man was cutting strips from its side and passing them out to a group of children. Two men seemed to be in the midst of wild argument, chopping at the air with their hands, their faces twisted with fury. But as Olive watched they suddenly embraced each other. She didn't see Delighty.

"No fortunes tonight." Olive flinched. A man stood beside her, frowning. "Get away now," he said.

"Delighty invited me. We, I mean I, brought her this present for the wedding."

He looked the velocipede over. "This way," he said.

"I'll just leave it with you," but he was already striding under the awning. She followed, holding on to the velocipede as if it were a shield. Her boots crackled over smashed candy. As she followed the man, the music stopped. The dancers trailed after her, making a ragged parade. The man ducked into a tent. Olive concentrated on the opening to the tent as the crowd thickened around her.

Delighty dipped her head out. She screeched and clapped her hands. "My machine." Her hair was a mass of oiled braids, her eyes ringed with dark powder. She wore a flouncy red dress. Gold coins jingled from her neck, wrists, and ankles as she walked towards Olive. "Where's your lover?" she asked. Everyone laughed.

Olive blushed. "She's sick."

Delighty's breath smelled of wine and honey. "This is a *Gajo* present for me," she said to the crowd. People moved closer, running their hands over the bars and wheels. Olive stepped back. The music started again. Several young men came from behind a wagon, prodding another man in front of them. He was dressed in red coat and shirt and wore knee-high black boots. He stumbled along, laughing every time he nearly fell. His friends lifted him onto the back of the machine and then lifted Delighty onto the front. She squealed and tried to twist away, but when she was seated she grabbed the front handlebars and screamed, "Make it work!" This made everyone go hilarious.

There were two men on each side of the machine and one behind. They jogged forward. Ilia tried to catch the peddles, but his big boots kept slipping off. Delighty held her legs out stiffly, her red dress hiked up to her thighs. She dropped her head back and screamed, "Wheee." When they reached the edge of the camp, the men gave a great push and sent them sailing off into the dark. Delighty's scream trailed away. There was a grunt of surprise, and then the slap of iron as it hit the ground.

The young men ran into the dark after the machine. Two of them came back helping Ilia, who held his hand to his bleeding forehead. Delighty stumbled into the light, slapping people's hands away. Her dress was ripped. She was crying. When Delighty saw her mother she cried louder. Her mother helped her to a chair and covered her with a blanket. She said something to her, Delighty nodded, and her mother moved towards the awning again. Everyone else seemed to have grown bored and gone back to the dancing.

Olive thought, I should go now. She sat down on the ground next to Delighty. There was a bit of ribbon candy stuck to the back of Delighty's neck. She was still snuffling. "I'm sorry you got hurt," Olive said.

"Oh, well." Delighty smiled and wiped her nose on her arm. "It was like flying, for a minute. Tell your lover I like it."

Delighty reached down and untied two of her coin ankle bracelets. "One for you, one for her." She handed them to Olive. Her fingers were sticky from sweets.

"Thank you." Olive made herself busy with the bracelets, lining up the coins. "Regina wanted to know why your mother doesn't have any hair."

"She asks too many questions. When my sister died my mother's hair fell out, that's all. It don't grow no more." Olive looked up and the mother was standing over them. As soon as Delighty saw her mother she began to whimper again.

Her mother sat down on the ground and pulled Delighty onto

her lap. She handed her licorice. Delighty sighed. She nuzzled against her mother's chest, sucking on the licorice stick. She closed her eyes.

Olive stood up. "I guess I'll go now. Don't let anyone see that velocipede. It belongs to General Hammond." Delighty's mother nodded. Delighty did not open her eyes.

Olive walked under the awning and into the dark field. She thought of the girl and boy in their scarlet clothes, perched over the spinning wheels, his dark boots, her dark thighs, the look on her face, like she had swallowed the whole world and was just licking her lips. It was almost frightening, how willing and beautiful they were. Then Olive heard shouting. She turned around.

Surrounded by his friends, Ilia swayed over Delighty and her mother. Ilia reached down and scooped Delighty into his wobbly arms. Delighty held on to her mother's neck so that her mother was pulled up and towards Ilia as he stood. When he stepped backwards, Delighty lost her grip on her mother's neck. She grabbed on to her mother's necklace. One of Ilia's friends yanked Delighty's arm. The necklace broke. Gold coins spattered everywhere. Delighty slapped at Ilia, screeched for her mother as he listed away. Everyone was laughing. Ilia carried her into a tent. People loitered around the entrance, joking, calling inside.

Delighty's mother's scarf had slipped off. Her bald skull looked shocking. It reminded Olive of the round stump of a leg that had been cut off at the knee. The woman kneeled and began picking the gold coins off the ground.

Olive glanced at the tent opening, then turned and walked across the field. The empty, dark miles towards Regina seemed endless. The moon was down. Soon the rain began to fall. Olive trudged forward, mumbling an old mining song to keep her going. She held the bracelets in the damp of her wool pocket, rubbing her thumb over the smooth coins as if they were the smooth skull of Delighty's mother.

* * *

As Olive walked up the drive she had a sudden certainty that someone had bolted the door. But it swung open easily. She re-bolted it and trudged to Regina's room with the same single-minded rhythm she had used for the long walk, not caring that her boots clomped hard on the floor, dropping ground candy and dirt. All the white of Regina's room—the quilt, the walls, Regina's nightgown—shone underwater blue. She sat down on the edge of the featherbed. She put her hand on Regina's ruffled shoulder.

Regina twisted up. "Olive?"

"I'm back," Olive said.

Regina wiped her eyes. "What happened? You're all wet."

"It's raining."

"You smell like you rolled in sugar and something rotten be-sides. Take off all those horrible clothes and tell me everything."

Olive pulled off the coat and scarf. She went to the basin and washed her face and arms. Her blood felt thin, rushing to her head and making her giddy.

"Tell me," Regina said.

"Her mother lost a daughter and it made her hair fall out. The girl said she liked the velocipede. She said it was like flying." Olive bent down and rummaged through the coat. "This is for you, from her." She handed Regina the string of coins. "She wore it on her ankle."

Regina held the bracelet to her own ankle. "Was she lovely?" she said.

"Yes. I ain't slept in two days," Olive said. "What am I gonna do about chores today? I can't be sick again, or they'll fire me sure."

"But I can be ill, and hysterical besides. So you'll have to spend the whole day calming me." Regina slapped the bed. "I have an idea. You get undressed. I'm going to bring you some surprises." Regina hobbled out of the room in her nightgown.

Olive didn't have the will to call her back to put a dress on or to ask her why she was limping. She took off her own dress and stood naked by Regina's bureau, sponging herself with a cloth. The cloth turned the water a rusty color that reminded Olive of iron dust. She wished she could wash everything off, all her life pooling in that white bowl.

Regina came in, her voice excited and whispery. "You look beautiful standing there, like a French painting. But close your eyes." Olive felt something warm and clean wrapped around her and knew it was Regina's white quilt with the dove design on it. She let Regina lead her to the rocker. "Just sit there and keep your eyes closed." She heard Regina lugging something into the room, and the sound of scraping and Regina's breath heaving. "Keep your eyes closed," she warned. Then she was scrabbling around by the fireplace. Regina was not used to making a fire, and Olive heard her crooning a long string of her favorite curses. Finally Olive heard crackling and smelled too much smoke. "There. Don't open your eyes. I saw them flutter. I have to fetch one more thing before old Fisk wakes up, and I lock us in here for the day." She left the room.

Olive's body felt light, hovering above the chair, surrounded by the quilt. Breathless, Regina was in the room again. "I was almost caught. It was this close." She heard Regina lock the door. "We're safe. Now, open your eyes." In front of Olive was the fire screen from the parlor. The stained-glass woman glowed blue and purple. The glass was thin enough so Olive could see the fire leaping behind the woman's legs, growing up past her thighs, licking her neck.

"That's not all either." Regina stood in front of her, her night-gown a big white bowl, cradling something in it above her knees. Then she turned it out, and oranges, pale and yellowish and soft, tumbled into Olive's lap.

"Where'd these come from?"

"There's a whole crate of them in the cellar. You look perfect sitting there. Like a queen. You see, Olive, about my fits. They give me whatever I want."

When Olive was a little girl the general had given each child an orange for Christmas. She had always tried to save hers, eating it section by section, but Ida would gobble her own down, then begin pestering Olive to share. The pestering half ruined the orange. Olive had always shared so Ida would leave her alone. As soon as the orange was gone, she had longed for another, would have traded anything for even one sticky, sweet section. "Regina, let's not ever go back to the Gypsy camp. It's dangerous."

Regina's face twisted. "What about the oranges? I thought you'd love oranges."

Olive stood up. The oranges tumbled off her lap. "What I really want is a hot bath."

"I don't think I could carry the tub in."

"I'll do it." Olive dressed, went into the kitchen, heated water, then dragged the tub into Regina's room. Kettle by kettle she filled the tub. There was something pleasurable in the hard work on top of the exhaustion. Regina was eating an orange. Olive undressed and let herself into the steaming water.

"Shall I wash you?" Regina said.

Olive shook her head. She began to scrub herself with a rough cloth.

After the bath, Olive slid between Regina's white sheets and fell into a sleep that was half a continual fainting. Every now and then she would wake up and see the figure on the fire screen. It was Rebekah, she thought. Rebekah at the well. She had always been comforted by the story of Rebekah, and now she saw Rebekah coming out to the well just after sunset, when the sky was all purple and blue, and there was the stranger. Rebekah was not dressed in scarlet and sucking on candy. She was a hard worker, and that was enough. Just because she was cheerful and uncomplaining, just by lifting up those pitchers of water until everyone had enough, Rebekah had drawn luck to herself, like water out of a well.

Once when Olive woke, Regina was sketching with a pencil, not restless or prone to have a fit. Olive watched her eat an orange off a yellow plate, the peel curling into an orange snake. Then she divided all the sections and circled them like rays from the sun. She ate a section at a time, her pinky finger arching daintily. And she didn't look at the orange while she performed this operation. Olive wondered who had taught her so good that she didn't have to look, and the gulf between their histories opened up before her. But it only made Olive wonder more, as if Regina were her piece of luck, her reward for uncomplaining hard work.

Once, Fisk knocked on the door: "We haven't seen you all morning, Olive Honsinger. What about Miss Sartwell's breakfast?"

Without even opening her eyes Olive heard her own voice slide out of her: "Oh, I got her breakfast early. She's been having a bad night. She's sleeping now, but I don't dare leave her. Got to keep her from making a racket."

"See that you do," Fisk said, but her voice was soft with something like pity.

The next time Olive woke, it was late afternoon. She sat up and let herself yawn and yawn. She looked around. The room was empty. "Regina?" she said. Olive got out of bed and went to the open window. There were deep shoe prints in the mud below the window, where someone had jumped from the sill. She turned back to the room. Orange peels were scattered everywhere. Mr. Cutter's clothes were gone. On the table lay a sketch of Olive's sleeping face. Regina had scrawled across the top: "Got bored."

Regina had walked quickly away from the house, straight across the backyard, and down the stone steps to the creek. Then she followed it upstream. Almost immediately her shoes were soaked in brown water, her skin itchy from brushing away the tall weeds as she pushed through them. The sun began to warm her in her filthy, heavy men's clothes. The black flies found her. When Regina stopped to lace her shoe, she looked over to the other bank. "What are you hicks gawking at?"

The boys slid their eyes towards each other, laughed nervously, studied their fishing lines. Regina pushed through a willow tree, moved on. Finally, the land by the creek rose and met the road. She passed a couple in a mule wagon. They stared. Regina slit her eyes and kept walking.

She reached the burned-out farm and looked across the field. The horses were hitched to the wagons. The Gypsies were loading up, taking down tents. Regina's heart began to shiver. She started a stumbling run across the uneven field until she got a stitch, then held her side and kept going. No one looked surprised or interested when she gasped into camp. She saw Delighty's mother tying a line of copper-bottom pots along the side of a wagon.

"I'm looking for Delighty." Regina pressed at her side.

Delighty's mother looked at her. "You're no boy," she said gently.

Regina pushed some of her hair back inside her hat. "But I still want to see your daughter."

"Over there." The woman gestured towards a tent.

Regina looked inside the tent. The sun glowed through the white fabric. Someone was snoring heavily on a mattress. "Delighty?"

There was a groan from the bed and Delighty sat up. The snoring continued. Delighty squinted. When she recognized Regina she slid her legs onto the floor. She was naked, except for her gold coin jewelry. Her hair was a loose mass of dark frizz. She sat with her elbows on her knees and her head in her hands.

Regina dropped down on a chair. She felt dizzy. The room was hot and close, filled with the smell of sweat and something strange and sweetish. From her seat she could see a man asleep on the bed. His mouth was open as he snored. He could have been Delighty's brother—the same glamorous high cheekbones and dark skin.

"My head hurts," Delighty said. "You missed my wedding." She wrapped herself in the blanket, leaving the man naked. Regina stared at him for one startled moment, then looked away. The man didn't stir. Delighty looked around the room until she found candy, then offered Regina a piece of black licorice. Regina shook her head. She sat down on a chair close to Regina and bit off a piece. She chewed. "You can have your machine back."

"That's not why I came." Regina looked away so she wouldn't stare at the opening of the blanket. She gripped the chair so she wouldn't swoon.

"Why did you come then, *Gajo?*"

"What's a *Gajo?*"

"Questions. I told you my head hurt." Delighty stood up. "Everything hurts." She walked over to the entrance of the tent. "We're leaving today. You better take your machine and go on home."

"That's what I came about." Regina watched her blanketed back. "I want to come with you."

Delighty laughed. She turned around and watched Regina. She sucked on her licorice. "A *Gajo* is you. All of you that aren't us." She glanced over at the naked man on the bed. Idly she tapped each toe with the end of the licorice. His foot twitched. She wedged the black twist between his smallest toes and left it there. "I didn't know he snored," she said.

"I so much want to come with you." It was hard for Regina to ask again.

The man in the bed startled up. He looked at Regina. "Who's that?"

"Nobody," Delighty said. He collapsed again. Delighty walked out of the tent, calling for her mother.

Regina had reached the place where she would leave the road and follow the creek. She started down the bank in a fierce struggle with the velocipede. She saw Olive coming along the creek. Regina pushed the machine towards her.

Olive's face was pale and filmy with sweat. "Did you walk down the road like that?"

"Like what?" Regina kept shoving the machine forward. Olive took the back handles. With two working, it was easier going.

"I'm glad you got it back," Olive said.

"I found another bracelet in the coat pocket," Regina gasped. "Is it yours?"

"I don't want it."

"She didn't want the velocipede. Or me, either." Regina stopped. Olive banged into her back. "She called me nobody."

Olive unpeeled one of Regina's hands. Regina's nails had bitten into the skin. Olive blew on the burning palm with her cool breath.

They hid the velocipede in the woods below the stone steps, until they could return for it in the dark. Dusk was coming on. Inside the house, Olive brought the fire screen back, then went to the kitchen to fetch the kerosene. Regina locked the door to her bedroom and searched for something to rip. She settled on her sheets. She started the cut with her teeth. Then she tore the cloth into long, ragged strips. She kicked the shreds under the bed, and sat down on the bare mattress. She raked her nails over the mattress to the rhythm of the words *There is a place for you to find.*

Olive walked into the parlor with the kerosene. Too late she was staring at the general and some man in a suit. "I'll come back later, sir."

"No, no, come in and make us a fire." Then, to the gentleman with his back to Olive, "My apologies, Judge, but these rooms are always chilly. A blessing in high summer, a curse until then."

Olive ducked her head. She put down the bucket of kerosene and went to the fire. She pulled the screen back. She lit tinder and blew on it from below, even though Mrs. Fisk had instructed her on the vulgarity of blowing. But the bellows were hanging up high on the chimney, and she didn't want to get out of her crouching position. Then the fire was lit. She stayed there, crouching.

Finally she pulled herself up and dragged the fire screen back over the fireplace. Then she took off the glass cover of the first lamp, unscrewed the well, and poured in some kerosene. She went to the next one. Slowly the conversation took on meaning.

"It's altruistic of you certainly," the judge said, "but we all believe you justly deserve the honor."

"But think of posterity. It will be a way to send a message through the ages. Now, just hear me out. I have a list. I know

~

Crown Point would be a difficult one to change, with its revolutionary associations, so let us leave that aside for now."

Olive was on her third lamp, unscrewing the well. The general unfolded some paper. "I would appreciate your honest opinion. For Irondale—what about Perseverance? Or Industry? I have a long list here. But those are the ones I favor. Hammondville, I was toying with Mary, after my sister. Mary, New York. Pleasing, with its religious associations. But perhaps something more muscular. Frugality. That has an honest ring."

Like God, Olive thought. She glanced up at the fire behind the stained-glass screen. The flames licked the shape of the blue Rebekah lifting the bucket. Olive stared at the body of the flaming woman until she was hypnotized. Behind the screen she saw Rebekah leaving town at dusk, walking across the hard earth to the well, filling her heavy clay pitcher with water for her father's house. Rebekah hauling more water for a stranger and his camels, lifting pitcher after pitcher, as if the weight were a pleasure. The sky turning dark, the desert cold. Her upper arms aching. No complaint.

If she kept staring at the flames, Olive could see right into the Bible times. She saw Rebekah called to wash the visiting servant's feet, and the feet of all those who came with him, while her own long, dark feet remained swollen and dirty. No complaint. The next day, her mother begged for just ten days to say good-bye. In her grief, the mother yanked out fistfuls of her hair, but Rebekah was still carried away to marry a stranger. The forward roll of the camels prying her fingers from her mother's neck, forever.

No complaint. Rebekah must be God's calm blue angel now. She was no longer hauling water, or was she? Was she lifting a golden bucket filled with sweet water to bathe the Lord's feet? Did her arms still ache from the lifting?

But then Olive understood. Rebekah kept silent, close to God, but when her teeth clenched, sparks leapt off, like two stones smashed together. The sparks might have scorched Him if He noticed. But He only noticed her breath, which sometimes smelled hot, like Indian spice, and He didn't wonder.

The kerosene was pouring onto the Oriental rug. She tipped her hand back up, crouched, began mopping up. The smell was strong. What if the general noticed? She crouched lower. She made her lips into one tight line to keep the kerosene from bursting into flame.

Six

REGINA WAS TRYING to yank Olive out of sleep. "This is important," her whisper went. "Will you please wake up?"

"Tell me tommorow."

"No, I might lose it by tommorow."

Olive opened her eyes to darkness. She pulled herself to sitting.

"Olive, will you please come to your senses?"

"What?" Olive's body was too heavy for her. She felt it sinking back down. Her eyes closed.

Something exploded into her head. She snorted. She choked. She threw her legs over the side of the bed.

"It's just the smelling salts," Regina said. "You sleep too soundly."

When Olive could breathe again, she said, "That ain't nice."

"I'm sorry. But I have to tell you about my dream."

Olive groaned. She began listing sideways.

"Don't start that again," Regina said. "Here now, get up, sit in the rocker." Regina sat on the footstool below her, her forearms resting on Olive's knees. "I've had an important dream. The woman was in it."

"What woman?"

"The one inside my fit. Pay attention. She was singing some

kind of a lullaby. There were so many sweet words, but I can't remember them now. Except for the chorus." Regina brought her voice down to a whisper. "Even the mother, the mother labors with her hands." Olive didn't say anything. "Olive! Are you awake?"

"Mhmm."

"What do you think it means?"

"You ate too much black pepper, could be."

"Don't be thick. What mother labors with her hands?"

"Every mother. My mother for certain, has all her life. Labored so hard, one hand's just about useless."

Regina didn't say anything.

"Can I go to sleep now?" Regina still didn't speak. Olive dropped back onto the cot. She closed her eyes, pulled the blanket up to her chin. "Maybe that could have waited till morning." Regina didn't answer. Olive looked over at Regina, just a crouching shadow on the edge of the bed. "Will you lie down? You're giving me the creepies."

"I know what it means."

"Tell me in the morning." Olive closed her eyes.

"I'm meant to throw in my lot with you, you and your mother. Your whole family. The place I need to find will be a place where your mother won't have to labor with her hands."

"I don't see how it could mean anything like that."

Regina slid under her quilt. She turned over and faced the wall. Olive lay in the dark, her eyes open.

May ripened slowly in Crown Point. Often frost would stiffen the nights, but by morning the birds were everywhere: sparrows singing on telegraph wires, robins, large-chested and self-important, yanking worms, woodcocks whirling in the fields. Swallows settled their nests over the kitchen, so that the door always opened in an explosion of birds. The house was ringed in wasps. They squeezed themselves through cracks in the windows and then banged themselves against the glass trying to escape. Olive and

Mrs. Fisk hunted them down and mashed them into handkerchiefs. Black flies swarmed, begging for blood.

Daffodils blossomed and wilted. Then the quince and crab apple bloomed, and finally the lilacs broke through—white and purple, sweet smelling. Olive brought them into the house in bunches. There was one lilac bush of the deepest purple that Olive stuck her face in every morning. It made her feel dizzy with perfume and good luck.

Olive didn't seem able to carry luck back up with her to Hammondville. She dug up a sucker from the Hammonds' purple lilac and planted it by the side of her mother's house. The sucker remained a bare branch stuck in the ground.

The spring didn't seem to sweeten Magnus Honsinger. His irritation crackled, shocking people in common conversation. At Sunday dinner, Florilla might say, "Olive, I was remembering today how your first tooth fell out while you was eating an apple. You don't remember that, do you?"

Before Olive could answer, Magnus's voice would cut in, startling them: "Look around you at this bald, no-tree land. People are saying Wisconsins is having so many trees, they don't know what to do. The forest in Wisconsins is going on forever, they say. Oscar Johnson says to me today, Old Man Hammond has ruined these Adirondacks. It's time to try this Wisconsins state. You know what I am saying to Oscar? These mountains ain't ruined 'cause they are never fit for people. Not even fit for animals. Only good for flies."

But Olive's mother would simply push on, her cheeks unnaturally pink, her words rolling over Wisconsin: "What could be keeping Ida? Wonder how that rash she had last year has healed up. Wonder if she's just as greedy for molasses candy. Remember when Submit first spoke, her first word was Olive—she said it Olla, remember that?" And then she would talk about the babies.

Nobody would respond. Even Magnus could not keep up. Finally Olive would say, "Hush now, Ma."

Her mother would answer, without pausing for breath, " 'Hush now,' you say? Why should I hush about my own children? You never told me to hush when you was a girl on my knee. Then you'd say, 'Just one more story, Ma.' I remember . . ." And she'd continue, stitching up the past to the present. Florilla didn't eat much. When she did, it never agreed with her, and she spent the evening between the outhouse and mixing up herbals for herself on the stove. She had become a thin, old woman, with a jutting collarbone and narrow wrists.

On Sunday afternoons, in bed, Olive lay on her back and let Ren need and enter her. He was not used to doing all the work, and sometimes, when he subsided, she would brusquely climb on top of him and move till he came, sighing a little so that he would think she was satisfied. She buried her face in his neck to avoid kissing him, but he didn't seem to notice. Then one Sunday his rhythm stopped. She thought he was spent, but he whispered, "Where are you?"

"Right here."

"Not here. Not all spring."

Olive didn't answer. She felt suffocated, pressed between the blue feather under the mattress and Ren's bony weight on top. "Olive, it ain't nice, keeping your mind down there to Crown Point with that rich girl while I'm living with your mother and working down to the mines every day and come home missing you, go to bed missing you. And on the Sunday we're seeing each other, one day a week, there you are, wishing for the big house."

"It's not the house."

He rolled off of her. "Let's just rest today." She lay in the exact position he had left her in, legs spread, staring up at the rafters. Finally she looked over at him, lying there pretending to sleep. She saw the child and the skinny teenager and the man, all in his pink eyelids and blunt, colorless lashes. "Ren," she said, and he opened his eyes. "You're good." She touched the lines that were already creasing at the edges of his eyes. She knew the goodness was true, but she didn't feel it, and when he kissed her and rolled back on top, full of kindness and passion, she felt herself dwindle down into a small lump in her stomach, far away from him.

Olive was standing on a chair in the parlor, surrounded by a sea of maroon drapes. She was trying to hang the lace curtains for summer. Her fingertips just reached the hooks, and she kept ripping tiny holes in the lace. And Regina would not leave her be.

Regina sat on the plum-colored chair, embroidering fitfully on a small balsam pillow. "Just try to imagine it the way I do. It's a white farmhouse on a hill, then behind it is the long, sloping field that runs into Seneca Lake. On the porch is a wooden swing."

Olive smashed a wasp between folds of lace. It left a yellow stain on the white. When she tried to rub the stain off, the lace tore. "It's a pretty dream."

"It is not a dream. It is a plan. There will be a linden tree in front of the house. Its clean, sweet smell will cover the lawn. We had a linden tree at my grandmother's."

"Is this a house you've already seen? How do you know the owners will let it go?"

"No, no, I haven't seen it. But there are houses all over the ridge above Seneca Lake. We just have to pick one out. We'll pick one with a good path down to the water. You just drift down, over the mown grass, through the peach orchard. The beach is covered over in oval slate-colored stones. They feel smooth on your feet."

The curtain was bunched absently in Olive's fist. She could see the pretty house in the gentle field that ran down to the long blue lake. She could see her mother rocking on the porch. She could feel her desire fluttering and growing.

"Now you add something," Regina said.

Olive reached up for another hook. "No."

"If you refuse to help me with this plan, I'm going to have to do something dreadful to myself."

"Stop it."

"You know I'll do it."

"Hand me the next curtain." Olive looked down. Regina smiled up at her. Three embroidery needles, each dangling a different color thread, stuck out of Regina's chest. Olive wobbled on the chair.

Regina laughed, grabbed on to the back of the chair. "They're just in my chest ruffles."

Olive smiled, shook her head.

They heard Dr. Corning on the landing. "My dear Mrs. Hammond, just take one step at a time, and you'll be downstairs in no time."

"And you'll see the lovely summer curtains you picked out." Mrs. Fisk was with them.

"Oh, Lord. I was supposed to have this done hours ago. It's your fault, filling my head with nonsense. Throw those old curtains behind the couch."

Olive hooked the rest of the lace on, cursing her stiff fingers. Regina dragged the yards of maroon fabric behind the couch. They could hear Dr. Corning's voice moving nearer. "I have had a great triumph at the medical conference with my paper concerning morbid tendencies during and after cessation of the menses. After I delivered this paper, eleven medical men stood to ask questions. Now, you don't want me to appear a humbug when I write of my star patient, do you?"

Mrs. Hammond swayed in the doorway with a weak, triumphant smile on her face, the doctor and Mrs. Fisk hovering behind. "Good afternoon, Miss Sartwell, I thought I'd—" Then she made a high, peeping scream and fell against the doctor.

"What is it?" Mrs. Fisk asked.

"Like some savage, in her breasts, to torture me." Mrs. Fisk half carried Mrs. Hammond back up the stairs. The doctor glared at Regina, who was searching for something in the rug, her back to the doorway. "Miss Sartwell, henceforth you must confine yourself to your room while in this house. Your presence profoundly disturbs my patient." He swept up the stairs after his patient.

Olive looked over at Regina. She was pulling needles out of her chest. "They won't put up with me much longer," Regina said.

Olive dragged the old curtains out from behind the couch. "Regina?"

"What?"

"In that Finger Lakes house," Olive said, "Do you think we could have a blackberry patch out back?"

Regina drafted businesslike letters to her father and to Maryanne, then planned the manner in which she would approach her uncle. She sent a letter to a friend of her grandmother's, inquiring as to a suitable house with shoreline acreage. Meanwhile, it was no longer just Regina's plan.

After the blackberry patch, Olive could not keep herself from adding lemon-colored paint on the porch swing and the shutters, and a little farm for Ren to putter around in: just a few chickens and sheep, some pigs and goats. A workhorse for the plow, and a smarter horse for the wagon. And then a little room off the kitchen for her mother's herbals. At times, Olive felt as if she were furnishing a doll's house. Other times, she thought of Regina's relatives, every one of them as rich as General Hammond. She imagined these people bought and sold whole towns without flinching. At these times, the small white house by the lake began to seem like a modest request.

Olive had hung four Oriental rugs on the line and was beating them with a broom. Dust puffed out with each thump, making her cough. Whenever she stopped to wipe her face, the flies came. She was whacking so hard at the rugs, sweat pouring down her back and beading up on her forehead, that she didn't notice SuSu standing next to her.

"Someone to see you." SuSu dug a hole in the ground with her toe.

"Who?"

"Some*one*. In the kitchen." SuSu ran away on tiptoe.

Olive couldn't imagine anything except bad news. She laid the broom down, pulled off her kerchief, and wiped her face with it. She wiped her hands on her apron. Then she followed SuSu around the house. When she opened the kitchen door, swallows grazed her head.

"Olive!" It was Ida, wearing some cheap, striped dress that puffed at the breasts and backside. She wore a hat with three long feathers coming out the back. Ida laughed. "Ma said you had some soft job as a lady's maid, but it looks like you've hired on as a chimney sweep, instead."

"It's not so bad." Olive touched her lip.

"Can you go for a walk with me?"

"Talk with me while I finish up the rugs, if you want."

Ida pushed a new wicker case into the corner of the kitchen and patted it. "Stay put now," she told it. She followed Olive around the back.

Olive stood in front of the rugs, broom in hand, watching Ida wave away flies with her hat. "Better change before you go up to Hammondville."

"I just come from Hammondville."

"You come all the way down here just to say hello? I got Sundays off."

"What's wrong with you?"

"Nothing." Olive began thumping a red and blue rug with the broom.

"Well, your smile's gone sour. I don't like it. And you don't seem glad to see me, neither."

Olive glanced at Ida. Her thick brown hair was coiled up high on her head. Ida was using her green hat to swat the flies, letting the feathers slide across her face. "I'm glad to see you, but you make me nervous, dressed like that."

"Ma hates me, so you might as well, too. She's mad 'cause I won't stay up to that ugly town and marry some ignorant, dirty miner."

"Like I did."

"No, you got this good job down here. That's why she wants

me to stay, so I'll take care of your husband while you're down here having fun. I can't do that." Ida coughed from the dust and stepped back. "I got a plan. I'm going to Boston." She patted her coiled hair.

"Boston?"

"Yep. My friend Agnes Wright, she was a neighbor of cousin Maureen's, she's already gone down to Boston and got a job in a gentlemen's shirt factory. And she wrote that I can come down and share a room with her. She says it's a great life. She taught me fancywork while she was still in Vermont. I stayed up late, rocking a colicky baby and stitching. That's what I been doing these last months—see, I got her customers when she left. I bought these clothes. I like money. I like ready-made clothes. And I hate Maureen's babies. I hate all babies. The smell of sour milk reminds me of Ma's suffering. And I hate Hammondville, too. Why don't you come down to Boston?"

Olive smacked the rugs.

"If we both said we was going, Ma'd have to follow. But as long as she has you, she'll stay."

"It's got to be something good to pry her away. She has her nursing and she has all the dead ones buried here."

"That's why I can't stand it up there. It's creepy. The house is full of ghosts. They pester me in my sleep. And Magnus Honsinger is so sour, he'd pickle cucumbers."

"Ida, didn't you notice that Ma's been sick?"

"She sure ain't as mild as she used to be. I believe she's gotten tougher. And she has that girl to boss around. I'll send money, too, once I get settled. Darn these flies."

Olive turned back towards the rug. "How can you do it?"

"Do what?"

"Leave the family when we need you."

"The only reason anyone needs me is 'cause you're down here."

"We need this money. Maybe we can get away on it."

"You ain't talking sense. You just said before Ma wouldn't leave. And I just told you I'd send money when I get to Boston.

You're the one that married that miner and chained yourself to this god-awful life. And now you like this soft job and you want me to ruin my life taking care of your husband for you. Sorry, Olive, but I ain't doing it."

"Not taking care of Ren. Taking care of Ma, Ida. It's your turn now."

"Ma don't need taking care of. You always been too helpful for your own good."

Olive heard the kitchen door slam. Mrs. Fisk scurried towards them. "Olive Honsinger, you forget yourself," she hissed. "Mrs. Hammond does not wish to have two common women screeching at each other in her backyard. It's disgraceful."

Ida said, "It's my fault, ma'am. I'm her sister."

"We cannot have sisters dropping in at any time."

"I just come to say good-bye. I'm leaving for Boston."

"Make your good-byes brief. And lower your voice."

"Yes, ma'am," Ida said.

Ida watched Mrs. Fisk's back. "If we work on Ma together, maybe she'll go with us to Boston."

"I got my own plan. You can come in on it, if you want."

"What kind of plan?"

"With Regina Sartwell."

"The epileptic lady you care for?"

"We're going to buy a house for all of us."

"Who's 'all of us'?"

"Our family and Regina."

"Why would the general's niece want to bother herself with our family?"

"Because—she likes me."

"How could she get her own house, anyway? I hear they won't even let her out of this one."

"She had a dream about it."

"A dream?"

"Yes."

"You was always the sensible one. Is it this job that's turned your head? That's what they say up to home. This job is turning your head."

"What was those dreams you had, Ida?"

"What dreams?"

"You said ghosts was pestering you in your sleep."

"Oh, them. I dream of Submit, mostly. She's climbing down the ladder in her nightgown. Her back is to me and I'm not sure it's her. But then I notice the blond fuzz on the back of her neck, and I know it's her. Then she turns and smiles. You remember how wide she smiled? And I get this feeling. This deep, relief kind of feeling. But then I remember she's dead." Ida shrugged, laughed a little.

"I dream like that sometimes. Or sometimes, I hear a baby cooing, right when I'm awake." Olive stopped hitting the rugs.

"Olive, give me a smile before I go, so I know it's you."

"I can't." She began whacking at the rugs again. "Ida, you go on to Boston. You get away from the mines."

"I want you and Ma to get away, too."

"Maybe we will." Olive could feel tears coming. She sniffed them back. "I don't know what's wrong with me. You write to us, tell us where you are so I can reach you if something good happens."

Ida stared at Olive.

"Go on now." Olive hugged Ida quick. Ida began to cry. Olive sighed. "These rugs are pretty well beat up." She began pulling them off the line. Ida was still standing there, swatting flies and crying.

"Ida, you better go or you'll get me in trouble. Mrs. Hammond don't want common women crying in her backyard."

"Good-bye, then." Ida's voice trembled. She picked up her skirts and ran to the kitchen, the way Olive remembered her running in games of tag, neck craned forward, not looking back.

Olive was ironing in the laundry room. It was a rainy day and she liked the steam that rose when she shook water over the white clothes, her thumb over the bottle's mouth.

Mrs. Fisk was rummaging through the basket of folded clothes, sighing and refolding Olive's work. "If I was you, I'd be getting home to your family."

Olive looked over at Mrs. Fisk, who continued to refold. "What do you mean?"

"Just what I say. Two dollars a week ain't worth a life of loneliness."

"My family's up to the mines, just like always."

Mrs. Fisk took the iron out of Olive's hand, spit on it to test for heat, then ran it over the petticoats herself, not looking up. "Maybe you think it's a true friendship, but it don't work like that. You make their bed, brush their hair, wash their back, carry their slops out every morning. The years go by, they marry, join their fine clubs, make new associations, and you're still carrying their slops. Their feelings grow away, but yours don't 'cause yours have nothing else to settle on."

"But Regina is an epileptic. How can she move on? She's got nothing."

"Nothing? That young lady's got something. A terrible will. Epileptic or not, she'll have everything she wants, sooner or later. I'd advise running from her faster than a weepy one like Mrs. Hammond."

"Regina and me have a plan," Olive said to the stiff profile of the housekeeper. Mrs. Fisk shook her head. She didn't stop ironing.

When the pile was finished and lay white and clean and starched and folded high in the basket, Mrs. Fisk put the iron in a bowl of water. It hissed. "Her name is Lydia," she said.

"Who?" Olive said.

"Mrs. Hammond. I used to call her Lydia." Mrs. Fisk walked out of the room.

"Tell me again. Tell me about our house."

Regina sighed, stretched her arms above her head. "Let me see, I

~

think the only thing left to plan is the privy. It will be painted bright pink and smell like roses."

Olive shook her head, picked at the seam of her blanket. "Be serious, now."

"Well, then, it will be a whitewashed double-seater, and it will face the lake. It will have a Dutch door so that we may take in the view, while still maintaining modesty." Regina's voice was filling up with sleep.

"Do you think Mrs. Fisk and Mrs. Hammond ever thought of having a little house together when they was young?" Olive had loosened the stitching on the seam of her blanket. She bit the thread off.

"What a strange thought. Those two, young. Aunt Hammond would have been a whiney, yellow-faced young thing. And Mrs. Fisk would have been pinched and scrubbed, a tattletale. They could never have agreed on a house together, though. Mrs. Hammond would have wanted a house of shells and shellacked bamboo, filled with hand-painted French porcelain. And Mrs. Fisk would not have stood for anything less than scoured stone walls, and cast-iron furniture."

"Why do we keep agreeing?"

"That's our secret."

"We'll have white china painted with those blue Oriental bridges and little men and birds on it. Like the ones they never use in the kitchen. And white muslin curtains."

"Fine."

"I'm happy."

"Good."

Regina and Olive reached towards each other at the same time, entwined their fingers. Olive drifted to sleep, their hands still clasped, their knuckles brushing the floor between their beds. In her dreams their arms became a blue bridge fixed forever on a white china bowl.

* * *

112

Martha Hoppey, the daughter of the owner of the dry goods store, was fitting Regina for a summer dress. Regina stood on a chair in her room. She kept her hand on Olive's shoulder for balance. Martha bustled around below, brandishing her measuring tape.

"Could you sew me a green dotted swiss?" Regina asked.

"Oh, no, ma'am. Mrs. Hammond already ordered cream muslin for summer." Martha had no chin and an overbite. She was measuring from Regina's neck to her feet now, while Olive held the top of the tape to Regina's collarbone. "Yesterday, one of them Quaker women, or is it Shaker? My Daddy says it's Faker. Anyways, they come into the store, two of 'em. They always travel in pairs. Daddy says they're 'fraid of temptation if it was just one alone. Like maybe they'd go all loony and buy something impractical, like a peppermint stick, so Daddy says. They order eighteen yards of grey poplin. Nothing else. What was they wearing? Grey poplin. What did they order last year? Grey poplin. I'd a fed my grey poplin to the hogs after one season. I know that. And their bonnets—it looks like they're wearing coal buckets on their heads."

"What are you talking about, Martha?" Regina said.

"I'm talking about the Shakers, ma'am. Hold that tape still, Olive. I don't see what there is to giggle about, neither, Olive. The Shaker women over to Paradox, ma'am. I heard there's a baker's dozen of 'em, and there ain't no man, and they do all the hard labor themselves, plus the inside work, and they take in fancy work and make baskets and mix cures for a pharmacy in Schenectady. Alls they do is wear ugly grey poplin and work. And I guess pray some. Daddy says they don't even pray to the Lord—they pray to a woman named Mother Ann who was just some grey poplin kind of woman who most likely killed herself from overwork, so they went and made her into a saint or something. And they shake and shimmy and blather and drool when they do it. Pray to her, I mean.

"All that giggling'll send bubbles to your brain, Olive. Daddy says the only men they think is any good is the Indians and the colored, and they used to hide the colored slaves in the root cellar, too. He says there used to be an old man there named Tobias, but he died, and who knows what goes on over there to Paradox now?" Martha rolled up her tape and stuck it in her apron pocket. "I guess I got all the measurements I need. Now, don't go gettin' plump on me while I'm sewing it, ma'am. Is Mrs. Cutter in the kitchen? I'll just have a cup of tea with her on my way out." Martha glanced at Olive. "Some people's heads are filled with bubbles."

Regina teetered off the chair. Olive grabbed her arm. "It sounds as if those Shaker women are all epileptics," Regina said.

"Martha doesn't know what she's talking about. They're plain, gentle women."

"Is it true they pray to a mother named Ann who labors with her hands?"

"As far as I know, you don't care 'bout God hardly, much less some Ann woman."

"It's exactly like my dream. We must make a visit to them."

"Paradox ain't near. It must be seventeen miles, over the ridge or around it, either way."

"We could take the surrey."

"I'm sure your aunt will say, Off you go now and take that fancy surrey alone all the way to Paradox to visit with them Shaker women."

"I'm sure they're proper ladies. I don't see why anyone would object."

"You don't even talk to your aunt no more. I know she would mind 'cause I'm the one does the asking."

"We won't tell her where we're going, that's all. We'll make up another excuse. How about charity work? I'm sure Aunt Hammond would approve of that."

Olive saw Mrs. Fisk carrying Mrs. Hammond's slops up and down years of stairs, her heart shriveling like an old apple. "What?"

"Olive, will you please pay attention? This is important. I said, couldn't we pretend we're doing charity work in Paradox?"

"I just have one question that I'm all confused on. How can your dream mean that you got to become a Shaker lady in Paradox and that you have to buy a little house on Seneca Lake where you can care for my Ma, both at one time?"

Regina's lips parted, but at first, nothing came out. "Why, Olive. I never said—"

"I got work to do—"

"Wait—"

"I said I got work to do. I'm a maid here, not some nothing-to-do-but-dream lady." Olive left the room. She climbed to the narrow third-story staircase. Her breath came in little squeaking gasps. "What's wrong?" she said out loud. She crouched on the stair and put her fist up to her mouth to keep herself quiet. She wanted Ren, she wanted her mother. She wanted to go back to that snowy winter night, and a full stomach, and the sound of the clock ticking, and her mother's voice reading, that night before Mr. Cutter banged on their door with Regina's message, before she had wanted anything. She thought, if I had that little card now, with that message from Miss Regina Hammond Sartwell—Please come—I'd rip it up and throw it in the stove and go back to bed.

Olive heard someone on the first staircase. She jumped up, tried to breathe normally. Mrs. Fisk stood on the bottom step. "Miss Regina is asking for you."

"I don't want to see her."

"I'll tell her I can't find you. You help Mrs. Cutter clean the dining room floor."

Olive slopped the mop around in the hot, soapy water, unable to follow Mrs. Cutter's conversation. She had to get down on her knees under the general's chair and scrape at the cigar ash with her nail. Every once in a while, she would gag on air and that ugly squeaking noise would come out. Finally she stood, dried her hands on her apron. "Mrs. Cutter, I got to see to Regina."

Mrs. Cutter smiled and thanked her for the help.

Olive stared at the top of Mrs. Cutter's little grey head, bent over the mop handle. "Mrs. Cutter, does everyone pity me for caring for Regina?"

Mrs. Cutter straightened, blinked, "Why, no. We think its generous. I was just saying to Mr. Cutter, that child is so sweet she could love anything." Mrs. Cutter began wringing out the mop.

Olive walked down the hall and into Regina's room. Regina was sewing on her balsam pillow. "Where have you been? I didn't mean that I was giving up our plan. I was just curious—"

"I can fix it with Mrs. Hammond, about visiting the Shakers. I'll talk religion and charity. And I'll tell her you'll be out of the house for the day. She'll like that." Olive felt her throat widen, her breath easing.

"You're too good. Olive, I'm sorry about before. I just don't think the Hammonds are going to put up with me much longer. The house on Seneca Lake is my absolute plan, but if I needed a quick escape, in the meantime, where would I go? You already have another place, but I don't."

"I guess I shouldn't put much faith in that Seneca Lake house."

"You should. I just need some insurance, a safe interim haven, in case the Geneva house takes longer than we planned." Regina handed Olive the balsam pillow. Her name was embroidered in orange thread—Olive Landry Honsinger. Regina Hammond Sartwell was in purple. Under it in big letters, Regina had begun embroidering FOREVER in a chain stitch.

The pillow smelled clean. Olive sat in the rocker and plumped it on her lap. "I'm acting mad, like you won't keep to the plan, but really, I'm just as afraid I won't be strong enough to convince my whole family to come along." She took a shuddery breath. "My ma does this crazy thing sometimes. She'll be talking 'bout one of the dead ones, or me or Ida even, and she'll do this with her arms." Olive spread her arms out and rolled them towards herself. "I don't think she even knows she's doin' it, but it's like she was gathering everything in. That's what I want to do. I want to gather you and Ma and Ren in, and I'm afraid my arms ain't strong enough."

Seven

~

"BROWN HORSES. BROWN dress. Brown hat. The Shakers ought to be pleased. Brown is almost as drab as grey." Regina tapped a fidgety rhythm against the wagon with her long fingers.

"You're frighting the Clydesdales, Miss Sartwell," Mr. Cutter said, fussing with the harnesses.

"Nothing could frighten those enormous things," Regina said.

Mr. Cutter slid his hands down the traces, dangled the ends in front of Olive, and began giving her technical advice. She nodded seriously, her pale face and orange hair floating over the high black collar of her best dress.

Mrs. Cutter tucked a wicker basket under the seat of the wagon. She winked at Olive. "Against doctor's orders for your outing. And, Mr. Cutter, leave them be. Can't you see them girls are raring to go?"

Mr. Cutter sighed and handed Olive the reins. He said he'd take them himself, if he wasn't so busy. He placed a shotgun behind the seat. "You won't have to use it."

He watched mournfully as Olive climbed up. He patted the brown horses and nuzzled their white faces and rubbery lips with his shiny forehead, whispering, loud enough for Olive to hear, "Sorry, old girls, nothing I can do about it." He helped Regina up.

~

117

Mrs. Fisk bustled out, shaking out a plaid wool blanket. She tucked it around Regina's legs. "Mrs. Hammond's orders."

At the last moment their plan had nearly failed because Mrs. Hammond could not decide between the elegant surrey or the farm wagon for their journey. Style meant the carriage, but she didn't think Olive could handle the high-stepping Morgan horses; yet it was humiliating to think of her own relative driven in a farm wagon by a work team. She deliberated for eight days, then came down with a headache and let Mr. Cutter decide.

As the horses plodded down the drive, Regina nudged Olive with her knee. "Hurry up. Before they think of something else."

"These horses don't hurry," Olive said. "So you best calm down and enjoy the ride."

Just after the widow's fork someone had planted weeping willows along the road. The trees brushed dew onto Olive's shoulders as they passed. Then they rode through miles of cleared land and blackened stumps, through Irondale where they stopped to pick flowers for Olive's family gravestones. She named them for Regina, tapping each monument as she went: her grandparents, old Tim Landry and his wife, Mercy Ann; Wealthy, her father; Submit; Baby Lynn; Baby Mary; Baby Tim, after her grandfather; and just Baby Girl, born dead and never named. "There's my mother's name, already chiseled in below my father's: Florilla. That's why it'll be hard to lure her away. The end of her life is all planned out."

In late morning they stopped under a tree at the edge of a farm, hoped the flies wouldn't find them in the shade. They ate their lunch—cold meat and chutney sandwiches, turned cider, oranges, and hard cheese. While they were eating, two farmer's children with wide, bland faces swung on the fence and stared at the oranges. Olive offered them some, but they shook their heads. As they rode away, the children were already searching the weeds, gathering up the orange peels.

Finally, near noon, they rode into the Paradox valley, past the blacksmith shop, the tavern, and then the schoolhouse. The school children left their lunch pails and ran beside the wagon, slapping the sides. Olive asked one of the older ones where the Shaker ladies lived. He pointed down the road. "The grand-lookin' one."

The sun was on the top of their heads now, their dark hats soaking up the heat, burning their scalps. A mile later, on the left, they saw a neat stone wall and behind it, on a rise, a white house. There were apple trees in the meadow beside it. Pink petunias grew out of two front window boxes. On the other side of the house there was a grey barn and a work shed. Someone had hung suet in one of the apple trees, and three birds were diving for it. A big, silver cat sprawled on the stone doorstep and eyed the birds.

Olive looped the traces around the hitching post. Regina was already knocking on the door. They could hear the sound of a scratchy violin. Regina knocked again. The violin sawing stopped. They heard scurrying footsteps. A chubby, moon-faced woman opened the door. She looked like some old-time Pilgrim in her grey dress, white shoulder cape, starched white net cap, and huge straw bonnet.

"Hello. I hope we're not intruding," Regina said in her gravelly voice. "My name is Miss Hammond Sartwell and this is Olive Honsinger. We've come from Crown Point." Regina handed the woman one of her calling cards. The woman didn't say anything, just held the card with two fingers, as if it were dirty. "To be frank with you, miss, I'm an epileptic. In my fit I had a vision. A woman came to me and said, 'Even the mother labors with her hands.' I thought you might be able to help me understand what she meant."

Olive smiled encouragingly.

The woman opened the door wider. She led them through an entranceway with identical long, black cloaks hanging on pegs. Inside the house, she said, "I will fetch our eldress. Sister Harriet."

They were left standing on polished floorboards in a long room with windows of shining paned glass. A white pitcher and washbowl rested on a side table with a white linen washcloth folded next to them. Chairs hung on the wall behind the long table. Everything seemed to be in scoured shades of grey and blond. The room felt cool, even on this warm day.

"It's so beautiful," Regina whispered.

"I think it could use some homey fixing up," Olive said. "From the outside it looks nice, but inside it's as drafty as a church."

The grey cat wound through their skirts, purring. Dustless sunlight washed the floor. The violin started up again. A woman sailed into the room so smoothly that she was beside them before they were ready for her. She was tall and pear shaped. Wrinkles spread out like sun's rays from extravagantly blue eyes. Her hair was white and wiry under her thin net cap.

"I've just been readying one of the gardens for planting." She held out her hand without taking off her work glove, so they shook cracked leather and dirt.

"I'm Olive Honsinger and this is Miss Regina Hammond Sartwell, the niece of General Hammond over to Crown Point."

"Regina and Olive." That still face was forcing nervous giggles up Olive's throat. Her lips twitched.

Regina said, "Can you tell me about your order?"

"Are you the one with the vision?"

"Yes, she's the one, miss," Olive said. "Why don't you two chat and I'll just take me a walk around the fields. Regina, you holler when you're done." Olive turned and left before Regina could say anything. She patted the horses a little in the hot sun. She wished for the fly-shaking skin of a horse. The horses were searching for grass between the stones, but it had been clipped away. She wandered around the south side of the house.

Here stood a little stand of trees she hadn't noticed before. They were planted in three neat rows, all about the same size, except a skinny poplar sapling at one end with a fence round it. When Olive walked closer she noticed that each tree had a plaque at its base with a name on it. Sister Harriet's name was under an oak. The poplar sapling belonged to someone named Sister Emily. Olive stroked the smooth bark of a beech tree, thinking, How silly. Then she envied them, each with her own sweet tree.

She walked around to the back. Three pale women, alike in their grey dresses and caps, were trying to coax a mule to move a large stone from the field. One woman encouraged the front of the mule, another pulled with him, and the third was heaving from behind. Olive thought, Just plow round it. She kept watching until she couldn't stand it anymore, then she walked over to help. The women smiled at her with gritted teeth. She heaved against the rock. Slowly it moved forward, rolling and shaking dirt onto their feet. The women and the mule rolled it downhill by the shed. Then the three patted each other on the back and wiped their faces with their sleeves. They looked at Olive shyly, from the side. They didn't speak. Olive followed them to a pump, and waited her turn for cold well water. She heard Regina call her name, and said goodbye. Two of them smiled and echoed her "Good-bye" in soft voices. The third studied the ground.

Regina was already on the wooden seat of the wagon. Sister Harriet was standing on the steps, stroking the grey cat in her arms. Regina was not smiling. Olive climbed up, waved good-bye to Sister Harriet. Sister Harriet held her palm up. Olive turned the horses around in a wide circle, and they began plodding back up the valley. She felt hot and uncomfortable, sweaty from helping with the stone. "So, what do you think?" Olive asked.

"Very little passion."

"A passion for cleanliness, that's sure. And hard work. In the back field, I saw three women and a mule pulling out a rock the size of an outhouse. I'd like to see you dressed in scratchy cloth, pulling huge stones out of the ground."

"I know you would."

"That elder, that Harriet woman? She was a mum one. Made me feel stupid, with those chicory-blossom blue eyes of hers. How was your talk with her?"

"Short and infuriating. I told her all about my visions. She said, 'Don't fret, that sounds common enough.' Those were her precise words. I said, What do you mean, 'common'? And she said, 'Mother Ann is generous; she visits many.' I said, I have no idea who Mother Ann is, but a Gypsy girl told me my fits would bring me a handsome husband and a good wagon, and that sounds just as reasonable to me."

"You didn't say that."

"I did."

"What did she say?"

"She in--ited me back on Sunday for their service."

"You made up an excuse."

"No, I said I'd go."

"What, to their service?"

"I know, it seems completely unsuited to me, but it fits the words so perfectly: Even the mother labors with her hands. It's like an itch, and I have to go back on Sunday and scratch it."

"They're too holy for you. Even for a—what did you call it?— interim safe haven. They're mourning doves and you're a cardinal or a mockingbird. You're not even a bird at all, you're—"

"What am I? I love this game."

"All right then, you're a dog. You're a terrier. When you get your teeth in something, you shake the life out of it, spit it out, and grab on to something else."

"And you're a cow."

Olive flinched. They both watched a small herd of Guernseys in a stumpy field.

Regina sighed. "I just adore cows."

Olive smiled. "I guess I wouldn't mind strolling in a pasture, chewing on a cud of sweet clover."

"I guess I wouldn't mind shaking the life out of something."

They let the horses make their own way down the road, Olive absently urging them on when they stopped to graze the side of the road. "I wonder how long it will take you to grow bored of these Shakers," Olive said.

"Not long, I expect."

Three hours later the sun was lower and they had reached the line of trees before the widow's fork. Regina was trailing her hand through the weeping willows as they passed. "What is it exactly that men and women do?"

"What do you mean?"

"At night. To have a baby. Or just for amusement, I suppose."

"You've seen animals together."

"No."

"Did you ever hear your parents on an afternoon? The noise?"

"My God. No."

"Ain't anyone ever talked to you about this?"

"Oh, sure, we all talked of it in boarding school. I know that men have this appendage. I saw one at the Gypsy camp. And it goes into the woman. I'm not exactly sure where. Where we bleed from?"

"That's it."

"And does it feel like the cramp on the first day you bleed?"

"No. Well, some women hate it. But with me and Ren it's—it ain't that much different from hugging and kissing in the feeling of it. Ain't you ever had a feeling down there?"

The horses wandered under a tree to graze new grass. They pulled the wagon after them until it rustled through a wall of willow and stopped under its canopy. Olive let the reins droop. The bowed, enfolding branches felt so much like their conversation that they hardly noticed where they were.

"Yes, I guess I have at night sometimes. It keeps me from sleeping."

"What do you do?"

"Rub against the sheet. It gets worse and then it sort of goes away and I fall to sleep."

"That's it, then."

"What's it?"

"That's the feeling."

"That's all?" Regina slid her hand down a willow branch. "Then I certainly don't need to marry. The sheet works just fine, and it doesn't order me about afterwards." Olive laughed, but

Regina grabbed on to her wrist. "What's that?" Dimly Olive heard yelling men's voices from beyond the widow's fork. Then the sound of breaking glass. She picked up the reins and pulled the horses' heads up. She trundled them farther under the willows.

"We can't hide. We have to see what the trouble is," Regina said.

The men's voices were coming nearer. The back end of the wagon stuck out of the drooping branches. Olive reached under the seat and lifted up the shotgun. She checked to see if it was loaded, then rested it against her skirted knees. She put her head down on her chest for a second, to clear away the dizziness. When she lifted her face, Regina was tapping her fingers on her knee. "You look greedy," Olive said.

She backed them out of the willow tree, the branches sliding over them. There was a curve before the fork, and they couldn't see anything around it. Olive kept the wagon over to the far right, skimming the edge of the trees, where they could see first thing around the curve. She stopped half in the last willow tree.

Regina saw about eight men, fifty yards ahead. Their voices banged off each other. She couldn't understand the words. They could have been yelling joy or grief. Urgent, aimless, they swaggered down the middle of the road, jostling together and apart. The men came to the farm before the widow's. There was a wooden wheelbarrow by the side of the road. A tall, thin man kicked it over. The other men's voices grew louder. Another, beefier man jogged over to the wheelbarrow and lifted it over his head. He crashed it down, again and again until it splintered.

The farm dog rushed down the drive, leaping and growling from a few feet away. The tall man charged it. The dog turned, yelping. The man chased it up the drive. Shouts of laughter followed him. Another man yanked off the door of the chicken house, ducked inside, and came out in a storm of screaming chickens. He kicked and threw, until the shack held only dust and drifting feathers.

A man with white hair and white skin picked up a rock. He weighed it, then heaved it through the window of the farmhouse. Regina heard Olive grunt, and then jerk back, as if she were the window. There was a scream from inside. A young boy ran out the back, took off across the fields towards Crown Point.

"The boy's off for the sheriff," Olive whispered.

The men didn't seem to notice or care. They moved on to the widow's house and stopped in front of it. The house was blinded by the blankets that covered the windows. The men jumbled around uncertainly. The white-haired man took hold of the sagging split-rail fence and began rocking it. The way he swayed it seemed almost gentle, at first. Then he yanked the fence. It fell in a shock of rails at his feet. Another man threw a rock at a window, but it just hit the blanket with a muffled, empty thud, and dropped off. No sound came from inside the house, as if the occupants were deeply asleep or deeply resigned.

Regina felt her pulse at her throat. "We can stop them. We can use the shotgun." She tried to pull it out from between Olive's knees, but Olive closed her hand around the barrel.

"Don't," Olive said.

"They're attacking the widow's home." Regina tried to jerk the gun out of Olive's hand, but Olive's grip was mulish and would not bend.

"Don't," Olive said again. Her lip had stuck on her tooth. She looked like she was snarling.

Regina didn't care. She yanked the gun up near her kneecap. With Olive's grip forcing the barrel skyward, she pulled the trigger. The recoil hit her thigh, hard. The sound hurt her ears. The rotten smell made her eyes tear. The big horses started, flinched their skins, shook their heads.

The men's heads swiveled around towards them. The white-haired one said something, and the men leapt over the broken fence and took off at a jog, cutting across the widow's field to the willow road, back up the way Regina and Olive had come.

Regina's leg ached. She knew there would be a bruise. Olive was watching the road to Crown Point. "What's wrong with you—"

"We couldn't tell who they was, right, Regina? When the sheriff comes. Say it was just some gang of men, too far off to tell. We shot the gun and they scattered. Say they was drunk."

"Who knows if they were drunk? They were savages."

"Say it anyway, Regina."

"Who were they, then?" They heard horses thudding down the road towards them from Crown Point. "Tell me."

"Miners. From Hammondville. It was my brother-in-law, Magnus. Keep quiet." Olive could see the sheriff and three other men on horseback. The young boy who had run across the fields clung to the back of one, bouncing behind the saddle. Olive started the wagon forward, and they met in front of the first farmhouse. The men reined in beside them. The boy slid down the rump of the horse and ran into the house.

"Miss Sartwell, ma'am." The sheriff took off his hat. Then he looked at Olive. "You seen some boys destroying property?"

"Yes, sir, we did. They was smashing things and swaying, all drunken. I shot off this gun in the air and they run."

"Which way?"

"Into the woods. I think."

"Where?"

Olive pointed away from the willow road.

"Were they miners?"

"I couldn't tell, sir. They was too far away."

"Are you the Landry girl?"

"Yes, sir."

"Did you marry a Swede—Magnus Some-such?"

"No, sir, he's my husband's brother. We don't get along too good."

"Was he there?"

"I'd tell you if I knew, sir, but I couldn't make out any of them." Olive coughed.

"Can you get Miss Sartwell home yourself?" Olive nodded. "Maybe Tom's family recognized 'em. Or the widow might have some idea what that Swede looks like." The men smirked. They turned their horses towards the farmhouse.

Olive and Regina rode home in silence. As soon as Olive reined in the horses by the shed, Regina jumped down and stalked into the house. Olive unharnessed the horses with Mr. Cutter. He patted and soothed them, worried aloud that Olive had let them graze along the road. Olive brought in the picnic things and washed them.

Then Olive went to Regina's room. Regina had thrown her brown dress and top petticoat on the floor, and she was pacing the room in the last petticoat. The bustle at her backside and the ruffles on her chest snapped and flounced with her pacing. Her thigh-high black stockings were slowly slipping down to her ankles.

"If you're going to be a Shaker woman, you'd best learn to pick up your own things," Olive said, draping the layers over her arm.

Regina stopped in the middle of her pacing and put her fists on her hips. "I don't care if he's your brother-in-law or your one-armed father come back from the dead." She started pacing again. "That poor widow woman."

"Don't even start." Olive began hanging Regina's things in the closet.

Regina stopped pacing. "What do you mean by that?"

Olive shrugged and kept hanging.

"Stop that. I detest it when someone begins something and refuses to finish it."

Olive shook out the jacket, sat down in the rocker, and began fastening the little velvet-covered buttons. "It ain't no mystery. I saw that greedy look in your eye, right from the start. If anyone would enjoy smashing things, it's you. You fired that gun 'cause you wanted to be part of the mess. Not 'cause of any poor widow woman."

"That is basely untrue." Regina sat down on the bed and crossed her ankles. She put the pillow on her lap, plumped it. "Mostly untrue." She brushed the pillow off her lap. "You're right that I envied those men their destruction. At the first farmhouse, I could feel the weight of the rock in my hand, the satisfying sound of shattering glass. But not at the widow's house. It was already broken. It was like watching someone who is very, very tired finally fall asleep, and then taking a rock and smashing in her head. But it was too late. It already felt as if it were my hand breaking that fence. And it scared me. And don't look at me like that. I did want to shoot that gun off to feel what it would be like, but I also wanted to end it. I really did. It was wrong. Why did those brutes do it?"

Olive buttoned faster. "You don't know nothing about it, that's for sure. You got a hard time, cooped up in here and having the fits that can't be cured, but it ain't the same hard time as they got up to Hammondville. You couldn't even spend one day up there without trying to kill yourself. I never want to tell you neither, 'cause I can't make it sound nothing but ugly. What do you think it's like breathing iron dust, so cramped up you can't stand up straight, twelve hours a day? You got a kerosene light on your head, and if you hit some gas in the rock, your head might explode, but you gotta have light. And you know if the flame starts to flicker, you're losing the air. And then they dynamite near you. You feel the rock shake right above your head, rock dusts down on you. You go to work in the dark, spend the day in the dark, you come out and it's dark. You think the sun might have disappeared and you wouldn't even know it. Then they cut your wages. You don't own or earn nothing now, but they cut your wages." A brown velvet button popped off in her fingers. She closed her fist around it. "They're fed up." Olive leaned her head back and closed her eyes. She could feel something simmering in her chest. She breathed in deep and easy, trying to draw in some cool air to douse it.

Regina didn't say anything for a while, and Olive imagined that she had left. Olive didn't open her eyes, just ran her thumb over the button, embarrassed and sad.

"How am I to know anything if you never tell me? I never thought about what it must be like. Is your life unbearable as well?" Regina was so hoarse, it was hard to make out the words tumbling around in the landslide of gravel.

"No, it ain't unbearable. But it's better with you and it makes me hate that mining town. I don't want Ren down there no more, he's dying, just like Magnus said. I only realize it just now. And the reason we're not leaving is 'cause of my mama's dead babies. And 'cause her name is on that tombstone. And 'cause Ren is too meek, just like me." Olive slid her hand over her face to smooth it out. "That's why I need that Finger Lakes home."

"We'll get that house. I should be hearing from my sister or my father any time now. But in the meantime, if they're going to smash something, why don't they come here and burn the general's house down? Those farmers haven't done them any harm."

"If they even got near this house, they'd all be shot down dead."

"What about the union?"

"We don't have a union."

"Then you must start one. They're all over the country. Just a few weeks ago I heard Uncle Hammond talking about some union men that came down from Plattsburgh. They were intending to organize, but Uncle Hammond had them run out of town. He confiscated their material. I'm sure it's in his office. I heard him reading from it to someone."

"You mean directions on how to do a union?"

"Yes. My grandmother was all in favor of unions. The workers band together and insist on better conditions and wages, then they force the owner to give it to them."

"That's what I never understood. How could they force him? He'd just sack them or throw them in jail."

"It's all in the material, I expect. We'll have to get it."

"Regina, this ain't a joke. It's not an adventure like sneaking out to them Gypsies, which wasn't no joke either. Messing with the general is like messing with dynamite."

"He's just an old, sentimental man. But I know how important this is to you. Which one was it?"

"Which one what?"

"Which one was Magnus?"

"The one with the white hair. The one with the rock."

"I knew it. The beauty."

They each took a candle and tiptoed down the hall. Regina had insisted on wearing the Cutters' son's castoffs, even though Olive had just gotten around to cleaning them a few days before. Regina hunched over in her baggy pants and coat and held her candle high, so that it made long, streaky shadows on the ceiling. "Sadly, we're going to burn the general in his bed. Set fire to his beautiful white whiskers. Beware, beware," Regina whispered.

Olive's neck prickled. "Will you keep quiet? He's away. We saw him leave. He's not here. We saw Mr. Cutter with his baggage."

"But isn't it marvelous? We're having the adventure of our lives, right in our own home."

"This ain't our home." Olive kept glancing behind her. She couldn't stop her back and neck from itching.

The sliding doors of the general's study made a horrible aching noise as they pried them apart. "Fisk ought to sand these," Regina said. "Someone should speak to her." They had a whispered argument about whether to close the doors. Regina thought the noise would wake someone, but Olive couldn't bear to have an open door at her back. Olive refused to move until Regina yanked them closed, but then the grating sound of the closing door reminded Olive of the lid of a coffin slamming shut.

Olive held her candle up. The light curved around a globe of the earth. There was a map of the mining operations behind a huge rolltop desk. There were green Oriental rugs on the floor and three green leather armchairs. It smelled of old cigar smoke and sweet whiskey. Books lined the walls.

"Look in his desk, Olive. I'll check through his file cabinet." Regina pulled out the top wooden drawer of the cabinet. Olive forced herself to walk over to the desk. The little key was in the lock. She was afraid to turn the key, pull up the rolltop, afraid of the sound, ridiculously afraid that somehow the general was crouching inside of it. The smell of cigar was making her sick.

"It's not under 'unions.' I'll check under 'strike.' "

Olive breathed in and kept the air behind her teeth. She twisted the key, pulled up the rolltop. Neat. No loose papers. She began opening drawers. She moved slowly, careful not to disturb anything. Her head was full of pins from not breathing.

"It's not under 'labor' either. Damn," Regina said. "What was the name of that union, anyway? I should remember that."

Olive slid open a little drawer at the far right of the desk. Inside was one flat book bound in black leather. She lifted it up. She opened the cover. The pages were filled with a curling script. A date topped each page. She stared at the handwriting: the extravagant loops around the Os, the elegant dashes after the Ss.

"Have you found something?" Regina asked.

"His diary."

"Olive, you're brilliant." Regina left the file cabinet and stood looking over Olive's shoulder. "All those pages of boring drivel." Regina made her voice into an affected whine. " 'Due to a mysterious vagary of nature, the Penfield bed nearly exhausted. Questions about the Hammond pit. Still, five hundred tons just this—' "

"Don't." Olive closed the diary. "I don't want to know." She handed the book to Regina.

"Fine, it's tedious swill, anyway. But let me see if we can find the date that those union men were here. You were away when I overheard the conversation. Which means it was a Sunday. Three weeks ago on a Sunday, I think. But then, the union men must have been the week before. I'll check the whole week. Blah, blah, grace of God, blah, blah, scurrilous agitators—here we are, here we are—Knights of Labor." Regina ran over to the file cabinet. "Knights of Labor, Knights of Labor." She slapped the files. "Nothing. I don't understand it. Men of business are always so organized."

"Let's go, Regina."

"Shall we read more of his ridiculous diary first? We might be memorialized in it."

"Let's go."

Olive slipped the diary back into its little drawer and rolled the desktop down. Turned the key. Regina pulled open one side of the study door. It creaked again.

"Who's down there?" It was Fisk's voice, sharp and afraid. They were standing just in the hall, outside the general's study. Neither of them moved. "Miss Sartwell?" They heard footsteps down the stairwell. Olive could see the light from a candle licking the bottom stairs.

Mrs. Fisk's frightened face appeared at the entrance to the hallway, glowing from the candle she held high. Her face soured. "What's this? Has she had a fit again?"

Olive looked down. Regina was on the floor, silently jerking and shaking. Saliva was running out of the corner of her mouth.

Mrs. Fisk came closer. "What is she doing out in the hall? What in the Lord's name is she wearing those rags for?"

Olive couldn't think what to say. Regina groaned Olive's name. Olive bent down. Mrs. Fisk shook her head. "She's scared you dumb. Get her cleaned up. We'll talk this over in the morning. And we'll lock her in at night from now on." Mrs. Fisk blew out her candle and walked back down the hall. They heard the angry thump of her feet on the stairs.

Regina jumped up. Olive jerked back, startled. Regina fled back to her room. Olive followed slowly. Regina was balled up on the bed, squeezing a pillow to her chest. Olive put her candle beside Regina's on the stand and sat down on the edge of the bed.

"Did it look real?" Regina rattled her teeth. She held the pillow to her mouth.

Olive squeezed her lips closed with her hand and began shaking with silent laughter. She hardly knew how it came to be that Regina was holding her hand, kissing her knuckles, whispering,

"Don't be afraid, don't be afraid," while Olive gasped for air, the pillow growing wet with tears.

The next morning, while Regina slept, Olive walked across the dewy lawn to the outhouse, rehearsing her explanation to Mrs. Fisk. "I woke up and she was gone. Sleepwalking. Went into a fit when I woke her," she mumbled to herself. Olive waved to Mr. Cutter, scything the grass beside the road. "Must have sleep-walked right into those old clothes I was using for a pattern. I've heard of things like that." She swung open the whitewashed door, breathed through her mouth to avoid the smell, checked for spiders, and sat down. She watched the light coming through the spaces between the boards. "Mrs. Fisk," she practiced, "good idea about locking her in, but I better keep the key in my apron pocket." She reached for the pile of newspaper, neatly cut in short strips. "Or, better yet. Mrs. Fisk, no need to lock her in. I'll keep a closer watch, is all." She glanced at the newspaper strip, an advertisement: "Ordered clothing for working men." She wiped herself, dropped it in, reached for another: "Mass Meeting, The International Working People's Association will meet in Waizmann's Hall, corner 23rd and Ash." She held the strip closer, mouthing the words over again. With her other hand, she slipped the hook into the eye on the door. She picked up the pile of newspaper strips and put it on her lap. Olive began sorting through them, reading the words in a mumble, smiling to herself.

It was Sunday morning, Olive's day off, but she wasn't on the train up to Hammondville. Instead, she was in the wagon with Regina. They had left early, at first light. It was a muggy, early summer dawn, the quiet broken only by a cackling rooster, then the sharp bark of a dog. On the seat beside Olive, Regina swayed in and out of sleep as they drove through Irondale. Olive ate the dry biscuits Mrs. Cutter sent with them, the reins drooping from her left hand. She ate all of them, in a trance, filling her lap with crumbs.

"Is that the turnoff to Hammondville up ahead?"

Olive dropped the last half biscuit down the front of her dress. She turned to Regina. Her eyes were sharp and awake. "Yes, but that's not the way I'll go. First I'll take you to the Shakers. It's maybe ten miles from here. Then I'll take a two-track that runs up the back side of the ridge to Hammondville. It's probably three miles, much quicker than coming back to Irondale again."

"And you'll return for me punctually on Monday morning."

"Yes."

"And you'll show Magnus Honsinger the newspaper."

Olive put a foot on the reins and reached under the seat. She pulled out the newspaper strips, looked at them doubtfully. "I don't see how they're going to be much help, though. Just half an article claiming that Jesus was the first union man, some slogans. Here's the announcement for a meeting . . ."

"But, Olive." Regina tapped the top of one of the strips. "I told you, this is the crucial information right here. The masthead. It has the address of the paper. You can write them for information, for help. That's what unions want to do—help other workingmen." Olive shrugged, but she tucked the bits of paper carefully back under the seat.

Regina smacked her own knee. "I just had a marvelous idea. Turn back. We'll both go on to Hammondville; that way I can meet your family. We'll have tea. You can take me down to Paradox afterwards."

"I don't have time for that today. I want to make it to church, and you got to get down to the Shakers for their strange Sunday doings."

"It must be shorter to go to Hammondville first."

"No, it's the same, ten miles from Irondale either way. Anyway, Mrs. Hammond wouldn't like it."

"She'll never know."

"I don't want to."

"Why not?"

"I didn't tell 'em you were coming. They're not ready."

"You're so scaredy all the time. Now, turn this wagon around and take me to meet your dear mama."

"The house might not be—" Olive gave up, set her mouth in a smile, her see-through eyebrows twitching. She turned the wagon. They rode into the burned hills. By the end, the road turned rough, the wagon bucking and tilting, the horses whinnying nervously. They didn't think of talking. They just hung on against the jarring motion. They drove into Hammondville past Reilly's boarding-house and Dog Alley.

Olive stopped the horses in front of her house. She watched Regina take in the weathered grey walls with rags stuck in the knotholes, the smoke-blackened roof, the rusted junk the snow had uncovered; the little poplar sagging against the house as if exhausted; the three skinned squirrels, headless and pink, hanging from the eaves by their still bushy tails.

Ren ducked out of the house. He glanced quickly at Regina and away, his face coloring. He forced himself to look back. Then he bowed stiffly from his waist, his chin jerking down several times. Olive climbed off the wagon. "Regina, or Miss Sartwell, I guess, this is Ren." Ren ducked his head again.

"Hello, Ren," Regina said. She was still sitting on the wagon, her hands in her lap.

"Ren, help her down."

Ren walked over and held up his big hand. "You'll be coming in, miss?" he said, polite and horrified.

"Of course she will." Olive rolled her eyes.

Mattie Stone was standing in her doorway, arms folded. "Ain't you got a fancy houseful this Sunday. The doctor and the epileptic lady both."

"The suicidal epileptic, if you please," Regina said. She took hold of Ren's wrist and eased herself down on a board that had been tossed over the mud.

Mattie Stone laughed, but she seemed embarrassed, as if she had forgotten that Regina could hear.

"The doctor's here?" Olive asked Ren.

"Yah."

"Why didn't you tell me?"

"I'm going to, as soon as I can."

Regina groaned. "Not that horrible Corning from Crown Point. What in God's name is he doing here?"

"No, no, its just Dr. Lenard, from Hammondville. My Ma works for him."

Ren helped Regina from board to board over the mud, her hand still on his wrist. He walked half backwards, looking as if he would trip over his long legs at any moment. Regina kept staring at him. As they came through the door, Ren kicked some chickens out of the way. A red hen and her three chicks bustled into the corner, squawking. "We bought them with a little of your money, Olive. They're yours," Ren said, smiling into the corner.

"You keep the chickens in the house?" Regina asked.

"Just till we can build a coop," Olive said, careful not to look at them. Olive watched Regina take in the heavy smell of stewed squirrel, the rickety chairs, the table whose fourth leg was a nailed-on birch branch. The doctor and Olive's mother were drinking tea. He held his chipped cup daintily with his long white piano fingers. The room was hot from the woodstove, but he was hunched over the cup as if tea were the only source of warmth in the world. He had on his blue scarf, as usual.

Olive watched the back of his head, studied his baby-pale fingers. She heard Dr. Corning's slimy voice calling her a fat-assed, giggling cow, before he had ever laid eyes on her. It was Dr. Lenard who had given him those words. She could feel her backside widening, her mind dulling. She realized she was about to giggle.

Regina stood in the doorway, grand in her brown velvet traveling dress, her flyaway hair pulled into a tight bun, her hand still circling Ren's wrist. She sighed loudly. "I feel as if I know all of you intimately already."

Olive's mother and the doctor turned their heads.

"Well, not all of you, but the family," she added.

The doctor scraped back his chair and stood up with a hurried flourish. He whipped off his hat.

"He's waiting to be introduced to me," Regina said, "In polite society the gentleman must be introduced to the lady before he addresses her, but only if she has given her permission to be introduced."

Olive watched Lenard's too polite face with its too wide eyes, his eyebrows pasted up near his scalp. His body bent forward, as if he were about to dash up and kiss Regina's hand, lick her boots, even. She watched a little sneering smile tip up Regina's face. Olive felt herself shrinking back into her normal self. The giggle disappeared.

Regina turned to Olive's mother. "You must be Mrs. Landry." She let go of Ren's wrist, strode over to Olive's mother, and shook hands with her. Ren held his wrist up where she had left it, like a hitching post.

"And this is Dr. Lenard, miss," Mrs. Landry said.

Olive sighed. Hadn't Regina just made it clear she didn't want to be introduced to that beanpole?

"You must be Miss Sartwell. I have heard of your case from Dr. Corning."

"I don't wish to discuss my case."

"Of course, Miss Sartwell, it must be very painful. But I may know some remedies that Dr. Corning might have overlooked. Perhaps I will call on the Hammonds one of these days."

"No need."

"Would you like a cup of tea, miss?" Florilla said.

"Please. But then I really need to be heading down the mountain to the Shakers."

"The Shakers, miss?"

"You don't know anything about our scheme, do you? I'm to spend the night with the Shaker women in Paradox." Regina winked at Olive. "And Olive has offered your Magnus to drive me down there this morning. Olive will collect me tomorrow."

"My Magnus?" Florilla said.

Ren coughed, cleared his throat. "That's a rough road to Paradox."

Flames lapped Olive's cheeks. Giggles came popping out.

"I'll take you, miss," Ren said, his wrist still offered up.

"No," Regina said quickly, "I wouldn't separate you and Olive on your one day together."

"It seems you are in need of an escort. I would be glad to offer myself in service." Dr. Lenard clicked his heels together. "A doctor would be ideal. That way, should you have a fit, I could be of additional service."

"I've told General Hammond that it will be Magnus Honsinger that drives me down."

"I'm sure the general would be just as pleased with his handpicked doctor as with that surly miner, don't you think so, Miss Sartwell?"

"I insist that Magnus Honsinger drive me down immediately." Regina's voice was a saw biting into wood. Everyone got quiet. "That's settled. I'll just have some tea if you will kindly give up your place, Doctor."

"Of course." He stepped away from the chair. Regina sat down to have her tea.

Olive watched this, blinking hard, mouth a little open. Then she walked up to Ren by the door. "Better find Magnus and tell him to get over here and drive Regina down."

"He won't be liking this. He already told us he ain't coming to services or dinner on account he's going down to Crown Point with some other fellows."

"Well, he can't."

"Maybe he is already going, Olive."

Olive brought her voice up to regular. "Ren, go get him. You heard Miss Sartwell."

Ren took his cap off the peg, muttering, "I don't see why I ain't driving her down myself."

Olive looked out the window and watched his long, ropy run towards the boardinghouse.

"You don't treat that boy nice anymore." Her mother's hot spruce-tea whisper was in her ear, startling her.

Olive didn't look at her mother. "What do you mean?"

"What I said. You treat him like your little brother."

"Sometimes I think he is, I known him for such a long time."

"Just because he's trying to accommodate more than most men ain't a reason to overlook him. You used to be like him yourself a few months ago."

Olive didn't know what to say, so she didn't say anything. The doctor was hovering over Regina's chair like a wasp. Olive went to the stove and began heating water for the washing.

"We can't be washing dishes now, Olive; we have to go to church in a few minutes. Just go change into your other dress," Olive's mother said.

Olive snorted. She climbed into the loft. She yanked on her good black dress. She might just go down there and say, Miss Sartwell, you must be mistaken. Mrs. Hammond never said for Magnus to drive you. She don't know him from Adam. In fact, she asked especially for Dr. Lenard to drive you. Olive heard the doctor drawling on about opera and books. She heard the downstairs door open and Ren and Magnus stomp in.

"Hello, there, Magnus," Florilla said in a cheerful, false voice. "This here is Miss Sartwell. You've the luck of driving her down the Paradox road."

"I hear this already."

Regina said, "It's a pleasure to make your acquaintance, Mr. Honsinger." A chair scraped back. "Thank you for your hospitality." Olive climbed down the ladder.

"Honsinger, you see you treat this lady as if you were carrying a cargo of gold, or maybe you'd treat her better if I said a cargo of whiskey, eh?" Magnus gave the doctor a look that made him take a step backwards and pat the scarf around his neck.

Regina grabbed Olive's hand in front of her whole family. Olive looked at her boots. "Come for me tomorrow," she said in her throaty, intense voice.

Olive nodded, head down.

"Not too late. I'm afraid to be left with those stern women too long. And don't you worry, I won't forget the privy paper under the seat."

The joke in Regina's voice forced Olive's chin up. The look on Regina's face was so purely herself, the nostrils flaring, the mouth twisted and teasing, the fox eyes squinty and sly. Olive felt a grin slide onto her own face. "I won't be late, then. First thing."

Regina squeezed her hand. "It's been a delight to meet you all. Olive, you're enchanted. Your mother is so kind, like the good woodcutter's wife in a fairy tale. And your husband reminds me of the mythic youngest son, shy and handsome and sweet. I wouldn't be at all surprised if that new hen of yours lays golden eggs." She swept out the door past Magnus, as if he were nothing to do with her.

"Have you gone crazy, woman?" Magnus scowled at Olive. "I thought you was learning something down there."

"Oh, shut up, Magnus."

Florilla gasped, "Olive!"

Magnus slammed out the door after Regina.

Eight

~

MAGNUS HONSINGER LURCHED the wagon onto the road. The wild roll of the wagon loosened Regina's topknot. She could feel it slipping, hair wisping into her face. Regina stared back at a group of grimy little girls. They screamed happily, sputtering against each other. A chubby girl broke away from the group and jogged beside the wagon, tapping the front wheel with a stick: "You got that holy sickness, ain't you, miss? Will you bless me, miss?"

"Get along," Magnus said.

The girl dropped back, but Regina caught the stick. "You're blessed with strength against your enemies. Evil miners will do you no harm." Regina let go, the girl stumbled to a stop, hugged the branch to her and smiled.

They left the town behind. The wagon skidded around the first switchback of the corduroy road. The gullies on either side were piled high with dead trees. It reeked of charcoal pits. Magnus Honsinger held the reins tight. His white forearms were snarled with blue veins, his blond-stubble jaw shoved forward. The big horses skittered, snorted. Regina gripped the side of the wagon with both hands.

A light, steaming rain began to fall. Regina's hair beaded with

~

water. A drop of rain was sliding past Magnus's ear, towards the cliff of his chin. Strands of hair stuck to Regina's face.

The right front wheel ground against a log. The wagon creaked, tilted. The horses heaved the wagon over the log. Regina was sure she saw steam hissing out of Magnus Honsinger's nose. "Are you angry about something in particular, Mr. Honsinger?" She gasped as the wagon hit another loose log, dragged it along with them, jumbled over it. "Or are you generally bad natured?"

No answer from Magnus Honsinger.

"It's the mines, I suppose."

"That's what Olive is telling you?" His *w* was a sharp *v* that made him sound meaner.

"I took an educated guess that mining was not a particularly pleasant occupation. Is there any chance you could handle these horses with a little finesse? I believe this ride is addling my brain."

"The road is steep and is wet."

Regina looked down at his hands. They were reddened, smudged with iron dirt, with a covering of white hair on the knuckles. There was a dark inverted moon of dirt under each wide nail. White flecks were scattered like stars over the pink squares. Regina liked the fact that he wore a night sky on each of his nails. She remembered that same hand had held a rock, smashed a fence.

"We may have things in common," she said.

His laugh was a nasty bark.

"If you are trying to irritate me with your childish pouting and your brutish dog laugh, you are succeeding. However, I arranged for you to drive me expressly so I could help you." No answer. "Even though I almost shot you last time I saw you." He didn't turn his head. "I should have realized you'd be a pig. It stands to reason that a grown man who would knock down a widow's fence for fun would turn out to be a coarse pig."

"Did you tell the sheriff, then?" Spitting the words.

"No. Only because Olive begged me not to. I think a whipping was in order myself."

"You got so many thoughts."

"And you have so pitifully few."

"And you know so much why I knocked the fence down."

"If there is some important information that I am unaware of, please enlighten me."

"Better not be asking me to talk. I ain't no doctor gentleman."

"I despise your manner thus far, so why not simply continue?"

"Good, then. The general's niece knows nothin' why I knocked the fence down or nothin' how the house she live in got built or who washes her geegaw dress. All she knows is that she has this sick in herself, this fit sick, and so poor, poor little lady, the poorest lady in the world—she need my brother's wife to do for her all day. Well, good then, because with that money we are free of her and her family." Blood flowered under his white face. Even his scalp was turning red. "And nobody suppose to say nothing bad about her 'cause ain't she the great general's relation, but people got something to say about the widow woman lives at the fork in the road. She ain't got no general to protect her. And what are they saying 'bout her if hers is the only house on the road that isn't messed with, yah? What if they coming in the night with a boiling bucket of tar and a pillow full of feathers? Then the general's girl sigh all pretty and say poor widow woman, and keep on wearing her lady dress and ordering my brother's wife." He snorted like a horse driving away flies. "I don't care, go tell the general all I said, I don't give a damn no more."

Regina jumped out of the wagon and fell on all fours. She immediately held Magnus responsible for her compromising posture and her stinging palms. She refused to notice that her healed wrist was pulsing from the leap. She began marching down the road, hand clenched against the throbbing in her wrist. She stumbled on a rock, kicked it, and kept moving. She blamed Magnus Honsinger for the dirty, fall-down woods, the irritating rain, and the whine of the mosquito near her ear.

He called out to her, "Two miles to Paradox in them rickety boots."

"Go to hell." She kept marching.

She heard Magnus's laugh behind her. "Jesus God. I will leave."
He urged on the horses and brought them beside her. "Get in the
wagon, now."

She didn't answer. She winced when rain slipped off her lashes
into her eyes.

"I ain't talking no more, the whole way." The horses skidded,
whinnied, heads up, struggling to keep the slow pace on the steep
road. "Yah, okay. I am the evil miner, full of hate for this mining
land and for the general's girl and her clever family. Get in."

She stopped. "Don't call me the general's girl."

"What am I to call you, then?"

"Miss Sartwell."

He smiled. "Miss Sartwell don't talk like no lady. And I'm
thinking I will never walk two miles in them boots myself." He
reached his hand down. Regina could have slapped it away. She
could feel the pleasure of the stinging slap, but there was that hand
with those starry nails. She reached her good arm up and he pulled
her into the wagon.

He turned her palm over. They both looked at the red scrape.
She yanked her hand away, touched her dress. They rode in silence. He brought the horses out into the narrow valley of un-
evenly plowed fields and log cabin farmhouses, all Sunday quiet.
Then he said, "What are you meaning you can help me? From not
telling the sheriff?"

"No. I have these clippings here. A newspaper." She reached
under the seat and pulled out the pile of limp paper.

Magnus glanced over. "What is it?"

"You can read them later. They'll explain everything."

"I ain't knowing how to read. Not in Swedish, not in English
either."

"Oh. I can read it to you. It's about unions."

"I know about unions. We ain't got one in Hammondville."

"That's exactly what Olive said. No one has one until they start
one. You can write to this address. They'll help you organize.
They'll send somebody. A specialist." She took up the first strip

and held it in her burning palms. Her wrist seemed to be swelling. "Let's see. *The Labor Leaf,* put out by the Knights of Labor. This first article is entitled 'Grim Determination on the Part of the Men.' " The article was only half there, neatly scissored down the middle of the paragraph, so she just read the calls for action in bold lettering. With these, she could guess the missing words: "The working people of this nation, white and black, male and female, are now sinking into a condition of serfdom . . . Oppression by corrupt and avaricious employers, causing poverty, misery, and death . . . In union there is strength . . . The workingman's effort is onward and upward . . . Jesus was the first union man."

"Keep your voice down." The blood still rushed under his cheeks. He wanted to hear the part articles about eight-hour workdays, organizing before trouble starts, a greenback currency system, life insurance, contracts, paid overtime. He asked her to repeat words, phrases. He made her read these parts over and over, slower and slower. The newspaper became soggy with rain.

Finally she closed the damp clippings up and put them back under the seat. "The ink is beginning to run."

"Is that all?" he said.

"Yes. Except for some advertisements."

"Olive asks you to give this papers to me?"

"Yes."

He stopped the wagon, gave the horses their heads. Regina looked down at her hands. "I learned to swear from the hop pickers my grandmother hired."

"I don't know if you do this for to help the miners or for Olive. I have not the courage to jump out the store window. I know nothing about having this fits, but still I think you are a good one to know." He took up her hand. He turned it over and blew on the scraped palm, cool breath over the burn, mocking smile.

Regina studied the wisps of white hair over the lips and the chin bent over her palm, and she decided to kiss him. Her heart started shimmying. She saw his rough lips getting bigger. She felt faint, she closed her eyes. The kiss ended up half on his lips and half on his stubbly cheek. She opened her eyes: There was his startled face so close, it took up everything. She jerked back.

He glanced over at the quiet farm they had just passed. "Why in hell will you do that?"

Regina took out her handkerchief, gave it a prim little shake, touched it to her lips. "I never kissed a man before. I simply wanted to see what it was like."

He laughed. "Better try again, then."

"No. I can't say I liked it." She looked away, breathing through her nose so she wouldn't pant.

"But you don't give a man a chance. Kissing is better than that."

"Make the horses trot, will you? I'm supposed to be with the Shakers."

"And instead you are kissing evil miners."

Regina smiled, but she still wouldn't look at him. "We're almost there."

They rode on. Once Magnus mumbled, "Maybe one of them knights will help us if we send a letter. We'll tell them about this conditions here."

He reined in the horses when Regina said, "We're here," but hardly seemed to notice as she climbed down and took her case off the wagon. "Good-bye. Good luck," she said.

He looked at her then. "I'll be seeing you, then."

"We'll never see each other again." She gave him a winning smile, swung away, all relieved and free.

"Never again until I drive you to the Shakers next Sunday."

Everyone had disappeared: Florilla visiting with Mattie Stone, Magnus driving Regina, the doctor doing whatever he did in his pretty house. Olive found the cracked corn and fed a little to the chicken, a kernel at a time.

Ren sat at the table looking down into his cup of thick black coffee, the dregs from the pot. "Like her?" he asked.

She had her back to him. "Are you going to sell them chicks?"

"It's for you to decide. You love eggs, I think."

She continued dropping kernels of corn in front of the hen. "It's damp in here, gives me chills."

"You want we go upstairs under the blankets?" Ren asked.

"I guess." He didn't move, so she turned to the ladder and climbed up. He didn't touch her ankle on the ladder. She hunched over in the dim loft. His dirty clothes lay in a neat pile at the end of the bed, his long underwear folded on his pillow, the quilt spread and tucked under the mattress. The mattress smelled of fresh straw. "You see that grand dress Regina was wearing just now?" she said over her shoulder. "The velvet one? Tonight she'll just toss it on the floor in a heap, maybe trample over it on the way to the chamber pot. Those Shaker gals will faint away when they see the way she treats her good things." Olive turned from the sound of him climbing the ladder. She pulled her dress over her head and slipped under the quilt. "That was nice, what Regina said before, about you and Ma coming out of a fairy tale, wasn't it? It was a nice thing to say." Ren didn't answer. Olive turned her head. "What?"

"I wonder how long it takes you to look for me."

"Now you know." She stared at his long feet in their wool socks.

He kneeled down. He smelled sweaty, strongly like himself. "You don't want this, do you?"

She shrugged. "Don't want what?"

Ren rocked back onto his haunches, his arms crossed over his bony knees. "I got something to say, but I been too afraid to say it."

"Don't say it, then." Olive laughed, looked away.

"It's simple. Only, I stay here 'cause of you. I married you 'cause I love you right from the beginning—your hair, your laugh, those hands. Mostly 'cause you seen me underneath—as with the reading when we was kids. You see that in class I cough over the words, can't read right, but you know I can read real good to my-self, and then I can read in front of you. Only other people I can read to is Magnus, and my ma. I could read Swedish back home to her, real good." He pressed his thumbs against his eyes as if pushing the memory back in. He opened them. "But now, since you been down to the general house, you only see the part that can't read good." He ran his hand over his face. "This is not the simple thing I want to say. It's only—if you don't like me no more, I'll go away. You will be free to—whatever it is you want, whatever they got down to the big house, maybe you can have it without me."

Olive's eyes traveled the long way from his feet to his face. "Remember last summer?" she said. "How I had to walk down the aisle by myself? I wouldn't look up. All I could see was everyone's black Sunday shoes. Then the room got to buzzing and fading. I knew for sure I was near fainting. So I look up. I fastened my eyes to your smile all the way at the end of the aisle. I just kept moving towards that smile that reminds me of geese." Olive's voice turned raspy. "My nerves quieted. I started laughing, remember? And everyone laughed back at me, as if they were saying—You're doing the right thing."

He patted her back. "Shh," he said.

"You saw how she is?" His hand stilled. "The way she looks, the way she talks. I think I been so stuck on Regina, I forgot you. I forgot to remember how you are, like Regina said, sweet. More than that, though. I forgot you're my family." He wiped her tears with his thumb. She ran her finger down the slide of his cheekbone, over his jutting collarbone, circled into the soft part under his arm. He brushed his hand over her breast. Olive felt an aching tunnel move from her throat down through her nipples, her heart and stomach, bigger and bigger until it pressed between her legs. "My family," she said on every breath.

Regina stumbled up to the Shaker house through the rain, dragging her leather case with her good arm. The cat appeared, whining. The round woman, looking scrubbed and smelling of soap, opened the door. The cat whisked past the woman's skirts. "Regina. Come in." She led her to a little room with a bed, a desk, and one small window. The woman straightened the edge of a linen cloth beside a white and blue mottled pitcher and bowl. "You will want to wash after your long ride. We were just moving to the meeting room for our service. I will wait outside the door for you."

"I thought you all slept in the same room," Regina said.

"So we do. But you are not of the family of believers, yet. So we welcome you to this room." The woman bobbed out, then eased the door shut.

Regina felt damp and itchy from the warm rain. She smelled sour, of nervous sweat. She stared at herself in the mirror. That botched kiss. She winced.

There was a light tap on the door.

Regina stuck out her tongue in the mirror. "Coming." She splashed water on her face, neatened her hair.

The woman walked ahead of her through the cool, bare house and then through a long hallway. They entered a high-ceilinged room with shining windowpanes, circled by grey benches. Twelve or thirteen shining wide pine boards, shining windowpanes; twelve or thirteen women in their grey dresses were scattered along the benches. Sister Harriet sat next to a girl with blond hair pulled tight behind big ears. The girl was either crying or had a cold. She snuffled and nodded as Harriet poured whispers into her ear. Harriet didn't look up when Regina walked in. One woman was unlatching the windows along the far side of the room. Everyone else sat silently, hands in their laps.

Regina smoothed down her brown bustle and slid onto one of the low benches. She felt Magnus's breath on her palm.

Sister Harriet put both hands on her knees and stood up, as if something were settled. Harriet glided to the front of the room. Everyone else rose and lined up two by two behind her. The young one with the big ears motioned for Regina to stand next to her. When they were all in this, two-by-two line, Harriet began a song in a resonant alto: "O, do feel more life, more love and union." The others joined in: "Now's the time to gather love, Pure love and union, Strive, strive to gather in, Gather in your portion,

Now's the time to be free, Come be in motion," and round and round. Their voices reminded Regina of a cedar closet.

As they sang, Harriet began to clap her hands. They all two-stepped forward. The sound of hard shoes scuffing over wood and the shush of their skirts mixed with the rain and the clapping. The room began to fill. Regina followed along, mumbling the song until she got the words. The women's voices seemed to grow stronger, the shuffling more vehement. The cool, rain-drenched air blew harder through the windows.

They changed to another song about Mother's Love Always Enduring and then another about Coming Down Right. They began a new song with a driving rhythm: "I do hunger and thirst, hunger and thirst for the bread and waters of life." The women danced forward, stamping hard on the words "hunger" and "thirst." Hunger and thirst lodged behind Regina's eyes and pressed there, aching.

The singing stopped. In the dizzying silence, Harriet motioned as if she were gathering something in, as if her hands were following the curve of an ocean wave towards herself. All the women took up the same wave, kept shuffling hard. Regina copied their arms. She felt a tingling below her navel, just where her hands met at the end of the wave. It made her woozy.

Harriet stepped away from the women. She began to speak while the women stamped in place. "Sister Emily is lonely. She says it is the spring weather." She waved her fingers for the girl with the big ears to come forward. The girl glanced quickly at Regina, smiled tearily, shuffled to Harriet. Some tears dripped down her nose. Sister Harriet gave her a handkerchief. The eldress continued, "Let us ask The Father and The Mother to lend her patience. Let us ask that the spring fill her with the sure knowledge that she is a part of God's earth, to fill her with the pure love of her sisters and so never lonely. Help us, Mother, to let her know that she is safe here." The women began a frontwards wave, as if pushing something away from their breasts towards Emily. They chanted in low voices, "More love, more love."

150

Sister Emily looked at the ceiling. She began to turn. The women clapped faster. She whirled faster. A few women began to moan. Sister Emily let her arms fly out, the handkerchief twirling at the ends of her pinched fingers. Regina watched the spinning girl open her hand. The tearstained handkerchief spun out and settled near Regina's feet. Regina picked up the cloth and squeezed it in her fist. It was still damp.

The round, soapy-smelling woman dropped to the floor, twitching and moaning. Regina started back. The round woman began speaking in a foreign language filled with harsh consonants and clicks of the tongue. The other women, except the whirling young girl, circled round her, clapping and moaning. She broke into a choking English: "They hunt us. Pray, my daughters." Another woman called out, "My daughters." Her upper body began to shake. The other women's shuffling and clapping seemed to drive the rhythm of their fits.

Regina forgot to clap. She dropped the handkerchief. More of the women were shaking and moaning. They sang one word, over and over, Love.

Regina began to twirl like the girl. The room and the women spun away in a grey blur. She allowed the dizziness to swallow her. Then she saw long, thin arms moving towards her. "You are safe," they said. She shrank. She was unborn, curled below her navel, circled by the arms. Muffled and far away, she felt her body shaking. Then, from that far-off place, someone gripped her shoulders: "Come back now." She enlarged until she was behind her heavy eyelids. She blinked. Her lids were so hard to lift, it was so easy to sink back down, but the voice and the grip persisted. She opened her eyes, rubbed them to keep them open. The light of the grey day made her squint.

Sister Harriet's blue-diamond eyes were sparking into hers. She smiled. "Sit up." She patted Regina briskly on the shoulder. "Don't be alarmed. The light has entered you." Sister Harriet helped her up. "Your wrist is swollen," she said.

Women pulled other women off the floor, brushed invisible lint off each other. "Good afternoon," they said to each other. The round woman dusted her apron. Patted back her hair. "Good afternoon," the girl with the big ears and shining, tearstained face said to Regina, holding out a sticky hand. It was raining harder now: Women went around shutting the windows and wiping up streaks of rain.

"We will eat now," Harriet said to her. "Then I will come sit with you." The round woman who had spoken the strange language led Regina back down the hall. Regina slid her hand along the smooth, smooth wall as they walked. In the dining room, Regina fell in love with the long table set with pewter dishes, mugs, steaming teapots, and bouquets of lady's slipper and gaywing. Two women were filling bowls of soup. The woman led Regina back to her room. As she was leaving, Regina said, "What was that language you were speaking?" Her mouth felt greased, new.

"Sioux. Not that I know a word of it now, of course. The spirit has left me." Another woman brought a tray with tea, one bowl filled with honey, another with cream, warm bread, and goat cheese. She set it on the table.

Regina drifted around the room, touching the starchy pillow, the rough weave of the blanket. She smoothed the polished edge and cool surface of the mirror. She bent down to run her hand over the bumps of the braided rug. She watched rain drizzle down the window. She ate a spoon of the dark buckwheat honey, felt her throat tighten from the sweetness, licked the sticky spoon. She tasted the mild cream, sour bread, bitter tea.

Regina looked up from licking the last of the cream from the bowl and saw Sister Harriet and the woman who spoke Sioux. Regina licked away her cream mustache. "Sister Tabitha," Harriet said, "there is a chill in here. Look, she is shivering. Would you get some wood for the fire, and I will start it." Sister Tabitha nodded, carried the tray out. "May I attend to your wrist?" Sister Harriet asked.

Sister Harriet packed ice chips in a piece of muslin and bound it to Regina's wrist. The eldress lifted another chair off the wall and sat. She took some beige knitting from the pocket of her apron. She hummed one of the songs from the meeting. She asked no questions. Tabitha came back with wood, and Harriet started a fire. She smiled, warmed her hands and went back to working her polished beige needles through her beige wool.

Regina watched, fascinated by the clicking rhythm. "I've never enjoyed a meal as well as this one. I even licked the bowls."

"Good."

"Don't you consider that wickedly sensual?"

"Eating is sensual."

"But if you accept sensuality, why is everything so plain?"

"Ornament is a distraction. It is too easy to forget what is important when surrounded by layers of things."

"I see," Regina said. "I'm an epileptic."

"I know. You told me on your last visit."

"Oh. But in your meeting I saw a woman."

"Who was she?"

"I don't know. Maybe Mother Ann. What did she look like?"

"She died nearly one hundred years ago and left no portrait."

"In my vision she has long arms. This time she said, 'You are safe.'"

"Hmmm." Needles clicking.

"How did you come to be in the wilderness, just twelve women? I thought you lived in big Shaker towns."

"That is a long story."

"Won't you tell me?"

"Yea, if you like." Sister Harriet's hands knitted by themselves. There were muted sounds of laughing and of pots clanking from the kitchen. "I was born near the Shaker community of Watervliet. When my mother died, my father, who was a Presbyterian minister, joined the Shakers. He brought me with him. I grew up in the bosom of the family of believers. As I reached my twentieth birthday, She began to reveal injustices to me in the Shaker life. Man and woman are equal in God's eyes, yet when we built our new meetinghouse there was only one entrance: for the men. The women, including the eldress, had to enter meeting after the little boys. The elder and eldress did not appreciate my bringing up this subject and other instances in which I felt the Shakers could move closer to God."

"What other instances?"

Sister Harriet waved a knitting needle. "Oh, I thought God must love music, so we ought to have music lessons for the children. What truly irked them was that I practiced the old style of worship, very enthusiastic, as you saw in our service. Shaker worship has become much more staid. So the elder and eldress turned against me. They felt I was vain. They instructed me to humble myself. They found a pretext to pronounce me wicked, and—pfft—I left with my father and a group of like-minded sisters. We went into the wilderness, like old Moses. And here we prosper."

"What was the pretext they found for throwing you out?" Regina asked.

"Ohhh." Sister Harriet smiled at her knitting. "We were young."

Regina liked that pleased-with-itself smile. She liked this story, of bad goodness. For the first time she liked those blue, blue eyes and that grey, wiry hair and that long, bending neck. "Won't you tell me, Miss Harriet?"

"Sister Harriet. Yea, I will tell you, as it makes a good lesson." She smiled, shook her head. "A man, a winter Shaker, came to us for a time at Watervliet."

"What is a winter Shaker?"

"One who comes for a short time in a period of difficulty, but doesn't have the true calling." Harriet raised one eyebrow. "This winter Shaker, Brother Joshua Anthony, was a college-educated man. He had a sweet singing voice, a baritone. He was a careful worker, but he enjoyed talking with the sisters. It came to pass that all the young women in our family—pfft—fell in love with him. He seemed to take a particular interest in me—he complimented my eyes and height." She told this story in a placid voice, knitting furiously. The rain dripped off the roof and slid down the window. "I confessed to the sin of lust, but it did no good. My work suffered. So did the work of the other girls. We were sorely tempted to talk of him while we labored, and we often succumbed to whispers and laughter. I felt far from God—all height and eyes. Finally, it came to me in a dream that I must submerge myself in the river. Lust is heat, I reasoned, and cannot remain in a freezing form. Remember, I was only twenty. I related my dream to the other girls and we decided to try it. We Shakers love group activities." Harriet laughed, in a short, hard, pleased way.

"We snuck down to the river. It was late October. The leaves were just past peak, ankle-deep beside the river, floating across it. We stripped off our clothes, unashamed. Nine of us. We left our grey homespun on the bank. We parted the leaves and waded into the water. The bottom rocks cut our soles. The water stung our skin. We went under and burst forth. 'It is gone!' I cried. All I felt was God, alive and cold and burning.

"Others laughed and cried out. I believe we all felt the same. We turned to leave the water. And it was then we saw that our clothes had been stolen."

Regina gasped. "Oh, no."

"Oh yea. Our kerchiefs and bonnets were strewn about the ground with the leaves. Our dresses had been hung in a tree several yards away. Then we spied two strange boys, cowering behind the very same tree.

"We sunk down to our necks for modesty. My teeth began to chatter uncontrollably. Sister Tabitha said she was losing feeling in her extremities. The world's people were shaming us. I gathered courage. I took Sister Tabitha's hand. I began to sing, 'Come, Come, Ye Virgins Bright.' I raised myself out of the water. Sister Tabitha took up the song, the others joined hands, and we waded out of the water, pale and goose-pimpled, fat and thin, short and tall, a chain of nine, singing like innocent babes: 'We have put our sins away, Lo! We stand in open day, And we will praise our savior,' " Sister Harriet sang in a soft voice, then laughed. "We looked neither right nor left. As we reached the tree where the boys were skulking, they hooted and ran, leaving us our clothes. We were victorious. We dressed and walked back to our home, still holding hands and singing, full of a clean, energetic godliness.

"But nay. Our trials were not over. The boys' father told the elder what they had seen. The eldress asked me to account for myself. When I told her she proclaimed me a sinner, said I must confess. When I refused there was a hubbub. I declared the brethren at Watervliet unenlightened. My father was the only one who believed in our innocence, so I left Watervliet with him and the nine like-minded sisters. We traveled in the wilderness until we arrived here, in Paradox."

"But did you ever see the man with the sweet voice again?"

"Brother Joshua left too, hounded out really, but we corresponded. He owns a dry goods store in Schenectady. He has been a great supporter of our medicinal herb and seed industry. He buys our brooms as well. And we still immerse ourselves in a cold spring all together, in our newborn state, on Mother Anne's birthday." Regina laughed. Harriet laughed too. "And you thought we Shakers led tedious lives. It is the life of the world that is tedious. We pare life down to its true drama—labor, the changing of the seasons, the worship of God."

"What would Mother Ann think of your immersion?"

"You are the one in conversation with her."

"Will you tell me about her?"

Needles clicking, rain clicking. "Yea. She was born in England, and cut velvet for a living . . ."

Olive and Ren lay under the quilt, their foreheads touching, their sides touching. Ren's foot snugged under the sole of Olive's foot. They drifted, listening to the rain on the roof, to the familiar drip where the roof leaked under the eaves. "I better put a pot under it," Olive said.

"Stay here." Ren made his hand into a bird, the thumb stretching out as one wing, the rest of the fingers, tight together and arched, the other wing. His mother had made the gull to soothe him to sleep when he was a little boy. He swooped his hand over her, just grazing her face, gliding up.

"Ren?"

"Mmm?"

"I got to tell you something."

"What?" The gull kept up its comforting, undulating flight.

"It's about a place called the Finger Lakes. It's a way we can have a better life."

The gull swooped in and landed on her forehead. "Tell me."

By Monday morning the rain had simmered away, leaving more black flies than ever. After breakfast, the sisters worked on brooms. Because the bugs were so unpleasant, the Shakers rarely worked outside until the end of June. Regina asked Sister Tabitha how it was, then, that the last time she had visited, the women were pulling an enormous rock out of the side field. Sister Tabitha blushed modestly. "That was my doing. The Sioux warrior told us that the rock must be moved, or our corn wouldn't grow rightly."

Sister Emily with the big ears helped Regina fasten netting around her hat and down over her face. She flashed friendly, shy smiles. She was just gulping, getting ready to say something, when Regina heard a soft knock on the door. She pulled away from Sister Emily's pinning. "That will be Olive," Regina said.

"It ain't nice out there, I'll tell you that, missy. Muggy and full of flies." Olive allowed herself to be led into the side workroom. Regina watched Olive while she was pinned into netting. Olive said, "You're just stuffed with secrets, ain't you?"

Regina laughed. Sister Harriet came to the door to see them off. "Will we see you next Sunday, Regina Sartwell?"

Regina nodded, winked at Olive. As soon as they climbed onto the wagon they were surrounded by the whine of black flies. Black flies gathered like a bracelet around Regina's bare wrists. She hid her gloved hands in the folds of her dress.

Olive sagged her shoulders, let the reins droop. She kept jerking her head and hands, scaring up the flies. "So," Regina said, "I danced and sang, fainted, woke up and became you."

"Me?" Olive said in a bland voice.

Regina laughed. "I must be losing my touch. No one seems startled by my conversation lately."

"No, go on. I'm just tired."

"Did your husband bother you all night?" Olive turned red, looked down. Regina rolled her eyes. "I went to the Shaker meeting. And the women sing and dance and some go into a sort of fit. Do you recall that girl who fixed your netting? She twirled like a whirling dervish."

"Sounds like some drunks I saw at a dance one time."

"Charming comparison." Regina rolled her eyes again.

"Finish the story, Regina."

"There's nothing more to tell."

"Don't pout. Tell me how you turned into me."

"I'm not pouting. I just enjoyed a meal for once, that's all I meant."

"I ain't the only one who enjoys a good meal. Near everyone does."

"Let's be quiet for a while."

The kitchen fumed with the sour smell of yeast. Mrs. Cutter had just punched down the bread dough. Olive was scraping the scraps off the wooden counter. SuSu was gathering bits of dough from the floor, sneaking them into her mouth.

Mrs. Fisk blustered in, her face all splotchy from exhertion and late spring wind. She unwrapped her scarf and placed her black hat on the table. "Tea," she said to Mrs. Cutter.

Mrs. Cutter took out Fisk's special rose-colored cup and saucer. She handed Olive a jar of vinegar to scour the countertop.

Fisk began sifting through a mess of envelopes, making piles. "Letter opener," she said to SuSu. SuSu choked on her last bit of dough, left the room, and returned carrying the miniature silver sword across her open palms.

Mrs. Cutter wedged a brick under the kitchen window for some breeze. Olive scrubbed, her nostrils tingling from vinegar. Mrs. Fisk slit paper and sipped tea. "Here's a letter for Miss Sartwell."

Mrs. Cutter came over to look. "Isn't that a pretty handwriting?"

Mrs. Fisk turned it over. "From Seneca Falls."

"Maybe it's someone offering to take her off our hands." Mrs. Cutter sniggered, coughed, lifted the dishcloths on her rising bread and peeked.

"Want I should give it to her?" Olive had not turned from the counter.

Mrs. Fisk laid the letter down, inched it away from herself. "I better run this by Mrs. Hammond. No telling."

"No telling what?" Olive said.

"Just no telling," Mrs. Fisk said.

Mrs. Cutter patted her swollen loaves affectionately. "Oh, give the crazy girl her letter. She ain't got nothing to look forward to 'cept the asylum come August. Let her have her small bit of pleasure." Mrs. Cutter wedged open the window a little farther. Sniffed the breeze. "Maybe it's an old sweetheart."

SuSu giggled, whispered, "Old sweetheart."

Olive screwed the lid back on the vinegar jar with a final twist for emphasis. "Well! I'm all done here. And Miss Regina is napping. Want I should bring the letter up to Mrs. Hammond?"

Mrs. Fisk didn't turn from her sorting. "Take these others too. Tell Mrs. Hammond I'll be up directly."

Olive picked up the bundle of letters. In the hall, at the bottom of the stairs, she stopped. She stared at the curling script: Miss Regina Sartwell. She turned it over. Sealing wax: cherry red. She picked at the seal with her thumbnail, glanced at the door to Regina's room, glanced towards the kitchen, picked a little more. The wax fell off in one gob and spattered. Olive looked up. SuSu was crouched in the corner of the entranceway, watching her. Olive shuddered. "You give me a scare. The wax fell off this letter."

"Is it good to eat?" SuSu whispered.

"No. It's just wax." Olive and SuSu watched each other. "SuSu, don't stare so. It's creepy." Olive climbed the stairs quickly, two at a time. At the top she turned back. SuSu was crouched over the spatter of wax. She licked her finger, picked up some wax, and examined it. Then she licked it off her finger. "SuSu, I told you," Olive called down to her. SuSu raised her wine-swollen face and watched her with calm eyes. Olive turned and knocked on Mrs. Hammond's door.

"Enter." Mrs. Hammond lolled in her blue armchair, one finger lazily tracing the windowpane.

"I got your mail here, ma'am."

Mrs. Hammond didn't answer. She slid her finger in arcs over the glass.

Olive piled the letters on Mrs. Hammond's dresser. She held Regina's in her hand.

Mrs. Hammond glanced at her. "Someone, at some time, somewhere, must have told you that it's rude to stare."

Olive looked down. "Miss Regina got a letter this morning. Should I bring it down to her?"

The finger was back on the window. "From whom?"

"I don't know. I can bring it down to her."

"Can you read?"

"Yes, ma'am."

"Read it to me, then." Mrs. Hammond clenched her hands together. "Go on."

Olive opened the loose flap. She lifted out a small lilac-colored sheet of paper and then a stiffer one behind it. She unfolded the bigger sheet: a drawing of a farm by a lake. The apples on the trees were perfectly round globes. She folded it back up.

Then she opened the lilac stationary: " 'My Dear Regina,' " Olive read carefully. " 'It was with unimaginable pleasure that I received your recent letter. How I wish your grandmother were still with us, but what sweet consolation it would bring if we were to have you in her stead. The Sartwells return to Seneca Lake.

How more than delightful. I do know of a house that may meet with your specifications. I've enclosed a sketch, rather crude—I'm just an old lady who enjoys working in pencil. Enclosed also is the name of the current owner if the house catches your fancy. I hope to hear of your impending arrival. Sincerely, Mrs. Roberta Tuttle.' " Olive folded the lilac letter up. "Should I bring it to Regina now?"

Mrs. Hammond's fingers freed themselves and began tapping at her knees. "How very odd. What could this mean?"

Olive's face twisted into her grimacing smile. She shrugged.

"Let me see the sketch."

Olive brought the envelope over. Held the sketch up for Mrs. Hammond. "My, it is crude. Carol, what is the meaning of this?"

"Olive, ma'am. It's nothing. Miss Regina just has a dream to move herself back to the Finger Lakes and live in a little house. Just a little house. So she'd be out of everyone's hair." Olive folded the sketch up, worked it back into its envelope.

"She plans to procure a house and live alone in it? How is that possible?"

"She'd hire someone to help her." Olive slipped the envelope into her apron pocket.

"You, no doubt." Mrs. Hammond's fingers were picking at her hair, ruining the swept-up look.

"Mrs. Hammond, ma'am, I can see it's hard for you to have her here. It would be so peaceful without her. And the farm would still be out of society, like her father wanted."

"She has caused my nervous system to deteriorate."

"I know, ma'am. What would be the harm of Miss Regina having her own little life out there to this Seneca Lake?"

"Who does she expect to buy this farm for her?"

Olive waited. "Maybe her father, ma'am."

"Why would her father bother with that when he has an ideal situation here, loading her onto elderly in-laws, knowing they could not sully the memory of his sweet wife by refusing?"

"Maybe if he thought you were tired of it . . ."

"That sort of rudeness would be impossible for the general and me. We must keep her, at least until August, then I believe Dr. Corning suggests a home of some kind, a ladies' rest home." Mrs. Hammond's hand quivered, then reached for the windowpane again.

"But, Mrs. Hammond, ma'am? If she did get the money someways, you wouldn't mind her going, would you?"

"Mind? Certainly not. God's speed. I will probably be completely undone if she maintains her frenzied presence until August." Mrs. Fisk rapped on the doorframe. "Oh, Fisk, I'm exhausted. Such a depressing conversation with Carol. Read me my letters and put a warm compress to my head."

Olive hurried out, head down, lilac letter in her hand. She held onto the banister, took the stairs at a rush, bumped open Regina's door with her hip. "Look here."

Regina popped up from her tousled bedcovers, eyes empty and startled. Olive bounced onto the bed, smoothed the drawing out on Regina's lap. "I was asleep." Regina grazed her eyes over the drawing. "What is it?"

"It's from that friend of yours, that Mrs. Tuttle, the friend of your grandmother's. It's our house."

"You opened my letter?"

"Fisk made me bring it up to Mrs. Hammond, and Mrs. Hammond made me read it to her, but just guess. She says she won't stand in our way if we can find the money for the house."

Regina snorted. "Olive. What do you mean, made you? Why didn't you bring it to me first? I believe it is illegal to open someone else's mail."

"I thought of bringing it to you, but then SuSu was staring at me in such a creepy way, like she knew just what I was thinking." Regina rolled her eyes. "Wake up, grouchy. Look what's right here in front of us. Our house." Olive smoothed it a little closer to Regina. Behind the house was the orchard with those perfectly round apples. Then the fenced-in pasture with sheep or cows. It was hard to tell which. But those were obviously chickens pecking in the yard, plump chickens as big as the door of the farmhouse.

"I'd like to have those two biddies arrested," Regina mumbled. "Give me the letter, or did they think it too dangerous for me to read?"

Olive handed it over; Regina's lips moved, smirking over the words.

The farmhouse had a high, peaked roof with two chimneys. There were hearts and clovers cut into the shutters on the four windows and a heart in the Dutch door. A rooster weather vane. The smoke curled up from the chimney right into the puffy clouds. The sun peeked half out of one, its long rays shooting to the ground. Olive traced her finger down a ray.

Regina dropped the letter onto the bed. "I remember Grandma once said Mrs. Tuttle is both a loyal friend and an utter feather-brain."

"I told Ren all about the house. I don't think he quite believes it, but we definitely got his interest."

"I wonder if there are Shakers in the Finger Lakes."

"Must be. Or if not Shakers, some other group like 'em. You said yourself there's spiritual groups everywhere nowadays."

"Olive, are there farmhouses on Paradox Lake?"

"Just hunting camps and big holiday houses for rich people."

"You said we wouldn't really be farming. Just puttering."

"You wouldn't even want to putter in the North Woods. To get anything out of this soil, you'd have to put your soul into it. And more."

"Let me see this sketch." Regina laughed. "Someone must inform Mrs. Tuttle that the earth is round."

"I like it flat, like a map of the land of milk and honey."

"Then you must hold it for safekeeping."

Olive touched the pad of her pinky finger to one of the apples. It just fit.

Nine

~

It was the third week in June. Iris, lupines, and foxglove bloomed in the Hammond gardens. Pea vines inched up their poles. Mr. Cutter stayed up all night and killed a woodchuck that had been looting the garden. Mrs. Cutter kept him company. "It was like a second honeymoon," she said.

On Thursday evening of that third week in June there was a knock on the front door—three clunks of the lion's head. Mrs. Fisk was busy with Mrs. Hammond, so Olive yanked open the great door that had swelled in the muggy heat. She brushed her sweaty, curling hair out of her face.

There stood Dr. Lenard, all close-shaven and perfumed and wearing his cerulean blue scarf. "Olive, my dear." Dr. Lenard winked. "Cat got your tongue?"

"No."

Dr. Lenard sighed. "Well, my dear, I've come to call on the Hammonds." He handed her a card with his name on it. Olive took the card, which had a crease down the middle: Doctor Laurence Lenard.

"The general ain't in, and Mrs. Hammond is ill."

Dr. Lenard raised his eyebrows. "A pity, but as I have ridden all the way down here from the mines, perhaps Miss Sartwell would entertain me for a few moments."

"I'll see." Olive turned to go.

"Olive, dear, I believe you're supposed to ask if I will wait in the parlor."

"Oh. Will you?"

"Yes, I will."

Olive found Mrs. Hammond in the unfinished bathroom. Olive put her eye to the crack in the door. Mrs. Hammond stood in the claw-foot tub with her nightgown on. Mrs. Fisk washed her legs, while Mrs. Hammond sponged underneath the nightgown. Olive knocked, then spoke through the crack in the door. "Mrs. Hammond, ma'am. Dr. Lenard from Hammondville has come to call. I told him the general ain't in and that you was feeling poorly, and he asked if he could see Miss Regina."

Through the crack Olive saw Mrs. Hammond look at Fisk— "Do you think that's entirely proper? Did he send in his card?"

Olive slid the card through the crack. Mrs. Fisk dried her hands on her apron and took it.

"Have they been introduced?" Mrs. Hammond called.

"Yes," Olive said, "by my ma."

"The maid's mother. What else should I expect?" Mrs. Hammond held the sponge still. It dripped on Mrs. Fisk. Fisk moved her head, kept scrubbing. "But if he is acquainted with Miss Sartwell, then he has no illusions as to her nature, so I need not forewarn him. Can you imagine, Fisk, if that Lenard fellow were to take Miss Sartwell off our hands? The Lord must be smiling on us today. Yes, tell him Mrs. Hammond is engaged, but sends her best wishes and hopes that her niece will be sufficient entertainment in her stead."

"What if Miss Regina is feeling poorly herself?"

"Make sure she isn't, and make sure she is as charming as possible."

Olive walked down the hall to Regina's room. She couldn't

keep the smile off her face. Regina was reading. "Mrs. Hammond says you got to see Laurie from Hammondville and be charming about it, too."

"Who?"

"Dr. Laurence Lenard."

"That mining doctor? I certainly won't see him."

"He's waiting in the velvet parlor. Can't you smell him from here?"

"Not funny. Tell him I'm indisposed."

Olive's smile crumpled. "Just for a minute or two."

"Absolutely not." Regina picked up her book.

"It is funny, the way he's all dressed up, preening his feathers. Don't you want to go make fun of him for a little while?"

"No." Regina didn't lower her book.

"But Mrs. Hammond said it's up to me to get you to see him."

"Tell her you failed. Tell her I was impossible."

"That won't be good for neither of us. She'll be irritated. Maybe she'll speak to the general."

Regina threw down her book. "Not the big, bad general. He'll huff and he'll puff and he'll blow us all down. Fine. Here I go." She caught up her sewing basket, flounced out of her room ahead of Olive.

"Miss Sartwell. So good of you to see me." The doctor was standing by the mantel, his hands behind his back.

"Dr. Laurence Lenard." Regina sat down on the plum-colored chair, took out her balsam pillow, and began sewing on it. Olive stood by the door with her arms folded across her chest.

The doctor glanced at Olive. "Would you be so good as to get me a glass of lemonade?"

"I'll fetch it," Regina said.

"Oh no, Miss Sartwell, don't bother yourself. I find I'm not thirsty after all." Regina sat back down, smirking. "May I congratulate you, you look much improved. Blooming, I should say. This six-month cure of Dr. Corning's may well be a success." He raised his eyebrows. He came over and took a seat on the yellow velvet couch, on the side closest to Regina's chair. "Surely you miss your great city. This little town must seem a veritable desert."

"This little town is a desert. And no, I hate New York City."

"What a trial to grow up there, then."

"I grew up with my grandmother—in the country."

"Ahh, a country girl. Good, good. And with your grandmother. I always find girls who spent their childhood with their grandparents charmingly old-fashioned." He raised his eyebrows. "May I see what you're sewing on? Some little keepsake?"

Regina held it up: "Regina" in purple thread, "Olive" in orange, and "Forever" still just chalked in.

"I don't have my reading glasses." He took one edge of the pillow, his fingers touching hers.

She yanked it away. "I'll read it for you—it says, 'Regina and Olive. Forever. And ever.'"

"How touching. You must be so lonely, dear, with no young people near you. How nice that you have befriended our Olive." He smiled in Olive's general direction.

Regina's mouth twisted. "Doctor, I find I am feeling nauseous. I must retire."

"I am a medical man. No need to be ashamed in front of me. It's convenient to be acquainted with a medical man, especially one who may have more . . . empathy than Dr. Corning." He put his hand on her forehead.

She slipped out from under. "Good evening, Doctor." She fled.

The doctor glanced at Olive, dropped his hand, and smiled. "You have the prettiest hair, strawberry blond, I believe they call it."

"It's orange. I got to see to Miss Sartwell."

"Of course. She's excitable—as are most women of my class, I'm afraid. Girls like you are calm as the sea, aren't they? More luck for your men." Olive escaped down the hallway. She heard Dr. Lenard call, "I believe you are supposed to show me out," but she opened Regina's door, closed it, and leaned against it.

"He's just standing there, waiting for me to show him out."

They stood grinning at each other until they heard the doctor struggling with the swollen front door. Then they collapsed on the bed.

"Silly ass," Regina said. "Did you see how he looked when I showed him the pillow? I think he'd hoped I was embroidering 'Larry Forever' on it."

"Next time he'll propose marriage." Olive waggled her eyebrows up and down.

Regina grabbed up the pillow from Olive's cot and hit her in the face with it.

Olive laughed, brushed it away. She reached for the envelope that had been hidden under the pillow. "Let's look at the drawing again."

"Oh, Olive. You must have memorized that terrible drawing by now."

Olive smoothed it over Regina's stomach. "I have. I'm going to bring it up to Hammondville to show Ren, maybe even Magnus and Ma."

"Don't do that."

"Why not?"

"You can't tell anything from that drawing. It might be a tumbledown chicken coop for all we know."

"How could it be a chicken coop?" Olive folded the drawing up carefully. She spoke into the envelope: "Why have you been so nasty lately?"

Regina kissed Olive so hard, she could feel the ridges of teeth pressed behind Regina's small, soft lips. "Because I'm a terrible person."

On Sunday morning, Olive tethered the horses to her cow shed. She opened the door for Regina and immediately felt the room was too full of restless men—Dr. Lenard at the table drinking tea, Ren on the ladder, Magnus leaning against the doorjamb to Florilla's room. Florilla was slicing bread at the table. She saw Olive and Regina. "Full house." She smiled in a confused way.

~

"A pleasure and a surprise." The doctor pushed back his chair.

"You didn't know I was going to be here, Doctor?" Regina said.

"Only hoped, only hoped, Miss Sartwell."

"Well, Mr. Honsinger," Regina said, without looking at Magnus, "I'm late. Would you mind beginning at once?"

Magnus smacked his hat against his arm, put it on. He nodded to Olive and walked out the door.

"Won't you rest a moment?" The doctor said, "It's unhealthy to rush about. You'll overexcite yourself."

"I'll overexcite myself if I stay here. I'll see you tomorrow, Olive. Good-bye, dear family." She wagged her fingers at Ren and Florilla over her shoulder on the way out.

Dr. Lenard raised his eyebrows. "Extraordinary girl. Bold. I overexcite her, she declares, and sweeps out of the room." He shook his head. "I'll just have another cup of tea, Florilla."

Ren and Olive smiled at each other from across the room.

Regina could think of absolutely nothing to say over the nearness of Magnus Honsinger. She could smell his sweat. She could see blond hair tufting below his collarbone. He had shaved. There were two small cuts on his chin. His shoulder almost touched hers. It seemed to radiate heat, dizzying her.

Just before the valley, he lurched the wagon off to the side. They sat there, not looking at each other. Finally she said, "You shaved."

"It's no good to kiss a man who hasn't shaved, am I right?" He smiled at her.

She turned towards him to say something snappy and rude, but she was distracted by his unruly eyebrows.

He kissed her then. She felt his tongue in her mouth. It shocked her. She touched it tentatively with her own tongue and felt another small shock. She felt the stubbly smoothness of his jaw on her cheek. She touched the sleeve of the arm that had nearly touched her on their ride down.

When he finally pulled away she was out of breath and coughed. "Someone might see," she said.

"You want we should go walking?" he asked. She looked at him. "It's for you to decide," he said.

"Yes," she said. He tied the reins to a bent tree. She held on to the wagon, her vision glazed, as if she had stood up too quickly.

He pushed back some pine branches. "How 'bout this way?" Needles brushed her face and arms as she went in.

"Which way?" she asked.

"You find us a nice place," he said.

The wagon was close. She could still see it through the pine branches, still hear the horses yanking up weeds. Magnus touched her back. "Changed your mind, miss?" His voice was gentle with sarcasm.

"No. I have made my mind up." She pushed through the woods. She was acutely aware of the feel of her skirts brushing against her legs, of Magnus Honsinger looming behind her. The forest didn't get any prettier as they walked in. Logged and ravaged by fire, it was full of charred stumps and piles of burnt logs. Spindly trees and scrub grew out of the ruin. Regina stumbled towards a glint of sunlight. She found a small clearing covered with moss. "Will this do?" she said.

"The deer are liking this too." He waved towards deer pellets. "Maybe the only nice place hereabouts." He took off his thin jacket and laid it down for her.

"I'd rather sit on the ground." She touched her palm to the moss. It was damp, elastic.

He threw his jacket to the side, eased himself down next to her. "I'm stiff," he said. She unpinned her hat. She felt a lick of sun on her neck. After awhile she took his hand. She lifted it up and laid it in her lap. She began running her fingers lightly over his nails, down the fingers with the white hair on them, over the chapped skin. They both watched her hand.

His hand began to grab up folds of her dress. Then he kissed her again with his shocking tongue. His hands went over her dress. He laughed in her ear.

"What?" she asked.

"You fancy ladies wear too many things. I ain't sure I have found you yet."

She grabbed his hand. "Show me everything. Show me what you do with that widow woman."

"I never met a girl like you for saying things. Is this what all American ladies is like?"

"No, of course not. I'm an epileptic."

"I like this epileptic's ways."

Regina stood up and unbuttoned the back of her cream-colored dress. She edged it off and laid it down beside him. Magnus touched an edge of the light fabric. She took off her first petticoat and handed it to him. She unpinned her bustle and the ruffles at her chest. She unlaced her corset and cracked it open like a shell. Magnus smiled. "Are we almost down to you?"

When she was finally naked she sat down and hugged her knees. She was not cold. She licked her lips, tasting what it was like to be naked in the outdoors, in front of a man. Her intellect seemed to have contracted, crowded out by her senses. Her mind was full of moss and sunlight.

Magnus traced the red corset marks over her ribs. "You're a skinny, hard little thing."

She looked down at herself. He came closer. "Take yours off first."

She watched him pull off suspendered pants and then an itchy-looking shirt. Underneath he wore a thin, baggy, yellowed cotton coverall. He didn't take it off. "You give me the fidgets. You got so much attention in you. You look so much, it might cause a pain." He came towards her again and touched the bones that jutted out from her hips. "We got to fatten you up, miss," he said, and his voice held that same sweet sarcasm. He kissed her.

He pressed against her until her knees came down, her arms uncrossed and opened. He touched her between her legs. She jolted. He touched her there again and she shuddered. He said, "You sure you want to do this, what you call everything?"

"Yes."

"Calm yourself, then," he said. "Close your eyes."

She didn't close her eyes. He was touching her again and then she felt something pushing against her. She pressed into the moss, away. "Don't worry," he said. "Lie back." She closed her eyes, forced herself to breathe, eased her muscles open. She felt the pushing again. She breathed rapidly through her nose. She felt a tearing pain. "Are you sure you know how to do this?" She opened her eyes: he was right on top of her, his white face and blue eyes.

"I'm inside," he said.

"Of me?"

"Yah." He laughed, but his breathing was tight. "What is it you feel?"

"It hurt, but now it's just sort of throbbing and sore." She squirmed. "Are you finished?"

He began to move, just tiny pulls from his hips. "Do you feel this?"

"Yes." She seemed to catch his labored breathing off of him. "Yes, I feel it. It doesn't feel so sore anymore. Or not just sore." He was over her, white hair under his arms smelling strong, something like hay, his chest hair rubbing on her breasts, his soft white hair on her forehead. She slid her palms over the moss. She turned them over, gripped the air, turned them back, dug her nails into the ground. Then he groaned and relaxed onto her.

He rolled off. They lay side by side, looking up into the spruce tree above them. "Maybe we should go," Regina said. "The Shakers will be waiting."

"Just rest a time," Magnus said. He arched his hand, swooped slowly in, and grazed her face with his palm, then up again. "A gull," he said. "Two wings of a gull." He brushed over her eyelids, brushed them closed. He blew, making the sound of wind, high up and far away.

She touched his arm. "I like the gull better than that other thing."

He laughed. "Another time, you like it more. The first time's no good."

Afterwards, they drove down the rest of the mountain and into the Paradox Valley, past the familiar farmhouses. Magnus's arm felt friendly, regular-sized as it brushed against hers. Regina felt tired and sore and comradely, as if they'd been through a battle together. "What are you thinking about?" she asked.

"That union business. Tonight me and Ren and his wife are going to write to them."

"Oh."

They didn't speak again until they were nearing the Shakers. "Clean them underthings, some blood maybe."

"Blood?" She felt her thighs tighten.

"Don't worry. Only a little blood. A little sore, maybe. Then never again."

"You mean it will never hurt like that again?"

"Yah, this is what I am saying." He nudged her shoulder. He stopped the horses in the Shakers' drive. Sister Harriet was stooped in the front yard, tying up some flopping tomato plants. She came down to them, carrying her shears, her bonnet a little askew, her cheeks flushed. "Hello. You've made Regina late." She winked a blue eye at him. "And had fun making her late, didn't you?" Magnus looked startled, then he smiled.

"What a striking smile you have, as if it were against your better judgment." Regina laughed. Magnus's lips twitched. He nodded to Regina, jumped off the seat, grabbed the horses by the bits, and led them through the turnaround. Sister Harriet smiled down at Regina. "I can certainly tease a man without committing a mortal sin, and that man has a lovely vessel."

* * *

173

That night in Hammondville they were having their supper. Olive moved from the stove to the table while Florilla served up. Magnus and Ren sat with their sleeves rolled up, elbows steady on the table. The only sounds were the crack and scrape of crockery and occasional grunts and sighs. This went on for a good fifteen minutes, until Ren took the bowl of gravy, sopped up the last of it with his corn bread, and handed the bread over to Olive. She ate it as she cleared the table. Then they all dragged their chairs closer to the stove. Olive carried the lamp over. Florilla went rummaging through her sewing basket. Magnus, Ren, and Olive gave each other the eye. "I've got a letter from Ida," Florilla announced. Magnus stared at Olive and Ren, but they turned away. Florilla read the letter:

> Dear Ma, Olive, and the rest,
> Here I am in Boston. They're working us long hours, and for some it's hard, especially the little girls. But for me and Agnes, when the work is over, we're off! Seeing the sights. There are too many sights in Boston for me to describe. I had to get me a new hat, but next month I'll be sending some money.
>
> Keep well,
> Ida

Florilla folded the letter up carefully. "That girl will grow tired of the fast life before long." She ran her finger and thumb over and over the crease in the paper. Nobody said anything. She sighed, "Olive, why don't you read to us? I could do with some Song of Songs."

Magnus thumped his knee. "She can't. She promises to write down a letter for me."

"She did?" Florilla said. Olive was up, gathering paper and pencil. Magnus and Ren dragged their chairs back to the table.

"I'll just go to my room."

"Wait, Ma. First I want to show you something, all of you."

"You have to show us this now?" Magnus asked.

"You'll like it." Olive took out the drawing paper from her apron pocket. She carefully smoothed it on the table. Florilla peered over her chair.

"Did you make this of the Finger Lakes house?" Ren asked.

"No. A friend of Regina's sent it to her. It's a picture of a house in a place called the Finger Lakes. This here is Seneca Lake, near a town called Geneva. Regina grew up around there."

"It looks nice," Florilla said.

"You're smiling like the cat that ate the canary," Ren said. He reached over, tickled Olive's neck.

Olive laughed, squeezed his fingers off with her shoulder. "Stop now." She looked at Magnus and Florilla. "We could move here, with Regina. Run the place for her. If everything works out."

Magnus snorted.

"Don't be like that, Magnus." Florilla smoothed Olive's hair. "When I was a girl, me and Polly Wagner would sit out back the barn. We'd take sticks and carve out our dream house in the dirt. We'd spend hours at it, mulling over where the beds should sit and so forth."

Olive pulled her head out from under Florilla's hand. "This isn't like that, Ma."

Florilla cupped Olive's chin in her hand and pulled it around so Olive was facing her. "Olive Landry, you got rings under your eyes, you near fell asleep in church today, and you're touchy. And didn't you tell me just last week you got aches? I'm going to make you up some comfrey root and leather shavings." Florilla turned to the shelves above the stove. Olive took her chin back.

"You say last week you will help us with this letter. Now you are too sick to help, yah?" Magnus said.

Olive shoved the drawing aside. It fell onto the floor. She yanked the thin writing paper to her and grabbed up the pencil. "Start," she said.

Ren reached down for the drawing and folded it carefully. He handed it to her. "I asked around about this Finger Lakes. It's western New York. They got good land there for farming, so they say."

Magnus slid the union paper's masthead over to Olive. "Copy the name off here."

Olive slapped the pencil down on the table. "Will you give me a moment to catch my breath?" Everyone watched her. Olive breathed in through her nose, held it, let it whoosh out her mouth. She picked up the pencil. "I have to write the date down first," she said.

The woman was cutting yards and yards of red velvet. Just sitting on a little stool in the corner of a white room, snipping the fabric that poured out on either side of her. When she noticed Regina, she smiled pleasantly. Regina asked, What are you making? And then Regina realized that the red wasn't velvet at all, but blood, pooling around the stool. And then Regina opened her eyes and saw the eyes of Harriet looking into hers.

She remembered that Harriet had lifted her up. And she had been trying to tell Harriet about her vision, but Harriet said, "Later," helped her to her room, and covered her with a shawl for the shivering. Then she had felt herself falling into a real fit. Next, she was on her bed and someone was sponging her legs. When the sponge was wrung out over the basin, rust-colored water seeped out. She wondered if the women knew somehow that the blood had originated in the moss-covered clearing, and then she had fallen asleep. Sometime in the night she woke to singing. She said into the darkness, "I'm so afraid."

She heard a voice: "Hush now. Sleep." Regina raised herself on her elbows. She thought she could make out Harriet, in the rocker, knitting and singing softly: "Come, feel more Life, more Life and Union." But maybe that was a dream, too, because then Harriet became her grandmother, and Regina slept deep and hard all through the night.

When Regina woke, the yellow sun felt sour on her face. Her

~

head was stuffed with wire brush. There was a tender bruise under the hair above her ear. The sisters wanted her to rest and eat, but she brushed them aside, insisted on helping in the back garden. Regina went to work, accompanied by Sister Emily.

They were weeding in amongst the lemon grass. Regina held up her hands. "The feel of dirt under my nails is disgusting." Sister Emily pulled off her own work gloves and handed them to Regina. For a while, Regina crouched, the sun burning her neck, the last of the black flies circling her head. She pulled and shook and tossed. Every once in a while she yanked lemon grass up, too.

Then Olive was grinning down at her, shaking her head, and Regina said, "Shut up," but she smiled for the first time that morning. She dozed most of the way back, her neck jilting around. When she arrived at the Hammonds', she pulled off most of her clothes and got under the quilt despite the heat. She fell into an immediate, sweaty doze that lasted the rest of the day.

That night Olive brought Regina water for a bath. She scrubbed Regina's hands for her, dug under the nails. She washed Regina's hair with egg and oil, then she brushed it out. Regina's head slid back with each stroke of the brush. "I feel peaceful," Regina mumbled. "I have that nowhere to go, nothing to do feeling you get from staying up all night and sleeping all day." Olive ran the brush over the bruise. Regina flinched.

Olive parted the hair, pressed the bruise with her finger. "What happened?"

"I fell."

"Are you having fits at the Shakers?"

"Just this one. I'm having something else too, like a fit but not as strong. But you musn't tell anyone. I don't want that hideous doctor to know. He thinks he's cured me, and that's exactly how I want it."

"I'll put some salve on it. I'll ask cook if I can make it up for you."

"Don't let anyone see you."

"I won't. But how come you have fits at those Shaker ladies'? Seems like they must be disturbing more than calming you. I'm worried the fits will damage your head sooner or later."

"Don't worry."

Olive braided Regina's hair. She turned the oil lamp low and shook out both their blankets, as she always did, searching for spiders and mice. She puffed up Regina's pillows, watched her settle into bed. "And another thing, is Magnus treating you right? When I asked him about you, he seemed strange." Olive swung her legs under the covers. She tucked the blanket down under her feet.

"I've seen Mother Ann in my dreams."

"But what about—"

"She grew up in England and her job was cutting velvet. She felt as if she were snipping away her life along with the fabric. And then four of her babies died. Her heart was broken. She began to pray to God. She prayed so fervently, she sweat blood. She was terrified, but she kept on praying. She sweat away her physical passion until all that was left was a skeleton, burning for God's love.

"She was a Quaker, did I mention that? I think the heat of her prayers infected the rest. Her whole group took up the crying and the shaking. But they held their meetings in private homes, and the neighbors complained about the noise. The authorities threw her in jail.

"She must have been down to skin and bones by then. She was in a sort of stupor, staring into the striped light of the jail cell, when He appeared out of the barred light. He entered her. And He never left. Later, she had a vision that she would come to America, and that's how the Shakers began."

"Who told you all this?"

"Sister Harriet told me most of it, and I dreamed the details. I swear I know her, back to front. Ann Lee."

"I never heard you mention Jesus before in your life."

"Jesus entered Ann Lee and now Ann Lee has entered me. Which means that I'm Jesus, three times removed."

"It's bad luck to talk like that. And I don't like that story neither. It's trying to be the Bible, but it's not in the Bible. It's a cheat."

"Close your eyes, now, sweet Olive." Regina made her hand into the gull. She flew it over Olive's cot. She whistled like the wind. "Shh now, go to sleep."

Olive sat up so quickly that the gull smacked her in the face. "That's Ren's gull, the one his Mama used to—" Olive swung her legs back onto the floor.

Regina hid her hand under the covers. "I'm a witch."

"No." Olive shook her head. "It's Magnus Honsinger showed that gull to you." Olive gripped her arm. "Oh my," she whispered. "What has happened?"

Regina pulled the covers over her head, giggling. Olive laughed too, but her laughter still held her shock. Regina said something under the covers.

"What?" Olive asked.

Regina lifted the covers off her face. "I said his hair is white, everywhere." Olive squealed. "Shush, shush." Regina picked up the covers. "Get in here." Olive climbed under the quilt. Regina threw the quilt over both their heads.

"Do we have to be under here? I can hardly breathe," Olive said.

They settled themselves with their heads above the covers. "Just tell me one thing," Regina whispered. "Is it supposed to hurt?"

"You went that far? I can't hardly believe it."

"Just tell me."

"Yes. The first time."

"That's a relief. I thought he might have wrecked something."

"I'm sure he knows what he's doing. I think he's had practice."

"He was so pale. Alabaster. One moment I would think he looked like some creature that had crawled out from under a rock, and the next moment like a Greek god. It was the same with his coverall. Worn, ugly thing. But afterwards, I had the sudden urge to keep it. I almost wish I had it with me right now. I'd lay my cheek against it."

~

"But did he force you, sort of talk you into it?"

"I can't imagine Magnus Honsinger pursuading me of anything. He hardly speaks, except occasional inarticulate ragings. I thought it might be my only chance. He's quite handsome, isn't he?"

"Everyone says so."

"He said it would be better next time. Is that true?"

"You'd do it again?"

"I might."

"If you do, make him wear something, so you don't get a baby."

"What do you mean, wear something?"

"A lambskin, on his peter."

Regina shrieked. Olive giggled. This time when Regina pulled the covers over their heads, Olive didn't protest. They tried to control their laughter in the hot dark, the dark that grew hotter with every breath, but one of them would say something, and the laughter would get away from them: "He kisses with his tongue." "So that's why he shaved." "He had cuts." "I saw 'em—"

There was a rap on the door. They put their hands to each other's mouths. "This is outrageous behavior. You've woken Mrs. Hammond. Do you think you are little children?"

They held their breath. They waited until Fisk's footsteps climbed the stairs. Olive pulled the blanket off their heads. They settled back on the pillows, gasping for air.

"My face hurts from laughing," Olive said.

"For some reason I was dreading you finding out, as if it would ruin it, but its only made it better." Regina turned her hand into a gull. She swooped the air over Olive's head. Olive made her own gull. Their hands glided over each other's faces, just brushing skin, slipping through hair. Regina's gull landed and lay still.

Olive swept her hand across Regina's cheek. "It's almost like we're related," she said.

Regina was already asleep.

Ten

~

JULY LAY ON the Adirondacks like an open flower. Swallows rose
and fell through fields of pink milkweed and tangled purple vetch.
The roads were lined with black-eyed Susans, daisies, orange lilies.
Mrs. Cutter opened the kitchen door before breakfast and didn't
close it till after she and SuSu drank their glasses of iced mint tea on
the back steps after supper. Pea pods began to bulge. The clouds of
black flies disappeared, replaced by deerflies, fat and lazy—easy to
smack.

Olive was digging out clean linens for Regina's bed from the
upstairs hall closet. She lay her warm cheek on the sheets, closed
her eyes, and almost fell asleep there, surrounded by the smell of
mothballs and lavender sachet. She sighed, pulled out the linens
she needed, hugged them to her chest. Dimly she noticed that even
that slight pressure set her breasts to burning. At the top of the
stairs, arms full of bedclothes, her right foot about to descend to
the second step, she stopped. Just like that, a feeling went through
her, more certain than any thought: There is a baby inside me.

Later, snapping the sheets over Regina's bed, she talked herself
out of it. She hadn't felt any movement. Her monthly was only a
week or so late. She might not have counted the days right. And
anyways, remember last autumn? She and her mother were so

~

sure, and it had come to nothing. Still, her body knew what it knew.

The Crown Point Fourth of July celebration was to be what Dr. Corning called "A momentous occasion for Mrs. Hammond." Her first excursion out of the house in nearly a year. Gripping the doily-covered arms, she was carried from her bedroom in her favorite blue chair. Dr. Corning convinced her to abandon the chair in the yard and allow herself to be lifted into the carriage on the laced fingers of Mr. Cutter and a stable hand.

Regina was already seated in the carriage, unconscious of the sneer that had settled on her face as she stared at Mrs. Hammond. Mrs. Hammond had developed an eye twitch for the occasion. Fisk sat up next to Mr. Cutter on the driver's seat, holding the picnic basket. On orders from Mrs. Hammond, Mr. Cutter had braided the horses' manes with flowers and ribbons. With the left-over scraps of ribbon Olive had braided pink satin and daisies into her and SuSu's hair. Now SuSu twirled at the end of her mother's hand, whipping the ribbon at the air, leaving a trail of wilted daisies as they walked beside the carriage.

The roads were so crowded that the walking servants stayed abreast of the carriage. Olive trudged slowly, fighting the urge to shield her tender breasts with her hands. Regina reached out and stroked the ribbon that ran through Olive's hair.

Mr. Cutter was having trouble keeping the carriage horses steady amidst the throngs of shouting people and farm wagons. They twitched, whinnied, rolled their eyes. A group of little boys, carrying pinwheels, ducked under the carriage and brushed against a horse's flank. The horse started. Mr. Cutter swore, wrapped the reins in his fist.

Mrs. Cutter turned to say something to Olive, and SuSu wriggled out of her grip. She was a ballerina, twirling the ribbon over her head and singing softly to herself. She pirouetted towards the neck of the horse, whipped her pink ribbon at the sun. The horse reared. Someone screamed. Olive saw the white-yellow hoof with its silver shoe in the air above where SuSu had fallen. She and Mrs. Cutter rushed forward. They both grabbed ahold of SuSu and dragged her away. The hoof hit dirt.

Mrs. Cutter and Olive looked at each other. Olive held a wad of SuSu's dress in her fist. Mrs. Cutter was gripping SuSu's hair. Then Mr. Cutter yelled at Mrs. Cutter. Mrs. Cutter yelled back, slapped SuSu, and brushed the dirt off her dress. They were both crying. Dr. Corning held Mrs. Hammond's hand. Fisk hissed that they were causing a spectacle. Regina was grinning. Mr. Cutter climbed off and led the horses through the crowd, humming to them.

Olive let people surge between herself and the carriage. She thought of that hoof raining down on her stomach. She cupped her hand over the turn of her belly.

Someone jostled her. She recollected herself, saw Regina's head craning from the carriage, searching for her in the crowd. She hurried to catch up.

Mr. Cutter and the hired boy carried Mrs. Hammond up a hill, above the throng. Cutter wheezed and poured sweat. They settled her on a woven folding chair underneath a canopy. Mrs. Hammond touched Dr. Corning's sleeve. "My dear friend." She smiled weakly. He tucked a blanket around her. Olive helped unpack the basket of food, then sat just outside the canopy, near Regina's chair. They drank lemonade and watched the spectacle.

General Hammond had condescended to lead the parade on his huge, stamping white horse, Old Knight. Old Knight was the grandson of the Old Knight that had carried the general through the War Between the States. After the parade came a live bear who would climb a pole for ten cents, and then a medicine show.

The medicine man filled a tin tub with lake water, into which he poured three drops of his miraculous chemical—The Amazing Elixir of Life. The water frothed and steamed. Then he began filling amber bottles and selling them for fifty cents apiece. Dr. Corning rolled his eyes, mumbled something about quackery and the ignorance of the masses. But Mrs. Hammond secretly sent SuSu with fifty cents to buy a bottle of that Amazing Elixir of Life. She gave SuSu a penny for herself to stop her snuffling. Mrs. Hammond teaspooned it right then and there, on the sly. She said it improved her considerably.

At dusk a specially selected group from the Hammondville free school recited. The girls quoted Bible passages and Tennyson while the boys shouted out war poetry, caps at their breasts. When Mrs. Cutter filled Regina's glass, she dropped a letter in Regina's lap, winked, and moved away. Regina stood up and motioned for Olive to follow her. As soon as they were a few feet from the Hammond canopy, Regina lifted her dress and began to walk quickly, stepping over blankets, swishing her skirts against children's faces. Olive followed as fast as she could. They reached the edge of the crowd and the edge of the mown grass. Regina waded into winter rye. Finally she threw herself down. Olive sat next to her.

"It's from my father." Regina tossed it to Olive. "Open it." She lay down in the rye and stared up at the darkening sky. Olive carefully ripped open the envelope. She drew out the paper and offered it to Regina. "You read it." Olive started to read, moving her lips. "Aloud, I meant."

Olive held the paper close, narrowed her eyes. " 'To my youngest daughter,' " she read, " 'I received your latest epistle with some consternation. If, as you say, your aunt and uncle Hammond grow tired of you, I fear you have only your own unlovely behavior to blame. However, we cannot rely on their generosity if you have become a burden to them.

" 'Regarding your plan, I have grave misgivings as to the feasibility of Geneva without a guardian. No matter how you rely on a trusted servant, her morals and refinement cannot substitute for a gentlewoman of one's own class. Yet, as in most cases, Regina, it seems as if you shall have your way. A letter has arrived from one of your grandmother's friends, a Mrs. Roberta Tuttle, who has offered to serve as your guardian if you move to Geneva. In addition, she says she knows of a suitable house of modest proportion.

" 'As you know, Regina, Geneva was my childhood home

before it was yours. And even if I later had differences of opinion with your grandmother, I still remember my boyhood with sentimental yearning. Perhaps there are those, like you, who, although they make admirable little girls, make very poor young ladies. If this is so, you may be happiest in semiseclusion, in the setting of both our happy childhoods, the place where you will be least likely to be forced to take on the habits and responsibilities of a lady. For better or worse, you have your grandmother's indomitable will. I almost wonder if these fits are not self-induced as a means to your end, eternal childhood. In many ways, I envy you.

" 'The arrangements may take six to eight weeks. I would not mention these plans to the Hammonds until all is in order.

" 'Sincerely, your father, Lawton Sartwell.' "

Neither Olive nor Regina spoke. Dusk was washing into blue evening.

"It came true," Olive finally said.

Regina sat up. "I can't believe it. Just like that—our future fixed."

"My child will grow up in the Finger Lakes," Olive said.

"But is this what we want?" Regina said. "Somehow I feel cheated, as if my father has made the decision for me. As if I really were a little girl."

"You wrote the letter."

Regina nodded. "You have a firefly in your hair," she said softly. "It looks gorgeous in there amongst the ribbon and daisies."

"You have a firefly on your arm."

"Our fireflies are searching for each other." Regina tipped hers into Olive's hair. She crossed her arms over her chest. "I don't like the way my heart feels."

Olive took Regina's hand. They watched the moon rise. They watched fireworks explode over the water. Each explosion brought a murmur from the crowd. Hidden in the grass, it was as if the hill itself were sighing in satisfaction.

* * *

185

The next Sunday Magnus and Regina lay on the moss. Regina wore her petticoat. Magnus was naked, slapping at mosquitoes. He swore, pulled on his trousers and shirt. He took a handkerchief out of his pocket and unrolled it. Inside a wilting cigar leaked tobacco. He sighed, struck a match on his teeth, and lit it. Regina sat up. They passed the cigar back and forth. They were quiet, watching the cigar smoke twist in and out of the shafts of sunlight, chasing away the bugs.

"Tell me about your widow woman. What's her name?" Magnus didn't answer. "I'm not jealous. I hope you give the woman as good a time as you give me."

Magnus laughed, took the cigar out of his mouth. "Ase. Ase Anderson. She has one daughter, Mary. Her husband, he fell off the roof and kill himself about four year ago. He is a Swede, so's she."

"Why didn't you ever marry her?"

" 'Cause I'm always planning on leaving this place, soon as I can."

"But you could take her with you when you go."

"When I go to be your stableboy in this Finger Lakes?" Magnus smirked. Regina blushed. "We don't need no union man," he continued. "We got Miss Regina Sartwell as union and mother and boss man all in one." He puffed on the cigar. "You will come to the barn sometime, keep me and the cow company? Or will I sleep in your silk-cover bed, maybe?"

Regina watched a mosquito suck the blood out of the back of Magnus's neck. She didn't tell him. "I'm growing to hate that childish drawing Olive carries with her everywhere. I feel as if I have played right into my father's hands." Regina took the cigar and filled her lungs with smoke. "My heart is filled with twigs." She coughed, passed the cigar back. She began dressing, her back to Magnus. "Sometimes I feel as if I'm falling and no one will grab my hand."

Magnus took the cigar back, tapped it out on his knee, folded the stub up in the handkerchief, and put it in his pocket. He reached into his boot and slid out a tiny pearl-handled knife. He examined it closely, rubbing his thumb over it. "My mother gives this to me before I go." He pressed a lever, and a thin blade slid out, sharp on both sides. He handed it to Regina. The handle was milky smooth. "This can maybe stop you from falling sometime." "Not the kind of falling I'm doing," she said. "But I like it anyway. The handle reminds me of your skin."

Magnus shrugged and pulled himself up off the moss.

Olive and Regina took a walk almost every night after dinner now. They liked to stroll in a grown-over hay field behind the horse barn. The field was full of milkweed, black-eyed Susans, pasture rose, and timothy. A small grove of poplar saplings spangled and whispered in the evening wind. Olive liked the swish of their dresses through the thigh-high growth. She liked to walk slow and steady, and sigh a lot, to get the day's work off her shoulders. She liked to breathe in hard to clean the smell of lye or simmering jam out of her nostrils. She wore the old green calico that had grown so thin, it was hardly a dress at all. She could feel the wind through it. She knotted her braid up on her head to feel the breeze on her bare neck.

Regina wore her new dress and a straw hat with a ring of wine-colored velvet roses around the hatband. She was restless, ripping up grass, walking backwards, running ahead, falling behind. She would give Olive lavish compliments: her hair, her posture, her sweet disposition. Caress her cheek with timothy. Kiss her knuckles. Tell her shocking secrets: "Lying with Magnus, just before the crisis, I feel a great rage. I barely keep myself from biting through the soft meat of his earlobe. But the rage opens, and I find myself stroking his shoulder, round and round, a hundred times."

Then Regina would insult her. "If there were a man with a knife after you, do you think you would stop plodding, maybe shock the world and break into a run? Your face is going to fat."

Olive wouldn't answer compliments or insult. She just smiled, brushed the palms of her hands along the tops of the flowers, walked more and more like she was in a grand processional.

On one of their walks, near dusk, they reached the far edge of the field where it met a stand of poplars. Olive stooped down near a drooping white flower. "This ain't supposed to be here."

"What is it?" Regina crouched next to her.

"It's bloodroot, but it's supposed to be gone by the end of May."

"What does it do? Maybe there's a reason it waited for us."

"If you need to spit. It helps you breathe clear. Ma calls it an exciter. But look at this." Olive broke the plant and lifted it up. She held the stem over her fingers. An orange-red juice dripped onto her nails.

Regina put her hand over Olive's and let some of the juice drip over her knuckles.

"They say the Indians used it for war paint." Olive pressed down the stem, and more juice dripped onto the back of Regina's hand. "I heard that when Captain John Smith forced those Indian girls to bed with him—they painted bloodroot all over themselves. They must've looked a deathly sight."

Regina ran her knuckles over her forehead, down her closed eyes. In the dusk the juice looked like two black bars over her face.

"Now, how are you going to get that off?"

Regina smiled. Her teeth shone in the last light. She held up her painted fist and came towards Olive.

"Oh no, you don't." Regina made a swipe at her. "Don't." Olive bolted for the far lights of the Hammonds'. She felt Regina's hand smear down the side of her cheek.

Regina fell down on the ground. Olive collapsed near her. They sat quietly for a while, watching the sky turn deeper blue.

"Know what?" Regina's voice was soft.

"What?"

"We can have everything."

"What do you mean?"

"Everything we want will be ours. All we have to do is

breathe." Regina took the wilted, drained plant out of Olive's hand and broke the stem in half. "Let's eat it."

"You can't fool with medicinals that way."

"As we will it, so it will come to pass."

"But we already got what we want."

"Absolutely everything, Olive? Every secret desire?"

"But what if our secret desires are different? What if they cancel each other out?"

Regina put the edge of the stem to her mouth and sucked. The bloodroot disappeared like a tiny green snake into a hole. Olive saw a drop of the dark juice at the corner of her mouth. "Bitter," Regina said.

Olive could feel the root's blood, dry and tight on her cheek. She took the little stem that Regina handed to her. She threw the bloodroot—it disappeared in the grass a few feet away.

"Stupid. Why did you do that?" Regina jumped up to look for it.

"It ain't safe, I told you that. Anyway, things are going just right already."

Regina parted the grass. "See?" she said. "I found this tiny stem amongst all the weeds. The bloodroot is already working its magic."

"Give it to me." Olive began to cry.

"You don't have to eat it. It's just a made-up game."

Olive grabbed the wilted stem and smashed it with her teeth. It tasted sour and hopeless, mixed with the salt of her tears. She gagged once, but forced herself to swallow. "Everything was fine until you started this," she gasped. "You're always so reckless. Why do you have to twist things, so we don't know which is up and which is down? You don't care what damage you cause."

"Olive, don't be silly. It's just a game."

Olive wiped her face. "I'm afraid it only works if you eat it right away, right when you think of it."

Regina pulled her up from the grass. "Don't take me so seriously." They walked home, watching bats swoop over the dark field, listening to their dresses rustle through the wet evening grass. The moon was rising. Their faces and hands felt stiff from the dried juice. They made for the rain barrel at the side of the house. Their stomachs began to twist and cramp as the bloodroot began its secret work inside them.

July ripened into August. Olive and Mrs. Cutter picked all the cucumbers and put them in brine. The cauliflower and beans were ready. Goldenrod spread over the fields. Five days after the bloodroot, Regina began to wilt. It was as if all her energy had leaked out in a single night. Her nose and throat were stuffed; she had to pee every few minutes. Olive made a tonic from the inner bark of a poplar. When that didn't work, and Regina continued to feel tired and queasy, Olive tried ipecac. Regina threw up and said she felt better. But the next morning the symptoms returned.

When Sunday arrived, Regina said she was staying home. "Tell Mrs. Hammond it's my monthlies," Regina said dully from her bed. Olive fussed over her, offering to stay and plumping up the pillows, but Regina had disappeared behind her eyes.

When Olive returned on Monday afternoon, she found Regina in her room, trying to embroider. She was pulling everything out, turning her work into a rag. Olive walked over, took the hoop out of her hands, began to undo the knots.

Regina snatched back the mess of threads. "It's mine, thank you very much."

Olive made Regina's bed, which was also twisted into knots. "Ma says you most likely got some kind of flu—just keep warm, drink water. I didn't dare tell her about the bloodroot. She would have thought we were loony."

"Olive." Olive didn't answer. "What does it feel like to be with child?"

Olive kept tucking in the sheets. "I never felt the quickening. But I heard of women who just know."

"I'm afraid I have it." Regina was staring at the snarled threads in her lap.

"Have what?"

"It—a baby—growing inside me."

"When was the last time you bled?"

"It should have come weeks ago." Regina tapped the hoop against her forehead. "I'm almost ready for another."

Olive walked over and kneeled by her chair. She stared at her face. "Do you feel a quickening?"

"A what?"

"Something moving in your womb?"

"You mean I would feel it wriggling in my body?" Regina's face twisted.

"Maybe it's too early for that. But you have been tired and sick. That's the body readying itself to make the baby." Olive smiled.

"What are you smiling at?" Regina sounded hopeful.

"Everything. Magnus a daddy." She laughed. "The coincidence of it all. I think I might be—"

Regina grabbed on to Olive's apron. "Isn't there a way to stop it before it grows?"

"Why would you want to do that?"

Regina yanked on Olive's apron and pulled her in. Olive could feel Regina's hot breath on her cheek. "Because I'm not married. I'm an epileptic. I may become a Shaker, for God's sake."

"Why can't an epileptic have a baby? Your womb's just fine, I'd wager. And you don't have that many fits, anyways, only once every month or so. A baby might regulate it. And Magnus is near twenty-seven. He'd marry. Think of it. I'd help you, and Ma would too. With the baby. We'd be sisters. Our children would be first cousins. Blood related." Olive's eyes went filmy with tears.

"Magnus and I aren't like that. We've no more thought of marriage than a trip to the moon. In any case, my people would never allow marriage to a common miner."

"I don't know about that. Like your father said, you got a indomitable will. What you will, will come to pass, like you said. Maybe this is your secret desire, outing from the bloodroot. We would be your family, Regina. It'd be practically like marrying me and Magnus both." Olive's hands pulled at each other.

"But, Olive—"

"We'd have everything we want. I could have Ren for comfort and you for passion, and you could have Magnus for passion and me for comfort." Olive stood up, pulling out of Regina's grip on her apron. "We'll have to make sure you don't lose this baby. I'll ask Ma what to give you."

Regina put her hand on her stomach. "My middle feels funny. Like I'm going to be sick."

"That's one of the principle signs," Olive said triumphantly.

For three days Regina didn't leave her bed. She barely spoke, except to whine that she felt exhausted and bilious. Olive fussed over her—asking Mrs. Cutter to cook bland foods, hot cereal, potatoes, biscuits, to soothe Regina's stomach. She kept the room clean and well ventilated, tried to convince her to go on walks. When Regina cried, Olive told her it was common for women in her condition to get teary, even cried along with her sometimes. She kept up a chatter, elaborating on their lives. Olive's face flushed when she told Regina she could picture the baby, shining, all covered with dew. She said Regina's face had taken on a glow.

On Friday, when Olive brought Regina her dinner, Regina was sitting up in the rocker. "You're feeling better!"

"I have to tell you something. And don't interrupt."

"Good." Olive sat down on the edge of the bed, folded her hands in her lap.

"You know I have agreed to the house on Seneca Lake."

"Yes, and I was the other day thinking of our babies, say I was to have one—"

"And, Olive, I love you. If I could marry you, if you could be my lifelong companion . . . But you are already married. And I do not want to marry Magnus. I don't even know how much I actually like Magnus. And even more, Olive, even more than not wanting to marry Magnus, I don't want to have a baby."

"It's natural to be afraid."

"Of course I'm afraid. My body is already filled with something that convulses me. I don't want someone else in there too. I would go mad. Look at what it's done already. It's poisoning me. When I picture a baby growing in there, feeding off my blood and bones like a cancer, and then that long-armed woman, feeding on my soul . . . it's too many. I'm not a damn hotel."

Olive winced. "Do you have to use that men's language?"

"I like it. It's strong."

"It's cheap strong. Unnatural strong. Selfish strong."

"The language?"

"Yes! The language!" Olive stood up.

"Olive, please."

Olive strode into the kitchen and found chores to do with Mrs. Cutter. Mrs. Cutter said Olive scrubbed the skillet so hard, it near had a hole in it. Olive combed the snarls out of SuSu's hair, until SuSu whimpered that she was yanking too hard. Mrs. Cutter asked if Olive was going to fetch Regina's tray. She asked SuSu to do it.

Olive insisted on rewashing the clean tablecloths. She hung them on the line in back of the house. It was a warm, windy day. She put her cheek against the wet fabric. She felt bile boiling up her throat, pushing at the back of her teeth.

When Olive asked SuSu to carry the supper tray in, SuSu shook her head and hid behind the stove. So Olive turned her face to stone. She kept the tray perfectly even—didn't spill a drop. Two military taps on the door. Regina didn't answer, but Olive could hear her crying.

Regina sat on the floor, her head resting on the bed. She was using ripped sheets to wipe her tears.

"Is there anything else?" Olive asked.

Regina unfolded herself quickly. She grabbed Olive's hand. Regina's hand was hot and dry. "I need you to take away this thing growing inside me." Her voice was nearly gone. "I'll do whatever you want. I'll marry Magnus if I have to, but just take this away. I feel as if I'm being murdered from the inside out." Olive tried to turn away, but Regina squeezed her hand until it hurt. "Do I have to disappear into your family to make you love me?"

"Stop this wild fussing. I just needed time to get over it. The baby." Olive's voice began to wobble. "I'm just getting over it is all." Crying, Olive pulled Regina up, wiped her face, remade the bed. Regina kept crying too, until their sobbing made them laugh.

Regina gasped, blew her nose. She tried to eat her supper. After the first teaspoon of chicken pie, she gagged. She stumbled to the chamber pot and threw up. The noise was a horrible scraping sound that went on and on. In between heaving, Regina moaned, "It won't stop."

With her hand on Regina's shaking forehead, Olive said, "Ma will know what to do."

Regina gasped and wiped her mouth with a handkerchief. She pushed the chamber pot away from her. "It's illegal, isn't it? To get rid of it."

"I guess it is. I don't really understand it." Olive brought Regina a glass of water. She blew her own nose. She kept talking, her everyday voice soothing them both. "When Dr. Lenard first set up his practice in Hammondville, he told Ma not to do any more abortions with home medicine. He said it poisoned the women. It was healthier to do an operation, even before quickening. Anyways, Lenard got to be the regular abortionist round these parts. He had a good business, and Ma would help him sometimes.

"But last year they made it illegal in New York State to cause abortions. They'll send the doctor to jail, or whoever done it. So he had to quit. It was peculiar because folks knew you could drink something to make you regular before you feel the baby growing. It's just your body making ready for a life. And if you can't feed it or you ain't married, you drink something. But then the preacher got a visit from the doctor down here, not Corning, the regular one. The next Sunday the preacher gave a sermon about abortion being murder. He says, what if the Virgin Mary had an abortion? What if President Lincoln's mother did? We was all surprised 'cause we never read that in Scriptures before, and the minister never said anything about it before neither. Then he told us the law was passed.

"Of course, we all know women who can make up the medicine, but now they're scared of jail and damnation. Don't worry, though, Ma knows all about it. She ain't afraid."

"You don't think it will poison me, like Lenard said?" Regina shuffled over to her bed, her shoulders hunched.

"Well, it'll poison you, but the poison'll get your blood flowing again. It won't kill you or nothing."

"Maybe if I have a fit, it'll loosen the blood."

"I think those fits poison you worse than any abortion medicine."

"They don't. You don't understand. It's as if all the movement in my body is on the outside, shaking, and on the inside there is just dark calm."

Olive was silent. The burning behind her breastbone had returned. She closed her eyes and squeezed her throat to keep it back.

That Sunday, Olive and Regina dressed in the hazy, early morning light. Olive opened the window, but even this early, the air was thick. They ate buttered bread and drank tea in the kitchen, standing up. When Mrs. Fisk came in, they left the house to look for Mr. Cutter. He was pitchforking hay into Old Knight's stall.

Olive hated to get near that horse. Folks said Old Knight's grandfather had been taught to trample foot soldiers in battle, and that the general had trained all the new Old Knights to do the same. The horse was enormous, with flared pink nostrils. Olive stared at him, while Regina asked Mr. Cutter to hitch up the wagon.

As they rode, the day heated up. Dew steamed off the fields. In Irondale the heavy sky was a lid, keeping the smoke of the forge from drifting away. It stank. Regina started coughing and ended up gagging. She wiped her mouth with the handkerchief. "I'm not telling Magnus."

"Why?"

"What if he wants to keep it?"

"He's allowed his opinion, ain't he?"

Regina didn't answer. They started up the rutted two-track to Hammondville. The horses slowed to a plod. The heat of the day lessened a little as they rose, but Olive still felt sweat sliding down her sides and back. She glanced over at Regina. She was sleeping, her mouth open, her head nodding with the pull of the wagon.

Magnus was sitting on the doorsill and Ren was on a stump, leaning against the house. They were whittling clothespins. Ren jumped up to help Olive with the horses. Magnus stood more slowly, showing his cautious half smile.

Olive didn't smile at all. She helped Regina off the wagon, draped the blanket around her shoulders. She held on to Regina's elbow and prodded her into the house. The men followed, confused.

Olive's mother looked up from her sewing. "You're here! Come in and sit down. It's a beautiful day, got some real warmth in it for once. There's a lily by the side of the house, did you notice?"

Olive led Regina to a chair. "Ma, Regina and me need to have a talk with you." She looked at Magnus. "Regina ain't goin' to the Shaker women this Sunday. You need to go down and tell 'em so they don't worry and send for news of her."

"Why?" Magnus's eyes were squinty and mistrustful.

"I need to speak with Magnus, alone," Regina said.

"If we go outside, we won't be alone. Outside is one big ear."

"What about upstairs?" Regina said.

"You can hear everything up there," Mrs. Landry said. Ren and Olive laughed.

"How amusing. No privacy in the entire town." She looked at Magnus. "I've missed my time. I want Mrs. Landry to make it come again. That's all."

~

196

Ren looked down, his cheeks striped pink. Magnus stared at Regina's middle. "You sure?" His voice was empty.

"Of what?"

He scratched the back of his neck, and Regina remembered watching the mosquito suck his blood. "Sure you don't want a baby?" Magnus finally said.

"Yes. Are you?"

He looked down again. "I don't want one. No."

The air in the room collapsed. Nobody spoke.

"I'll head down for the Shakers, then." Magnus nodded at Regina. He left the house. Ren stood for a minute in the house full of outraged women. Then he said, "I'll go with him."

After the men were gone, the women kept still while the air slowly inflated again. Then they all sat down at the kitchen table.

Olive's mother said, "Now, Miss Sartwell, I'll make up the mixture and give it to you. Then it'll take an hour or more until the cramping starts."

"What will happen?" Regina stared at the skinny woman with the flat face and big hands. She concentrated on the wise-looking wrinkles around her mouth.

"There'll be pain, maybe some vomiting—depends on how your body takes it. They'll be more blood than your usual time. Then you'll want to sleep. The blood will keep on for a few days, heavy. And you'll want to keep to your bed. But you don't usually get home until evening on Monday, and once there, stay abed. So it'll just be the wagon ride down the mountain tomorrow. Should be fine." Florilla patted Regina on the hand. It made tears leak out of Regina's eyes. She shook her head and the tears stopped. "Now. There's more than one medicine for unblocking a woman. But some needs the cooperation of the full moon, which we ain't got today. Then there's some stronger than others. How many times you missed your time, Miss Sartwell?"

"Once, but I'm about to miss another."

"Let's see what I have." Florilla pulled herself up and went to the shelves above the sink. She took down several small, rusty tins and opened them. "I got borax and saffron but no myrrh. Myrrh is hard to come by, I believe it travels all the way from Africa or Palestine. As the Lord was made a present of it, it must be one of those. I got me some Seneca snake root left. Put the water on to boil," she said to Olive, "Alls we need is enough for one cup."

Florilla took out a dried root from one of the tins and began chopping it up. "Is that water simmering?"

"Yes, Ma." Olive hovered behind her mother. Regina hunched in her blanket at the table.

Florilla swept the finely chopped root into her palm, made a sweeping motion across the counter, gathering up the dust. Then she dropped it all into the bubbling water. "We don't want that to boil," she said, sliding the pot so it perched half on, half off the heat. When it was done she stretched a cheesecloth over a cup and poured the yellowed water into it. She threw out the shriveled root. Then she dropped ten white grains into the water. Next came ten grains of something that made her eyes water. She jiggled the cup, peered into it. She handed it to Regina. "Drink this."

"I'm afraid."

"That's right," Mrs. Landry said. "But we'll be sure you come out fine."

Regina took a sip. She gagged. "It's so strong," she said, when she got her voice back.

"Here," Olive said. She moved behind Regina and plugged her nose for her. "Ma, will you fetch something for her to drink afterwards?"

"Don't want to water it down."

"Ready, get set, go." Regina drank it down. Olive let go of her nose. Regina gasped.

"Don't vomit, Miss Sartwell. The medicine will come up without doing its work." Olive held on to her hand, letting Regina squeeze her fingers until it hurt too much. Gently she moved Regina's grip to her wrist. "You're not breathing, Miss Sartwell," Florilla said. "If you don't breathe, the pain'll be worse when it comes. Follow me." All three women breathed together. After a

~

while, the others broke off and started a quiet conversation. Regina didn't seem to notice.

"They're here," Regina finally said in a tight voice. "The cramps." Olive and her mother helped Regina to Florilla's bedroom and onto the straw mattress on the floor. She curled around her stomach. Olive held her hand. It was slippery. Her face was yellow, covered with a fine sweat. "Can I vomit now, please?"

Olive looked at her mother. "Can she?"

"The medicine has grabbed on. She can't bring it up now." Olive's mother came back with a tin pail. Regina threw up.

"If you stay with your friend, Olive, I'll just start dinner. Folks might stop by to see why I'm not in church." Olive's mother went into the other room. In the bedroom Regina rolled with the pain. "Breathe," Olive said, and Regina breathed. But often she hissed instead, "It hurts. It hurts." Later, Regina whispered, "I feel wet down there."

Olive called her mother. She came in with cornmeal on her hands. She returned with some old faded calico fabric and began cleaning Regina up. When Regina saw the bloody rags, she vomited again. Olive's mother packed more rags between Regina's legs. She took the first ones into the kitchen. Olive heard her opening the stove door.

Regina sipped some water. She closed her eyes and slept.

In late afternoon, Magnus pushed aside the curtain and watched Regina whimpering in her sleep. He let the curtain drop and walked back into the main room.

They ate a cold Sunday supper.

"Didn't hear, did you?" Magnus said to Olive. "What's come of your grand union. We get a letter this past week."

"They said they was glad we wrote, glad to know about us," Ren said.

"Yah, glad, but they say the Hammond mines ain't ready for unions yet. Man who wrote's named Chapmen. Unions is just for Irish, I guess."

"That's all you've ever cared for, isn't it?" Olive said.

"Hush," Florilla said. "Olive, you keep an eye on Miss Sartwell. I have to check with the doctor, see if he needs me. Hopefully it won't take long."

Olive nodded. She couldn't eat. The house was close and hot, wreaked of blood and vomit. Her insides burned. Olive heard Regina calling for something to drink. She brought her a tin cup filled with tepid water. She helped Regina drink, but when Olive tried to give her another sip, she shook her head and curled back onto the bed, already asleep again. Olive walked back into the front room and put the tin cup on the shelf.

There were three crisp knocks on the front door.

They stared at each other.

The knocks again, louder and more impatient.

"Who is it?"

"General Hammond and Mr. Putney." The chief engineer's voice stammered.

Olive opened the door. "Sir," was all she could think of to say.

"This is Olive Honsinger—" the chief engineer began.

"She is a maid in my home," the general said. Then he directed himself to Olive. "I was having supper with our chief engineer when I was told my niece, Miss Sartwell, lay ill in your home. I found it difficult to credit the story."

Olive's voice went so high, it scraped her throat. "She meant to go down to the Shakers, sir, like she always does, but she fell ill with female troubles and couldn't make it. But my mother has been nursing her, sir."

"We'll move her to Lenard's."

"I don't think she can be moved, sir."

"Miss Sartwell couldn't be comfortable in these conditions. Completely alien to her. I'll send some of my men with a pallet."

"Sir, I'll bring her to the doctor's. My ma is there now."

"Meet us at the doctor's. We'll go there directly. And, Landry, I hold you responsible for this unorthodox situation."

"Yes, sir."

Olive closed the door as soon as the gentlemen turned their

backs. She went to Regina. She put her hand on her hot forehead, stroked her hair. "Regina, you can spend the night in a real bed, at the doctor's house."

Regina whimpered, turned over.

"I'll stay with you. And Ma's there too."

Regina sat up. Olive helped her dress. She packed fresh rags between her legs. Regina's head kept listing towards Olive as they walked into the front room.

Magnus pushed back his chair. "Want I should drive her over in the wagon?"

"Just get her in. I'll take her over." Magnus lifted Regina up onto the seat of the wagon. He seemed awkward with her, as if he couldn't remember how to touch her. Finally he patted her leg. "Feel better now?" he asked her.

She looked at him. She touched his cheek. She put her hands back in her lap and turned forward. Magnus walked back into the house.

It was overcast. The night air was full of water. Olive drove the few hundred yards up the embankment to the doctor's house. She held the reins with one hand, the other arm across Regina's front to keep her from tipping over.

"I'm a mess," Regina said.

Olive shook her head. "How did this happen?" Olive helped Regina totter into the doctor's house. Olive thought she would choke on cigar smoke and loud men's voices. The general perched stiffly in a huge armchair. The chief engineer sat on the edge of the couch, tapping a rhythm on his knee. The doctor bent over a cabinet, the forks of his coat parting over his rear end. The general's other foreman stood by the door. Olive's mother was at the sink, washing dishes. She gave Olive a grim stare.

"Miss Sartwell, we have a much more appropriate room here in the doctor's house," the general said.

"I was fine at the Honsingers'," Regina croaked.

"But I should have been notified," Lenard said. He drew his head out of the cabinet and stood up. He brushed a hand over his hair. "Florilla was over here and never even notified me you were ill. I told her myself that simply wasn't right."

Dr. Lenard slid a glass filled with brown liquid onto the top of the cabinet. He sloshed a little on his hand. "Still, what's done is done. She is safely with us now." He licked his fingers, then walked over and put the sticky hand on Regina's elbow. "Right this way."

Olive followed behind the doctor and Regina into a little room. There was just a single bed with a beige satin coverlet. "I'm afraid this is the best I can do on such short notice. Now, if you'll excuse me for a moment, I'll just wash my hands."

Regina sagged down onto the bed. "Sleep here tonight, Olive. I hate this place."

"I will."

Olive heard her mother from the other room: "I'm finished cleaning up. I'll see my daughter and be on my way." No one answered. As soon as her mother came through the door, Olive realized it was fury that had whitened her face and pulled her mouth taught. "I will work for that drunken devil no more." Florilla's voice was a poison whisper.

"What happened?" Olive's teeth began to chatter.

"All these years calling me Florilla and whining for help. And then in front of the general he speaks to me as if I were a dog. He'll not have to bother with me no more."

"Ma, I'm going to stay with Regina tonight," Olive whispered.

"You be careful. I don't trust that devil."

The doctor returned in a cloud of cologne. Florilla swept out, lifting her skirts as if the room were dirty. He nodded to her in an absentminded way. "I'm ready to examine the patient now."

"It's female illness," Regina said.

"Who shall make the diagnosis, the doctor or the patient?"

"I want Olive to stay with me."

"That won't be possible. I need privacy."

"I won't be no bother," Olive said.

They heard General Hammond call out, "Tell that Landry girl to make us some strong coffee."

"I'll be right back," Olive said to Regina.

Lenard closed the door after Olive. He fussed with the latch. He leaned his back against it. "I believe this is the first time we have actually conversed in private, Miss Sartwell."

"I am in no mood to converse. I wish to sleep."

"I have a confession to make." He ran his hand through his hair, twice. "Miss Sartwell, I am in love with you."

"You are drunk."

"Only a little, for courage." His breath was raspy. He tottered towards the bed and dropped heavily onto one knee.

"Dr. Lenard, I cannot imagine what you are thinking. This is a bedroom. You must leave at once."

"I assure you that your epilepsy has become only a further fascination."

"This is a disgusting exhibition. Get out of here."

Dr. Lenard lurched off his knee and gripped her arm to steady himself. "I pledge to care for you, in sickness and in health."

"You drunken fool." She pulled away, but he was leaning his weight on her. They toppled onto the bed in an awkward jumble of arms and legs.

"Get off me." Regina tried to sit up.

His pasty face was close to her. "Oh, my love, our passion overwhelms." His wet lips attached to her neck. She grabbed a fistful of his lank hair and tried to pull him off.

But the doctor was moaning, ripping at the buttons over her chest. He was pushing his hand inside her dress. The hand wriggled under her petticoats. She felt his fingers on her breastbone, crawling towards her right nipple.

She brought her knee up. She tried to pull the pearl-handled knife out of her boot. It took three tries. Lenard's lips felt enormous, suffocating on her neck. She finally had the knife. She gripped it. Her sweating hand slipped a little over the handle. She put her thumb on the lever. His nibbling was at her cheek now, moving towards her mouth. His other hand was on her breast, pinching her nipple. It hurt.

Regina pressed the lever. The double-edged blade slipped out of the handle. With the knife in her fist, she felt with the side of her hand for his left breast. Her hand was so wet, it was hard to hold on to the knife. She found a vest pocket.

She jabbed the blade into his vest. There was resistance. She pushed her palm against the end of the handle with all her strength. The knife seemed to poke through something. It slid in easily up to the hilt. Regina let go.

The doctor lay still. She wondered if she had killed him already. Then he reared back, slipping to his knees by the side of the bed. He looked at the knife sticking out from under his arm. He looked at Regina, his mouth a little O.

"Don't worry," Regina said. "I missed the heart."

Olive heard Dr. Lenard scream. She dropped the cup of coffee. It broke, splattered dark liquid. The general strode to the door of the room, coffee dripping from his knee. He turned the knob. It was locked. The other men gathered around the door. A foreman bashed his shoulder against it, but it didn't give.

Then someone was fumbling at the other side, unlocking it. Men crowded into the entrance of the little room. Olive stood on tiptoe behind them, straining to see. Over a shoulder she saw Regina in the far corner of the room behind the bed. The doctor was stumbling around, tears and snot dripping down his face. At first Olive thought he had gone crazy, then she saw the small knife sticking out of his armpit.

"Olive!" Regina screamed. Olive tried to push between all the dark backs of the men, but they were a wall, keeping her out. One of the foremen grabbed Regina by the shoulders. The doctor sat down on the bed. "I feel faint." He continued to cry. His voice rose, as if he were trying to wake up the men who stared at him. "My God. I've been stabbed."

Regina kicked at the foreman.

"Let go of her!" Olive began to sob.

The general shoved Olive out of the room. He locked the door. Olive knocked on it.

"He attacked me," Regina screamed.

"It's epileptic fury!" the doctor wailed, his voice more hysterical than Regina's.

Then Olive heard General Hammond: "Lenard's fainted. Telegraph Crown Point that we're coming down with the epileptic and the doctor. Find some chloroform for the epileptic."

The door opened. The chief engineer slipped through the crack. His eyes were wide and terrified. "Telegraph," he mumbled, stumbling for the front door. Someone drove the bolt back, relocking the door. Olive heard one of the foremen say, "I think she's going into a fit, sir." Something fell over and broke.

The general's voice sounded loud and calm. "Lay her down on the floor. Bind her arms."

Olive banged harder on the door. The skin on her knuckles stung. "Please, let me in. I know all about her fits. I'm her only friend. I'm her maid."

"Get rid of that blathering idiot outside the door before we have to chloroform her, too." The bolt was thrown back. The door began to open. Olive turned and ran.

Eleven

~

REGINA WOKE ON those tumbling boards in the cold of March, just after her leap. Someone was bouncing the boards on purpose, trying to pry her loose from her jumbled bones and skin and heart, and she was almost ready to accede. *Here are my skinny bones, my lump of heart, my pile of skin. Take them, I am too weary to hold them anymore.*

She thought, *I have spent my whole life on these two jolting boards, damaged goods, hauled by shop boys.*

She was soaked with snow or tears. Her limbs were broken: She couldn't move them. She smelled alcohol and sweat, smoke and damp air. She heard horses snorting and human groaning. She was blind.

No, her lashes were gummed with dried tears or scum or blood. She couldn't move her hands to rub at them. She strained them open.

She was not on boards, it was not March. She was in a three-seated buckboard, at night, jammed into the last leather seat between two men in rumpled frock coats. She was tied. In front of her she could see the general. He sat catty-cornered, alone in the middle seat, his legs crossed. In the front seat Dr. Lenard and the chief engineer were crammed in next to the driver. The chief engineer was holding a cloth to the side of the doctor's breast. Both men's faces glistened sweatily, both sighed and groaned in some shared language of commiseration. Dr. Lenard's head lolled around. He wheezed, as if his breath were coming up through something shredded. The engineer's knuckles shone white as he gripped the back of his seat. He shouted, "Faster, I think we're losing him."

"Simply can't go any faster down the Irondale Road," the general said. "Horses stumble and we'll all lose our lives. He's only fainted, in any case." His voice was round and deep. His eyes were closed. Regina stared at his wrinkled face. His eyes slid open. "You have shamed your family."

She looked away. "Are you going to tell my father?" Regina's voice came out high and painful, as if her lungs had shrunk.

"It's time you knew the facts of the matter. Beforehand, Mrs. Hammond and her physician insisted that the truth would retard your progress."

"What facts?"

"Your father suffered a stroke of palsy nearly four weeks ago. According to reports, his entire right side is paralyzed. He cannot speak, except for nonsense syllables."

"My father . . . But then, my sister Eliza could—"

"She has responsibility for the care of your father, as your eldest sister is traipsing about the world and you are incapacitated. Eliza has asked me to take over your legal guardianship. Her husband cannot face the task." The doctor moaned.

The chief engineer moaned: "There's so much blood—it just keeps seeping and seeping."

"The first rule of blood: Looks like more than it is," the general said. Regina smelled woodsmoke. The rattle of the coach sounded more hemmed in, and then they slowed and turned in to the general's drive. The suddenness of it dazed her. Regina noticed she was matching the doctor's ragged breathing, breath for breath. The two men beside her shifted. Her vision seemed to dim at the edges, but she thought she saw the driver and the engineer carrying the groaning doctor off the surrey.

"Now, Miss Regina," the general said, "if you can comprehend me, I must ask you to be very quiet when we bring you into the house. You won't be there above an hour, and I don't want to alarm Mrs. Hammond."

"Where am I going?"

"To the state lunatic asylum in Utica. We just must ask the judge over to sign the papers. I believe Lenard and Corning can be prevailed upon to sign as the requisite two doctors, and then you'll make the first train south, at seven-thirty this morning."

Regina's lips and chin began to shake. She frowned to steady them.

"No tears, now. This asylum is got up in the best way. Corning's cousin is the assistant superintendent, and thus we've heard all too much about it. It's a perfect model of society. The classes are separated. They may be able to bring you to your health and senses where we have failed."

"I'd rather go to the Shaker ladies." A few sobs got out. She frowned again.

"You've been visiting them these last many weeks, and what good has come out of it? My guess is they're too meek to manage you."

"But it would just be for a short time. You see, my father has procured a house for me, in the Finger Lakes."

"Let me impress on you that you have attempted murder. I'm afraid there'll be no houses in the Finger Lakes for you."

Regina swallowed, clenched her teeth. Her throat was so tight, she felt as if she were suffocating.

They carried her out of the coach like a piece of furniture, one man with his arms under her shoulders and the other heaving at her knees. They laid her out on the bench in the hall.

From her sideways position she stared at the wallpaper, which she had somehow never noticed before. It was a robin's-egg blue, with two kinds of flowers, one rounded, the other pointed. The general sent one of the dirty-jacketed men to fetch the judge.

Regina decided they had laid the doctor out in her room. She pictured him in her bed, his face shiny with sweat, his mouth quivery with held-back tears. He seemed frail and pitiable, and she would have liked to offer him a handkerchief.

The chief engineer stumbled into the hall. He held on to the doorframe of the parlor: "It just keeps seeping," he mumbled. Then he mumbled something about feeling dizzy. He lurched over to the yellow couch and fell across it. His breathing, too, was quick and shallow. Regina thought she would like to hold his hand.

The general leapt up the stairs, three at a time, invigorated by catastrophe. He came down with Mrs. Fisk. Regina could see the white of Fisk's nightgown.

"I need you to pack Miss Sartwell's things, Fisk. Immediately."

Regina heard Fisk gasp. "Sir, what's happened? Is she hurt?"

"She has suffered an attack of epileptic fury. She has lost her mind."

"But why is she all tied up in that way? Is she bleeding? Where is Olive Honsinger?"

"Her services are no longer needed. And I have grave doubts as to the efficacy of her good influence, or whether the influence was ever good at all. This one is tied up because she attempted to murder our doctor. It is his blood on her."

"Dr. Corning?"

"No, no, Corning is upstairs. The doctor in Hammondville— Lenard. Now, Fisk, go pack her things."

"Yes, sir. But where is she going?"

"Never mind now."

"But shouldn't I clean her up if she's traveling home? Does she know, sir? Her father—?"

"We can't untie her now. She would be a nuisance, and yes, she has been informed."

"But, sir, she smells . . . and, sir, I think that blood ain't only—"

"Fisk! Miss Sartwell must leave this house at seven. It is now quarter past six. Go and pack before Mrs. Hammond is wakened."

"Yes, sir. But, sir, seeing as she is a relation, shouldn't she look presentable? She is your niece, sir."

"This one is an aberration. She bears no relation to my sister. None. Go."

Mrs. Fisk turned and slipped away, down the hall.

Regina thought, Mrs. Hammond must be partial to blue. She began to name all the blue in the house—the blue of the fire screen, this blue wallpaper, the blue-bordered plates in the dining room. Regina saw the skirts of Mrs. Hammond's morning robe, blue, on the landing. "Hammond? Are there thieves?"

"No, dear, go up to bed."

"Who is that tied on the bench there? A thief?"

"No one."

"I believe it is Miss Sartwell. Has there been an accident?"

"She has had an attack. We're taking her away."

"Not like that, sir, please. I can smell her from here. What would her people say?"

"They will clean her up at the asylum."

"General Hammond, you must clean her up and make Carol Handslinger escort her to Saratoga. That is where they take neurasthenic ladies. Saratoga water is a natural tonic. But she'll need new dresses if she's going. The ladies there wear a different dress every day. Maybe Dr. Pierce's sanitarium in Buffalo—that might be less grand."

"Don't you worry, Mrs. Hammond. We'll talk about it in the morning."

"Is Fisk awake? Where is Olive Handsinger?"

General Hammond walked up to the landing. Regina could see up to their chests. The general had hold of Mrs. Hammond's elbow. "I'm afraid she has tried to harm someone. We must take her to the lunatic asylum in Utica."

"But that's no place for a lady."

Regina forced words through the vise of her throat: "Aunt, please, don't let them take me there."

"Quite right. Mixing with those dirty lunatics. Hammond, I insist."

"She is a criminal, Mrs. Hammond. It is either the lunatic asylum or prison for her now."

"Well, I can't think, but you must clean her up, even for there."

"Yes, yes. Just go on up—"

"Your blue robe," Regina yelled to her, "the blue fire screen, the blue china bowl on the dining room table, the blue flowers on the wall." Mrs. Hammond was sitting on the stair. It was as if Regina were looking into a mirror. She could feel the reflection of her wide eyes and round mouth on Mrs. Hammond, and feel her hands over Mrs. Hammond's ears.

And then another hand was trying to press some wet, bitter cloth to her face. She strained her face as far away as she could, but the cloth followed. Daddy, Daddy, I'm afraid. Then she was falling into the dark, all alone.

Olive stumbled down the hill, skidded her boot over some thin-stemmed pansies. The door opened. Olive squinted in the light: "Mama?" she said.

Then Olive could feel her mother running her hands over her, searching for hurt or break. She could feel the two men, their wide bodies behind her mother, shielding her from the light. Olive somehow couldn't tell them it wasn't her, it was Regina. Her mother prodded her over to the rocker. She wrapped her in an old quilt that smelled of camphor and mildew. Her mother sponged her face with a wet cloth. Magnus built up the fire, even though it was a July night, and the stove coughed soot and smoke. Olive's mother brought her a piece of corn bread in a bowl of warm milk. Ren massaged her shoulders. "It's Regina," Olive said.

"Eat first," her mother said. Florilla and Magnus sat and watched her, while Olive drank down the tea and sopped up the bread and milk. Standing behind the rocker, Ren smoothed her hair. The tears kept leaking out like sweat. Her mother handed her a handkerchief, and she blew her nose.

Exhausted from the heat, Olive closed her eyes.

"Breathe," her mother said. "Ren."

"Yah." His hands stopped smoothing Olive's hair.

"Make her some tea from that third jar on the left." She could hear the worried clucking of the chicken. Her mother must have heard it, too, because she said she was going to make up a soft-boiled egg.

Olive concentrated on her breathing. She blew her nose again. Then there was some tea in front of her. The mug was hot, and she drank the tea down, the minty taste drying out her mouth. Then there was a soft-boiled egg, and she ate that too, although she was so sleepy, she could hardly spoon it in.

"It's late," her mother said. "The men got to work in the morning. Why don't we all go to sleep."

"Good," Ren said. He picked up the candle.

"Wait, I ain't told you what's happened."

"That's right." Magnus sat down opposite her. Her mother huffed to the sink and fussed around, her back to Olive. Olive could feel Ren's fingers walking her shoulders, finding the sore spots and keeping a steady pressure on them.

"What's happening to Regina?" Magnus said.

"Shush, now," Florilla said from the sink. "Let Olive get her breath."

"Regina was in the bedroom and the doctor went in to see her. He must've done something bad because then there was—I don't know what happened, but I do know Regina has taken that pearl-handled knife Magnus gave her and stuck it into the doctor." Magnus hissed. She took a breath and on the exhale felt an urge to laugh, big bellows of laughter that would roll out of her like storm clouds. A few tears burned down Olive's face like heat lightning.

Then Olive felt her mother's hands on the side of her face. "You need a good night's sleep," her mother said. Florilla's hands ran over her eyes, over and over, the way she'd soothed all her babies to sleep. "Ma, Regina had a fit, afterwards. When they threw me out they were ripping—"

"Sha, sha sha, sha." Florilla pressed her hands over Olive's eyes. "Ren, blow that candle out." The room went dark. Olive let her mother transfer her to Ren, who led her up the ladder. He helped her undress and shook the covers over her. He rubbed her back until she fell asleep.

Olive woke up hard, as if she'd been smacked. Eyes pulled wide to early grey morning. A bird squawking. Everyone shuffling around downstairs. She yanked herself out of bed, pulled on her dress, and struggled with her boots. She grabbed her basket and stuffed her other dress in it. She climbed down the ladder.

Ren and Magnus were at the table. Florilla was cleaning up after breakfast. They all turned to her. Olive's mother took one look at the basket and busied herself. "And where do you think you're going, Olive Landry Honsinger?" she said.

"To the Shaker women. Maybe they'll know what to do. I should have left last night. I already wasted too much time." She went to the bucket, poured some water, and washed her face in it. Her eyes ached.

She felt Ren's hand on her shoulder. "You want I should come with you?"

"How can you? You got to work." She heard him cross the room and climb the ladder.

Magnus put down his mug of coffee. "What will you get from them Shakers, huh?"

"Maybe they can keep her from prison. Or more likely from an operation or from the lunatic asylum. That's what they've always had in the back of their minds."

Magnus walked over to her. "That's not for rich ladies. They ship her to one of these fancy rest places. Here they stuff 'em full of milk and lamb, and bathe 'em and make 'em sit in chairs in the sun. You don't need this rushing down the mountain." He wiped some water off her face with his sleeve.

"But they said if she didn't get better, they'd send her to the insane asylum. They said they might operate on her."

"If they do this operate, then she'll have her own room as big as a house with a private maid, just as pretty and nice as you most likely."

"You've already forgotten her," Olive said.

One side of Magnus's face jerked. "What's that you want, I to run down there and save her? Carry her away? I ain't a prince." He took a breath, found some reason in his voice. "We can't save rich ladies from rich gentlemen. We can't even save ourselves." Florilla faced the stove, saying nothing. Olive knew Ren was in the loft, listening, waiting.

"I'll see to Regina myself."

Magnus kicked the counter. Water sloshed out of the bowl. "Goddamn it. You got no sense. You're all mixed up in crazy love. You forget your husband needs you."

"He'll just have to do without me, till I get back."

Magnus gave her a glare like broken glass. "You know nothing, trouble-starting girl, trouble to my brother from the start. Now you run off and leave him for a rich girl." He yanked open the front door. The door smacked behind him.

Olive's eyes burned. "I'm not leaving you all," she said to the door. "I'm bringing Regina back so we can start our life in the Finger Lakes." Florilla didn't answer, just stared through the little window over the sink, her hands resting in the greasy, pot-filled water.

Olive saw Ren's long legs hook onto the ladder. He climbed down. He handed her some paper money. "This is for you," he said. "It's yours. From the work down to Crown Point. I been keeping it under the bed for you." Olive took the money and held it in her fist against her chest.

She looked at Ren, who was looking at his boots. She touched his soft hair. "You're good," she said.

"You bring Miss Sartwell back here. We'll give her a bed in the kitchen. We'll string a curtain up so Magnus don't bother her."

Olive smiled. She touched Ren's hand. He didn't look up, but he squeezed her fingers.

Olive got her summer shawl. "Ma," she said.

Her mother turned. She was gripping a jar of molasses to her middle. "It ain't safe to go running off somewheres to help a near stranger. It ain't natural."

"I won't be gone longer than I can help."

"At least eat something before you go. For strength."

"I'm full from the egg and all. Be careful down there to the mines, Renny." He nodded.

She stood by her mother, who was fussing with the lid of the jar. She kissed her mother's ruddy, veined cheek. Her mother still wouldn't face her, so Olive hugged her sideways. Olive wrapped her shawl around her shoulders, picked up her basket.

"Olive, it ain't safe for you to go."

"Ma, I'm not a baby."

"You ain't, but you're carrying one."

Olive looked at Ren.

"Come back," he said.

She opened the door and closed it behind her.

Regina was on the train. On each side of her sat those silent men from the buckboard. One was pudgy, the other had a doglike face. In front of her sat Dr. Corning, taking notes in a little book. His lips moved silently as he wrote. On the other side of the aisle was a woman, a man, and a baby. The man had a very long mustache. For hours no one had taken that seat. People would begin to settle themselves, then notice her bound hands, or maybe smell the dirt and urine and blood, and their faces would contract. They would nudge each other, raise eyebrows, and move on. But finally the coach filled, and the couple with their young baby had nowhere else to sit.

The woman and the baby smelled of sweet-sour milk. Once Regina woke, and the baby was crying. The man and woman looked embarrassed. They switched seats so the woman was walled in by the man. She and her baby disappeared under a cloak, but Regina could hear the sucking sound. Regina thought, I'll take the baby, I'll be the baby, I'll help, just help me.

Another time she woke and felt blood sliding down her legs—there was cramping. She could feel the sodden fabric in her drawers. Dr. Corning was asleep, his mouth open.

She dozed in and out, half aware of her head swaying back and forth on her neck, her jaw loose. Even in sleep she did not try to lean against the two men on either side of her.

Later, when they changed trains in Schenectady, she had a fit. They had seated her on a bench. The men were drinking coffee and eating sandwiches near her. She had been hungry: She could smell the roast beef and butter, and she kept touching the back of her teeth with her tongue. Suddenly her teeth seemed to grow into white pillars. She was her tongue darting between them. Then she opened her eyes. She was staring at some lady's pointed boots moving past. She tasted the blood of her own tongue. She was on the dirty, wooden floor of the station in Schenectady.

"Let's us get her into that train. We'll miss it and be stuck with this for the whole day. Am I right, Doctor?" one of the men said.

The two men carried her by the armpits into the compartment. She slept then, jerking awake when her head grew heavy with sleep and tipped.

They were bumping along in some kind of coach. She could hear the pounding hooves of several horses. She was tilted at a strange angle, but she could see partly out the window. They were in the country. She smelled cow manure. They began to slow down. In front of her was a sprawling lawn bordered by shrubs and then a high, iron gate. Behind the gate and the shrubs she could see a huge, grey stone building, a domed center and long wings on either side.

"Who does that building remind you of?" she said to herself, but the men somehow heard it. They laughed, uneasily.

"Delusion," the doctor said.

They passed through the gate and up a drive that ended at an entrance with high, fluted Greek columns.

As they carried her in, the doctor patted one. "Corinthian," he said. Regina touched the back of her teeth with her bitten tongue.

They dragged her by the elbows into an echoing, high-ceilinged room with stiff-backed chairs and horsehair sofas. They shoved her onto one of the couches. The men sighed, relieved of a burden. They both went over to a sofa on the other side of the room and poked tobacco behind their bottom lips. Corning disappeared.

Regina felt the scratchy sofa on her cheek, so she must have fallen over. She could feel the sticky, dried blood on her leg, and more blood kept leaking. She thought, I am near death now. I hope.

A door opened and the men were called to haul her into the office. Inside stood Dr. Corning. A man sat behind a large desk and another perched on the edge of it, swinging his leg.

Both men breathed in. "This is what you have been referring to as a lady?" the one with the swinging leg said. His voice was slippery with condescension.

"She was convalescing until only yesterday. Then she declined."

"What is your name?" the one behind the desk asked her.

She looked at him.

"Do you know your name?"

She felt that if she spoke her name, the words would take on the strength of Samson. They would shake the building until those two large columns swayed, cracked, and fell. But she could not get her voice out. She cleared her throat. It sounded like the whinny of a horse.

"We will take care of it." The man's voice held something close to pity.

"Her aunt has sent along money for her to buy painting materials and cloth and embroidery thread for fancywork."

The condescending doctor snickered. "Does she do fancywork, Corning?"

"Well, cousin—" Corning laughed nervously"—she did. I assure you hers was a rapid decline." He cleared his throat. "But I will be asked to describe the conditions of her new residence to Mrs. Hammond."

"Tell your Mrs. Hammond that the first ward has linen table-cloths and silver. That they take walks each day and eat wholesome food. Tell her there is a piano."

"Fine, good then. General Hammond will remit payment on the first of the month. They will probably send along her things soon. Ah, is there anything else?"

"Everything seems to be in order," the man behind the desk said.

The other one said, "You might have brought her here before she attempted murder."

"Well, it seemed that she was improving under my—"

"Only an expert can treat lunatics. If I remember correctly, you consider yourself a ladies' specialist."

"Yes, but there is a new book that links epilepsy with—"

"Epilepsy is a form of lunacy. It is a brain disease, as you should know."

"Yes, however, her aunt wouldn't give her up until now."

"Corning, you should prescribe to the patients, not the other way round." He swung his leg, stood up. "We will see what we can do with her. There is medication, you know."

Dr. Corning hovered near her. Finally he patted her on the shoulder. "Good-bye now, Miss Regina. Stay well, or rather—" He turned and left.

The doctor behind the desk laughed a little. "You were hard on your poor country cousin."

The other one laughed back. "Just setting him on the right course." He called for an attendant. "I'm not surprised he became a ladies' specialist. He was always saving damsels in distress when he was a boy. I'm sure he still believes he's Sir Galahad." They both laughed.

"Regardless of that, if this little humiliation serves to keep him away from epileptics, it will be all to the good. Look at that poor creature. If we had been able to treat her sooner, her prognosis might have been hopeful. But now . . ." Regina heard several people at the door, men and women. "Another one for ward eight, I'm afraid," the man behind the desk said.

She was being heaved by her armpits down a long corridor. Her feet skimmed the floor. Her armpits burned from the pressure. They climbed down a floor to another, darker corridor. A woman was ahead of the two men, leading the way. "Where are you taking me?" Regina asked.

"It speaks," said one of the male attendants.

"Ward eight," the other attendant said.

"What does that mean?"

"That means the dangerous and dirties, that's what that means." The woman had a Welsh accent.

"But I know my name," she said. "I know it." She heard her own voice: "Regina Sartwell. Regina Hammond Sartwell." And the words sounded powerful and unfamiliar, like incantations. She waited for the walls to come tumbling down.

Olive could feel the raw blister working on one heel. It wasn't noon yet, but already hazy with heat, and the deerflies kept sticking in her thick hair. Her forehead was wet with sweat. She trudged around the last bend, came down the last dusty incline, and there was the white house. She walked up the stone path. The big cat was dozing in the sun, its tail flicking. It opened an eye and looked at her, closed its eye again. Olive stood on the path to get her breath. As soon as she stopped, sweat began to spout from all her pores.

Purplish grey lavender grew on each side of the door. White butterflies hovered over it. She felt like crushing the lavender and the butterflies.

The short, chubby woman opened the door. "I need to see your, what do you call it, head woman," Olive said.

"You must mean our eldress." The woman brought her into the dining room.

"May I bring you a glass of water?"

"Yes."

The woman came back with a mug of cold well water. "If you would like to wait in our guest room, there is a pitcher and bowl . . ."

"I know I'm all sweat and dirt," Olive said, but she followed her in. When she was alone, Olive poured water from the blue and white pitcher into the blue and white basin. Then she stuck her whole face under. She unbuttoned her dress to her waist and soaked a cloth, then pressed it under her arms and let the water run down her sides. She glanced out the window. A tall woman in netting stood in front of a stack of wooden drawers. There was a dark cloud of bees around her. The fat woman who had let her in went up to the tall woman and spoke. The tall woman moved slowly away from the wooden drawers, the dark cloud thinning and streaming away behind her.

Olive heard footsteps. She pulled her dress up. She smoothed her hair and felt it spring back stubbornly against her hand. Sister Harriet entered the room. The color of her eyes shocked Olive all over again.

"Olive Honsinger. Sit down. I was just seeing to the apiary."

Olive sat. Sister Harriet fitted her wide bottom into a rocker. And kept her see-through baby blue eyes on Olive.

Olive looked down at her hands. "It's Regina, ma'am."

"Call me Harriet."

"It's Regina, Mrs.—Harriet. See, there's this awful doctor up to Hammondville and he was always bothering her, keeping after her, trying to court her or something. And she hated him and then she was sick and he said he was going to inspect her, look her over, or whatever they call it, and then he tried something, to get her, you know, to compromise her, I guess you'd call it. My mother's a good woman and even she called him a drunken devil, which he was. So Regina had this little knife from my brother-in-law, Magnus, and she protected herself with it. And he might die, I guess. It was just in the armpit, but I think that's where the lung is, but anyways, the general has packed her off to a lunatic asylum or had them do an operation on her—I don't know what or which. But I know she's going to need our help." Olive took a breath and looked up.

Harriet sighed, all her wrinkles flat lines on her no-expression face. "Why did that boy give her a knife? You see where weapons lead. Swords into plowshares."

"But if he hadn't, the doctor might have got her."

"Yet is even purity worth another's life?"

"Mrs. Harriet, I mean just plain Harriet, Regina ain't even pure in that way, you might as well know. But Regina would never sit back and let someone take something that's hers to give away."

"Yet there are other ways to do battle besides the sword. However, it has been done, and Regina now needs help, as you say. I suggest you go to Crown Point and find out what has become of her, as the first step. We will take you there. And you may need some financial support. Now, when you speak to Regina's people, let them know that Regina has a place with us. She may seek asylum with the Shakers." Sister Harriet's smile said, no need to thank me. She began to stand.

"Wait, Miss Harriet." Olive pushed her words past her steaming face. "That ain't enough. I need all of you to come see the general. It'd be hard to stand up to a whole bunch of you in your grey dresses and bland faces all the same, like an army."

Harriet shook her head. Her eyes turned downward, the lids making two little frowns. "That is a very romantic rescue you have planned. Unfortunately, summer is the season of vegetable growth. We cannot leave the fruit to rot on the vine. I believe this will be a journey for you and God to make alone."

"But you don't understand. There's nothing I can do alone. I can see that you need some of the women to stay and work the farm. So then, how about just you come along?"

"Olive, we ourselves are alone, in the wilderness. We have no others of our faith for support. My sisters depend on me for guidance." Sister Harriet stopped and thought. "It is not even the guidance. Our mother fashioned me tall and calm, and I believe it is my physical presence that reassures my sisters. As if they were living in the company of an oak tree." She smiled.

Olive spoke to the floor. "Regina hoped to make a home with you, and now she's been snatched away by an evil man and you got too much gardening to give her a hand. That don't sound like Christian mercy to me."

Sister Harriet stared at her, her eyes frowning. Olive stared back. Harriet said, "Let me think a moment."

Olive willed her face to stop flaming. She reached up and untucked her dry lip from her tooth. She kept her breathing even.

"Olive Honsinger, I can do this. I will call the sisters together. I will present your dilemma. If anyone feels called upon to make the journey to Crown Point with you, and perhaps beyond, as you say she may have been placed in an asylum, then that sister may go. That is what seems right to me."

Olive watched Sister Harriet's curving hips move through the doorway. She looked out the window. She could see the glare of her reflection in the glass. "I'm growing bold." She smiled out the window at the drawers full of bees.

Olive waited almost an hour, long enough for her to fall asleep. Then she heard two sets of footsteps walking towards the room. Sister Harriet opened the door. Even her mouth was frowning this time. "Here is Sister Emily. She insists she has been called on to make the journey." Sister Emily edged past Harriet's hips. She was a skinny girl with hunched shoulders, arms crossed over her chest, hair tucked behind big ears, little green eyes that looked like they'd been crying. Sister Emily's face opened in a big, trembling smile.

Twelve

~

REGINA WAS ON a raised cot. Her arms crossed over her front in some shirt that tied under the bed. She felt something brush the cloth that covered her fingers. "What is it?" she asked. Her voice sounded bald in the dark.

"It's one of them rats. I can see it under there, scurrying and nibbling," someone said from the floor near her. She twisted around in her jacket, but she couldn't pull loose. "Get me out of here!" A chorus of rising moans from the floor answered her. "Someone, help."

Her cry echoed from the floor, in a thin voice: "Someone, help?" A light shone in the doorway. The lantern swung across straw mattresses with one or two women on each. Many of the women were chained to the floor with handcuffs. The voice of the Welsh woman called out: "Who's making all the dem noise? I can't sleep in my room all the ways down the hall for it."

"It's me," Regina said. "Will you please remove this shirt contraption? I believe there's a rat under my bed."

The woman laughed. "You really are a lunatic, ain't ya? You come in here dangerous and dirty—we know you've killed a doctor, and now in the middle of the night you wish to be untied 'cause there's a rat under your bed. Wells, I smell a rat. I untie you and you turn on me, am I right? Have I guessed it?"

"No, you haven't guessed it. Why would I want to hurt you?"

"Very tricky. Now just keep your mouth shut so's we can all sleep."

"Will you just untie me? Untie this damn thing."

The woman threaded her way between the pallets and slapped Regina's face.

Regina spit up at her, but most of it fell down on her own face. The woman laughed. Regina laughed back. "Now keep your mouth shut," the woman said. Her voice was less harsh, as if they'd gotten acquainted. Regina watched the lantern sway back towards the door. Her cheek stung, and she wished she could wipe the spit off her nose.

This time she clearly felt the slick hair of the rat's back slide under her fingers. Just the thin piece of cloth in between. She heard it scratching near the top right leg of the cot. Regina clenched her teeth to keep the tears from tipping out. The thin voice rose again from the floor: "Someone?"

Sister Emily stood outside the farmhouse, watching the others load the wagon. She kept her arms crossed over her chest in a defensive position, then she cried out and fled into the house. Olive could hear her rushing up the stairs. Sister Harriet disappeared.

The round woman, whose name turned out to be Sister Tabitha, said she would drive them to Crown Point in the farm wagon. The heat rose as it neared noon and glazed the earth like icing spread on a warm cake. Olive sat by herself on the stone steps near the lavender.

Three Shaker women were loading wooden crates into the back of the wagon. There were crates filled with seed packets, dried bundles of sage, lavender, tansy, wormwood, and yarrow. Other crates held little brown jars of summer-flower honey, syrup of mullein, lily, and marigolds. At the end of the wagon the women crammed in empty burlap sacks and reed baskets.

Sister Tabitha clapped invisible dust off her hands. "We'd best be on our way." She looked up at a window on the second floor, and as if by force of the stare, Olive heard someone moving down through the house. The front door opened, and Sister Emily came out in full Shaker regalia: grey dress, black boots, napkin pinned on her head and a huge bonnet over that, a little poncholike shawl over her rounded shoulders. She smiled that trembly smile at Olive and mumbled some general good-byes as she climbed up on the wagon seat. She mopped at her eyes with a handkerchief and blew her nose.

"Remember God on your journey," the eldress said to Olive. "And Olive Honsinger." For the first time she lost her oak-tree confidence. "Sister Emily has not been happy of late. I don't know if the Shakers will see her again, I don't know why she has been called to this journey or even if . . ." Sister Harriet adjusted her headdress and braced herself with a small laugh. "Here now. A great adventure awaits you. This is life, Olive Honsinger. Glory in it."

The ride was dusty, hot, and bumpy. The jars and bundles jostled each other in the back. The bugs were bad. In the front seat the women's hips pressed damply against each other. Sister Emily sat squeezed between Olive and Tabitha, snuffling into her handkerchief. Finally Olive said, "Do you have hay fever, Emily?" She shook her head. Sister Tabitha was pink and gasping. They rode along Old Furnace Road, past the turnoff to Hammondville. It ran up and disappeared among charred stumps and blackberry brambles. Olive looked away.

In Irondale, Sister Tabitha said, "This seat is too small for three. I believe I am suffering from hay asthma myself. Sister Emily, will you sit in the rear? And don't crush any of those dried bundles, please." Emily crouched in the back the rest of the ride, gripping on to the side, her head snapping over the ruts.

The soot and the smell of the ironworks met them, then faded again as they neared General Hammond's house, protected by trees. Olive jumped down. She forced her voice into normal. "I can meet you at Hoppey's General Store, if that's where you're going."

Sister Tabitha nodded. Emily was up on her haunches in the back.

"Do you need her to help unload?" Olive asked Tabitha.

"No. The clerks help." Sister Emily jumped out. She smoothed her traveling outfit. Sister Tabitha turned the horses.

All the windows looked like spying eyes. Emily stood in the dust of the road, a little distance away. "Shouldn't we go ask for Regina Sartwell?" Her voice was a whisper.

"You go to the front. I'll go to the kitchen door. That way, the general and Mrs. Hammond won't know I'm here. Maybe Regina is inside and I can walk right into her room."

Sister Emily looked at her shoes. "I never been to the front of a house like that," she whispered. "What should I say?"

"Just say you're from the Shakers and you're inquiring after Regina 'cause she never shown herself yesterday." Emily repeated the words in a whisper to herself, but she didn't move. "Go on now, it'll be all right." Olive put her hand on Emily's back.

Emily squealed and skittered away from her. "You give me a start. I'm ever so ticklish."

"Fine, I won't touch you, just go." Head down, hands folded, Sister Emily walked towards the lion's-head knocker.

Olive's nervous smile came back, widening for no one but herself. She knocked on the kitchen door. Her neck shivered like someone was sneaking up behind her.

SuSu opened the door. When she recognized Olive, she closed it. Mrs. Cutter pulled it open again. "Olive! Mrs. Fisk got most of yer stuff—she packed it all up. Just wait here." Olive smelled cinnamon and blueberries. Mrs. Cutter was back in a minute. She handed her a parcel wrapped neatly in brown butcher paper.

"Wait, Mrs. Cutter, I need to know about—"

"SuSu, bang on that pot real loud if someone comes into the kitchen. Bang on the pot real loud now, honey, if someone comes in the kitchen." Mrs. Cutter looked behind her, then pulled Olive round the back side of the house. She pressed against the lilac bush. She whispered, and her spit hit Olive on the neck. "It's bad, Olive, real bad. You don't want to be seen. Of course, he's not here right now, but he could come back any time, you know that. He's always in and out."

"Why, what's happened?"

"The young doctor's near death. At first he seemed to rally, but now I believe the wound's gone bad. His room smells of it, that I know. And it sounds like he's strangling—real ugly. I wonder every time he grabs another breath. I heard the general speaking of you and it weren't complimentary. And Mrs. Hammond has had a shock and won't leave her room, or so she says."

"But what about Regina?"

Mrs. Cutter pressed even farther into the lilac bush. Her little eyes were all wide and her eyebrows pressed up near her hairline. "They've sent her off to a lunatic asylum, the one in Utica. Fisk says she looked awful, like she was a real lunatic, when they packed her off. Like an animal, Fisk says. And Fisk says they wouldn't let her clean Miss Regina up except put her in an old black dress and wipe her face. But no one's supposed to know that. The general wants people to believe she gone off to Saratoga to the baths, and the doctor is dying of some illness, but I don't think they've invented which illness yet."

The sound of her own voice seemed to calm Mrs. Cutter, and it rose into her normal range. She moved until she was standing beside the bush instead of in it. "The paper was all set to publish an article about the whole mess tomorrow, not mentioning names, but clear exactly who it was, but the general stormed over there early this morning and put a stop to it. Seems the editor got stubborn. I heard he's just going to print a big black space on the front page tomorrow where the article should've been. If you ask me, that editor is playing with his future."

Olive thought she heard the front door opening. "I got to go. Thank you for the news."

227

Mrs. Cutter grabbed her hand. "We'll miss you." Her eyes got teary. "Wait here a minute." She waddled into the house and came out with an edge of baked piecrust, covered in cinnamon and sugar. She handed it to Olive. She waited until Olive put it in her mouth, then she nodded, sad and satisfied.

Olive hurried away with a mouth full of sweet pastry and her parcel pressed to her chest.

Sister Emily was crouched in the ditch by the road with her dress hiked up. When she saw Olive she jumped up and brushed her skirt down. "Had to go. Always got to go when I'm nervous."

Olive started walking towards town. "Did they tell you anything?"

"That housekeeper took the words right out of me with her 'Speak up, speak up!' And then when I finally drew courage and spoke up, she said, 'Quiet down, Mrs. Hammond is ill.' Whoever Mrs. Hammond is, I don't know. She says to me that the doctor in the house is gravely ill of a fever, and that Miss Regina Sartwell has gone to Saratoga for a rest. Is that the same doctor Regina Sartwell stabbed with a knife?"

Olive nodded. "Regina's been sent to the state lunatic asylum." Olive stopped in the middle of the road to get her breath, but she gasped even more than before. She put her hands on her hips. She pulled her face long to keep the tears back, but they came anyway.

Sister Emily jerked back as if Olive had touched her. "Why are you crying?" she whispered.

"I'm crying—" Olive knew she was spitting the words out in a nasty way, but it was the only way to keep her voice strong "—because Regina is so far away. And I'm crying 'cause I have to go far away now too. To find her." Olive's voice shuttered, then the tears stopped, and she said in a plain voice: "I never been to Utica."

Sister Emily crouched down in the dirt of the road. She picked up a handful of dirt and pebbles and scattered it. She stood up. "I been to Utica."

"You have?"

"I been most everywhere. Utica, Schenectady, Albany, Ticonderoga, Fort Ann, Lake George, Glens—"

"How come?"

"With my pop. I'll go to Utica with you."

"All right."

"All right," Sister Emily said.

They started walking again, Olive limping from her blister. "Let me borrow that old handkerchief," Olive said.

"You got the hay fever?" Emily said. Olive smiled.

Martha Hoppey met them at the door to the dry goods store. "Olive Honsinger! You're just the girl I wanted to see." She pulled Olive over to the pickle barrel. "The whole town's talking, and you're the one that knows the truth." The sour, salty smell of the pickles made Olive realize how hungry she was. "Is it true she's a crazed murderer? To think I fitted a dress on her. With a mouth full of sharp pins, too!" Martha fished into the barrel and pulled out a pickle. She bit off the top and then passed it to Olive. "Did she ever try to murder you?" Olive ate up the pickle. Martha handed her another one. She ate that too.

"Can I have another?" Martha fished in the brine and handed one over. "It's for my friend. Good-bye, Martha."

"But—"

Olive met Tabitha and Emily out at the wagon. There were still two crates in the back. "Wouldn't sell?" Olive said.

Sister Emily looked at the ground, but Sister Tabitha smiled at her. "On your way to Utica you will stop off in Schenectady and drop off these boxes. You may spend the night with a friend of the Shakers and make your way to Utica the next day."

"I don't know about that," Olive said.

"Surely you will need a place to stay. You cannot make Utica today. Why, it's nearly five o'clock." She heaved herself up into the wagon. "And there is nothing wrong with performing a homely task in the midst of a great adventure."

Sister Tabitha had to drive them down to the lake to catch the Delaware and Hudson. The station sat in the middle of the ironworks. Black clouds of soot and noise belched out across the long, blue expanse of Lake Champlain. Olive looked across to Vermont, where she had never been. Emily hunched over her pickle, caught up in the dilemma of eating in public.

Two hours later, Olive and Emily were on the train. The porter had shoved the heavy boxes under their seats. The sky glowed orange over the lake. They wouldn't arrive in Schenectady until after dark. The line of cars chugged away from Crown Point, south along the lake, a direction Olive had never gone before.

Two female attendants unhooked Regina from the jacket that held her. They led her down to the basement, to a room with five large wooden tubs in it. Mold grew in the cracks between the slate floor. A woman lay in one of the tubs, her head thrown back, her eyes staring. She looked dead.

"What are you going to do?" Regina's voice echoed.

"Clean you up." The attendant yanked at the buttons of Regina's dress, then pulled it off her shoulders and down. Regina had no underthings on. She crossed her arms over her chest. "If you will give me soap and a cloth, I will clean myself."

"None of that. We've been told what you done. Anyways, the ward doctor is coming through today and we don't want all this blood and piss on you. You stink."

"Get in, now," the other one said.

Regina lowered her foot into the water. Gooseflesh shivered over her. She pulled her foot out. "It's too col—" One of the attendants hit her hard in the back with the flat of her hand. Regina grunted and fell forward. She felt a hot scrape as her other leg dragged over the side, then the shock of the cold stopped her breath. She came up squealing.

The two attendants laughed. "Dunk down now, so's your hair gets wet, too." Regina tried to climb out of the tub. The attendant put her hand on Regina's head and shoved her back down into the cold. Regina jerked around trying to get out from under the hand, panicked that she was being drowned like the woman in the other tub. Finally the hand slipped off. She came up coughing and sputtering.

"You can get out now." They held up some kind of sack dress for her to put on. Regina dropped back into the freezing water. She held her breath, her cheeks puffed out. She opened her eyes and saw the wavering slats of the barrel. She pressed her legs against one side and her butt against the other, wedging herself under. There was a splash. A hand fumbled for her chin and began pulling her up. She clamped her chin to her neck and pressed her feet harder into the sides. Her chest hurt. She felt another hand dig into the roots of her hair. They dragged her up. Hauled her out by her armpits: dropped her on the slate floor. Her hip burned as it hit the slate. They were all breathing hard. One of them gasped, "I hate this job." They pulled her to her feet and shimmied the sack over her head.

Later, Regina began going into fits. They came like waves crashing over her, again and again, and she welcomed the jolt and terror, because once she was down, through the raving tunnel, the company comforted her. Her thin-armed woman was no longer mysterious. She was just a girl named Ann. Together they cast a velvet net, hauling in teacups full of mother's milk and oranges, anything they needed. Her best friend Ann. Her only friend Ann.

Emily dozed, but Olive watched as the landscape turned from orange to navy blue to black, afraid they would miss their stop if she slept. Her shoulders and neck ached by the time the conductor called, "Schenectady, Schenectady, next stop Schenectady."

The conductor helped them from the train to the platform. Immediately the sultry air of a hot night puffed around them. A porter dropped the two crates of honey, seeds, and medicine at their feet. Olive thought she heard a crack and hoped it wasn't a honey jar. He stood in front of them, aggressively close, his face passive. Emily handed him a coin. He disappeared.

They guarded their boxes as people streamed by them. There was yelling, about trains and pretzels. Men were threading through the crowd, offering rides. One looked her up and down, glanced at Sister Emily, and moved on, asking a woman with a huge bustle, "Ride, ma'am?" On one side of the raised platform Olive could see the dark Mohawk River, and on the other, Schenectady tumbled out below her.

Olive looked over at Emily: She was groggy, one side of her face impressed with the nap of the velvet seat she had been sleeping on. "I guess we're here then." There was no emotion in Emily's voice. Olive didn't answer. "I guess we better get a cab. I been where we're going."

"Good," Olive said.

"Want I should find a man?"

"Yes," Olive said. Emily walked over to five men who lounged at the edge of the platform on an empty baggage trolley. She scanned all of them and picked out the only one who wasn't chewing tobacco. Olive didn't hear what Emily had to say, but the man walked over, tossed the crates onto a trolley, and began rolling it so briskly down the platform that Olive and Emily had to rush to keep up. In the main station throngs of people moved past long wooden benches. Emily grabbed on to Olive and then on to an edge of the man's coat with her other hand. The man didn't turn around.

Out on the street he loaded them into a hansom harnessed to a swayback horse with blinders on. The man drove from a raised seat behind them, down a wide, cobbled road called State Street with gaslights and tall buildings. They passed The Hotel Schenectady— all windows and chandeliers, with fancy gentlemen and ladies eating inside. Olive glanced into an alley and watched three dogs attacking a mountain of garbage. The streets were full, though it must have been ten at night, and the man drove recklessly, yelling at people trying to cross the street. He stopped for a few minutes to have a talk with another cab driver. Then he turned down Altamount Avenue. It curved away from State Street at a confusing angle. They turned down another road, Olive didn't catch the name, and she thought, I could never get back to the station now, and I don't know where we're going either.

But Emily's pointy face had a clever look. She mumbled the names of the streets under her breath. Once she called out to the driver, "Turn here." They rode down smaller streets, the houses shuttered and dark, the road empty. The sound of hooves on cobblestone gave way to hooves on dirt. The horse slowed to a trudge. The driver stopped in front of a brick building with a red-lettered sign on the front: Anthony's Dry Goods Store, and underneath in green letters, We Sell Everything. Sister Emily paid off the driver. He unloaded the boxes and left them on the dark street.

As soon as they stood in front of the shuttered store, Emily whispered, "I got to pee."

Olive didn't like the empty street. Across the road a pig was snuffling in a dark pile. Not far enough away, she could hear young men shouting.

"This is it," Emily said.

Olive waited for Emily to knock, but she stood there, pressing her legs together, so Olive banged on the door. They waited, then Olive banged harder. The pig raised its snout, snorted. She saw a light moving through the store and then behind the door a man's rough voice: "Who is it?"

Olive looked at Emily, but Emily said nothing. Olive said, "The Shakers sent us, sir. Sister Harriet from Paradox." The door opened. The man had on a clean, white apron stretched tight over a barrel chest that looked as if it had grown with age to include a hard, round belly. He was tall, with wavy, grey hair and little round glasses.

"Emily Ciminiski!" He shook her by her narrow shoulders. "You look much improved. Don't regret it for a minute, do you?" Emily crossed her legs and grimaced and didn't introduce Olive.

"I'm Olive Honsinger, sir. We brung two crates of various goods from the Shakers."

"Pleased to meet you. I was just sitting down to my supper. But there's enough for all."

They stood beside full shelves that smelled slightly of mildew and flour, while Mr. Anthony heaved the crates into the store. Then they all climbed the stairs to his apartment.

They ate ham with quince jelly, scalloped potatoes, and coffee off his small round kitchen table. His kitchen was tiny, and surrounded on all sides by clean, stocked shelves. Above them huge cast-iron pans hung from curved hooks. The steaming food made them sweaty and tired. Mr. Anthony insisted they call him Brother Joshua. He said that he had been a Shaker once, and Olive imagined him in a long grey dress with a napkin on his head. He asked Emily many questions about the Shakers and didn't wait for the answers. Each question was a stepping-off place for a sea of his own memories, each kept afloat with words like "silence," "simplicity," and "beauty." "It was a simple life, but the beauty and the silence sustained me," or "Once I stood outside the window and watched a Shaker girl ready our simple repast. Her gentle hands her grey dress, the pewter dishes—there was a simple beauty to it I cannot describe."

After supper, he served them hot milk and honey by the fire in his crowded parlor. An enormous brocade sofa took up one whole wall of the room. Two overstuffed chairs were jammed into the other corners. Without introduction, he began to sing in a rich baritone. His voice became pure mahogany as he turned the words out: "Sisters, now our meeting is over, sisters, we must part, and if I never see you anymore, I'll hold you in my heart. And we're bound for the shore, and we're bound for the shore . . . to have peace forevermore." Olive leaned her head back against the hard couch. She closed her eyes and held the empty cup of milk.

Emily and Olive shared his sleigh bed with the headboard that curved all the way up to the ceiling. Brother Joshua slept on the hard couch. Street sounds settled over Olive in hot layers: the huff of an engine far away, the snort of a horse, glass breaking, a man and woman arguing.

"Emily, how do you know Mr. Anthony?"

"He's the one introduced me to our eldress."

"Was that here?"

"This was the last place I lived before the Shakers took me in."

"You mean this store?"

"Near here. A few blocks is all. I shopped here for the place I worked."

"What kind of place was that?"

"A bad one."

"What was wrong with it?"

"Olive Honsinger, are you quick to judge?"

"I don't think so. Nobody ever asked me to judge them, so I'm not used to it."

"My pop was a peddler. We're Polish. Well, he was Polish. I never seen the old country. We had a red wagon with our name on it in gold letters—Ciminiski. The dots over the *i*'s were gold stars." She was quiet, staring at the ceiling, rubbing the sheet between two fingers. Then she said, "We traveled all over this part of the state. Our wagon was chock-full of necessaries. Pots, pans, spices, dishes, needles, oh, thimbles, can't even name 'em all." Emily turned on her side and rested on her arm; her skin-and-bones elbow touched Olive's cheek. "But we also carried wind-up music boxes and oh, toys and ribbons, and some tassels, canary yellow ones, I ain't sure what those was good for. My pop loved to spread out all the pretty things for a lady, right on her kitchen table, and we would all marvel at 'em. Maybe he'd give her a ribbon, just for nothing. We sure loved pretty things."

"I love pretty things, too," Olive said.

"I thought so," Emily said. "We slept in grand hotels sometimes, if we had the money, and sometimes we ate in restaurants too."

"But how did you meet Mr. Anthony?" Olive asked.

"Mr. Anthony bought thread from my pop. They was friendly, not bosom-friend friendly, but Pop played the fiddle and Mr. Anthony likes to sing. Pop died when we was in Schenectady."

"That's a shame," Olive said. "My father died too."

"That's the thing about parents, ain't it?" Emily said. "They most likely die. That's why it's good to have a friend. Mr. Anthony helped me sell Pop's things—the wagon with the four golden stars, our horse Yola, the harmonica, everything. I didn't know what to keep, so alls I kept was a real gold thimble that belonged to my grandmother Ciminiski in Poland who I never saw, and my pop's shoes." Emily Ciminiski sniffed in. "Are you tired of my life yet?"

"If you don't finish telling me, I swear I'll stay awake all night wondering about it."

"Well, then. Let me see, I had the money and Mr. Anthony found me a little room in a boardinghouse. He said I should go to school, but I never gone before, so I wasn't going to start now. I sat on my bed a lot. I kept my pop's shoes under the bed in a box and I'd take 'em out and stare at 'em sometimes. Then I started shopping. I bought myself a tea set with bluebirds on it, lace curtains, a yellow canary in a golden cage. Oh, I got me some pretty things. I bought this lacquered box for my pop's shoes. It had dragons painted on, from China, I think. Pretty soon my money was gone. So I got me a job in a bad house."

"What do you mean?"

"You know, a house of ill reputes. I just cleaned and bought groceries. Nothing more. Mr. Anthony said not to work there, but at first it wasn't bad. I moved all my pretty things into my little room there off the kitchen. The painted ladies were my friends.

"But soon when I was fourteen I started whoring myself. One day Mr. Anthony sees me on the street and he asks why don't I do the errands no more. I tell him, and he gets all choked up and says, 'You come down to the store tomorrow, I want you to meet someone.' And next day there was the eldress and she told me come live with them. She told me to come to them as unencumbered as the day I was born. It's clean and warm and safe, she says. I give all my pretty things to the whores. But I put on my papa's shoes over my own, and I sewed the gold thimble into the hem of my dress. And then I gone off with the eldress."

"It must have been hard to give away all those things you loved so much."

"It was worth it. To get away from the men."

"Emily Ciminiski, I'm glad you came."

"I didn't mind." Emily breathed in and out through her nose and closed her eyes. "Good night, now."

Brother Joshua woke them early and insisted they eat a huge breakfast. Hot air was already gusting through the windows, meeting the fire in the stove and the steam from the oatmeal and eggs and bacon. Olive kept glancing at the clock and wondering, "How long will it take to get back to the station?" while Brother Joshua laughed at his own jokes. Finally he belched behind his napkin, said he supposed he must take them away. He got his wagon and drove them back through the streets. There was a traffic jam on State Street, caused by a milk wagon that had cracked its axle. Drivers were cursing. Horses whinnied nervously and stamped. The sun glared hazily. Then a gang of teenage boys descended, crowding from buggy to buggy, demanding money. Olive pressed her back against the seat. Brother Joshua gripped his whip tightly and mumbled to himself. Emily did not seem interested. When the boys were only three carriages away, traffic began moving again, and Olive watched their ugly, jeering faces as she rode by.

Brother Joshua insisted on seeing them onto the train, and then when he'd found someone to watch his horse, and they were walking through the station, he found out for the first time that they were going to Utica. He became confused and intransigent and must be explained to. He kept saying, "Now, you're not running away from the Shakers, are you? I haven't been aiding fugitives, have I?"

"No, no, sir. We're visiting a friend in Utica. Sister Harriet knows all about it," Olive repeated again and again. Emily said nothing.

Brother Joshua asked Olive why she wasn't wearing her bonnet and dress. He asked Emily how she was getting on in Paradox.

They stood in a line in front of a desk. Finally Brother Joshua asked the fat gentleman when the next train to Utica was. "Right now, sir. Track ten."

"And the next one?" Brother Joshua asked.

The man took time looking it up. "Next one would be four this afternoon, sir."

Olive looked wildly around the station, saw a sign for track ten in the far corner. "Thank you, sir," she said, grabbing her basket out of Joshua's hands. She and Emily ran through the station, dodging slow-moving people. The train was already huffing and steaming on the track, but a conductor pulled them on just as it was jerking forward.

Olive sighed. "I'm glad to be rid of him."

Emily nodded. "Pop and me always felt the same way. Not that he ain't trying to be nice."

They couldn't find seats together. Olive spent some of her precious money on the ticket, round trip. She listened as three seats down Emily bought a one-way.

They reached Utica at high noon on what had become a stunningly sunny day. Some moved sluggishly in the heat while others were caught behind them, cursing softly and trying to squeeze around. Women whipped fans around; children whined sweatily. The Utica station was even bigger than the Schenectady one, and not raised, so that they entered Utica in the midst of its crowded center. Olive's neck hurt. She felt pummeled. They couldn't find a hansom cab driver to help them, so they walked out onto the street. Somewhere in this steaming city was Regina.

"We could stay there." Emily pointed across the street: The Utica Hotel. It was the twin of the one in Schenectady. A man in a red suit with gold epaulets stood in the doorway.

"I don't think we have to stay anywhere," Olive said.

"We surely won't find Regina, get her out, and catch a train back to Crown Point, all in one day."

"That place looks too expensive."

"My papa and I stayed there once. It ain't so bad. Anyway, I got fifty-eight dollars from the Shakers."

"But that's their money."

"Our money. I'm a Shaker too, you know."

"I forgot."

"We could bring Regina Sartwell there, before we go home," Emily said.

"It doesn't seem right, somehow."

"You'll like it," Emily said, already crossing the street.

The man at the desk eyed them strangely. A boy insisted on carrying their things up. Emily paid him off.

The room was heavily decorated in brown velvet: bedspread, drapes, and chair. The dark fabric seemed to be storing heat. Olive opened a window, but more heat and soot and noise came in. "We need to cool ourselves down," Emily said. She led Olive down the hall to a door with a painted silouette of a lady on it.

Inside the little room was a huge, claw-footed white bathtub with brass fixtures. Two cherubs blowing trumpets sat on a shelf above the tub. The room smelled of roses. Emily closed the door and latched it. She turned one of the brass handles on the tub and brown water came out. "You got to let it run awhile," she said. When the water ran clear she put a china stopper in the drain, and the tub began to fill. Olive stood on the pink braided rug and watched. Emily hummed under her breath. She took a bottle out of a mirrored cabinet and poured some liquid under the faucet. Bubbles began to rise out of the water. She took another bottle and shook it over the tub. "Rose oil," she said to Olive.

Olive was sniffing some soap shaped like flowers. She looked up and Emily was standing naked in front of her.

Olive looked down. "I'll wait in the room."

Emily stepped into the tub. "Get in."

"I don't think there's room for both of us."

"You must be used to bathing in a tin pot. Get in."

Olive turned her back and took her dress off, pinned her hair up, sunk into the warm, rose-oily water. Emily's slippery calf rested against hers. Olive pulled her leg away. "Sorry."

Emily drooped her leg back against Olive's. "Don't worry, it's only when I get scaredy that I can't abide being touched. I used to take a bath like this every day," Emily said. "After we save Miss Sartwell, I expect you'll both be joining the Shakers."

"Oh, no. We got a plan." Olive sunk to her chin, her legs sliding to Emily's shoulder. "Regina's father is giving us money to buy a little farm. It's in a place called Geneva, near Seneca Lake."

"What's the farm like?"

Olive closed her eyes, rested her head back. "White, with a porch swing, an orchard out back. A flowering quince bush in the yard. Red shutters . . ."

"Were you born lucky?"

Olive smiled. "This tub feels so good. My feet were aching."

"Think there's room for one more on that farm out to the lake?"

"That's up to Regina, Miss Emily."

Emily sighed. "Your hair's so pretty."

"Anyone would feel pretty in a bath like this. I wish my ma could try it. I wish Ren could try it."

"Is that your man?"

"Uh-huh. My husband."

"You got a baby in there, don't you?"

Olive opened her eyes. "Why do you say that?" She pulled her knees into her stomach.

"You got the look. Believe me, at the bad house, we got to keep an eye out for the look. Breasts swollen, skin blotchy, stomach bulging already. But you knew, am I right? I can tell by the way you're careful with yourself, like you were carrying a china cup." Someone knocked on the door. Emily stood, suds sliding down her toothpick legs. "Got to get out." She stepped over the side, wrapped herself in a fat towel.

"In a minute," Olive said. She stayed just where she was, her chin on her knees, her body curled around her belly in a tight circle.

When Olive returned to the room, Emily was stretched out naked on the brown bedspread. "Wouldn't you be surprised if there was a knock on the door and in come Brother Joshua, singing away."

"We should find Regina," Olive said.

"Now?" Emily sighed.

"That's what we come for." Emily dressed and followed Olive downstairs. Olive prodded Emily until she asked the man at the front desk about getting to the asylum. The man looked haughty and tight-lipped. But he said he could order a conveyance for them.

Emily nodded, but Olive said, "You mean a private one?"

"Of course, ma'am."

"How far is it?"

"I've never been, I assure you, but I would estimate a half hour's drive outside the city."

"Isn't there a public coach?"

"I will inquire." He went in the back and talked to someone, then returned and told them where to meet it. They walked to a coach station, and waited outside until one came by that went out to the asylum. Several people got in, all looking disheveled, hot, and sad. They rattled out of the city into farmland. Olive breathed in the manure smell, watched the open space, and felt calmer. Emily whispered, "If we'd rented our own cab, it'd been nicer for Regina Sartwell on the way home."

"Regina isn't as particular as you think," Olive said. They came to a huge stone building with iron gates. The driver said a coach would return in two hours' time.

They walked into a large, empty room with a domed ceiling. Olive looked over at Emily. She had begun blowing her nose and walking awkwardly, squeezing her crotch.

"Not now, Emily."

Emily nodded.

Olive sighed. "Is there any rhyme or reason to when you get scaredy?"

Emily shrugged.

"I guess I can't count on you to speak up for us, then?"

Emily shook her head.

There was an office, which the small, straggling group from the coach filed in and out of. Some were led away and others sat down on the horsehair couches around the front room. One woman opened up a basket, took out some sausage, and began to eat it. The man next to her whispered something in her ear. She gestured to the right wing with her sausage. "Cherry's in there; that's the girls' side." The spicy smell drifted across the room. The last person was just filing out of the office. Olive walked across the floor, Emily trailing behind, stepping on her heels. Their shoes clicked loudly on the marble.

A man sat behind a little desk in a little room, writing something.

Olive said, "We're here to see someone, sir."

The man looked Emily up and down and sighed wearily. "Not the prevention of cruelty society again. Don't you people ever go on holiday?"

"No, that's not us, sir. We are here to see a friend who is staying with you," Olive said.

He still seemed weary. "Who is it?"

"Miss Regina Hammond Sartwell."

The man went to a glossy wooden file cabinet and slipped his fingers over papers. He stopped, went back and forth for a while, then pulled out a file. "Her guardian is General Hammond of Crown Point," he said, accusingly.

"But. I'm her maid, from the general's house. We'd just like to visit with her." He didn't reply. "I been sent."

"Have you a letter?"

"A letter? No."

"She's a violent patient. She isn't allowed visitors, excepting her guardian."

"But." The man went back to writing. Olive felt her eyes stinging. "Excuse me for bothering you again, sir, but isn't there someone we could talk to, to get permission? I think Miss Regina would be happier if she could see us."

The man sighed, gritted his teeth. "You'll need an appointment with the superintendent, then."

"How do we do that, sir?"

He sighed again. He looked through his book. "Next Thursday, three P.M."

Over a week away.

"Sir, I work for the general, and we can't be away that long. We got to see her tomorrow, at the latest."

He huffed, flipped through his book. "I can squeeze you in day after tomorrow at ten in the morning. I can only give you seven minutes, though, and the superintendent will have to go without his coffee break to do it. Who do you think will hear about that?"

There was nothing else to do but wait for the coach for an hour and a half in the large, empty room. Olive whispered to Emily, "I feel as if we should shout her name, just to let her know we're here."

"They'd kick us out sure or maybe lock us in."

They returned to their broiling room in the broiling city. Emily took a nap. Olive tried to find a park. She discovered one with a large monument of a soldier holding a sword at its center. She sat on a bench by herself, near the tip of the sword, until a man tried to talk to her, then she walked back to the hotel. She became a little lost. When she finally got to the room she tried to open the window for some air, but it now seemed stuck. She banged at the frame. Behind her, she heard Emily's sleepy voice. "Did you have a nice walk?"

Olive rested her forehead against the window. "It's too hot, and

I'm the wrong one to help Regina. Saving her calls for never giving up. It goes against my grain."

"It's 'cause you got a baby in there. It makes you go moody."

That night, Olive dreamt of finding Regina. She was ushered into a sunny room with a flock of fancy ladies sitting about, embroidering, tittering at a story Regina was telling. Regina looked up, a little surprised and just a little irritated that her story had been interrupted. What are you doing here? she asked.

Someone had forced a spoon into Regina's mouth. She felt the bitter click of the metal on her teeth and then powder scalded down her throat. They choked her on that white powder more than once. With the powder inside her, everything slowly turned solid and everyday grey.

Regina was handcuffed to a straw pallet, wearing a sweat-stinking sack. On one side of her lay a melancholy opium addict, and on the other, a teenaged girl who claimed to have been born in the asylum to a lunatic mother, who claimed there was nothing wrong with her, and who claimed to be drugged every night and raped by the doctors. In another life Regina might have been fascinated by the opium addict, whose hair was shorn jagged, as if she had done it herself, or by the young girl who spent all day telling her story and endeavoring to stay clean, brushing her dress off, wiping her face with a piece of cloth, and sighing over and over again that she hurt between her legs. But now, Regina was deeply uninterested. She snapped at both of them and at Mrs. Wickner, the Welsh attendant, who seemed to be amused by it.

For breakfast, Regina ate potatoes and bread. For dinner, radishes and bread pudding; and for supper, bread and butter. She already felt puffy and potato like.

After what felt like weeks of this fitless life, Mrs. Wickner told Regina she hadn't had an attack in twenty-four hours—"a bloomin' miracle," she said. "Them doctors know their job, they do." She unlocked the handcuff, told her, "Mind yourself," and let her loose in the ward. Regina found a stretch of wall that wasn't cluttered with beds. She walked the length of it: eleven steps.

She took up pacing. Of course, she remembered the lioness in the zoological gardens in New York. That cat had a slinking, eel-like grace, its head facing its audience, swinging. Regina slunk her shoulders and swung her arms, grimaced and stared. It relieved boredom to become the lioness. Eleven steps there, eleven steps back. If she fumbled and came up twelve, she growled. It worked off the potatoes.

A woman shuffled into her path. She just stood there, with her frying pan face, right at step nine. Regina glided sideways to avoid her and hissed in her ear, "Out of my way, or I'll scratch you with my claws." The blob woman refused to move, so on the way back, at step two, Regina gave her a hard shove in the back. The blob stumbled forward, mewed, and was out of her path. Regina swung her head around. Others had seen. They giggled nervously.

They left her alone until dinner. She ate her bread pudding on her pallet, hid the radishes underneath. The opium addict stayed as far away from her as she could, but the teenaged girl said, "Mrs. Gottfried's a killer, too. She says you can't have all that space to yourself." Regina growled.

The girl sang, "I dropped the baby in the dirt, I asked the baby did it hurt, And all the little thing could say, Was wah, wah, wah!"

After dinner and some pacing, a big woman with fat ankles stood in her pacing space. She folded her meaty arms and wouldn't look at Regina. Regina paced up to her and shoved. The woman looked surprised and stumbled back, almost fell. Regina heard Mrs. Wickner say, "What's this now?" The woman shook her head and charged Regina. They fell on the floor. The woman was hitting Regina in the stomach, which hurt and made her gag, but Regina hardly noticed. She was too busy pulling hair, raking the face, banging the head by the ears, kicking and kicking at a shin. She could not hurt her enough.

Regina kept trying to get in as much hurt as she could before they were pulled apart, but no one pulled them apart, and finally the big woman heaved herself away on all fours. Regina tried to catch some air. She thought she might throw up. She looked around. Mrs. Wickner was laughing. "You're a tough one, you are. You bested Mrs. Gottfried. Best out of three, though, I say."

Thirteen

OLIVE HEARD SOMEONE say it was the hottest summer in a hundred years. Children sagged on stoops. Olive saw an old man wobble on his ivory-topped cane, then keel over in a faint. Stray dogs panted in the shade of trash cans. It rained the first morning after her visit to the asylum. The brief, thunderous downpour steamed away within the hour.

The heat enveloped her in its warm sea, lulling her until she was dull with lack of desire for anything but rest. It took all her will to roll off the bed in the morning, to remember Regina.

Olive and Emily took their meals in the ladies' dining room: "Magnificence on a modest scale for women unaccompanied." Three times a day they sat at the same table and ate heavy food with French names. Every dish had a sauce: raspberry, cream, gravy. Olive felt queasy and sleepy afterwards, but Emily sopped up everything with her roll, picked up her grey skirts after the meal, and waded away from the table. The combination of heat and sauce seemed to give Emily buoyancy.

Dinner was crowded with chatting women in enormous hats, but at supper there were only three couples. Three old ladies still had the sloping posture and billowing dress fashionable before the War Between the States. An old woman and a young girl argued through each meal. And two middle-aged ladies wore clothing so constructed, Olive thought they must surely die of heat.

Between meals, Emily wanted to window-shop. Emily could stand for half an hour in front of each store. Olive shifted from foot to foot, glancing at passersby, hot and cranky, ankles swelling. Late in the afternoon, beside a uniform store, Emily found a little shop that sold curios. She said some of the keepsakes in the window were Polish. She went in. Olive followed her. Emily hopped around, her head cocked to one side, gazing at every glittery item in the room. She twittered. Then her hand latched on to something and flew it up to the counter. The round-cheeked woman behind the glass case seemed happily dumbfounded at this greedy little Shaker.

Emily picked out six handkerchiefs embroidered with peacocks and a shawl embroidered with blue birds. Two pillowcases with lace tatting. Dangling red glass earrings. Green glass earrings. Yellow glass earrings. Seven pairs of kid gloves in seven different colors—periwinkle blue, magenta, emerald green, white, black, tan, and clay.

Olive did not know what to say. She helped her carry the parcels back to the hotel, while Emily hummed and babbled. Emily said hello and smiled to people who passed. She told Olive the green glass earrings were for her, to go with her orange hair, as well as three of the handkerchiefs. Olive didn't even bother to tell Emily she didn't have pierced ears. The red glass earrings were for Regina Sartwell. It was too hot to say anything. Apparently Emily must keep all seven pairs of gloves as she had always wanted to wear a different color each day. Back at the hotel room, Emily spread out the shawl so she could gaze at it. She generously laid the two pairs of earrings on Olive's dresser, glancing at her modestly. She pushed back her straw bonnet and slipped the yellow earrings on her jug ears. She inched on two different-color gloves at once and twirled her wrists in front of the mirror.

Olive was sunk in the brown velvet armchair, sweating. "Will Sister Harriet let you keep all that?"

Emily shrugged a little. Sniffed.

"What will you do with it all, then? And are you sure Harriet wanted you to spend all their money on trinkets? What about Regina's ticket?"

"I got twenty-nine dollars left."

"And you haven't paid the hotel bill or the return tickets."

Emily shrugged. "I guess I'll just give this away if I go back."

"What do you mean *if* you go back?"

Emily was having a hard time pulling the gloves off her moist hands. "I ain't sure if I'm cut out for a Shaker."

Olive snorted. "But you're spending their money. What else would you do, anyways?"

"I don't know." Emily stroked the blue glove against her cheek. "I feel safe there—that's nice. There's plenty of food. I'm learning the violin. That's nice—Pop would like that. But all the sisters are older than me. I'm lonely for a friend, and I'm lonely for pretty things. I think I could live without one or the other but not without both." She reached over and touched the red earrings. "If Regina Sartwell goes back to the Shakers, maybe I will too."

"But I told you she's going to the Finger Lakes. You wouldn't take up whoring again, would you?"

"In whoring I got the pretty things and the friends," Emily said, her voice stubborn and high. Then it collapsed. "I couldn't do that. But how come there's only two choices? In this whole big world how'd I get down to only two choices?"

Olive lay back on the bed. "In this heat I only have strength for one thing—keeping up my nerve to help Regina. I can't be talking sense into you all the time, too."

Finally the molasseslike day passed. On their third morning in Utica, Olive woke early and bought two rolls and two cups of tea at a bakery and took them back to their room. Emily offered to stay home because the asylum gave her the willies, but Olive forced her to come. To Emily's satisfaction, they had to hire a private cab to the asylum to get there at the appointed time. They arrived at five minutes to ten. Olive rushed in, terrified of missing their seven minutes. As she was charging towards the office she realized she had not planned what she would say to the superintendent, how she would convince him to let them see Regina. The mean little man was gazing into his papers again when they arrived. Olive tapped on the doorframe.

"One moment," he said, and bent his head more furiously into his work. Finally, he sighed and looked up.

"We have an appointment to see the superintendent at ten," Olive said.

"What? Speak up."

Olive moved closer. "We have an appointment to see the superintendent at ten, about Miss Regina Hammond Sartwell."

He looked in his book. "You're mistaken. Your appointment is at eleven-fifteen. Surely someone taught you to write appointments down."

"Are you positive? Could you check again, please?"

He gasped in irritation and attacked the appointment book. He jabbed his finger at a place that Olive couldn't see. "Eleven-fifteen. Miss Sartwell. You are Miss Sartwell, aren't you?"

"What?"

He covered his face with his hand. "Miss Sartwell. If you will go out and sit on a couch for one hour and fifteen minutes, I will then admit you at your appointed time."

Olive walked out. She sat down on a couch. Emily sat next to her, very close. "What could it mean?" Olive said.

"He thinks you're Regina Sartwell," Emily whispered.

"Not Regina. We never said we was Sartwells. One of her sisters must be here to see her." Olive's hands began to smooth her dress. "We'll just have to wait and see. It could be her sister Maryanne or her sister Eliza." Olive tapped her foot. "But not her sister Eliza because she's married and has a new name. I'll just have to tell her family I'm her maid. They'd never believe it if I said I was her best friend." Every few minutes she got up and crossed the hall and looked out the great door at the road. No one came. Emily went to find the outhouse. There was a clock in the secretary's office that Olive could see if she stood in front of his door at a certain angle. Finally it was eleven-thirteen. She counted to sixty, five times. Still no one. Emily returned. Olive heard a hansom pull up.

Olive smoothed her hair, unhooked her lip, and put on a smile. The two glamorous ladies from the hotel sailed in. They did not seem to be in a hurry. They did not glance about. They walked like the prows of ships. Their hats alone were large and sturdy as ships. Olive did not know how to stay their course. They surged into the office. "I'll see them when they finish," she said miserably.

After a while a gentleman walked out of the room with the two ladies. They met a fat woman in a long white apron and a floppy cap at the entrance to the right wing. The woman unlocked the door and led them inside. Olive jiggled her knees back and forth in her skirt. Much later, they came back. They went into the office again.

After another half hour, the two ladies glided out of the office. They walked in that same way, as if their movements were predestined. The plump one held the thinner one's elbow. It was clear now that the thinner one in blue was Regina's sister. She had Regina's fine hair, though darker, and Regina's warrior nose, straightened. Her figure was more curved than Regina's, but that could be the dress.

Olive almost let them pass again, as if she were watching an armada from shore. Then, in a panic, she rushed and caught them on the steps. "Excuse me. Would you be Miss Sartwell?"

"What do you want?" The thin lady looked unfriendly.

"I wanted to, wished to, speak with you, ma'am. I'm Olive Honsinger. Miss Regina's maid from the Hammonds'?"

"Of course, that was in Regina's letter, remember, Maryanne?" The plump one smiled at Olive. "Whatever are you doing here?"

"I've come to see Miss Regina, but they won't let me in. I was worried. Did you see her, ma'am?"

Olive directed her words to Regina's sister, but the plump one answered. "We would like to talk with you further, but Miss Sartwell is feeling indisposed at the moment. Will you join us for supper at the Utica Hotel at six?"

"Yes, but—"

"We really must go. We will converse later, my dear." The two ladies were helped into the cab that had been waiting for them. The cab man leapt onto his seat. He made a smart click, click sound, flicked his whip, and the horses trotted off. Olive stood on the steps in the dust of the hansom. She walked back inside. Emily was asleep, her neck curved down on her chest like a goose. They had to wait another two hours for the public coach.

Emily insisted on wearing her yellow earrings and her white gloves, along with her usual Shaker headgear. She was so happy about having supper with the two pretty ladies that Olive could not tell her she hadn't actually been invited.

At the door of the dining room the waiter began to lead them to their usual table. "We're eating with those two," Olive said. The man looked at them suspiciously. "We're invited," Olive said.

"One moment, please."

"I never heard the word 'please' sound so mean," Emily said loudly.

The waiter walked over to the ladies. They nodded. He came back. "This way, please," he said.

The waiter held the chair out for Olive. She had a hard time finding the seat, then edged the chair in herself. Meanwhile, Emily had already sat down.

The plumper one was called Mrs. Hartson. She was gentle and asked how they were, glancing in a worried way at the skinny Shaker in the yellow earrings and white gloves.

Olive said, "This is Emily Ciminiski. She is from the Shakers over to Paradox. Regina visited with them many times before she was taken here."

Regina's sister rolled her eyes like Regina would. Olive fell half in love with Miss Maryanne Sartwell immediately because she had

Regina's nose and hair, and deeper than that, because the blood that ran her had a secret family affinity with the blood that ran Regina. But Maryanne seemed to feel nothing for Olive at all.

Regina's sister gripped her spoon furiously through the soup course. "I don't know who those idiots believe they are fooling. I'm very suspicious. They showed me all over their first ward, as they call it. Oh, they insisted that was where Regina would be going as soon as she completed her intensive chemical treatment. They said they had already cured her of epilepsy. But of course, they would not allow me to see her. It's outrageous."

"Is it a place Regina would like, ma'am?" Olive asked.

"I wouldn't know. When I left, Miss Sartwell," she said pointedly, "was a happy schoolgirl. I have arrived to find she is an epileptic in a lunatic asylum. Did she actually try to murder a physician?" she asked, as if it were Olive's fault.

"She was just defending herself against him. He was taking advantage of her. She had to," Olive said.

"Repulsive," Regina's sister said, and Olive wasn't sure who or what she was referring to.

Their suppers came. The pork loin was covered in a creamy mushroom and shallot sauce, with beet greens and brandied peaches on the side.

Olive tried to make friends with Maryanne. "It's a wonder you got here so fast. You must have flew across the ocean." She smiled.

Maryanne rolled her eyes. "We did not leave the continent to visit my sister in a lunatic asylum. We returned because I received notice that my father was in grave condition. I didn't learn of my sister's situation until I arrived in New York three days ago."

"But what about Regina's letters to you?"

Maryanne's voice sounded exactly the way Regina's did when she was speaking to Dr. Lenard. "I knew she was an epileptic. I had yet to learn she was a murderer."

Mrs. Hartson picked delicately at her food with a fork. "It seems to me that our foremost responsibility before we leave is to ascertain exactly what Olive has just asked, that is, is your sister being treated with care, and is she receiving proper medical attention for her malady."

"But there's nothing wrong with Regina—Miss Sartwell, I mean," Olive said.

"How did you come to that conclusion?" Maryanne asked.

Olive couldn't think what to say.

Maryanne chewed silently but viciously. "Tommorow we will enter that asylum and see her for ourselves."

"That crazy house gives me the shivers," Emily said. It was the first thing she had said all evening. There was cream sauce dripping off one of her gloved fingers.

Miss Maryanne glared at her. She put down her fork. She picked up her napkin and pressed it to her lips. "If this place is curing her, well and good. And if not, money will remove her."

The next morning Mrs. Hartson and Miss Sartwell left again in their private hansom. When Olive knocked on their door in the afternoon, Mrs. Hartson answered it, her hair a little frowsy. "Miss Maryanne is down with headache. I'm afraid she won't be able to talk with you. We didn't see her sister either. The superintendent seems well meaning, though, and he's an expert on brain diseases. He assures us that when next we visit we will be pleased with her progress. We'll return in the spring. If you would like to meet us here in May, we'll do our best to get you in for a visit."

"But if you didn't see her, how do you know she's all right?"

"We just must trust the experts, I suppose. You seem so devoted, dear. Thank you for being kind to Miss Regina." Olive didn't move or say anything. "Do you need money?"

Olive shook her head.

"So nice to make your acquaintance." When Olive still didn't say anything more, Mrs. Hartson gently shut the door in her face.

Olive walked to her room. Emily was napping. She wrote her a note: "I'm going home tomorrow." She watched Emily snoring on top of the brown bedspread. She added to the note: "I don't even know if you can read." She dropped the paper on the pillow beside

Emily. Leaving the hotel, she entered the glaze and stench of the city.

In her little park she walked up to the grey statue and clenched the end of the stone sword in her fist. It felt cool against her hot fingers. She imagined snapping it out of the soldier's hand, holding it over the little man at the asylum, demanding to see Regina. Her hand slid off the point. "I ain't a prince," she said.

She began the long walk back to the hotel. She passed the store that sold Polish trinkets, walked to the end of the block, and stood at the large intersection while horses and carriages breezed past. There was a brief commotion in the crowd waiting to cross on the other side of the street. Then the road cleared, and people began streaming off the sidewalk. Someone lay on the ground behind them. Olive shaded her eyes. The man on the ground shook as if the earth were quaking under him. A gentleman stepped over him.

Someone pushed past her. "Are you crossing the street or not?"

Olive crossed the street. She stood over the man. He lay still now, his clothes twisted around his body, his brown hair flat with sweat. One muddy boot had fallen off. Olive picked it up. More people shoved past them. "It's like she never seen a fit before," someone said. The man's eyelids fluttered and he opened his eyes. He scowled at her.

Olive stepped back. "You had a fit."

He waved her away. He pulled himself to a sitting position, his head drooping. He kicked out at a passing leg.

"Here's your boot," Olive said.

He took it from her and began shoving it on.

"Do you want me to walk you somewhere?" Olive asked.

"Get on, now!" the man said wearily, "Go help someone else."

Late afternoon, Olive stood outside the asylum, steadying herself against a column. Her heart scared her with its clunking. She climbed the steps and walked quickly into the main room, her shoes shouting over the marble floor. She perched on the edge of one of the couches, staring at the door to the little man's office and then watching the door that led to the women's wing of the building. She had no plan. She just sat on the edge of the couch, waiting to see what she would do.

She heard a cooing-sighing kind of racket, like pigeons. A line of crazy women came jumbling through the main entrance into the hall. They all wore misfitted coats and hats. One of the women suddenly made a break for it, a shuffling run towards the men's wing of the building. Her mashed-in straw hat fell off her head and skimmed the marble floor. Two attendants in big aprons charged after her. The women left in the main room seemed nervous, fluttering their hands and cooing louder. Someone began to whimper as the remaining attendant herded them towards the women's wing.

Olive thought she might faint as she watched herself lift the straw hat. She followed after the group. The attendant unlocked the door to the wing. The women began to crowd in. Olive stood at the end, moving closer to the door. She began to raise her arms to settle the hat on her head. The attendant holding the door was watching her.

Olive brought her arms down. She handed the attendant the hat. "One of them dropped this."

"Thanks." The attendant opened the door wider for the two aproned women who held the struggling runaway between them. They prodded her into the hall.

"I've come to visit a friend in there." Olive waved her hand down the long, dim hall with its double row of doors.

"See the assistant to the superintendent," the attendant said, and shut the door. She heard the bolt slide in.

Olive felt reckless with failure. She walked to the office and knocked on the side of the door. There was the assistant to the superintendent, head bent over his notebook. He held a long finger up and kept writing. Olive watched the bald spot on the back of his head. He looked up, not deigning to recognize her. "Yes?"

"I've come to see Regina Sartwell, sir." Olive's voice came out high.

"You've come before.

Olive nodded.

"And what did I tell you?"

"I need to see the superintendent to ask permission." Olive said miserably.

"Have you an appointment to see him?"

"No, sir."

He sighed and began flipping through his book. "We're into next month . . ."

Olive backed herself against the wall opposite the desk. She clenched her fists at her sides. "It has to be today, sir."

"Impossible."

"I'm leaving town today. I've been here four days and I don't have any more time left. I just want to see her for five minutes."

"You do not seem to understand. We have procedures. Either make an appointment or leave the office."

Olive pressed against the wall. She felt as if she had a fever. "I ain't leaving until you let me see Regina. I'll stand here all day if I have to."

The man slapped his book closed and stood up. His mouth twitched. "If you don't leave this moment, I'll call for an attendant to evict you." His own voice came out high and screechy.

The door to the superintendent's office opened. All Olive could see was his gold-ringed hand on the knob. She wished she could step into the wall. "Is there a disturbance, Mr. Termening? You know I'm meeting with Mr. Whiting."

Mr. Termening stood on his toes indignantly. "There is a woman here who refuses to leave the office until she sees one of our inmates."

"Let her see him then. And no more disturbances, is that clear?" The door closed.

The assistant shook himself, his mouth twitching more. "I want you to know," he said to Olive, "I was not persecuting you personally. I treat all visitors in the same manner."

* * *

An attendant led Olive down the hall. Olive glanced into the thick glass window of each door as they passed. In the first three, worn-looking ladies were knitting or doing fancywork. In the corner of one of the rooms a well-dressed lady was crying into a handkerchief. Another lady was playing "Oh When the Saints," over and over on a piano. Olive could hear the tinkle of it through the heavy door.

The attendant unlocked a door at the end of the hall and walked down a flight of stairs. Olive followed her to a damp, windowless lower floor. She heard whimpering and scraping. The attendant knocked on the door.

A stocky, aproned woman opened it and stepped into the hall, closing the door after her.

"She's come to see Sartwell." The first attendant sat down on the stairs. "I'll wait here."

The stocky woman put her hands on her hips. "And who are you?"

"Just her maid, from before. I need to see her so I can rest easy."

The woman laughed. "Well, we sure want you to rest easy." She unlocked the door.

Olive was positive it was the wrong room. It was full of dirty women and dirty pallets thrown on the floor. It was dusty and there were no windows. She breathed through her mouth to avoid the stink. On one side was a huge, sooty fireplace and on the other a long, pitted table without benches. Most of the women seemed to be tied down, but a few wandered around. There was a swelling feeling in the room, as if the air in the room would soon force someone to strike out.

The attendant laughed. "Sartwell, she's one of the baddies. Don't budge yourself into her pacing. She owns that space, she does. Over there." The woman pointed.

"What's wrong with her?" Olive whispered.

The attendant laughed. "She's loony, that's what's wrong with her."

Olive didn't want to cross the room, and she didn't want to meet Regina at the other end.

"Think you'll have sweet dreams now?" the attendant said.

"I better go ask how she is," Olive whispered. She walked towards Regina, threading her way through the beds of women. One reached for her ankle. Olive jumped ahead. She felt skittish, ready to bolt. Her skin shivered. She neared Regina.

Olive stood a foot from her, but Regina didn't look up or stop pacing. "Regina," Olive tried to whisper, but her voice caught.

Regina swung her head up. "I'll scratch you with my claw."

"But—it's me."

Regina paced away, swinging her arms. She stopped, paced backwards until she was next to Olive. She looked at Olive's feet. "Who?" she hissed. "Tell me quickly or I'll scratch."

"Me. Olive Honsinger." Her voice broke. She began to cry.

"Olive," Regina said flatly. Her eyes went up to Olive's chin. Her hand reached out, Olive brought her own hand up to meet it, but Regina snatched hers away. "Don't."

Regina began to pace in front of her, three steps up, then three steps back. "Stop now, stop it. You're confusing me. Don't say anything, don't grab."

"I won't." Olive was concentrating on not making any sobbing sound.

"What'd you say to her?" The attendant stood in front of her. "You leave now, you're making her strange." Regina whipped her hand out. Olive felt the pads of Regina's fingers on her face, pressing. The attendant grabbed Regina from behind. Regina's nails raked down Olive's cheek and chin. Regina struggled. Both she and the attendant were grunting. Regina reached for Olive. Olive stepped back.

"Help me," Regina said.

Olive stumbled between the beds. She banged on the door until the attendant in the hall let her out. The attendant led her back through the locked halls. Olive's chest hurt. She forced herself to plod as slowly as the woman in front of her. She was finding it hard to breathe.

When the attendant finally opened the door to the main hall, Olive bolted. The attendant yelled, "Hold up," but Olive ran through the hall, through the entrance room, down the stairs, and across the drive, out onto the hot, dusty country road. She kept running until she couldn't breathe, then jogged until the pain in her side became unbearable. She moved down into a stumbling walk. The scratch on her chin pulsed. "There was nothing wrong with her before. Only a week before," Olive said. As soon as she said this, despite the sharp pain in her side, despite the thick heat, she began to run towards Utica.

The sun broiled. Three times men spoke to her, asking her if she needed something, a ride, a drink, some money. "Leave me alone!" she yelled, as if everyone were lunatics, including herself. She kept walking. It must have taken three hours. Her blisters opened again. Her feet swelled until she had to remove her shoes. Her hands tingled, then itched, turned fat and blotchy red. She held them above her heart. One whole hour was spent in the city, wandering around trying to find the hotel without asking any-one.

When she finally found it, the guard in that glaring red uniform grabbed her arm as she passed. She said loudly, "Leave me alone. I have a room here." He let her go. She climbed the stairs to Regina's sister's room.

Mrs. Hartson opened the door. Her face crumpled with worry when she saw Olive. "Come in," she said.

Miss Maryanne turned to her from the window. "You again?" she said.

"You have to get her out of there. Now. It's wrecking her. A week ago she was just fine and now she's . . . something's wrong with her now. They keep her in the basement, in a room you wouldn't keep cows in, dirtier'n a barn. That place done it to her. It would do it to anyone. It's that ugly."

"But how could you know that?"

"They let me in. I saw everything."

"We shall see," Maryanne said. The two women calmly put on their coats and hats and gloves. Mrs. Hartson gathered up her large purse. They became the twin ships again, sailing past Olive and down the stairs.

Olive walked up to her room. She sponged the blood off her heels and told Emily a small bit of what she knew. Emily took up all her store-bought items and left the room. Olive didn't ask where she was going. She limped over to the mirror on her toes. She cleaned the cut on her chin. A lightning bolt, Olive thought. She said to the mirror, "I am so tired out." She tiptoed over to the bed and lay down on it, still in her dirty dress. The afternoon sun soaked the bed with heat. She fell asleep.

There was a sharp knock on the door. Olive swung her legs over the bed and groaned. The blisters had tightened. The sun was gone. She tiptoed to the door. A bellboy gave her a card. She took it and closed the door. She heard him mumble, "Bitch." She realized she'd forgotten to pay him. She didn't care.

The card was engraved: Mrs. Drew Hartson. In round handwriting on the back: "Miss Regina Sartwell, Miss Maryanne Sartwell, and I request your presence in the ladies' dining room at six-thirty. You may bring your Shaker."

Olive washed herself in the lesser heat of dusk. The only other dress she had was her good black wool. She took off her filthy calico, scrubbed it, and hung it in the window anyway. The sounds and smells of the city through the window had become familiar, and she no longer heard it. She climbed into her black dress, gingerly keeping the cloth from her heels.

Emily returned at six. "It was easy to give everything away," she said. "They thought I was a Shaker, doing charitable works. I expect I was a Shaker doing charitable work." She seemed pleased with herself, as pleased as she'd been buying everything. "I didn't keep anything. Not even the red earrings for Regina Sartwell."

"We're to meet them all for supper in a half hour. With Regina."

"Good." Emily seemed happy but not surprised, as if she had expected it. She pinched her pale cheeks in the mirror.

Olive sat in her black dress and waited.

At six-thirty they walked down to supper. Olive stood in the door of the dining room. Regina sat between the two ladies. She was wearing a white dress with little pearl buttons and a spray of lace at the neck, and a small white plumed hat. White powder on her face. She looked like a painting, like the first time Olive had ever seen her. Olive touched her scratch with her fingers. She felt pretty and gentle, as if white feathers were waving above her own head.

Regina still hadn't seen her. Emily whispered, "Ain't we oughta go on in?" Then Regina looked up and there was her small, amused smile. She raised her chin in a rude, come-here gesture. Olive tiptoed to avoid the blisters, as if she were dancing. She tiptoed past tables covered in shining silver, under crystal chandeliers, in the wavering light of a dozen white candles. She felt as if she were Cinderella, tiptoing through happily ever after.

Olive and Emily slid into their chairs too quickly for the waiter to help them.

Olive could not think of a thing to say, but it felt fine.

"This is a celebration," Mrs. Hartson said. "I know Americans believe it's vulgar for a lady to drink in public, but I think we ought to have sherry all round."

Olive smiled at her plate. Olive could not yet look at Regina. The soup course came, a creamy squash. Mrs. Hartson ordered a bottle of sherry.

Regina said, "Olive. You should have seen me. What they put me in to leave." Regina's voice was higher than usual, straining for something. Bravery, Olive thought. "First they took my photograph in my old sack. Then they did my hair all up and rouged my cheeks and stuck a horrible bow at the top of my head and dressed me in mismatched layers—I looked like some ridiculous doll. They took my photograph again to show how they'd cured me. Before and after the asylum."

Olive looked up and smiled a quick smile. She looked down at her soup again. "Where'd you get them pretty new clothes?" she said softly.

"Oh, Maryanne was horrified. She rushed out in a panic and bought the entire ensemble. Everyone seems to want to dress me." Maryanne snickered.

"But," Olive said. "Why'd they let you out?"

"Because they are money-grubbing cretins, that's why," Maryanne said. "Mrs. Hartson simply offered some of her dead husband's money for a donation to the asylum. Then he said, 'Desperately overcrowded,' and paroled her for a month. In a month's time we apply for an extension of parole, with more money. I believe it happens this way all the time. Routine."

"But they did cure her of her malady," Mrs. Hartson said. "They gave us medicine to keep it away."

The waiter cleared their bowls away and brought the sherry. The sherry singed Olive's throat and glazed the crystal. Olive's hand felt graceful on the narrow stem. She drank all the syrup down. The waiter's arm appeared at her left, filling her glass again.

Maryanne set her napkin on the table. "We must settle your future, Regina. Mrs. Hartson and I will be sailing back to the continent. I think you ought to come with us. This country does not seem safe for you, as long as that annoying uncle of ours is in it. And because of the difficulty with the physician. Surely you could use a long rest."

"I can just imagine you under a blanket on ship deck and then lolling about our back garden in Nice. You can see the Mediterranean from the back garden." Mrs. Hartson's voice sounded kind, but her face had that crumpled, worried look.

Olive thought, Poor Mrs. Hartson, I guess she might not want Regina lolling in her back garden. She looked at Regina. Regina was showering her smile on her sherry glass, tilting it to catch the light.

"Regina Sartwell," Emily said, in a formal voice. "Eldress Harriet wants you to know you have a place with the Shakers in Paradox."

"Pardon me?" Maryanne snorted.

Regina smiled at Olive. "Are those all of the adventures offered?"

"Our Finger Lakes house." The sherry was thick and red, and Olive's voice was brimming over with it.

"You mean Grandmother's farm? That is long gone."

Regina didn't say anything, so Olive said gently, "Regina's father is giving her the money to buy a house on Seneca Lake."

"My sister's husband has control over our father's money. And I very much doubt he'll part with a penny of it."

"My father's had a stroke of palsy," Regina said. "He's gone."

"But the letter—" Olive said.

"What letter?" Maryanne said.

"He sent Regina a letter, promising to buy her a farm."

"Where is this letter?" Maryanne said.

"It must be . . . Where is it, Regina?"

Regina said, "Where is my Gypsy princess when I need her?"

Maryanne stared at her. "What about the trapeze lady from the circus as well?"

"I'm not being absurd," Regina said. "There was a Gypsy princess. Olive knows." Olive touched the cut on her face with her fingers. "In any case, I want to go with Ann."

The waiter brought the main dish, roast beef in a wine sauce with cranberry jelly on the side. Regina waved him away. He stood uncertainly, holding the last two plates, then slipped them down anyway.

Emily said shyly, "My name is Emily."

"I know who you are, that whirling girl from before. None of you are Ann. Ann was the only one who stayed with me." She touched her napkin to her lips.

Emily said, "Could you mean Mother Ann?"

"Not a mother, a friend," Regina said.

"What are you talking about, Regina?" Maryanne said. "Do you realize you're not making sense?"

"I am going back to the Shakers in Paradox. Can you comprehend that?"

"You're an idiot," Maryanne said.

Mrs. Hartson put her hand over Maryanne's. "Maybe Regina knows what's best for herself." Her relief that her garden had so miraculously emptied out showed on her bright cheeks. "Why don't we visit this Shaker place with her? The Shakers are a pious, cleanly group, I believe. A restful place, perhaps."

Olive watched her hands on the knife and fork. She watched her hand pick up her fourth sherry and bring it to her mouth.

On the way out of the dining room, Regina and Olive walked up the stairs together. Olive wasn't sure where everyone else was. Regina seemed to be pulling herself up by the banister, but that was fine because Olive needed to do the same.

Regina walked into her room. Olive followed her. Olive lay down on the big maroon bed she found in there. The bed began to whirl, so she sat up. Regina was pulling open the drapes. The gas lamp outside the window threw a band of light across the room. Regina stared at her reflection in the glass of the window. She began wiping the white makeup off with the heel of her palm. Under it, her skin looked yellow. She unbottoned the tiny bottons on her dress, then the petticoat underneath. Olive watched as Regina pulled the dress off her shoulders, the sleeves hanging below her waist. Her chest and small breasts were so pale, Olive could see the dark veins fanning out under the skin.

Then Regina was lying next to her, her pale shoulder shining in the dark, her sweet breath on Olive's eyes. "The farm is gone, isn't it?"

Regina kissed her on the mouth. It tasted like sherry.

"But why couldn't we find the letter? It must be at the Hammonds'."

"Don't think, Olive," Regina said. "Let's not think." Regina kissed Olive again, and the kiss went deeper and deeper, and Olive didn't think, but she felt: This bed is like sherry, Regina's skin is like sherry. And she didn't think, The farm is gone, but the words rolled over and over in her head, and the sherry tasted like mourning and the rhythm of Regina's circling hand on her breast reminded her of the rhythm Florilla commenced in the rocking chair after each of her babies had died.

In the middle of the night Olive woke up with a terrible thirst. She stumbled to the water pitcher and drank three glasses without stopping. On the way back to bed she thought she saw Regina pacing by the window, her arms swinging from her shoulders. Olive fell back on the bed.

Miss Maryanne knocked on their door early in the morning. They untangled themselves. Miss Maryanne walked into the room. Olive and Regina stood beside the bed, naked. "How French of you, Regina. With the maid. But you must always lock the door." She opened the curtains, poured water into the washbowl. "We leave within the hour, as the journey to Paradox will take all day." She strode out.

Olive's head felt parched, even her eyeballs. Regina sat down heavily on the bed. "You'd better go pack," Regina said. By the time Olive had woken Emily and gathered her things into her basket, Mrs. Hartson was settling the bill. "Don't concern yourselves with this." She smiled at Olive and Emily. "The coach is waiting by the curb." They walked out the door. The red-suited man took their bags and put them in a trunk behind the coach. Then he helped them inside.

Maryanne and Regina and Mrs. Hartson sat on one side, and Emily and Olive faced them. Regina had that makeup on again, making her look like a porcelain doll.

It seemed to Olive that she blinked and the city disappeared. Wait, she wanted to say, I will never see the Hotel Utica, or anything like it, again. The coach flew. They raced a train for a while, and the engineer blew his whistle at them. Once a huge freight wagon rattled towards them. There was only room for one vehicle on the road, but neither driver would pull over. At the last possible moment the wagon careened over the side of the road and tilted into the ditch. The wagon driver shook his fist at them as they thundered past.

After a few hours, Emily fell asleep, her head on her chest, her breathing clogged. Mrs. Hartson fell asleep on Maryanne's shoulder. Maryanne fell asleep, her cheek resting on Mrs. Hartson's head. Regina moved across and sat between Olive and the window.

"It will be all right," she said, and patted Olive's leg.

"I know," Olive said. "I can visit you every Sunday."

Regina nodded. "Do you remember how you found me in there?"

"No, I don't," Olive said.

Regina's smile came back. "I'll change my name and dye my hair so the general won't know me. Maybe I'll paint my lips." Regina's voice came out like the screech of breaks on a train. Mrs. Hartson sighed in her sleep, a pretty puff of a sigh. They were both quiet for a while, letting the screech disappear.

"I guess the bloodroot worked for you. You got what you wanted. The Shakers."

"Do you remember last night?" Regina took Olive's hand.

Olive nodded, smiled, blushed.

"Do you feel—strangely—about it?"

Olive shook her head.

"Nor do I." Regina reached into Maryanne's bag and slipped out a dark bottle. Regina held it up so Olive could get a good look at it. The label was scrawled over with directions. It contained powder. Regina tossed it out the window. They didn't hear the smash: The coach was moving too quickly. No one woke. Regina took up Olive's hand again.

"Regina, I'm going to have a baby."

Regina tightened her grip on Olive's hand. She grimaced.

"Don't think about that," Olive said.

Regina smiled, sighed. "Can it be my baby, too?"

Olive nodded. Regina pillowed her head on Olive's shoulder. "I guess the bloodroot worked for you, too." She closed her eyes. "I'd already started my baby when I ate the bloodroot. I wanted the farm." Olive's eyes stayed open for a long time, then she cradled her arm over her stomach, rested her cheek against Regina's head, and closed her eyes.

That evening the coach arrived in Paradox. Groggy, they shambled out into the dark smells of pine and cedar and wet earth; the raucous yelling of the crickets and tree frogs. The sisters gathered around like a flock of doves, cooing over them. Emily kept smiling and smiling, as if she had brought Regina back single-handedly.

Mrs. Hartson was thoughtful enough, even in her confusion, to ask the coachman to take Olive up to Hammondville. The coachman grumbled until Mrs. Hartson gave him more money. Olive walked up to Regina, who was introducing Maryanne to Harriet. Olive touched her on the shoulder. Regina turned. The makeup had peeled around her mouth. "See you on Sunday," Olive said.

Regina glanced back to Maryanne. "You're not staying the night?"

"No."

"Oh." Regina squeezed her arm. "I'm all in a tizzy. See you on Sunday." She turned back to the ladies.

Olive watched out the window as they climbed. The horses slowed to a plod. She could hear the coachman cursing up top. Olive gripped the side of the window and imagined her mother and Ren and Magnus. She smiled. The adventure was over, and it was hers.

Fourteen

THE COACH DRIVER let Olive off just below Hammondville. She stood for a minute where the fallen and chaotic forest opened up onto the bare rock. The night was clear—a parasol of stars. She held onto a skinny sapling, and it swayed in her hand. The dark, humped shapes of the houses looked like the homes of small animals, mice or beaver. Olive felt tender, like a mother looking at her bedraggled children. She walked across the top of the mountain towards her home.

She could see a small light in the window of her mother's house. The oil burning after everyone was in bed. She imagined stroking her mother's face, saying, That light was for me. She walked more quickly. Then she stumbled over a leg.

"Olive Honsinger?"

"Who is it?" She moved closer. She made out the delicate features of the chief engineer. He was sitting on a log. He smelled like liquor. "What are you doing out here, Mr. Putney?"

"Perspective. Hammondville is so inconsequential from here. It doesn't matter at all."

"You best take yourself home, Mr. Putney."

"Is Miss Sartwell safe?"

"Why do you ask that?"

"I noticed you were gone. I thought you must have left to find her. You're braver than me. This operation is collapsing and I'm too frightened to leave."

"I'll help you home." She took his elbow, but he pulled himself up. "I want you to know that I tried."

"I'm sure you did. Night, now."

"I gathered my courage. I told him the men wouldn't put up with another ten percent cut. How can a family live on that wage? I said. But he gave me that sharp-eyed look, and I couldn't go on. Frightened. Tell the men I tried, Mrs. Honsinger." He swayed, sat down heavily. "I think I'll just rest here a little longer. You go on."

Olive left him. The houses had regained their rightful size. Olive stubbed her toe on a wagon wheel. She knocked on her door. Knocked harder. She heard Magnus's rough voice. "Who is this?"

"It's me."

The light flared up behind the door. The door opened. Ren smiled. If she lived to be a hundred, she would never have enough of that smile. He took her hand and held it. She pushed forward until she was under his arm, in the middle of his smell.

She felt Magnus's hand on her head, yanking some frizz. "We give up on you this time."

Her mother came out of her room in her high-necked night-gown, her hair in its skinny braid over her shoulder. She gasped, pulled Olive to her, pressed at the scratch on her chin, searching for infection. "Where you been?" she kept saying, as if Olive were a little girl late for dinner. Florilla made everyone mugs of strong coffee. They sat around the small table so that their elbows and knees made a jumbled circle.

"Tell us your story," Magnus said.

Olive shook her head. "I don't know where to begin. First thing, it turns out they did send Regina to the lunatic asylum in Utica. So I took the train there."

"That's a long ways," Ren said.

"All alone!" Florilla said.

"No, a little Shaker came with me, Sister Emily. She was a nice girl, but she had her peculiar ways. Every time she got scared, she had to pee, no matter where we were." Her family laughed. "Anyways, when we got to Utica we stayed in a fancy hotel, I can't describe how fancy. With indoor hot water from pipes. And the food. There's just too much to tell all at once."

"Tell about Miss Regina," Florilla said.

"They wouldn't let me see her. And then I went to the asylum and refused to leave until they let me see her."

"You didn't," Florilla said.

"And they finally gave in. As long as I live I'll never forget that place. I told Regina's sister and they paid to get her out."

"Where'd you find Miss Regina's sister?" Ren asked.

"Didn't I tell you that already? She was there all the time, staying in the same hotel."

"And where's Miss Regina now?" Florilla said.

"She's with the Shakers."

"So close. That's nice for you." Florilla stood up and began clearing the mugs.

"She's joining the Shakers, then?" Ren said.

Olive looked down. "The Finger Lakes house is gone. Her father is too sick to give it to her."

"Did you ask Miss Regina to come stay with us?" Ren said.

"She wouldn't come here. Anyways, Regina can be tiring. Even more since she come out of that place. Maybe two miles is the best distance for us."

Olive's mother brought over a pot of warm water and witch hazel bark for Olive's heels and sponged some on her scratch. "Any changes, in your belly?" Florilla asked.

"No."

"You're lucky, with all that traveling in this heat. I'd say you won't feel movement for another few weeks."

Magnus pushed Ren's shoulder. "Daddy."

~

271

Ren smiled.

"You folks seem cheerful. I was afraid to come in after I met the chief engineer. He told me about the cut."

"What cut?" Ren said.

Olive looked at their tense faces. "Maybe he was wrong. He was drunk, rambling on about how the general decided on another ten percent cut."

"I knew it," Magnus said. "Renny, you is saying today, don't worry, just rumors. Now, here it is. Another ten percent. He's paying us in stones soon." Magnus went over to his bedroll and began furiously folding it up. "We pack up. Enough now."

"We'll strike," Ren said.

"Yah, strike. The union man says we ain't ready."

"I'm ready." Ren stood quietly, his hands clenching and un-clenching at his sides.

Magnus stopped folding. "When are you ready?"

"Now. Tonight. Give the general a little surprise in the morn-ing." Ren's smile twitched at the edges.

Magnus stood up quickly, his bedding falling in a heap at his feet. He nodded, several sharp jerks of his head. "We'll wake the others. We'll wake the whole goddamn town."

"We'll have to be ready long before the whistle blows. We'll need a start on them." Ren noticed he was gasping. He took a big gulp of air. He looked at Olive. "What do you think?"

Olive nodded.

Ren and Magnus pulled on their coats, jostling each other. They nodded at Florilla and Olive and hurried into the dark.

Olive pushed off the blanket her mother had draped over her. She stood, her body aching. Florilla was looking out the window into the blue predawn. "Looks like a crowd over to Pit Twenty-one."

Olive came over to the window. "Let's go up there."

"Eat some breakfast first. The boys stopped by about an hour ago and had theirs." Olive thought she would have to force the food down, but once she started, she plowed through corn bread and molasses, fried eggs and milk.

It was just getting light when Olive and Florilla trudged up to Pit 21. More people began to gather. The women and men and children bled into each other. The sharp morning wind hissed around them. Crows circled, scolding.

Everyone was talking at once, in three languages. Some looked angry, their voices loud and threatening. Others were grinning, shoving each other. Some smelled of their breakfasts and seemed confused. Olive found Ren in a small knot of Swedes. He squeezed Olive's hand. He was explaining something in Swedish, his voice soft even in its effort to be heard. If one of the listeners spoke, the others shushed him. He was listing something off on his fingers. The men nodded seriously.

Magnus was in the middle of the crowd, yelling about unions and tyrants to no one in particular, to everyone. Several young women cheered.

They jostled each other's shoulders, reined in each other's children: A crying Irish baby was passed to a Swedish woman, and finally a French-Canadian girl quieted him by sticking her pinky in his mouth.

Olive noticed a Frenchman, Veral Benoit, with a large group around him. He was full of pepper, hopping around on his toes, his face red, reading a list of demands from a piece of paper he waved in his hand. People were laughing.

Someone passed out sparklers. Olive could smell the gunpowder and hear their hiss and sizzle. She watched a young boy raise the sparkler over his head and let the pale fire pour over him. Etta Clark was telling all who would listen that her uncle had died in the war to end slavery, and she wasn't about to settle for slavery on this mountain, now. A boy was banging a drum. Someone threw an old Union army cap into the air. Olive heard a girl say, "Is this the Fourth of July?" and her mother answered, "I ain't sure what it is." Children dodged in and out of the crowd, quick as needles, stitching them all together.

The foremen shuffled nervously at the far edge of the group, frowning. Olive saw the chief engineer's curtains slide open. He was watching out the window. The store manager walked out on his stoop, his shop boys crowding behind him. He locked his door and rested the butt of his shotgun on his potbelly. Hardly anyone noticed. No one cared.

They could hear the first train of the morning coming up the mountain. Its whistle was blowing. It was early. The yelling lessened a little as they listened to the hustle and rush of the train.

"Just a half hour since I telegraphed," the store manager called out. "Must be some kind of record getting up this hill—couldn't've taken more'n fifteen minutes." His voice cracked.

Everyone clumped together more, but their voices had shrunk, like sap in deep cold. Ren let go of Olive's hand. He called in his soft, calm voice, "Strikes is legal. Stand your ground."

The train burst around a curve and shrieked to a stop. The sheriff of Crown Point climbed off the train, along with ten men. They passed rifles down to each other. They gripped their guns, hefted them, bounced them a little, getting comfortable. Two of them jogged along the tracks. They slid open the doors of the last car. Olive thought they might have a cannon inside, but then she heard snorting.

The two sheriff's men jumped back from the opening. General Hammond's horse, Old Knight, clattered off the car. Someone was standing inside, holding the reins. He mounted Old Knight: It was General Hammond, in his Civil War uniform. His coat flared down to his knees. It had two long rows of shining brass buttons, blue velvet at the cuffs and collar. His gold epaulets carried stars. A silk sash wound around his waist. An eagle and three bobbing, white ostrich feathers rode the crown of his black hat. The general's beard shone white. His horse glowed pearly white.

Cantering over to the sheriff and his men, the general leaned over gracefully and had a word in the sheriff's ear. He straightened up, pulled down his jacket. He drew his sword. The general trotted over to the strikers, his back stiff, his sword held easily, unsheathed at his side. The sheriff and his men leaned against the side of the store, a few feet away, with the shop boys and store manager, their rifles propped against the wall beside them. Smirking now, the foremen joined them.

Old Knight was nervous, snorting and cantering from side to side. The general bellowed: "I won't allow this kind of disloyal rabble on my personal property."

No one said anything.

"If you are not satisfied with your employment, settle your accounts and depart." He paused; no one moved. "I'd like to know who started this trouble." Silence. "I'll warn you right now that the troublemaker, who I'm willing to bet my life was not born on American soil, deserves to be run through on my sword. I've given you a good home, a decent job, a moral environment, a baseball team. A school and two churches. A Christian life. Will the traitor have the courage to step forward?"

Women called their children to their skirts, hid their babies in their shawls. People slipped around strangers, found their own. Ren was staring at his shoe, his neck bulging veins. Magnus watched Ren, his face so full of fury, Olive had to turn away. Olive imagined that silver sword running through their bellies.

Olive pushed her way through the crowd. She broke through the circle and stopped, a good ten feet from Old Knight's stamping hooves. "This strike was started—" Her voice was too high. She forced it down. "This strike was started because we can't live with another cut. We won't be able to eat."

"You're the maid," the general said.

Laughter broke out in the crowd. The horse spooked at the noise, and the general had to concentrate on reining him in. There was more laughter. The men against the store stood straighter, picked up their shotguns.

The general pointed his sword at her. "You and your family must be out of my town by tomorrow morning." He had regained his orator's voice. "I will give you that time to leave, if your bills are paid. If not, we will have to jail you until those debts are secured. The rest of you," he shouted, "disperse. Return to honest work!" The mine whistle blew as if on command, startling them. The men with the rifles cocked them noisily and began to walk towards the crowd.

A gash opened, and everyone leaked away. The miners drifted towards their holes. The women hurried their children, not looking back. Olive watched a man sweep up a tiny girl into his coat and shoo three more children towards Dog Alley. He was crying.

The only people left by Pit 21 were Olive and her mother, Magnus, Ren, and Veral Benoit, testing out his toes, still clutching his list of demands. The general called for his sheriff. The sheriff gathered Ren and Magnus and the Frenchman together. Then he herded them away with the butt of his rifle. He walked them behind the company store. The sheriff's men poured after them.

"Come back," Olive said. She started for the store, but her mother grabbed her arm. Olive yanked away. She turned on the general, her chin pointed towards him, up there on his saddle. "Where are you taking them? I just told you why the strike was started." The general was talking, but she couldn't hear him.

"There's nothing bad about these men. They're hard workers. We just need enough to live on. They'll work even harder if they think you're paying them fair." She stood right by Old Knight's side now, right by the shiny silver stirrup. She felt as if she'd caught a fever from the neck up, but the heat seemed to have scoured her brain and left only steaming logic. "I can make you a list. The money we get on one side, the money we need to eat and pay our debts on the other. It doesn't match up." Olive could see Old Knight's skin quivering. It was really mouse pink, not white. A man came over and gave her a hard shove with the shotgun he held in both hands across his chest. She fell on the ground and skinned her hands.

She got up. He kept ramming her down the hill with the side of his rifle. She kept talking and falling. She didn't give him a glance, kept her attention on the general: "I've seen how you live. Why don't you spend a week with us, then decide if you'll cut the wage. Even the chief engineer knows. Ask Mr. Putney." She looked over at his window. The curtain dropped. The man who was pushing her seemed to be shoving harder. She turned her attention to him. He was just one of the shop boys from the store. He didn't even shave yet—plumes of reddish hair grew out of his chin. "What in God's name is wrong with you?" she said. "Stop that."

He looked as if he were about to cry. He widened his eyes and stuck his lower jaw out. Then he smashed the butt of the shotgun into the side of her head.

The mountain was tilting, trying to jerk her off her feet. Then her mother was sponging her temple and singing some soothing hymn to her. Her mother was crying. Olive vomited in the tin bowl her mother held for her. "Nothing hurts," she said to her mother. "Where's Ren? Nothing hurts. Where's Ren and Magnus?" She had an idea she was repeating herself, but her memory twisted away from her. Everything solid had become limber—the table legs bent and stood straight, the stove bowed. Her mother's face kept shrinking and growing. Somewhere far away there was a dull ache. She put her head in her hands and waited for things to come right.

She noticed she had been sitting in the rocker with the quilt around her for a long time. Her vision was clear and dull. She had the kind of headache that made tears come without sadness, sour tears like slicing into onions. She stood up. It was worse. "Ma?" she croaked. Her mother was in her room, folding things into small, neat piles. "What are you doing?"

"Packing. Go on and sit down. Remember your baby."

"They haven't come back?"

"Not yet." Olive concentrated on not thinking, which wasn't too hard because of the headache. She moved slowly, helping her mother sort through her things: a pile to go, a pile to give away. Olive's mother talked in a bland, pass-the-salt voice. She needed to write to Ida. Had Olive heard that Lenard hadn't died after all?

They sent him off to a rest home to recover. Should they keep this green cloth for something?

They heard someone fumbling with the door. They looked at each other. "Stay here," her mother said. Olive's head hurt too much to be afraid.

"It's them—our boys."

Olive walked quickly, despite the pain. Ren had a blackened eye. The left side of Magnus's face was swollen. That was all the hurt Olive could find. She could feel her shoulders dropping down. Then she saw the neat slices across their throats, twin red lines, dripping blood. "Ma." Olive pointed.

"They're shallow." Ren sat at the table. Olive went down on her knees and put her hands in his lap. He twirled his fingers in her hair. No one said anything more.

Olive's mother was putting water on to boil, grinding herbs, and all the time, out of her mouth, as fluid and rhythmic as a hymn: "Those sons of bitches, those evil, shit-breathing dogs." Ren and Magnus laughed. Olive watched Ren's Adam's apple bob against the cut at his throat. She was afraid the laughter would burst his neck at the seam. But she laughed too, and the laughter hurt her head, and felt only a little better than crying.

Florilla curtained the windows. She started a fire with the little charcoal they had left. She fussed at their wounds, healing them.

"That Frenchman was kicked in the gut a lot," was the first thing Magnus said.

"Now, why didn't you bring him home?" Olive's mother said.

"He didn't want to come," Magnus said. "See, he made the mistake of going on the ground and curling up, but then maybe it wasn't a mistake 'cause he kept his arms over his head. His gut must've hurt, but his face looked good."

Olive dropped into a chair. "I can't understand," she said. "Just some women talking reason got Regina out of that asylum, but here there was strong men, families, all of us together. It don't make sense, why one would work and not the other." There was silence in the room, as if they all knew the answer except her, as if they felt sorry for her. "Just tell me, if you think you know."

Ren said, "It's the money made the difference."

"What do you mean?"

Magnus said, "As soon as I hear your story, I know it is only them rich ladies' money that does it. If we have this kind of money, we don't need nothing else."

"I think it was because strikes need more planning," she said. Her family said nothing. "Anyway, it wasn't just the money." Still, no one spoke. She reached into her pocket and pulled out her leftover wages. "Well, if it was just the money, I got some of that good-luck stuff right here." They all smiled.

"You should've heard Olive, giving the general a dose of the truth." Olive's mother smiled some more.

"We hear, but not the words. What does she say?" Magnus said.

Florilla began spreading a paste on Magnus's face. "Just the truth, that's all." Ren stroked Olive's head.

As late afternoon came on, they limped around their home, packing. Ren swept the money off the table, led the cow out of the shed, and went away. The cow's swishing tail seemed sweet and confused. When Ren came back he had a swayback horse and a sturdy raw-board wagon. "They wouldn't sell me nothing at the company store, but I settled up," he said. They didn't ask him any more.

Mattie Stone stopped by. Olive's mother gave her three china cups. Mattie gave them a small sack of smoked, leathery meat and two jars of blackberry preserves. Mattie helped Florilla pack her medicinals, and they seemed to create excuses to brush against each other. Olive watched the two old women's backs. "Ma, I'm sorry," she said.

"I ain't sorry we're leaving," her mother said, not turning around. "This place don't deserve us. It don't even deserve our bones." Mattie patted her mother's hand.

The mine let out, but no one came over until Florilla and Olive were putting food on the table for supper. Then Benoit knocked on their door. He walked tenderly, cradling one side. Florilla wanted to have a look at him and make him stay for supper, but he refused. He had the same shallow red slit across his neck. Olive watched him and Ren and Magnus conferring at the door.

At supper Magnus said, "The Frenchman says we oughta come with him over to Pennsylvania. They're hiring on at a steelworks there. Steel's the future of the industry. By the Monangahela River." He said the name carefully, because it was strange and because it held their fate.

Olive said, "What about farming, out west?"

"He says they already got a union there—Amalgamated Association of Iron and Steel Workers." Magnus didn't look at them.

"I guess steel's one step up from iron," Olive's mother said. "That's spit in the general's eye."

After supper they all slipped away on their private errands. Florilla said Olive would probably want to go by way of Paradox tommorow, so could Ren take her down to the Irondale cemetery tonight? Magnus said he'd catch a ride to Irondale and then walk the rest of the way to the widow's. Olive's mother told Olive to keep the latch string in. Ren said they'd be back soon. Then they were gone.

Olive sat in the rocker, alone in her house, and let the one candle gutter out. She did not rock. If she held herself completely still in the dark, she felt only a gnawing ache just below the skin of her forehead. There she sat, silent, in pain, in the dark, but still, the general had failed to erase her. Olive had never felt so present. She could feel the pores of her skin blossoming. She heard the mouse scrabbling in the loft as if it were scrabbling at the turn of her ear. She heard the quiet crunch of gravel as someone walked by their curtained window.

Her pores opened wider and she could see her sinewy old mother in the black dress that faded into the black night as she moved between the stones, housekeeping in the cemetery. She watched Florilla gather up the ghosts, packing them for travel. Through her pores Olive could see her mother burrow into the dirt, pull up jumbled bones, blow on them to raze the dust, then polish them with her handkerchief. Florilla hid the polished bones in the folds of her skirt, for safekeeping.

Through her pores she could see her baby for the first time. The baby was curled in the bowl of her stomach, its head resting on her heart, all ten fingers gripping her insides. This baby would not be shaken loose.

Then Olive thought: Regina. Her pores shriveled. She was only in her rocking chair in the dark, empty house, crying from the pain of a terrific headache.

Late that night, Olive's family returned. When they lit the lamp, the glare hurt her head. Through her squinted vision, their packed home looked bare and sorry. The chicken squawked from her crate. A woman Magnus called Ase ducked her head, busying herself, making a bed of blankets on the floor for her daughter. The little girl, Mary, swayed, eyelids fluttering, and refused Florilla's offer of a cup of milk. Ase had high, reddened cheekbones and white hair, broad shoulders and a round middle. Her face looked windburned. The blue eyes of both mother and child were round, their eyebrows raised, as if they had spent a long time searching for something precious and small.

Olive climbed the ladder, too tired and pained to notice how Magnus treated his new family, whether he tucked the blankets around Mary or patted her head, whether he slept with his arm around Ase. She climbed the ladder and fell into bed next to Ren. Her exhausted sleep held no dreams.

At sunrise a small knot of people gathered around the wagons in front of the Landry house. Swedish men helped lift the stove onto the wagon. They seemed afraid of the cuts on the Honsingers' necks, and kept their eyes on their business. Somewhere, Magnus had acquired his own ramshackle wagon hitched to two old mules. Veral Benoit arrived with a bundle tied up in a jacket. He threw it into Magnus's wagon, climbed in, and said something to Mary. Olive saw her smile for the first time.

The whistle blew, and the Swedes drifted back to the mines.

Three foremen with shotguns started down the hill. Their neighbors touched Olive and her mother quickly, scattered back to their homes. It was laundry day.

They drove the wagons down the rattling hill towards Paradox. Olive couldn't keep her eyes off the cut on Ren's neck. It had hardened into a scab. At one edge she could already see the new pink skin underneath. She longed to rip off the red strip and throw it away. She wondered what Ren had to say or do to keep that knife from pushing deeper.

Down in the Paradox Valley the same old, raggedy farmers were working their land, the mean winters and the rocky, thin dirt sucking all the sap out of them. At the Shakers', Magnus pulled up beside them. "I'll wait for you by the twin falls up there a few miles. Tell Regina I say good luck." Olive nodded. Ase bored her wide-open eyes into him. The little girl dozed with her head on Ase's shoulder. Even in sleep she had a worried look on her face. Veral Benoit winked at Olive from the back of the wagon.

Ren and Florilla stayed outside with the horse. One of the sisters she didn't know told her to wait in the dining hall. Olive sat down at the long table.

Regina hurried in, dressed in Shaker clothes. The grey dress made her look even bonier. The hairnet paled her face. Her old broken wrist was newly bandaged, the fingers purpled. Her eyes were dark circled and swollen, her lips dry and whitish, with a crusted, yellow sore flowering on one edge. "Olive!" Regina sat down next to her on the bench. She took Olive's hand. Regina's hand felt clammy. It was shaking. "I didn't think you'd be here until Sunday. Look at me! I'm impersonating a Shaker. Can I pull it off, do you think?"

"Is it all right here?" Olive said.

"I've already gotten into a fight with Eldress Harriet. My fits have come back, and I tell her it's just the same as worship in meeting, and we ought to be able to worship anytime, not just on Sunday. And that makes the fusty, old eldress nervous. Especially because this morning right at breakfast, which is supposed to be perfectly silent, Emily fell off the bench and shook and sang off key on the floor." Regina laughed. "It was a poor imitation of a fit, if you ask me, but the others seemed impressed."

"You're going to ruin them." Olive smiled.

"Oh, I know. I'm the heretic in the family of believers. Will you spend the day? I've got to show you what I've been doing. It's a big secret." She slid off the bench and rushed away. Olive glanced out the window and saw her mother and Ren waiting by the wagon.

Regina came back. She held a sheaf of paper. She laid it on the table. "This is the secret of the Shakers," she whispered. "They're called spirit drawings. They're sacred, heavenly visions—gifts from the Mother." She turned the first one over. It was a tree with leaves in neat rows on each branch. Perched in the branches were bright birds and bright apples. "One of the sisters did this. It's the tree of life or something." Regina flipped it back over. "More of the same," she said, flipping paintings.

She turned the next one over. It was all in shades of blue. In the center plant roots dangled in deep blue. In the lighter blue at the top of the painting blue flowers grew out of the plant. A smudgy woman with long arms reached in a half circle around the flowers. In the deeper blue at the bottom a baby floated in a crosshatched net. "I did this one."

"I know," Olive said.

"I'm going to do a million of these. I love spirit drawings."

"How is Emily Ciminiski?" Olive asked.

"Oh, I adore Emily," Regina said.

Olive picked up one of the other paintings. "I come by because we're leaving."

"What do you mean?" Regina gripped her own painting.

"The general run us out of town."

"But where will you go? Why don't you stop here? The Shakers will put you up." She smiled excitedly.

Olive studied the tree on the paper. "We're going to a place called Homestead."

~

"Why?"

Olive shrugged. "They've got a union and they're hiring."

"It's all settled then."

Nobody said anything. Olive counted the apples on the tree.

"Homestead is a pretty name," Regina said.

Olive nodded, traced the trunk of the tree. "On the Monongahela River."

"I like that," Regina said.

Olive ran her finger over the word "peace." "Will you be all right?"

Regina looked down at her own fingers gripping the blue painting. "Yes. They don't really mind me here."

Olive stood.

"Wait. Are you leaving right now?"

Olive put the painting of the tree back on the table. "You should try alum and egg white for those puffy eyes."

"My eyes are puffy?"

"Lenard didn't die."

"I know." Regina flipped the edge of her painting.

"Magnus said good luck."

"Oh, him. I just liked him because he was related to you." Olive stepped backwards. "We promised," Regina said. "We promised on the pillow, we promised on the bloodroot. Two nights ago, in the hotel, that was a kind of promise, wasn't it?"

"You're blaming me for broken promises?" Olive said quickly.

"What do you mean?"

"In the restaurant. Your sister asked where the letter was."

"I didn't have the letter."

"You could have found it. Mrs. Cutter could have found it for us."

"It wouldn't have worked."

"Because you didn't want it to work."

"Olive, you hate me."

Olive shook her head, looked away. "Maybe I do."

"Because you saved me, and I promised to save you, but I didn't."

"I didn't save you. Mrs. Hartson's dead husband's money saved you."

"That's not true. They were going to leave me there to die. I can save you, too. From that hideously named river."

"No, you can't."

"Yes, I can. With Mrs. Hartson's dead husband's money." Regina took a little Bible from the pocket of her smock. She opened it and slipped out a thick envelope. "Maryanne gave this to me. Escape money." She held out the envelope to Olive.

Olive looked at Regina. She smiled. "We can all escape together."

"Just take the money. Go find that house in the drawing."

"But why don't you come? It ain't healthy for you here. We'd fatten you right up."

"Because you are all encumbered, with husbands and mothers and babies. I wouldn't be good at playing the spinster aunt. I'd destroy everyone, trying to get at you." Regina pressed Olive's fingers around the envelope, patted her hand briskly. "And because I'd rather be visited by sacred visions here than be a shaking, drooling lunatic in the Finger Lakes."

Olive squeezed the envelope in her fist. "You'll visit. Once we get settled."

"We'll write," Regina said. "I can't cry. I feel like a piece of burnt toast." Olive laughed, and then began to cry. She turned to go. "My best friend. My baby," Regina said. Olive nodded. She left Regina standing in the dining room.

Olive climbed up into the wagon, and they started down the road. The wagon bed was full of junk: herbs, broken furniture, chipped crockery, and ghosts. They all jumbled against each other, singing and clanging and complaining in the back of the wagon. On the front seat, Olive's mother took her hand and held it in her skirt. Ren kept glancing at her. Olive wiped some tears from her face, pulled her hand out from her mother's, and crossed her arms over her stomach. "Regina's given me money. We're going to the Finger Lakes."

"What? You took the lady's money? And what about Magnus?" Florilla said. "What about that union?"

"He's welcome to come along," Ren said. He gave the reins a bright snap.

"And I'm going to name the baby Regina. Or Reginald if it's a boy. Reginald, the Gypsy King." Olive laugh-sobbed.

Her mother shook her head and smiled. "You're a mess. There's no controling you, is there?"

In the pretty, polished wood dining room of the family of believers, Regina stood holding her painting, as if she were listening for something. Her hand began to spasm. Regina watched as the painting shook and waved, then fell and skimmed the smooth floor. This was something new—only one arm. But then the spasm began to rise. She felt glorious and terrified.

"Dear Olive," she thought, "I am going down."

The Stories After

BEFORE THE CENTURY could turn, a cheaper, higher-grade midwestern ore drove the Hammondville mines out of business. The remaining miners stayed on only to dismantle the town, to throw the hacked-up shacks into piles and burn them, to load the company's valuables onto the train. They pulled up the tracks behind them, and Hammondville was gone. Crown Point and Irondale shriveled.

The decades wedged against the new century were filled with fire. As the men logged, they stripped branches, left the slash knee-deep, covering dried stumps and roots. It stopped raining. The slash turned brittle. Any spark could ignite it. And sparks did, again and again. The dead forest flamed over thousands of acres. Even the dirt burned. Root fires sizzled underground, until they crept up a living tree. Suddenly a white pine would explode, spontaneous combustion, the warning hand of a god. With no roots to keep it steady, the earth skidded down the mountains in terrific mud slides.

The old money who summered in the Adirondacks did not appreciate the charred scenery after the fires had passed through. A Vermonter wrote a book claiming all great civilizations doomed themselves by cutting down their trees. The state legislature grew afraid of prophecy and wealth. In 1892 they declared the Adirondacks a park.

Now, start at the Paradox road. Still unpaved, filled with ridges. Stop at the Shaker house, now owned by a city lady as a vacation home. It would have cost twice as much in Vermont, and here it stands, in a small tangle of trailers and aluminum-sided ranch houses.

In the attic of the house, behind a broken rocker, this city woman found a sheaf of Shaker paintings. She brushed the dust off their pleasing, bright faces. "Oh, how pretty!" And how rare. She sold nine of the paintings at auction, and the money paid the mortgage—it was as if the house had given itself to her, a gift.

She kept the blue watercolor, at first because it had a rip down the middle and because the dealer said it didn't look Shaker. But now she climbs the stairs to the attic often, in the heat of the afternoon. She keeps her hands in front of her face until she can find the string to the bare bulb, worrying over spiders. She looks into the corners for rats or even rabid raccoons, who knows, in the country? Then she crouches cautiously down in front of the blue painting she has propped against a trunk. She stares at it, brushes it with her hand, wondering. There are things swimming in the blue, figures she can barely make out. She is sure she sees a baby tangled in the roots of a plant. It is so hot up there, she can't stand it for long.

Sometimes she thinks of carrying the painting sideways down the narrow attic stairs, getting it repaired and cleaned, then hanging it, close to her. Other times she can imagine the satisfaction of sticking her fingers through the cracked blue middle, ripping, finishing the business. Her dreams are strange.

Surrounding the Shaker house are those ranches and trailers, including one painted green camouflage. They are the descendants of the Swedes and French Canadians and New Englanders who hung on, who love this lonely, ramshackle land that holds their ancestors' bones. But still, they dream wistfully of developers. Although they don't know it, they dream the general's dream, that advancing civilization will someday remember, gather them in. That it will be different this time.

And then, past these houses, no people at all. The forest is tumbledown, awry, crowding the road. The valley school and farms and blacksmith are all gone. In the sixties, a commune appeared, a decade's burst of color and noise, and then they, too, packed up their geodesic domes and moved on. The valley is nearly empty now, just a beaver swamp, two blue herons, circled by trees. It is hard to find the Hammondville road. Look for the signs: No Trespassing. Danger. Deep holes covered only by a thin layer of earth. It will frost early in Hammondville, and the hoarfrost is beautiful on the frozen leaves. Deer step delicately through the missing town. Coyotes howl at its center.

Trespass. Climb the old two-track. Out of breath, at the top, at first there is nothing to see—the tousled woods have taken everything back. Nothing except a scatter of gun cartridges from last fall. But move carefully, look closely. Here are foundations, circles of rock. Touch the cool stone, still flecked with dark iron. There is a bucket, the bottom a lace of rust. An old green bottle drowns in a tangle of blackberry brambles.

Some of the mines are still open, jagged wounds with aqua water streaming down their sides. Tread carefully. Some shafts are hidden. You can tell when you are standing over a hole: Crouch, brush away the dried twigs and leaves until you see black earth. Rest your hand flat on the ground until you feel a gust of cool, moist air rising. Crouch still. Hold your breath. Listen. The mines are filled with bats, and the sound of their fluttering at dusk is like the sound of a hundred quick hearts. The cool air feels like breath on your palm: Keep breathing. Hope the past will bear you up.

Acknowledgments

I BEGAN THIS book while at the Blue Mountain Center. I continue to be grateful and nostalgic for that month.

I wish to thank the Blue Mountain Museum, the Hoops, curators of the Penfield Museum, and the Miller/Endre's library for allowing me access to their collections. Ileen Devault kindly checked the union material for me.

I owe a great debt to the authors of many journals, memoirs, cookbooks, medicinal and etiquette books, especially to Jeanne Robert Foster's Adirondack memoirs, and Clarissa Lathrop's memoir about the state lunatic asylum at Utica.

Joe Mahay, Naomi Tannen, Bekah Perks, Deborah Tannen, my editor, Bob Wyatt, and my agent, Suzanne Gluck, carefully read early drafts and kept the faith. Thanks also to Gigi Marks and Paul Cody for reappearing at the right moment to render crucial support and advice. Alison Lurie acted as guardian angel. Finally, I am grateful to my grandfather, Eli Tannen, for remembering so much, including the story of his aunt Regina.